THE OMEGA PLAN

BY KURT S. JOHNSON

Fairway Press
Lima, Ohio

THE OMEGA PLAN

FIRST EDITION
Copyright © 1992 by
Kurt S. Johnson

All rights reserved. No portion of this book may be reproduced or utilized in any form or by any means, electronic or mechanical including photocopying, without permission in writing from the publisher. Inquiries should be addressed to: Fairway Press, 628 South Main Street, Lima, Ohio 45804.

7933 / ISBN 1-55673-483-2   PRINTED IN U.S.A.

To many Sauls who could be Pauls.
To many Pauls who once were Sauls.

Foreword

We don't live in times friendly to the premise that Jesus Christ is Lord. Many people work to ensure that all faiths get equal representation — or that no faith gets any representation. Unfortunately, this also ensures that any faith which actually is the truth will not be recognized.

Meanwhile, unprecedented trends are developing on this planet. From lower life standards to higher costs of living, from global warming to cooling economies, there's much evidence to suggest that big trouble may be ahead. Anything could happen. Why not, then, *The Omega Plan*?

I hope you enjoy this book. I enjoyed writing it. Fair warning though: it's rather biased. *The Omega Plan* is an adventure based on end-times biblical prophesy, specifically in Daniel, Matthew and Revelation. Is it plausible? You decide.

Thanks to my wife, Liz, and to many good friends, who waded through earlier versions of the manuscript with great patience and insightful perspective.

By the way, Jesus is Lord. Deal with it! A good tussle with God never hurt anyone, and it's much more exciting than hiding behind the legalisms and busyness of this life. I hope in some small way that this book will help you let go for a few hours of the weighty cares of your world and come on a freedom walk into a future that just might happen.

Chapter 1

By the time they'd reach the eighth tee Michael Ames had to squint. It wasn't just the onset of dusk that made vision difficult — it was the strange pink cast in the air.

Tommy Thompson stood silently nearby. Michael waited for his chiding. At the last outing he'd done poorly on Number Eight, to Tommy's unending delight. But this time he felt sure he'd blast the ball far beyond that stream lurking in the dusky shadows ahead.

Michael blinked as he lined up the shot. The pink sheen on the ball appeared to be deepening. He looked up toward the pine thicket to the right, nearly black now in fast-approaching darkness. The light of the rising moon gave a faint glow to its needled outline. That too, he noticed, seemed pink. A strange sensation gripped him. He broke out of his stance and wheeled around.

Tommy stood with his back toward Michael, staring into the sky. Just beyond the finger of his outstretched arm Michael saw the newly rising moon still partly hidden behind the clubhouse, very large, its outline clear but faint against the deepening blue of the evening sky. But the moon this night did not glow with its familiar cream color. Instead, it was like an alien pink eye peering at them from behind the roofline.

"Look at that," Tommy breathed.

Michael leaned his club against his hip and rubbed his neck, summoning an amusement he did not feel. "Must be your rose-colored glasses," he said.

"No, look! It's pink!"

"Tommy, there's so much junk in the air it wouldn't surprise me if it was polkadot. Come on, it's getting dark."

"Thre's no pink like that pink."

"Forget it, Tommy! Let's get going!"

"Yeah," Tommy Thompson turned and pulled a driver from his bag.

Michael struggled to hid his eerie irritation. He stepped up to the tee and pulled the club back. His body uncoiled, and the club head swung through the ball in a powerful, fluid arc. The crisp "whack" of the impact signalled a good shot. Both watched the ball lift into the deepening pink sky, then drop onto the shadowed fairway and bounce out of sight.

"Nice," Tommy said.

Michael glanced at the moon, fully exposed now, and very large and round. Its pink tone had deepened, and the darker areas — the face of the man — were an irridescent crimson.

"That is strange," Michael said, putting his club back in the golf bag. "It's gonna be a big night for the werewolves, Tommy."

"That's not funny."

"What're you so tense about? Werewolves are only imaginary . . ." Michael suddenly feigned horror and scrambled behind his friend, partly hunched over and pointing toward the pine thicket with a quivering finger. "Help, help! There's one now, in the pines, Tommy! He's baring his teeth . . . wait. It's not a werewolf. It's Rob Peary. Aargh . . . he's got me, Tommy . . ." he grasped his throat in mock chocking, staggering in front of his friend.

"You're hilarious, Michael." But Tommy wasn't smiling.

"Hey buddy, lighten up!" Michael stopped his charade. He liked his friend, but he wasn't the same Tommy Thompson of years ago when they'd both worked for Robinson A. Peary Associates. Somewhere in the intervening years Tommy had changed. His driving need to always be the center of attention had disappeared, and his appreciation of the ribald humor which characterized their early friendship had faded. Michael snorted, angry all over again, and fearful that something was now happening that he didn't understand.

"You don't think that moon has anything to do with all that religious nonsense you're always talking about, do you?"

Tommy looked at him for a moment, then turned back to the moon without replying. Its glow cast an eerie reddish tinge over the golf course. Across the ravine the clubhouse lights glimmered, and the faint laughter from the crowded patio bar was lessening.

"What time is it?"

Michael checked his watch. "Eight forty-five," he replied. Darkness was coming quickly. "We'll never finish now, Tommy. It's too dark. Let's go."

"In a minute."

They were both distracted by the strange moon, now high enough that atmospheric distortion could not be a factor. When it was lower it was seen through miles of dirty, hazy air, often taking on strange colors and sizes. But it had always risen above the airborne muck of progress and recovered its familiar cream-colored purity, reassuring all those below that it was indeed the moon they saw as a child.

Michael's disquiet increased. He squeezed his eyes shut, then opened them wide, shaking his head vigorously as if to clear his mind. Silence reigned and hypnotized the countryside. Tommy and Michael watched the distant figures on the patio far across the ravine spread out around the corner of the clubhouse silently staring at the moon. It seemed to grow and deepen in color as it rose in the sky, yet its light was not lessened. It glowed with unusual strength. But it glowed with a rich, fearsome, deep-bright crimson. No twig stirred or bird twittered, no laugh or sound floated across the ravine. All eyes watched the rising of the blood-red moon into the cloudless midwestern sky that summer evening.

"What time is it?" Tommy whispered.

Michael's watch reflected the clear red light. "Almost ten," he said, surprised. The stiffness in his body confirmed that more than a few minutes, indeed, has passed. He put his hand on his friend's shoulder.

"Let's go."

They climbed into the cart and pressed the pedal down. Its whirring electric motor seemed almost sacrilegious as they lumbered along the cart track and on toward the clubhouse, bathed in crimson light.

"This is one more sign, Michael."

They had trundled along the path through the ravine in silence, each lost in his own thoughts. Michael was startled that Tommy's statement had so accurately mirrored the question that was pushing and probing into his own mind.

"Sign of what?" he retorted impatiently. "It's just dirt in the air. No big thing."

"Maybe. But when you add this to everything else that's been happening . . ." Tommy eased the cart into the paved area next to the clubhouse and shut off the motor. "Even you, Michael, have to admit that there may be more to it than just dirt in the air."

"There aren't always mystical reasons for everything!" Michael spoke with more anger than he'd intended, regretting it immediately.

"Sorry. I don't know why I feel so irritated."

"Forget it. But if you want to talk . . ." The invitation hung like a dangling jewel.

Michael laughed, hiding his tension, and clapped his friend on the shoulder. "Anything but that Christian stuff, Tommy. I don't know what got you into all of that, but it sure has changed you."

He was surprised by Tommy's pleased expression.

"Come on, I'll buy you a beer — even though you are strange."

They walked up the path to the clubhouse, golf shoes clacking on the flagstone path.

"I thought Christians didn't drink beer," Michael gibed. They guffawed and shoved at each other as they went through the door.

Chapter 2

Ben's back wound, though healed for forty years, was painful on this early fall afternoon. He shuffled along the littered sidewalk, trying not to limp, squinting his eyes against breeze-driven dust. Few walked on this side of the city, even now during the daily exodus from the tall office buildings rising like shrines into the skyline just a few blocks north.

Passing the sandwich shop on the corner, Ben waved to Digger. A hand that was missing two fingers waved from the shadows behind the counter as Digger returned the greeting.

Ben turned the corner, feeling inside a pocket of his trench coat. The paper his fingers touched gave momentary hope, but proved to be only the ad he had clipped out announcing a Binzoe crusade meeting. Ben read its invitation to all to come and hear Gabriel Diehl.

"I'll be sure to be there," he mused, smiling. He put the clipping back into his pocket and continued searching. Familiar waves of hunger increased as he ran out of places to look. He found a quarter lodged in the sweater watch pouch, as well as a small hole he hadn't noted before. He made a mental note to close it with a piece of gum — better that than to risk the loss of precious coins. A nickel popped out of the pocket of his trousers.

He leaned against a graffiti-clad building and poked the two coins around in his palm, tasting his hunger.

"Soup," he said. His stomach burbled. "All right, friend stomach, all right. Four days of soup alone is too much, I agree. Tonight we'll have more than that! I'll have to dig into my savings, though."

He grunted as he bent over and pulled off a worn sneaker. Reaching inside, he pulled out a damp folded five dollar bill. "Ah, yes," Ben said. "Friend stomach, you and I will eat tonight!"

He pushed his foot back into the sneaker and relaced it, then stood upright slowly, thinking delicious thoughts. A cup of hot soup and his favorite sandwich, shredded beef and lettuce with catsup, would cost $3.85 at Digger's. Then, refreshed, he would stroll the block to his room and spend the evening going through his precious books.

The day had been busy but that's how it had been all summer. Binzoe's population was increasing rapidly in these days. Some had been defeated in the squeeze of an economy reeling from global catastrophes and growing world tensions. Others had succumbed to their own habits and excesses, cocktail coke sniffers who had played with the dragon until it had stamped them flat. They were frightened, lost, despairing — shunned and unforgiven by the one from whom acceptance was so important — themselves. The times when friends are most desperately needed are often the times when they're most scarce. Ben knew that. Today he had counselled with four new arrivals at the shelter where he spent much of his time. He spoke their language. But usually he helped just by listening. He was listened out, now.

"Yes, an evening with the books is a perfect idea," he said to no one in particular.

He turned back around the corner toward Digger's. A large truck rumbled by in the nearly deserted street, hurling papers and dust into its windstream and shattering all thought in the noise of its bouncing along the potholed street. Ben nearly missed hearing his name called from behind him.

"That raspy voice could only be Meg," he said with delight. She had been missing for a while and he was worried. He turned, squinting into the sun, and spotted Meg in all her ragged heavy-set splendor shuffling toward him. He waved and hurried toward her, all but forgetting the pain of schrapnel still imbedded just above and behind his hipbone.

"Ben," Meg breathed, stumbling up to him. Her toothless grin had been changeless across the twelve years they had known one another. He recalled his feeling of repulsion the first time he'd seen the grin. One side of her lower lip was pulled in a little, and the look of a simpleton was in her eyes. But he had noticed the Binzoe regulars treat her gently most of the time in that terse sort of way that enabled hard life to be survived. Meg was one of them, as integral in their life support system as any. Now she puffed up to her friend and rummaged through an old shopping bag, extracting a folded newspaper page.

"Look Ben!" Meg said triumphantly, drooling, and a bit too loud. She looked up at the kind face towering nearly two feet above her.

"It's good to see you! Where have you been, woman?"

Meg's eyes closed a little, and a frown appeared. "Been gone, Ben. Hurt."

Ben's eyebrows raised with concern.

"Hit, Ben. See?" She lifted oily matted strands of hair from her forehead, revealing an ugly red wound with the look of lingering infection.

"Crowns hit me," she said, looking down and talking almost like a shy pouting child.

"The Crowns," he thought, marauding a neighborhood where there was no money, but only helpless people. The Crowns had to be a particularly cruel strain, gathering their dregs of enjoyment by beating defenseless people. But the anger rising in his large frame changed to compassion even as it appeared.

"I okay, I okay," Meg said. "Look!" She waved the newspaper pages in front of him. Ben recoiled at the headline: "ANOTHER SUPERQUAKE HITS ATLANTIC. TIDAL WAVE DESTROYS JERSEY COASTLINE!"

Meg grinned with delight, not comprehending the depth of tragedy those headlines announced. Ben took the paper and slumped down on a nearby door stoop to read more. Meg plopped down beside him, drooling.

> Atlantic City NJ — Thousands are missing and feared dead in a second disastrous tidal wave which struck the New Jersey coast shortly before dawn. Roads were jammed by thousands fleeing the resort areas since the Prime Alert was issued. Wave height was sixty feet. The tidal effect was felt from Long Island Sound to the Chesapeake Bay, and as far inland as Philadelphia where the Schuylkil River is expected to crest several feet above its banks. Damage

is estimated at several billion dollars. The entire resort area including 13 casinos and 16 hotels was levelled. Cottages and homes for miles along the beach are gone. "We have no idea of the casualty count," a local official was quoted as saying. "What we know is that land on which 45,000 people lived has disappeared."

Ben put the paper down without reading further and hung his head, remembering days so many years ago when he had walked the wooden planks of the Boardwalk, full of hope in himself and youthful avarice for the world he had intended to conquer.

"Is 'at sumthing Ben?" Meg said loudly. "Today's! It new!" She nodded vigorously to emphasize her point.

Ben stared absently at her as the shock of realization that there was no more Atlantic City sank in.

"Are you hungry, Meg?" he finally said, softly and with resignation.

"Ya, Ben. I hungry."

"Come on. I'll buy you soup and a sandwich."

"Oh Ben, we gonna celebrate?" Meg's innocent toothless grin pushed the tidal wave and its tragic enormity away.

"Yes, we'll celebrate your return to the street and the healing of your head bump!"

They got up slowly, Meg retrieving the paper and stuffing it into her sack.

"You know when I got hit by the Crowns, don'tcha?"

Ben's thoughts had returned to the Atlantic City that was, and to memories of people he loved.

"What, Meg?"

"When I got hit, Ben. You know, here." She lifted her hair away from her forehead again. "It was the time the sky was red. 'Member? Hope I don't get another bump. This one aches all the time."

Ben wrestled his attention away from painful thoughts and studied her worried face. He put his ragged arm around her heavy, sagging shoulders and led her back toward Digger's. "Don't worry. You'll be fine."

"Good Ben, good. I don't want trouble now with this head. It hurts." She stumbled along helplessly beside her friend.

Chapter 3

Michael Ames was involved in the most important account of his career. This was the one, he often said to Debbie, which would move him into a vice presidency and provide access to people of considerable power and influence. He would, after years of hard work, at last be a player.

It was more than an opportunity — it was a crossroad. By the unwritten rules he knew so well, the time had come either to rise and conquer or to be forever relegated to windlowless offices and "what's-his-name" roles. He had to succeed.

Michael had made very few errors. He had the knack of sensing the real issues of his clients — rarely those upon which the initial consulting relationship was established — and the instinctive ability to develop the right strategies to address them. On more than one occasion this had proven to be quite lucrative for his company. But always, he felt, someone else got the credit. His role had usually been a minor one. It was more through his force of personality within the firm that his insights influenced the approach ultimately presented to clients. Those approaches usually succeeded.

As he climbed into the BMW he savored a brief recollection of his meeting with Rob Peary eight months before. Peary, as usual, got right to the point. "You can only be on so many successful projects in a row, Ames, before I start thinking that maybe you, more than the others, are the one who's making all the business happen," he had said. Then he had ushered Michael into his conference room for a moment as sacred as any moment could be at Robinson A. Peary Associates. Peary would call his Account Directors into session around the gleaming, polished conference table, as indeed he had done on this occasion. Small crystal goblets, the Peary logo engraved on the surface and each filled with a costly liqueur, would be handed to each director without a word. They knew why they were there.

When tension had peaked Peary would toast the one he had chosen to manage the next major account. This was the first any of the directors knew who had been given the nod, including the appointee himself.

Michael pictured that particular meeting and Ron Peary's double surprise.

"Gentlemen," he had intoned, "congratulate our newest Account Director, Michael Ames!" Michael recalled his heart leaping at the discovery of his promotion.

But Peary wasn't through. He had then lifted the dark blue briefing folder from the table and extended it toward Michael.

"Yours, Mr. Ames. Prantzer Defense Group — the largest account our firm has ever had. The contract . . . ." Peary peered over his glasses at the stunned directors . . . "is over three million dollars."

Then came the traditional speech for these occasions, stroking or striping each director according to the ever-delicate balancing act of keeping motivation high and competing political pressures stable. He had extolled qualities Michael didn't even know he had as the shrewd owner of the well-known business services firm levelled the playing field. Michael remembered his mind dancing between Peary's accolades and the large increase in income this promotion would bring.

Michael turned the key and the car responded obediently. He paused at the end of the driveway, admiring his Georgian home a hundred feet up the gentle slope of the front yard. Frosted in the early winter air, sun not quite peeking above the horizon, he admired its imposing white pillars, double chimneys lifting over the peak of the slate roof, the enormous blue spruce across the driveway.

It would have been a perfect morning had he and Debbie not quarreled. Her objections to his work schedule were becoming more frequent, and her bitterness more intense. As far as Michael was concerned, there was no choice to make. She just didn't understand.

He pushed the argument out of his mind and eased down the silent street, turning his thoughts to the critical meeting coming later that morning. This was it — formal presentation of the Prantzer reorganization plan — four hours with one of the toughest, most intense executives he'd ever met.

Turning down Claypool Drive, he inserted a management cassette into the tape player. Just as it began he sensed, more than heard, a low, rumbling sound.

"Detection of hidden agendas is important," the voice intoned.

Michael felt vibrations. He pulled over to the side of the road. Rumblings and vibration continued. He checked the instruments, finding nothing wrong other than that the fuel guage was on empty. He looked around with the quick movement of a bird sensing a nearby cat. A tree shivered slightly. Suddenly the car felt as though it had been hit and the rumbling increased as if a speeding freight train bore down on him. The trees across the street shook noticeably. Then all became still.

Michael felt adrenalin pumping. His breath came in short shallow puffs. He waited a few moments, then eased his car back onto the road.

"A strange morning," he muttered, accelerating. A sense of foreboding began to build. His thoughts were overtaken by memories of other recent occurrences. The earthquakes in the Atlantic two months earlier, the terrorist massacre in Kansas, the red moon all converged in his mind. He did not understand, and that disturbed him as much as the events themselves.

The car phone interrupted his thoughts.

"Ames," he said impatiently, cradling the receiver against his neck.

It was Debbie. She was hysterical.

"Slow down!" Michael barked. "What happened?"

"The power's out, Michael!" Debbie sobbed. "And the wall is cracked!"

His irritation increased with his wife's incoherent chatter. He almost ran a red light, jamming his foot hard against the brake pedal at the last moment before traffic surged across his path. The BMW swerved to a stop.

"The yard split open too — I think we had an earthquake! Oh Michael, I'm frightened! The dishes fell and the spruce is leaning . . ."

Michael heard the wailing sounds of distant sirens then. A quake! In the middle of the continent!

"Debbie, get hold of yourself!" he said sharply. "We don't have earthquakes here. Call the fire department. I've got a very big meeting in an hour — can't you get that through your head?" He slammed the phone into its cradle and pressed the accelerator to the floor as the light changed. The car leaped and disappeared into traffic approaching the city. As far as he was concerned there was too much at stake to be distracted. Whatever had happened, Debbie would have to handle it. He was blind to the signs of the world around him.

Chapter 4

Born into affluence, Pankie Quille Retson's parents were shot to death as she watched, frightened beyond scream, at the age of eight. "Burglars," the news had reported, "panicked into shooting while caught robbing the Retson estate." In the years following that horrific experience she suspected there was more to it than that. But that brought no consolation.

Pankie shuttled from boarding school to boarding school and governess to governess throughout the New England states. Bored, confused, and irretrievably hardened, she found her only delight in creating anguish for her warden, headmistress, or nanny of the day. Abuse, molestation, and repeated rejection, whether of desperate attempts to control her reckless independence or to take advantage of a wealthy teenager out of control, had become Pankie's lesson in what life was about. She determined to be tougher. By the time Pankie was fifteen nothing could shock her.

Before she turned seventeen she met Boze, and for one fleeting year her life might have changed. Boze was a huge man, not easily intimidated, and patient to a fault. He loved Pankie from the start, seeing through her coarse hardness into the heart of a fearfully hurting young woman with extraordinary intelligence, talents and beauty.

But even his saint-like patience could not withstand the repeated and unprovoked attacks, insensitivities, humiliations, and unfaithful excursions. He had tried. But it could not work. Pankie stormed out of their marriage eleven months after it had begun, leased the penthouse suite in the Charlemagne Hotel, and slept and drank with anyone she could find to fill for a time the gaping tear in her soul.

Two months later she was rushed to Lake Shore Hospital, battered and stabbed, near death. She awoke to her eighteenth birthday. Boze was leaning over her bed. Pankie screamed, and kept screaming. Boze left, never to be seen again. Pankie became catatonic.

Her slow recovery became the forum in which she shaped her life. Strapped to her bed, she lay helplessly enraged in a private hospital room. Gradually anger transformed into ruthless purpose. And she thought it through.

The power of her intellect moved cautiously down that torn and scaly tunnel of her past, confronting and conquering the dragons along the path. She willed her way into the gunbarrel of her future and deliberated every option and every opportunity. If she had awareness of shadowy figures appearing now and then at her bedside, of the occasional attempts at conversation, of the frequent bite of the hypodermic needle, she paid no attention. If she slept, upon awakening she picked up her thoughts exactly where she had dropped them. In poverty of soul and power of mind, Pankie worked her life out until she had answers . . . clear, crisp, black and white answers.

Only memories of three other people had invaded that process during those weeks of recovery and relentless appraisal.

The first was Miss Carlson, a governess during the summer of her junior year in high school. Visions of white, tightly pulled-back hair, eyes blinking through thick glasses, and wonderful aromas of fresh blueberry pie flooded through her. She remembered the setting — Miss Carlson on the porch of her Victorian house in a rocker, creaking back and forth with maddening regularity in the afternoon sun. Her wrinkled, chubby face rocked up close to hers, eyes peering through those heavy spectacles.

"Child, you've got to make a choice," she said. "You've got to go the way of good or the way of bad. There's no middle ground — only people who think there is." Pankie took Miss Carlson's gift deeper than words can plunge. Good and bad . . . how is one known from the other? But all of one or the other? Absolutely. No more uncertainty.

The second was a professor. Pankie had attended few classes. She could take almost any exam, especially where expository writing was required, and do well with little study or class time. But she never missed Dr. Biggs' economics lectures. He was a brilliant light in an otherwise drab unstimulating world, and when he taught it was as if the oracles of wisdom had opened.

The professor never knew how Pankie's heart, in the last days of sputtering feeling before her iron will had suffocated it, yearned toward him as a father figure. It was one of her few indulgences. But had he known, he would not have treated her any differently. Dr. Biggs treated all of his students with kindness and respect, regarding them each as a precious gem. He would shuffle back and forth in front of the lecture hall, engrossed in his subject and unaware of himself, pouring forth jewel upon jewel of knowledge. He himself was the precious gem, the incarnation of caring and worldly wisdom, and his students knew it with each fresh insight into the financial checks and balances which powered things of the real world. Pankie could remember his words almost verbatim.

"Money is power and influence. It is the doorway through which freedom is realized and control is exercised. But you must manage your money wisely, young people, or you will lose it all. You must establish priorities and stick by them. You must not live wantonly, but you must live in the style of those who have what you want. You see, already," he had said, "this is not the sort of lecture one can offer in the public schools." Pankie recalled the twitter of privileged laughter. Students at that institution came with a very different financial background than most people had ever dreamed of.

"Without capital you are common, without means," he had continued. "With it, the doors open. You must make your choice now, while you are young. You must learn to be wise as well as energetic, young people. You must turn from your emotions if they would put your capital at risk. You must become hard. You must get more than you give, if you please."

"Only a few are able, and these few are the leaders of this world. They will yield control into those hands which belong to kindred spirits and to no others — yes, only those who are wise enough and hard enough to take it from them."

Certainty and capital. The shape of her future began to form.

The third was Boze. Husband. She rolled the word around in her mind — it seemed like a right shoe on a left foot. Yet her eyes filled as he came to her thoughts. Big, patient, loving Boze. How many times had a man said he loved her? By that measure the word love was among the most cynical cruelties the world had thrust at her. But she knew Boze meant it. It was the only time in her life she had felt loved.

But she could not love in return. Knowing not what to do with such abundance, unable to rely upon its treasure, and fearful of its loss, she had rejected it. And in that rejection, Pankie had wounded Boze with deliberate thoughtlessness, helpless against herself. Once wounded, all that remained had to be killed. That love was so beautiful as to be frightening, but too beautiful to be flawed. Pankie persevered through her own torment until she had crushed that love. Self-hatred borne of her uncontrollable will to destroy grew, unresisted, until it became her master.

Boze was the single matter she was unable to resolve. All else except love yielded to the pattern she was forming. So Pankie set the imponderable aside and developed her philosophy until the imponderable itself had been destroyed. Good or bad — one or the other. The self must be its own guide, and it must pull everything to it. There was no basis for sharing. And therefore no basis for love.

In the recesses of her mind a door slammed shut, and an iron bolt shifted and locked it tight. She saw a key drop from her hands and tumble end over end into a glowing pit until it was lost. The memory of Boze, and what he might have been to her, faded away.

Many days had gone by when Pankie stirred in her restraints and opened her eyes. In the darkness of her room a nurse sat reading a magazine.

"Water," Pankie rasped.

The startled nurse jumped from her chair and scurried through the door. Pankie heard her in the corridor announcing that Miss Retson had finally awakened.

Chapter 5

Pankie blinked, surprised her thought had drifted to that formative hospital room ten years before. She shifted in the uncomfortable gallery chair and returned her attention to the hearings. The congressional panel investigating global catastrophes had been in session for over six hours, receiving testimony from members of the world's scientific community.

She scanned her notes. "129 quakes above Richter 5.0 — loss of life at least 3 million. 43 volcanic eruptions — two new, in Egypt and New Zealand. Increased global temperature over the past decade of 1.9 degrees — drought throughout northern hemisphere, famine killed three to six million — AIDS-3 virus now thought to have infected 20 pecent of the Region, and found in Europe . . . ."

She looked up and took a deep breath. It was too much. Something far beyond human understanding was at work.

The last witness, Dr. Emerson Prantzer, approached the bench. Pankie noticed the silence in the chamber as he took his place at the microstalk. Dr. Prantzer was highly respected and world-reknown. For her, he was dangerous. She hoped Senator Ashton had enough gumption to control him, although she doubted it.

Dr. Prantzer testified at length of unexplainable aberrant occurrences in the Region's defense and communications systems, focusing particularly on the failure of instrument networks to recognize obvious short range changes in environmental conditions. By the time he finished no one doubted that something was seriously and inexplicably wrong.

"Thank you, Dr. Prantzer," Senator Ashton said, leaning into his microstalk. "Panel, questions please."

"Dr. Prantzer," Ms. Dunwright, the senator from South Dakota, said, "the Washington Post reported yesterday that there was another shift of the earth's axis. Is that true?"

The scientist leaned back to consult with a colleague seated behind him. Then he turned back to the microstalk.

"The earth's axis normally oscillates very slowly and predictably. Two months ago, instruments on Satellite Beta detected a one degree shift from correct polar orientation. Beta rejected the readings within four hours of the automatic monitor report, concluding that no such shift had occurred. All instruments were in working order."

"Dr. Plaines of the Sacramento Ground Station advises that the Beta instruments reported another shift two days ago. Once again we were unable to verify the report."

"Can you say whether this will happen again?"

"The normal variance in oscillation is almost nil. The axis has never shifted out of predicted position since measurements were begun. If these deviations did occur they are highly significant — indeed, incredible. We've been studying the matter since the first occurence but have no explanation."

"Dr. Prantzer," a deep voice from the end of the panel table called. "Are you implying, then, that external forces or powers are responsible for these extraordinary occurrences?" The voice spoke with pretentious drama. Pankie swore softly. Moe Cummings was grandstanding again.

"What do you mean by 'external,' senator?"

"Why . . . anything not of this world."

The scientist hunched over the microstalk. "Senator Cummings, I know of only one way to respond to that question, but the 29th Amendment constrains me."

"The False Doctrine Amendment deals with public gatherings," Senator Cummings replied. "This is a closed hearing. Please answer the question."

Dr. Prantzer wiped his brow. The lights were hot. "Very well then. I do not believe these phenomena will ever be explained scientifically or rationally. They simply happen, and are happening. No man-made or natural force could in my opinion be responsible."

The hearing chamber grew very still.

"There would seem to be only two possible explanations, both involving forces beyond those of our world. Either alien intelligent life forms are creating cosmic disturbance of sufficient magnitude to have these impacts, or we're entering the time which has been described as the end of the age."

Murmuring rose. Pankie scribbled furiously, fuming over the senator's clumsiness. It was just like that pompous buffoon. He'd set Prantzer up with all the cleverness of a grapefruit and given him an opening to say what Pankie feared he would say.

The chairman gavelled the chamber back to order.

"Dr. Prantzer," Senator Cummings continued, trying to smooth what he realized by then was a blunder, "it's unseemly that a scientist of your stature would indulge in such thoughts. Surely there must be a rational, not fictional, explanation."

"Senator, scientists throughout the world have searched for possible explanations. We've compared data and tested every conceivable hypothesis. Governments, as you well know, responded to our circular letter of last May with massive additional equipment and resources. We have so far found no rational explanation. Yet earthquakes, famines, volcanic eruptions, new and lethal viral epidemics, and unprecedented global pyschological distresses are increasing. It does not seem rational to me to insist that there is a rational explanation at all."

"Dr. Prantzer," the woman from South Dakota interrupted, "If alien beings are indeed creating these disturbances, surely the World Alliance Orbit Laser Network would have detected such energy crossing our communications or defense fields, would it not?"

"The World Alliance Astrotechnical people are more qualified to answer that than I am."

"But your company designed and built most of the hardware which makes up the Network. And you were one of its architects. What is your opinion?"

George Ashton gavelled and spoke with an edge to his voice. "Dr. Prantzer, these sessions are investigating unparalleled changes in world stability. We don't know, yet, even the beginnings of the implications, if indeed there are any. Please respond as best you can. That's why you're here."

A heady mindfulness of his role came upon Em Prantzer. Since receiving the summons to testify he'd wondered if it would come to this. He believed the world was near the time of the promised return of Jesus Christ. And he had begun to sense that he, somehow, would play a part in it. He had confided this to his good friend, Gabe Diehl. "Don't shirk from that which the Lord Jesus asks of you," Gabe had advised him.

Em Prantzer knew himself, and he knew the years of disciplined thinking during which he had contributed so much to the application of the sciences. He knew his mind was as sound as ever. He'd tried to shake off his conviction that the

Day of the Lord was nearing. But it would not shake. The Day was near, and his God would have him testify of His Word. He held the knowledge to himself as, he reasoned, any rational fifty-seven year old scientist would do. But its realization had prepared him.

He felt the tension. If he held to data and facts he would bear no risk. But if he spoke that which was poised in his heart he would no doubt bear heavy consequences.

And Pankie Quille Retson was there, he noticed. The brash, arrogant leader of the influential SelfGuide movement could be expected to raise a terrible hue and cry.

Knowing the moment, he sought relief from it, afraid at this moment of action that he might have misinterpreted his Lord's call. Even as he fought the inner fight he knew its outcome.

"Dr. Prantzer," the chairman said, banging his gavel, "we await your reply."

He looked up. "I must make three disclaimers. First, most of the data is not yet verified. Information is pouring in at a much faster rate than it can be processed. We don't have a complete picture at all. Second, my views are not a scientific consensus."

As he spoke he tried once more to turn from the awesome proclamation pushing for release from deep within and hold the course of accustomed scientific familiarity. Yet he knew he did not wish to resist. The incongruity seemed overwhelming, that he, master scientist known for rationality and logic, would be under power and command to bring such an announcement forward.

The Lord helped him get to the point he was there to make. His third "disclaimer" trailed off into gibberish. The chairman pounded his gavel. Em Prantzer realized what had happened and ended his rebellion.

"Dr. Prantzer! Would you please repeat that last statement?"

Yielded now to his duty, he felt filled with peace and confidence. As he began to speak again his voice took on strength and purpose. None could remain neutral to what he said as he removed his glasses and pushed his briefing papers aside.

"I have dedicated myself for more than thirty years to the disciplines of structured thinking. I am merely one of many who are equally or more gifted in these regards. Yet for some reason I have been touted as a 'master of logic.' I ask you to remember this now."

"I believe we are entering into the last days of this world as we know it before the return of the Lord Jesus Christ, the Son of the Living God. The time is short."

He paused. Stunned silence yielded to open shouting. Pankie Retson was on her feet before she knew it, her body shaking with outrage.

"Mr. Chairman!" she called in a shrill voice which had bested many a shouting competitor. She turned on the scientist without waiting for recognition. "You dare to stain this hearing with personal feelings declared to be false by the Twenty-Ninth Amendment?" she screamed.

Chairman Ashton gavelled sharply and stood. Pankie was no match for his microstalk.

"Order!" he boomed. "Order! Ms. Retson, be seated!"

"Mr. Chairman, this is ludicrous hypocrisy . . ."

"Be seated Ms. Retson, immediately, or your gallery privileges will be revoked!"

Fuming and breathing hard, Pankie stopped under the chairman's glare and sat down. She knew she'd gone out of control, and the hot embarrassment was intolerable. Slowly the chamber quieted and the chairman addressed the scientist who sat quietly in the witness chair.

"Dr. Prantzer, your statements are inconsistent with national policy and the Declarations of the World Alliance. There is no basis for unfounded opinion in this or any hearing chamber of our government. Retract your statements and continue, please. Clerk, strike his comments."

The clerk reached for the editing dial on the FOX-100 transcribed computer. His hand froze at Dr. Prantzer's command. "Do not strike my comments!" he barked into the microstalk.

"Mr. Chairman, my statements are neither unfounded nor are they opinions. You've put no special conditions on my responses — in fact you insisted that I respond. It seems to me that an injustice is done to any witness and to our legal system if my comments are struck from the record."

The chairman held a hurried whispered conference with other panel members, then gavelled sharply.

"We remind you of the standing rules of expert testimony. Remarks must be confined to conclusions based on demonstrable facts, hypothesis based on reasonable justification, and speculation only when asked, and tempered with professional discipline. Did you not already agree to these conditions?"

"I did, of course."

"Proceed."

"It is accepted, Mr. Chairman, that any document supporting an observed event is legally submissible as evidence whether it precedes or follows the occurrence itself. Last month the moon came up blood red. It caused a major stir throughout the world and within the scientific community. Well before it had passed across the sky, intracell bulletins were issued with an explanation designed to ease world-wide concern."

"Yes, yes, we all remember," Ms. Dunwright said impatiently. "It was merely refraction of light through the ozone layer disrupted by ash from Vesuvius and Krakatoa."

"This explanation, Mr. Chairman, was wrong," Em Prantzer continued. "If a scientist composed it he is a charlatan. Alpha base reported that the lunar viedotapes and data on atmospheric chemical content, color scans, and trajectories showed no abnormal conditions. Electronically speaking, the moon was normal. Atmospheric composition was normal. Earth and lunar trajectories were exactly as they were calculated to be. There is no scientific basis for the appearance of the red moon seen by the entire world that one night. And there is . . . ."

"Dr. Prantzer," Chairman Ashton interrupted, "that's in direct conflict with the Official Lunar Report confirming the intracell broadcast and providing extensive data supporting its conclusions. What you are saying would incite panic into an already nervous and fearful population. Is that your intent?"

"We seem to have an ability not only to dissect the mechanics of natural phenomena, Mr. Chairman, but to construct whatever case for their cause best meets the needs of the Regional Alliance. I do, however, direct your attention to another document relevant to the blood red moon."

George Ashton had no choice other than to allow him to continue. The scientist pulled a small book out of his pocket and thumbed through its pages.

"I submit this in evidence of what happened, and more importantly, why it happened. I quote directly . . ."

"Identify your source of data."

"Yes — this document predates the event of the blood red moon, and other phenomena, by more than two thousand years."

"It's title, sir."

He quickly prayed for guidance. There could be no basis for the chairman to terminate his testimony.

"It is a letter written by an eyewitness to the statements made which forecasted the red moon. The title is 'The Acts of the Apostles.' "

There was whispered conversation between the chairman and panel members. The chairman turned back to the microstalk, glaring, but said nothing. A sense of energy seemed to fill the chamber. He adjusted his glasses and began to read.

> "I shall in those days pour out my Spirit, and they will prophesy. I shall present wonders, too, in the heavens above and signs in the earth below — blood and fire and smoky mist. The sun will be turned to darkness and the moon to blood before that great and conspicuous day of the Lord arrives. And it will be that whoever will call on the Lord's name will be saved."

The chairmen stared at him. "Does that complete your testimony, Dr. Prantzer?" George Ashton's voice was dull.

"No."

"The panel is not inclined to hear more of the nature you are offering. We find no value or relevance . . ."

"If you do not hear this testimony now, Mr. Chairman, while there is still time, you will hear it later when it is too late. This document is highly relevant. It obviously names the specific phenomenon, the red moon, which is one of those under investigation."

The panel was in a difficult position. Because the hearing was closed, they had no legal basis to prevent testimony from anyone called to the stand unless hearing rules were violated. He could not be gracefully stopped. Dr. Prantzer clearly would not be put aside until he had had his say.

Ashton sighed audibly and motioned Dr. Prantzer to continue.

"I cite another document which predicts these events."

"The title," the chairman sighed, resigned to hearing him out.

"The Book of Matthew."

Senator Ashton leaned back in his chair and folded his arms across his chest. Dr. Prantzer thumbed again through his small book until he found the page he wanted.

> "You will be hearing of wars and rumors of wars. See that you not be troubled; for they have to come, but that is not the end. For nation will rise against nation and kingdom against kingdom, and there will be famines and earthquakes in various places; all of these are but the early pains of childbirth. Then they will hand you over to be persecuted, and they will kill you, and you will then fall away and betray one another and hate one another; and many false prophets will arise and will deceive many, and due to excessive lawlessness the love of many will grow cold. But he who endures to the end will be saved."

Not a sound was heard. Indeed, the book from which he read had been banned from public use for thirty-three years.

Few had ever heard the words before. Those who may have had long since forgotten them or had relegated them into the blends of ancient fables. He looked back to the book and continued.

> "And this good news of the kingdom will be preached all over the world to testify to all the nations, and then the end will come. When you, therefore, see the desolating abomination mentioned by the prophet Daniel, set up in the holy place, then those in Judea should flee to the mountains; one on the roof must not go down to fetch things out of his house, and one in the field must not turn back to pick up his coat. But alas for those who are pregnant and those who are nursing children in those days! Pray that your flight may not be in the winter or on a Sabbath; for then there will be such great tribulation as has never been experienced from the world's beginning until now, nor ever will be."

Dr. Prantzer removed his glasses and returned the book to his jacket pocket. The room remained silent. Pankie Retson's eyes burned with hatred. The World Alliance Surveillance representative scribbled furiously. Members of the panel looked down at their scratch pads.

"The red moon is one of the signs signalling the imminent return of the Lord Jesus Christ. Our days are numbered. I implore you all to return to your senses and stop this charade which the world, under the auspices of WOEC, the World Alliance, and all the rest, have been acting out for an entire generation. Disasters are occurring all over the globe!" Em Prantzer swept his arm through the air for emphasis.

"Desert areas have quintupled in the last twenty years. Half the eastern shoreline was pushed six miles inland by a massive tidal wave. Eighty-six of the world's 139 national communities are at war! Violent crimes have tripled each year for the past five years. Two hundred acts of terrorism occurred last month alone. Gangs plunder our streets. Economies stagger. Viral epidemics are rampant even in high-civilization communities!''

He was on his feet now, his voice clear and strong, his finger stabbing the air to drive the message home.

"Doesn't all this strike you as a bit odd? 'Of course,' you say, 'that's why we're holding these hearings.' Balderdash! These hearings are nothing but mindless futilities. You who represent the leaders are treating events prophesied and foretold thousands of years ago as if they were just one more budget problem or probe. While you fiddle . . ." He jabbed his finger at the panel . . . "people are growing more frightened, more confused, and more leaderless. You are damning billions. And you will be accountable for the monumental ignorance and arrogance which this hearing symbolizes!"

Em Prantzer glowed with energy. Those who knew him were astonished. While he was a courageous man of integrity he was also a gentle man who rarely spoke so strongly on any matter and, when he did, spoke in soft, shy tones.

He sat down, putting his hands on the witness table, and spoke again, softly, with urgency and compassion.

"Turn away from all of this, I beg you. Turn back to God. Our nation and our world are engaged in games. We've created a fantasy which is crumbling before our eyes. We are so caught up in ourselves that no one can see the truth. It's too big for us to see. We're too small to see it. We are a filthy, futile people, and love has dried up and gone cold. Repent and return to God."

George Ashton allowed the emotional charge of Dr. Prantzer's impassioned plea to diminish. When he spoke his tone was cold and condescending.

"The future cannot be dealt with through tools of the past. The future is in OUR hands. We are determined to prevail. This panel notes your testimony with disappointment. You are a public figure and you carry public responsibility on that account. Your views violate the Agreement of Testimony which you yourself signed. They mock the collective efforts of a diverse planet at last becoming united under the World

Alliance. We are seeking permanent solutions to our most basic problems. This hearing is a small and humble cog in the process. You have turned it into a forum from which to proclaim musty doctrines deemed empty by the thinking of the world's best minds. Your position defies intelligence, Dr. Prantzer."

He paused and wiped his brow. Emerson Prantzer sat quietly.

"I hearby find you in contempt of this hearing and order your appearance at Regional Alliance headquarters' Public Values Office tomorrow morning. Further . . ." the chairman glanced toward the hearing clerk . . . . "I ORDER this testimony struck from the record. Clerk, you will comply immediately and without interruption!"

The clerk hastily spun the Fox-100 dials and signalled confirmation.

"Finally," the chairman concluded, "I remind everyone of the confidentiality of closed hearing sessions. We end this day with regret. The interests of the United States, the Regional Alliance and the World Alliance have, despite commendable earlier testimony, been ill-served today. This hearing is recessed until ten o'clock tomorrow morning."

He rapped his gavel, rose quickly, and disappeared through the door in the rosewood wall behind him. The others quickly followed.

Half an hour later it was quiet again. All who remained in the huge empty chamber were Emerson Prantzer and the security monitors standing stiffly at attention around the perimeter. It was quite some time until he sighed and slowly walked toward the door. Two of the monitors broke ranks and escorted him out. He would indeed appear the next morning at the Public Values Office.

Chapter 6

Michael jumped into his car, ebullient. The meeting had gone well. It was not by any compliment that he knew he'd succeeded — the Prantzer Defense chief executive was not that kind of man. Rather, it was the terseness Franklin used to put down his minions' foolish objections to the proposal which Michael had boldly presented.

He had orchestrated the presentation carefully, taking senior Prantzer Defense executives through each step of the plan well in advance, designing security and influence into the new structure for those who were part of Franklin's inner circle and eliminating those who were out of favor. Franklin himself was no stranger to boldness. He had not risen to head a twenty billion dollar world defense company and in five years triple its sales without calculated risk-taking.

Prantzer Defense Group had sufficient insight into the plans of the World Alliance to see unprecedented oportunity. Michael knew something was in the works because of his close association with the huge company. Had he known more specifics — that the World Alliance chairman had set a course toward selected private company ownership of the smaller countries of the world — he would have been privy to knowledge with implications beyond his comprehension. Prantzer Defense Group intended within the next three years to acquire European and African countries and their resources, skills, military and trading base. Along with another dozen carefully chosen international firms they would form an industrial defense complex whose total revenues were projected, within the panelled inner offices of the World Alliance Headquarters, to be more than a third of the world asset base. Therein lay control.

The directive Franklin had given Rob Peary and Michael, that the new organization be patterned after the structure of the North American Regional Government "for maximum business advantage at the highest points of leverage," seemed to be a shrewd approach conceived by a seasoned business leader, and nothing more. Neither had an inkling what was behind those instructions.

He eased his car into the late afternoon city traffic. To save time he decided on the shortcut through Binzoe. He hated the thought of driving his BMW along those potholed streets, hated the sights and sounds, the odors and squalor. But traffic would be much lighter. He turned on the radio to get the news as he cut across several lanes of traffic and turned south.

The news report had more than the quake update to capture his attention. There had indeed been a minor earthquake in the area that morning. Damage had been isolated, concentrated in the very affluent suburb in which Michael lived. He wondered how badly his beautiful spruce tree had been damaged. The news continued. At the mention of Dr. Emerson Prantzer's name, Michael was immediately attentive.

". . . among several distinguished scientists who testified today at the Congressional Hearing On Global Catastrophes. Our Capitol correspondent has more on today's sessions. Bud?"

The Washington reporter's voice crackled through the radio. "Dr. Emerson Prantzer is reported to have gone beyond the bounds of scientific data in today's closed hearings," the correspondent said in soft, clipped words. "Pankie Quille Retson, colorful leader of SelfGuide, was said to have accused the well-known scientist of 'departure from rational norms.' However, she declined further comment when questioned, stating only that 'disclosure of Dr. Prantzer's remarks would be in violation of the False Doctrine Amendment.'

"This Amendment," the correspondent continued, "prohibits reference to the Bible and other religious books in public gatherings. It would seem, then, that Dr. Prantzer's remarks, as alleged by Ms. Retson, were based on religious views. What might he have been referring to? Whatever it was, it raises a question. Is the magnificent mind of Dr. Emerson Prantzer beginning to lose the disciplines and creative genius upon which his reputation is based? Or had Pankie Quille Retson found opportunity in her innuendo to create a new target in this gentle man of science? Neither option appears plausible. Any way we look at it, there's more here than meets the eye."

"Thanks Bud," the local anchorman said. "We'll have an update on the brewing Prantzer-Retson battle at our 10 p.m. report. In other news . . . ."

Michael thought it through. Franklin had directed him to structure Dr. Prantzer into an isolated commerical research group, citing deteriorating mental stability. Others as well were to be named to that group, most of whom, Michael found, had been long term associates of the Prantzer founder.

Yes, it fit. Emerson Prantzer's top drawer was sticking a bit. Michael shuddered at the decisive ostracism of a man of such wide respect and reputation, and coveted the power of those able to issue such a directive.

The BMW jolted sharply on a pothole, shaking Michael's attention back to the road. He slowed down, bouncing along partially upheaved cobblestones in the dusty shadows of dilapidated Binzoe buildings. Derelicts slumped in dark doorways and shuffled along what once had been a sidewalk. A shanty leaned against the brick wall of a dry-cleaning plant in a weed-infested, trash-filled lot. Michael viewed it with scorn.

An old car without front fenders roared toward him, bouncing almost off its wheels, it seemed, and swerved away at the last minute, raising tired clouds of dust and debris. Michael spotted South 19th Street ahead and took the corner to the right without slowing. The big BMW engine suddenly coughed, increasing the tension already building from his near-collision a moment before. A glance at the fuel gauge reminded him instantly of his error. The car lurched for half a block, then sputtered again and died. Frustrated and angry, he coasted to the curb, fuming that he'd get home late and probably end up in another argument. He slammed his hand on the dashboard and swore helplessly.

Shadows along South 19th Street had deepened to that point where shapes blended together in a dirty dark gray. Neon signs sprinkled here and there told of a neighborhood of bars, pawn shops, and surplus stores. Michael could see no gas stations.

He'd heard enough about Binzoe to have more fear than he cared to admit. There was no way he intended to leave the safety of his car in this God-forsaken part of the city. He grabbed for the car phone. It slipped from his hand and tumbled to the plush carpeted floor. As he reached to pick it up he sensed he was not alone. He looked up.

A large, ugly face was pressed against the passenger window, leering and grinning in a way that sent spikes of panic up and down his spine. He pressed the automatic door lock. Too late. The door opened and a huge grimy body attached to that face heaved itself into the front seat, reeking of old sweat and alcohol. Michael stared in raw, breathless panic.

"Nice car, man."

Michael's throat was frozen.

"Get out."

Michael went rigid. The invader moved closer. "Get OUT, man."

Michael worked his mouth but no words came. Then he noticed the others surrounding his car, clones of the filthy creature beside him. His presence of mind returned at least enough to speak. "Hey, man," he croaked, "you seen any gas stations?"

The invader flicked a long knife open, looking bored. He pointed it at Michael, his eyes glowing like a leopard's nearing the kill.

"Last chance," he hissed.

Michael's words flooded out. He pleaded. He bribed. He was babbling incoherently about a wife and good job when a searing pain shot through his right arm and instantly silenced him.

The invader pulled his knife back and wiped the tip on Michael's trouser leg. A fearsome loathing oozed through every grimy pore. Michael grabbed for the door latch, shoved it hard, and scrambled out of the car.

They were waiting. If he hadn't blacked out from the first blow to his soft belly he was only merciful moments away from fainting with fright.

He regained consciousness laying on the broken pavement with his head on the curb. He sat up slowly, nauseous and jolted with pain. His arm felt like a heavy fire. His car was gone. A lone street light threw grotesque shadows around a scrap of debris nearby. Michael groaned with despair. Every part of his body ached. He looked at his watch: it wasn't there. Neither, he found, was his wallet.

"Let me help you, friend."

Startled, Michael looked up. A fresh wave of nausea swept through him. A large man clad in tatters stood ten feet away. Michael gaped at the two different shoes he wore, at the baggy trousers and open wrinkled overcoat revealing a sweater buttoned along the front. At the top of the buttons he looked upon a surprisingly kind, grizzled face.

Gently the man knelt beside him and moved his fingers carefully over the bruises and welts around Michael's eyes and jaw, checking each wound. Michael noticed that his hands were strong and steady. And clean. When he came to the stab wound he shook his head sadly but said nothing. At length the makeshift examination was finished.

"Can you walk?"

"I think so."

Supported by the stranger's strength, Michael stood, leaning on him until the dizziness passed.

"You'd better come with me. I live around the corner. Those wounds need cleaning."

Michael felt comforted. The voice was reassuring. In this strange turn of events this man was not at all like he thought derelicts were. For all Michael's derision of anyone he thought to be lesser than himself, here was one upon whom he now depended. Then fear surfaced. He was still on the street where he'd been beaten and robbed.

"They'll be back," he said, shivering. "I'm not safe here."

"You'll be okay with me."

"They're animals!"

"The Crowns. Don't get your kind very often. Usually they just beat up on the weaker of our people. Not many others foolish enough to be here."

Michael knew the man was right. He'd done a very stupid thing. With his arm over the man's shoulder, they made their way across the vacant lot to the shanty he'd noticed earlier. An old blanket and some tar paper hung over the doorway. They had to stoop to enter.

Michael felt exhausted. His wounds throbbed. He slumped down on a mat while his rescuer lit some candles. The light revealed a room about ten feet square, barely high enough to permit standing. The bed mat, a small shelf, and makeshift bookcases nearly filled the room. The shanty wall formed by the brick of the dry-cleaning plant had a metal exhaust tube elbowed upward through the tar paper roof. The shelves were filled with books. Michael gaped at the sight, astonished.

The man shuffled over with a small black bag, noticing his expression.

"My treasures," the man said, motioning to the books. Michael looked at him, then at the black bag.

"You're . . . a doctor?" he said incredulously.

"Veterinarian. Take your jacket off and roll your sleeve up.

Michael obeyed. The stab wound was ugly red, swollen and matted with blood. He lay helplessly as the man's sure and steady hands cleaned and dressed the wound.

"You're not badly hurt. But you should get antibiotics. I don't have any. You've been in shock, but that's receding. How do you feel?"

"Better." He looked around. "Where's the phone?" His question sounded as stupid as it was as soon as he said it. He hoped he hadn't offended his helper.

"Across the street and around the corner. Place called Digger's. He's got a pay phone. I'll walk you over," the man said, snapping his bag shut.

Michael felt stronger, and his head was clearing. He rose to his feet unsteadily and reached into his pocket. Empty. New despair set in.

"I wish I could pay you something," Michael stammered with embarrassment.

"I don't need money, friend. Just glad to help."

Michael studied the man's kind, craggy face, acutely aware of his surroundings. 'Right,' Michael thought, amazed. "Who are you?" He had to know.

"Name's Ben."

There was a long pause. "You live — here, Ben? You, a doctor?"

"I live here, friend. It's warm and it's cheap." The kindly eyes crinkled in a smile as he motioned toward the cleaning plant's exhaust stack. Michael nearly fell back on the bed mat. Ben chuckled softly. "It must seem a little strange to you."

"Strange? It's incredible!"

"Come on. You'd best be on your way."

"Why do you do this? Did you lose your license? Is that it?"

"Not exactly, no. Here now, grab my arm. I'll help you through the doorway. Your wife must be worried."

The morning's earthquake, Debbie, and the huge spruce tree returned to Michael's thoughts. "Yes, yes, I need to go."

With Ben's help they ducked through the doorway and into the chilly night air. The crisp cold cleared Michael's head. Ben pointed across the lot toward Digger's, visible under a yellow mercury vapor light across the street.

"I really appreciate what you've done for me Ben," Michael said, turning to go. He was surprised — he felt sad to leave the acquaintance of this strange man. There was something about him that compelled liking him.

"I'll come back and pay you," he said determinedly.

Ben waved him off: "No, friend. No payment is necessary."

"But surely you must need something!" Michael found himself pleading.

"I have all I need. But thank you for your kind thought. Goodbye."

Michael looked at the man who'd gone to great trouble to help him. Then he turned and limped toward the street light, his mind a turmoil of confusion and gratitude. Ben stood by his shanty, watching him go. Michael could not stand the unanswered questions flooding his mind. He turned back.

"Why? WHY, Ben! You went to all this trouble for nothing!"

Ben's face creased in a slight smile. Michael thought he'd never seen a man so much at peace. He envied that peace, and realized suddenly that he'd never had it. Just as suddenly, he wanted it badly.

"There is One who did much more for me than I have for you. It was for Him that I helped you. Now go. I'm sure your wife is worried."

Michael's mind stopped in its confusion. "How do you know I have a wife?"

"They took your ring, friend. But they didn't take its imprint on your finger."

Michael looked at his finger. The wedding band was missing. Even that, he thought, more sad than angry. He turned slowly and walked toward the yellow-shadowed street corner, suspicious than Ben must be an angel.

Two of the Crowns hunched in the shadows across the street looked beyond Michael toward the shanty where Ben stood in the weak halo of the street light. Two enormous men, fully a foot taller and thickly muscled, bare to the waist even on this late autumn night, stood by him, one on either side.

"Forget him, Sauce. Those two big guys are back."

"Yeah. Again."

Michael disappeared into Digger's Diner.

Chapter 7

Gabriel Diehl stepped to the dais with an air of loving urgency and without a trace of exhaustion. His ministry spanned the nation, and his schedule strained him with long days, heavy travel, and the work which took him into the hurting lives of hundreds of men and women. But he felt increasingly driven to hold the pace. God's message overflowed within him, and the compulsion to share the good news with all who would listen was his source of energy.

Born of middle-class parents, educated in middle-class schools, and sheltered from what the world really was, Gabe had listlessly prepared for emergence into adulthood. He came from good honest stock. Hard work and personal integrity were important. His parents were quiet, unassuming Christians who lived in a style which Gabe openly rejected as often as he secretly admired.

In the midst of his apathy, Gabriel Diehl caught the fire.

It began in a familiar way. He would be wrapped up in whatever issue captured the moment. Usually it was quite trivial. Suddenly he would lose concentration. When he tried to focus on the matter at hand it became irrelevant. That which compelled his attention like a magnet one moment would, in the next, become a source of boredom. Depression would come as he contemplated the emptiness of it all and realized he knew no way out of that emptiness. Attraction, repulsion, irrelevancy, depression. The pattern had, more and more often, become his cycle of life.

He was filling out his college application in his room one wintry evening when the cycle appeared. He leaned back and tossed his pen on the desk. Snow was falling hard outside the window of his bedroom. He could see several inches on the ground, drifting up against the fence.

Normally Gabe knew that it really WAS a trivial activity which preoccupied him. But college was not a meaningless pursuit. He sighed and tried again to concentrate. But it was no use. He thumbed through a sports car magazine. The modified Maserati was on a thumbworn page near the back. Gabe often thought that to own that car would be one of the great experiences in life. He admired it now, coveting its sleek lines.

The voice of an evangelist his parents often listened to on the radio drifted up the hallway. Suddenly Gabe knew the evangelist was speaking directly to him.

". . . the righteousness of God through faith in Christ Jesus for all who believe . . ."

Gabe locked onto those words as if drawn to the core of creation. Dawn had broken. His heart felt like rupturing, and tears pushed into his eyes. He leapt from his chair and ran down the hallway to the living room. His parents sat the way he'd seen then a thousand times and had come both to love and hate in that near-perfect contradiction of adolescence unknown to children and forgotten by adults. His mother was in the overstuffed chair clasping her worn Bible. His dad was stretched out on the couch, stockinged feet propped up on one armrest and head on the other.

"What was that? What did he say? I have to know!"

His dad pulled his hands from their clasped wingspread behind his head and sat up. "Are you all right, son?"

Deep, heaving sobs coursed through Gabe. A part of him stood detached, though warmly, observing and keeping him aware of his experience. A burden of enormous remorse forced him to his knees.

"Gabe . . ." His mother stopped in mid-sentence. Recognition came, and her fading beauty lit up with happiness. She glanced at her husband. Tears streamed from his eyes, freely, silently, as exquisitely true gratitude and joy filled him up. Both knew what was happening. Seventeen years ago they had experienced the writhing pain of the birth of their son. Now they witnessed the pain of his rebirth, the birth of his spirit.

"I'm sorry, I'm sorry," he sobbed. "All those times . . . I've hurt you and made your life so difficult . . ." They held their silence, barely able to contain the sweetness. Gabe leaned against the big chair and sighed. He was frightened by the strangeness, not by any fear, of the power inside of him. He struggled to bring rationality back, to preserve at least some adolescent dignity. Even as he spoke, different words came out.

"What's happening to me?" It was what he'd really wanted to say.

His dad put his strong hands on Gabe's shoulders. "Son," he said, "you're under the convicting power of the Holy Spirit. God Himself is touching you this night."

Gabe felt excitement trembling in those hands, and knew it was true. The weight of conviction came on him again, and he sobbed unashamedly until the hardening framework of an emerging worldly adult melted away.

He saw in his heart the terrible potentials which lurked there, and the insights were wondrous if fearsome. He saw the power to hate not merely as ugly emotion but as an insidious toehold toward the justification of vengeance, even to murder. He saw in his glandular delight with Jeannie not just sportful play but the seeds of abasement sprouting into an ugly thornbush. He no longer found virtue in his abilities to manipulate and compromise; instead he found bitter oceans of self-deceit. Once adrift, he found he would forever be without linkage to truth, forced to write new scenes for new plays from new imaginings until at last he would be awarded the permanent emptiness of his drifting.

Piece by piece, the prized elements of his maturing desolation fell under the power of God's conviction, their empty places washed and cleansed for occupancy by a higher calling. The last to go was his pride, pride in who he had acted like and in who he had intended to become. It was drawn from him in climactic convulsions after there was nothing else left to take pride in.

Then, exhausted, he had a vision of tottering on the brink of a pit. In it was all that had been exorcised, calling for him to follow. It was as if his very arm, torn from his body, now lay on the floor and demanded to be reunited. Squirming in the depths of that pit, his rebelliousness masqueraded as freedom and his self-centeredness grinned alluringly. His inclination toward sarcasm winked and insisted that without that he was defenseless. His impatience leered, urging him to reclaim it before it was too late. Gabe fought the battle with himself. It was his own choice.

He felt emptied, as if rid of a huge but hidden infection and cleaned all out, but not yet wrapped with fresh ointment and dressing.

"What do I do?"

The question raised a cornucopia of memories for his parents — the broken bike and the helping hand, the stolen toy and the guiding word, the ball team strike-out and the consolation of a father's love.

"You know what to do. God is touching you with His power. Your mother and I received Jesus Christ quietly, without apparent experience, years ago. But God seems to be calling you in a more profound way."

Gabe would have reacted with sneering rejection even three hours ago. Yet now he hung on every word, and he knew the answer was true.

"You know who Jesus is. We've told you many times. Respond to Him, Gabe. Receive Him into you. That's what He has prepared you to do."

At the mention of Jesus' name tears again flooded Gabe's eyes. And in an instant he knew the Savior Himself as if he had stood at the foot of His cross and shared His agony. The noise of his pride, impatience and self importance dimmed as a membrane of Love stretched over that pit. He knew Jesus was the answer, the hope for all things. His freedom of choice flitted across his consciousness. He plucked it out of mid-thought and confirmed his decision, laughing the spontaneous laugh of released joy. "I do receive Jesus!"

The membrane thickened and toughened, and the brash clamorings faded away. Gabe had never before felt such perfect harmony. It was as if a jumble of dissonant sounds suddenly blended into a triumphant and mighty chorus. He was filled with welcoming brightness and freshness of being, and knew he was reborn into the loved family of God himself. His wounds had been dressed with the incorruptible dressing of the Holy Spirit, and would heal.

Few experiences are sweeter than the birth of a new Christian in the presence of prayer warriors whose faith has at last been answered. The new Christian is bathed in a quiet joy and peace which eludes understanding and envelopes him in the arms of a boundless love. And the leap of joy in the hearts of those who prayed with perserverance on his behalf is a leap which knows no landing.

So it was in the Diehl household that night. The presence of the Spirit of Jesus Christ filled the room. They simply sat on the floor, smiling and laughing in the clear clean glow of utter truth, blessed certainty, perfect love.

Gabe found his half-completed college application years later in a stack of papers as, newly graduated from seminary, he prepared to serve in his first church. He lasted four months before being asked to resign. His outspoken denouncements of the Twenty-Ninth Amendment were "inconsistent with congregational consensus." But he refused to be silenced. He had not only railed against the False Doctrine Amendment, but had begun to challenge the structure and the leadership of the World Organized Ecumenical Council. The religious community, itself in a state of turmoil, closed him out.

So Gabriel Diehl went to the streets in tent meetings and preached with power against the organized hypocrisies and their complicities with deception that characterized those times. He was effective. Arrest inevitably came. The young preacher spent two years in prison for subverting social values. He was released only in the general amnesty extended by the North American Region Government, a move intended to ease controversy around the Regional Alignment Plan to unite individual and state values. That amnesty put him back on the streets again, with burning conviction of the futility of the world's direction, and with a renewed sense of mission to help all who would hear and understand the unalterable and crucial message of Jesus Christ. The matured Gabe Diehl, and others who, sooner than any could possibly realize would be recognized as final day prophets, spoke out with vigorous urgency. And slowly, many began to listen.

Gabe's message and call always threaded the same needle: all matters of the world are temporary futile vanities. The saving relationship with Jesus Christ, man's way back to life and meaning, was the essential need of every one. And there was not much time left to fill it.

The religious community had become divided into two camps. One, numbering five out of every six churchgoers, were members of established denominations who were party to the World Organized Ecumenical Council (WOEC) and had signed the Pledge Of Loyalty. The smaller group, steadfastly pointing to Jesus Christ alone as the author and finisher of their faith, refused to participate in WOEC or sign its Pledge.

When the False Doctrine Amendment was enacted, these two groups comprised half the nation's population. Five years later they were less than a third, the larger group losing people to apathy and disillusionment, the smaller to intensifying persecution. Fears and uncertainties were growing. Many began responding to the message of Christ preached by Gabe Diehl, Amy Greene, Warren R. Heath, and others. Their social stigma faded. Even in the highly organized social structure of the United States in the days of Regional and World Alliance, new churches emerged. Though ridiculed by WOEC denominations and legally required to conform to public gathering laws, their Christ-centered ministries were never diminished. Those who had perservered in faith in Jesus Christ through the difficult years of social upheaval, increasing war and violence, and focused persecutions of those who held that Jesus Christ alone is to be worshiped, were not fooled. Once the truth is found, the counterfeit no longer can satisfy.

Gabe Diehl was called to one of these churches. Membership quickly doubled, then tripled. He mounted the dais of that church now. More than a thousand people were crowded into the hall for this first of three worship services. As he came forward he watched the government monitor seated on the platform. The usual disapproving glare was in place. Earlier that week the monitor had paid him a visit, ostensibly to warn him of infractions of the law he repeatedly committed while leading worship services. But Gabe thought he'd been touched, too, by the message of Jesus and, like Nicodemus, wanted to find out more. He had special hope for Harry Hawkins, servant of the state. But his expression showed him more resolute than ever in rejecting the tug of mercy Gabe sensed was working in him.

He'd chosen to speak this morning about the Savior. It was a violation of national statute, and therefore, a risk. But then, any stand for Jesus Christ was risky.

"Some of you may be confused and frightened because of the terrible calamities which have touched us all. Know that as you are here with us, you are among people who love you in Jesus' name! We love you because He loves you. It is Jesus Whom we worship — the Christ, the Lord of Lords, the King of Kings, the Son of God.
"He knows our quiet desperations, our afflictions, our torments. He sees us tangled in arguments, greeds and selfishness. My friends, Jesus offers living hope to a dying world. I know this is true by my own experience. Will you hear about the Savior?"

Gabe glanced toward the scowling monitor. The man shifted and scowled more fiercely.

"Jesus came to us not to judge but to save. He revealed God's truth to all who would hear, untainted by worldly influence of compromise. Humble in spirit, powerful in obedience, fearlessly tearing out the falseness and traditions which deadened and separated people from God, Jesus preached and taught and healed. He proclaimed a new covenant of Love.
"The religious leaders decided to kill Him — He had become a threat to their own power. He had revealed Who He was. Stirred by those leaders, the people began to reject Him. He prepared to give Himself for them all. He knew His purpose, and He knew our need."

Jesus and His disciples walked together into Gethsemane. The torches of the city winked through the dust of her festival celebration. Traces of laughter floated over the wall, across the valley, and through the olive trees. Jesus moved off to pray. The energy of Creation coursed through His body with such power that perspiration seeped from Him like droplets of blood and dripped onto the ground. God the Father, Magnificent, All-Powerful, and Splendid in His Heavens, now looked upon His beloved Christ kneeling despondently in the garden, and released Him to suffer alone and to die. Why? So that people could be saved from God's Own Wrath! And what is God's wrath? It is His leaving us to the outcomes of our own nature. Jesus died for us. God gave His only begotten Son, that whoever would believe in Him would not die, but have everlasting life! Yet many harden their hearts and refuse to receive Him."

"Pharisees and soldiers followed a nervous Judas into Gethsemane. They grabbed Jesus. His disciples ran. He was marched away to trial. Caiaphas, the leader of the Pharisees, questioned Him. 'Are you, Jesus of Nazareth, actually who you claim to be?' Jesus looked steadily at him and confirmed the truth Caiaphas had spoken. Then Jesus was presented to the people. Pharisees whipped up the crowd gathered there against Him. He stood on a balcony bloodstained, exhausted, silent. 'Crucify him!' they shouted, 'Crucify him!' "

Gabe glanced again toward Harry Hawkins, the monitor, gauging whether he would be shut off from talking further. The monitor's expression was strange, as though a listening heart desperate for Peace struggled with a mind long since yielded to the traditions and values of human nature. Harry Hawkins trembled behind his stoic mask of habitual unpleasantness. There was hope enough in that, Gabe realized. The lost do not even tremble.

"They laid the beam on Jesus' shoulders, raw and aching from whippings. He struggled up the cobblestone street to Golgotha. The beam was fitted across a pole lying on the ground. He was shoved down upon it. Then He convulsed as spikes were driven through His wrists and ankles. The world spun as the cross was lifted upright with heavy ropes, its base dropping into a socket dug into the Judean clay. Agony flooded Him as it rammed into place.

"All of Creation watched the Christ suffer and do final spiritual battle, knowing that the fate of each of us across all time depended on the choices which the Son of God would make in the coming hours. The crowd saw a Man hanging on a cross. But spirits saw the forerunner of Armageddon that day. Attacks from every evil crashed against the Savior like violent storm-driven waves pound against the rocks.

"The crowd taunted. 'If you are God, get off that cross!' But He did not. He suffered in humiliation and pain, and battled in majesty, for us. No nails held Him to that cross — it was His unconditional Love for US which did so.

"Finally in incredible pain and loneliness Jesus looked up to Him Who had turned His face away for our sakes. 'It is finished, Father. Into Your hands I commend My spirit.' A mighty crash split open the sky, and rains hammered the earth. Jesus died then, and took the crushed powers of sin with Him into Hell."

Gabe suddenly spun around. Harry Hawkins sat, looking down, sobbing. Gabe spoke with urgency.

"If the way does not lead you to safety it is not the Way. If the truth is flawed it cannot survive and is not the Truth. If life ends in death it is not life. Jesus is the Way, the Truth, and the Life. He broke the power of sin and death by His willingness to endure the cross. Then He rose from death and consummated His victory — a victory which all who are reborn in Him share. Everyone will enter the valley of death. Those who follow Jesus follow Him through that valley and into the safety of the other side. Those who do not follow Jesus have no other way out."

Many received Jesus Christ as their Lord and Savior that morning. One was Harry Hawkins. Broken and convicted, he became just a man without pretense, who discovered that he is Loved by name just as he is, and that there is nothing strong enough to overpower the risen Christ.
"There is rejoicing in the presence of God's angels over one sinner who repents." It was one of Gabe's favorite passages, and he delighted in its truth. But some had decided it could not be even before they got through the doors after Gabe's sermon, and left with a mocking spirit.

Chapter 8

Debbie met Michael at Lake Shore Community Hospital after midnight. Both had forgotten their pre-dawn quarrel and the day's events, relieved that Michael would be all right, and grateful for his strange encounter with the man called Ben.
As they turned into their driveway an unaccustomed bump rocked the van where paving bricks had heaved in the earthquake that morning. The spruce tree leaned toward the house at an awkward angle.
"Maybe it can be straightened," Michael said hopefully. He patted his wife's knee.
Debbie nodded and smiled, surprised at his calmness. The garage door yawned open, and the fastidiously clean space

for the BMW glared back at them empty. Debbie pulled in and shut off the engine of the van, steeling herself. Michael's griping irritability was sure to come with this reminder of the loss of his metal mistress. She expected him to slam the car door and stomp off into the house, seething with his misfortune.

They sat in silence inside the dark garage, Michael neither irritable nor impatient. His head was back against the headrest, eyes half-closed. The Binzoe experience had forced parts of his life into perspective, and raised questions successfully ignored until now. Vulnerability made its unspoken case with the persistent throbbing in his arm. The creature who had stabbed him could just as well have rammed the blade into his side. Micahel did not feel angry — he felt spared, and grateful for it. He might have been dead now, with all he had worked for blown away like mist. What of it, then? Nothing. And that was the point.

The word "nothing" stuck in his mind. Is that where it all led? Debbie would grieve for awhile — perhaps — then adjust her life and go on. His clients would quickly forget him. What would Debbie have lost? Certainly not his time or attention — his ambition had taken that from her years ago.

Moonglow filtering into the garage highlighted Debbie's brown hair, making the auburn strands dance and sparkle. 'She is beautiful,' he thought, savoring the tiny lift to the corner of her mouth and the shine in her eyes. He thought sadly about how little of himself he'd given to her over the years, and how much of their fighting and tension he knew he had really caused.

Debbie almost worshiped her husband. Nothing affected Michael quite as much as the look of deep hurt which crept unavoidably into her eyes at his thoughtlessness and selfishness. A flood of love filled him as if it were the first time they'd met. She saw, and responded. A tear of gratitude for whatever the powers were that had brought her husband back to her this evening glistened in her eye.

Michael winced from the pain in his arm. The evening had touched him in ways he did not understand. The Michael he had grown accustomed to and come to loathe would have cursed his misfortune. Despite the hour he would have gone into his study and worked long after Debbie had gone to their lonely bedroom and sobbed herself to sleep.

"Something big is happening, Deb." His own words startled him. He hadn't intended to say it, and he didn't know why he did. It just came out.

Debbie kept silent, both in instinct and by good breeding, and took his hand. But Michael had no more words. He leaned over and kissed her, ever so gently.

"I love you."

It was enough. They climbed out of the van and went together into their house.

That night Michael had three mysterious visions, vivid and rich with symbolism, beckoning him toward unknown places in his soul. He understood none of them, yet they became irresistible companions to his waking thoughts.

He found himself floating through an utter void in which specks of light appeared mercifully as darkness sought to smother him. The twinklings increased like handfuls of sparkling diamonds thrown against the blackness, and seemed to grow brighter, as if moving rapidly toward him. He found that he was growing, expanding far beyond the speed of light itself, shrinking the void in which he was suspended.

Light specks took on form and color as they approached, and he could discern shimmering, intricate crystals orbiting in majestic whorls of energy. Now the size of moons in the skies, they revealed interlocking patterns of perfection which changed his panoramic tapestry into spiralled cords and webs of matter.

He felt as though he'd been woven into cubic cloth. Yet still he expanded, and the warp and woof of dense fabric grew finer and more pure. Blackness yielded to a deep emerald green with a glow of its own, and cell-like structures emerged and increased in strength. Far above, he saw a lighter, more intense translucence, as if he were rushing upward through the waters of the sea toward its sun-crested surface. And then he popped through, but gently. Delicate filaments of chlorophylled nourishment beckoned greeting, and the leaf yielded him to that which lay beyond.

For just an instant he was his own size, and his planet stretched before him, its beauty billowing with perfection from every different countless blossom and sunkissed pond.

He grew again, rising amid the landscape of earth until he floated over the seas and touched the mountaintops. Graceful white clouds scudded under him across the blues of the oceans and browns of the lands, designs in a living carpet. Forests languished in the sun, and rainbows spawned in new rains offered their promises. As he rose it became a whole globe turning with hope and teeming with the life of all to whom the Creator had granted pilgrimmage there. He gazed at the world with a hungry soul, and wished never to be released from the beauty it now revealed. The moon raced by him, ebbing along its sideward arc. Great glowings of orbiting light moved harmoniously through the heavens, sculpting networks in their perfectly obeyed pathways. As they diminished, others joined the throng, gleaming their farewell and speeding away until they were, once again, barely discernible flecks against the black stillness of the outer heavens.

"I have created as many such cycles as there are stars in the evening sky. What is man, that I am mindful of him?"

The unspoken words came into Michael's mind, and his eyes opened. Banal intrusions interrupted the peaceful ecstasy of his journey as familiar forms and shadows of the darkened bedroom restored reality. Debbie's steady breathing brought peace of a different kind. In moments he fell back asleep.

Soon he was in an obviously expensive restaurant. A grotesquely fat man with a huge napkin tucked into the folds of his chin sat a few tables away, unmindful of his presence. An enormous plate piled high with exotic foods was in front of the man, who lustfully ogled the burgeoning platter.

Michael glanced through a large window expecting without knowing why to see gaunt, impoverished faces pressed against the glass, peering in. But there was revealed only a row of dark, dirty buildings, ghastly under the harsh glow of yellow street lights.

With arrogant ceremony the huge man shovelled his fork into the food, lifting enough for three or four mouthfuls. He chomped and drooled without appreciating in the least the exquisite rarity of his nourishment. Suddenly, as if coming through a zoom lens, Michael was moved toward the man's face, which soon filled his range of view. Pig-like eyes, glinting behind folds of flesh, watched him draw nearer. The mouth continued to churn and chomp. Michael seemed about to be pressed against the drooling, oily chin when the mouth suddenly gaped open very wide. Inside the foods had become dry, choking dust. In an instant the huge man turned to powder and collapsed into a pile on the chair, spilling over like sand onto the expensive oriental rug. A lion appeared with a carpet sweeper in its paws and moved it over the dust until all traces had disappeared.

Michael awoke, trembling, realizing the man was himself. He took some time to fall back asleep.

Not long afterward he stood beside a high tower, its stone wall glistening with condensation in pale, suffused moonlight. He was cold and very hungry. Then he sensed a movement in the shadows, and peered through dark fog at that which approached him. A figure emerged from an alley, robed in a white tunic, tall and slender. His face was without expression and he walked more as one who had practiced the movements of another than as he himself might have walked. His eyes burned with their own luminescence. They were eyes of power and malevolence. Michael shuddered involuntarily. The figure stopped before him and held out its hand.

"I've been looking for you, Michael. Take, and eat."

Resting on its outstretched palm was a frosted wafer about the size of a sugar cookie. It looked delicious. Michael felt the emptiness of his stomach. But for a strange fear he would have seized the morsel and eaten without hesitation.

The figure eyed him closely. "You are hungry, are you not?"

"I am," Michael heard himself say.

"Then take — it will give you what you want."

"Will it give me what I need?"

"Is there a difference?"

Michael shrugged. His mouth salivated in eager anticipation. "Why not," he replied, reaching for the wafer.

Then he heard a faint moan from the alley. A bent-over form crawled painfully into the glow of dim light reflected off wet stones and raised his head.

"Don't eat that, Michael. It will kill you!"

Michael wished to question him, but he slumped over suddenly and collapsed on the ground, motionless.

"And what of that?" Michael said indignantly.

The figure shrugged. "It's your choice."

"But he said it would kill me!"

The figure's eyebrows arched. "Oh? He's lying. Think about yourself and your hunger. He suffered because he did not eat, not because he did. Feel your own stomach, Michael. Does it please you?"

Michael agreed that his hunger was unpleasant.

"Lick the surface of this wafer as a test. You will find it sweet, and you will know then what to do."

That seemed fair enough. Michael brought the wafer to his tongue and tasted its surface. It was sweet indeed, a curiously compelling sweetness which urged him to devour the morsel whole.

"Did I not tell you the truth?"

Michael nodded, pleased.

"Then you can trust me. Take, and eat."

Michael was still uncertain. But the sweetness lingered on the tip of his tongue, and there were no consequences. He stuffed the wafer into his mouth and brushed the crumbs from his hands. The taste was sweet, exhilarating, intense. Then he swallowed. Without a word the figure turned and walked away with that curiously awkward stride. Michael watched the figure depart, and suddenly fell to the ground in shock. Cloven hoofs were where its feet should have been. His stomach began to burn then, and the wafer became like a hot rock in the pit of his stomach.

The figure spun around. His eyes were like red coals and his leer was void of hope. The pain in Michael's body filled every muscle and joint with fiery agony. He writhed on the ground, doubled over and clutching his arms around himself.

"Why?" he gasped. "I didn't know . . ."

The figure laughed. "I needn't waste another lie, so I will give you a truth. The warning of a friend is weaker than the temptation of a stranger. You were no challenge. You did my work for me." The figure swished its robe and disappeared into the alley.

Michael groaned in great misery. Screaming for mercy, he staggered to his feet. But the pain pulled him back and he crumpled in a heap onto the hard ground, screaming for deliverance.

His eyes blinked open then, and found Debbie's worried face close to his.

". . . Michael, Michael!" she said softly, soothingly. "It's all right now — you must have been having a nightmare."

He sat bolt upright and looked around, assuring himself that it had never happened. His bandaged arm ached painfully and he was damp with perspiration. But he was greatly relieved. Shaking, he lay down. Debbie stroked his forehead until sleep finally overtook him.

Toward dawn the house trembled, accompanied by the low rumbling of another small earthquake.

Chapter 9

If Pankie had unusual strength beyond well-endowed intelligence, it was in her ability to dominate using caustic harshness and ruthlessness. She had nurtured these abilities carefully, and they had returned many victories during the building days of SelfGuide.

She had also learned the value of compromise and was skilled in the art. Now, behind her large glass desk in the Self-Guide offices, she blinked a short night's sleep from her eyes and checked the clock. Its readout showed "SAT 06:28 AM." In a few minutes she would have to use her skills deftly.

The office was dawn-still save the gentle intermittent hissing of a silver coffee urn. Surveying the distant reaches of her mirrored suite, she admired her reflection. A good foundation, she thought, thinking over the struggles to achieve and the distance yet to be covered. She thought, too, about the boldest plan of all, the plan that would soon be put into action.

The call had come several days before from a senior aide of the World Alliance chairman. They had met once before, when SelfGuide, WOEC, and other groups were first being aligned with the World Alliance. She recalled her furious resistance to the alignment process.

But Ing Hammock, then Deputy Chief of World Alliance Public Relations, had paid a special visit to her hotel room in Geneva. She found him to be a kindred spirit, and soon became convinced of the rightness of the association. The financial benefits, certain privileges, and Ing's personal assignment to help Pankie accelerate SelfGuide's public education activities, had helped her decide to cooperate.

Her attention drifted to the words etched into a small solid gold bar on her desk. "Power is everything. Use it." Ing had given it to her, a memorial of South Africa taken from the president's private cache during the crash of the apartheid government.

Power she certainly had. Her influence and personal wealth were providing access and leverage into leadership and opinion-setting circles. Acquaintances today, perhaps, but friends, and comrades in arms, tomorrow.

'The Iron Maiden,' she mused with a tight smile, thinking of the epitaph Ing Hammock, only half-joking, had assigned to her. Not iron. Steel. And certainly not Maiden.

She checked the week's summary her secretary had placed on the desk. Revenues, membership, and pledge backlog were strong, but the dramatic increase during recent months was slowing. She reviewed her schedule . . . senate hearings, press meeting and WOEC banquet at the Charlemagne . . . the week demanded much, and glittered with opportunity. SelfGuide had become big business. One of its last hold-out critics had called it "the hula hoop fad, but more expensive." Pankie had attacked the critic through the press, stoutly defending the deep values of SelfGuide and its intrinsic worth and abusing the hapless wag until he retired without honor and disappeared. No one could speak poorly of her organization without facing confrontation to the death.

She sighed impatiently, feeling like a tightly wound spring. Moe was late. The Omega Plan waited. Pankie knew, of course, that Moe Cummings was connected in various ways with hidden power elements, into those linkages which made things operate while propaganda continued to be spewed out into the visible world. She didn't care about the degree of integrity, or lack of it, with which the senator plied his trade. It only mattered that he was useful and that she continued to be useful to him.

Carpet-muffled footsteps sounded outside of the office suite. Senator Moe Cummings came in, dripping wet.

"You're late," Pankie snapped.

Moe opened the mirrored door to Pankie's private washroom and tossed his soaked overcoat across the rim of the tub.

"They've gone crazy," he grumbled. "Got any coffee?" He sat on the white oversized couch. Pankie motioned across the room to the silver urn.

Moe grunted and got up. "You're taking this SelfGuide stuff too seriously, Pankie. Whatever happened to executive hospitality?"

"Make mine with sugar," Pankie retorted.

"You're in a fiesty mood, Ms. Retson," he needled. He passed a steaming china cup to Pankie and sat down across from her.

"Don't you want to know why I'm soaked?"

"Does it matter?"

Moe ignored her comment. "Would you believe they're rioting again? Went on all night."

"Of course I know they're rioting." Pankie touched a sensor on her chair. A holographic image of an EBC newscaster shimmered above the titanium plate on her desk and began in mid-sentence with the morning's headlines.

". . . University students are at it again. The Public Guard was forced to use gas tranquilizers and water cannon to quell an all-night protest against the new ruling which prohibits personal slaves from campus housing. The demonstration became violent at 4:30 this morning . . ."

Pankie clicked the image off, looking smug. "Impressive," Moe said. "We've only had those things a few months ourselves."

Pankie smiled. "So, senator, you who elude the subtle darts of Regional politics are soaked by a water cannon." She laughed scornfully. "It fits."

Moe reddened. He was accustomed to deferential treatment almost anywhere he appeared. Pankie was the exception. He had met her, two years before, within a day of disparaging remarks he'd made about SelfGuide during a press interview. Pankie had stomped into his office unannounced — no small feat in itself — and barked the senator to attention. He knew immediately he had a big problem. Their verbal barrage accelerated furiously, trading abuse and accusations like heavyweight boxers going for the kill. What cowed the senator was not the vehemence of the battle, but the fury in her eyes. That fury bore into him mercilessly, and defeated him.

This did not happen solely by the force of Pankie's personality and will to fight. She had used the time between ignorant senatorial remarks and bold confrontation digging up everything she could about the senator's past. She was amazed how much could be learned in twenty hours.

If she was amazed, he was stunned. They quickly became friends in that special sort of relationship fused whenever vulnerability and amoral determination meet and find mutual utility.

The senator ran his fingers through his damp thinning hair. "My driver lowered my window instead of raising it as we passed the riot area. Just then the cannon blasted. Spray poured in on me and everything else within a hundred feet."

Pankie lit a thin cigar and leaned back in her chair. She liked to put Moe on the defensive. It was one of the few things she did with him that she did not find boring.

"So," he said, seeking a change of subject. "What can I do for you?"

Pankie exhaled a plume of smoke. "Emerson Prantzer."

"Yes. He went too far, didn't he?"

"You wouldn't know it from the stupor you seemed to be in during his testimony."

"Listen Pankie . . ."

"You were pathetic!" she interrupted savagely. "You let him babble on with talk in direct contradiction to SelfGuide. You blew it again, both as a senator and as a member of our board!"

"The hearing was closed, Pankie, and it would have been awkward to stop him. Besides, Ashton's the one who let him go on."

"Of course it's awkward, once you let him get into it. Why didn't you cut him off at the beginning?"

Moe felt his anger rising. "You know it wasn't clear where he was going until he was already into it. Appearing to censure testimony is deadly. Ashton used good judgment. It wouldn't have worked to undercut him."

Pankie's eyes creased in a sneering laugh. "Do I detect a note of fear?"

Moe's pulse throbbed and his breath quickened. She noted the change with satisfaction.

"Get Emerson Prantzer out of the way," Pankie said sweetly. "He's too well known and too willing to speak out. You know those types. They'll preach from that book every chance they get. They're poison to the world!"

Moe squirmed in his chair. The gleam of vengeance in Pankie's eyes was unsettling.

"Will you handle it, Moe?"

He rubbed his chin, mocking thought just long enough to appear to have considered the matter. "All right. The subcommittee discussed this only yesterday. For the good of the country and the Region, we must do something."

"Yes senator, I quite agree," Pankie snorted. She stubbed her cigar into the ash tray and pulled a laser disk out of her drawer. "Here," she said, flipping it across the desktop toward him. Moe looked at it, puzzled.

"The way you bumble around, Prantzer would die a natural death before anything constructive happened. This . . ." she jabbed her finger at the disk . . . "should expedite matters by a few months." She picked up the disk and went to the other side of the office, brushing up against Moe as she did so. He turned in his chair to watch her. She inserted it into a small computer built into the wall. A large screen came alive with static. Then a slender well-dressed man appeared. A digital voice began its recitation.

"This is Michael J. Ames, white male, age thirty-six. Six feet one inch — one hundred seventy-seven pounds. 11 Plum Grove Drive, Cabington Borough, Glen Ridge, Illinois. Married to Debbie Bower for twelve years. No children. Citizenship — North American Region and United States, by birth; Global, application pending. Clearance Five. Military — none. Health — excellent. Belief — Neutral Scale Zero. Radioactive exposure — none."

Pankie pressed 'pause.' "Not bad looking, eh Moe?"

The senator grunted with disgust. "Maybe for you. What's this all about?" Pankie pressed the sensor again. The voice resumed.

"Employed with Robinson A. Peary Associates, Management Consultants — Account Director, eight years. Current responsibility — Prantzer Defense group reorganization project. Prior — Wallich Financial Inc., Training Manager, seven years. Education — B. A. Cornwall University, Magna Cum Laude; M.B.A. Cornwall University, Cum Laude. Income — Two hundred twenty-seven thousand. Assets — Five hundred forty thousand. Liabilities — Seven hundred fourteen thousand. Hobbies — golf. Skills — photographic memory.

The screen displayed a series of photographs of Michael in personal and professional settings. Then it went blank.

"I've heard of Peary Associates. They worked with Bell Observatories when I was on their board. Pretty impressive stuff."

"As usual, your laser-like mind homes right in on the crux of things."

Moe flushed at her sarcasm. Pankie laughed. "Easy, senator. Don't take it personally."

"Yeah." He pushed himself out of the chair and refilled his coffee. "So what's the connection? Consultants work with Prantzer Defense all the time."

"Ames is working directly with Franklin himself. And the reorganization project involves Emerson Prantzer."

"Interesting. But I can see Franklin directly if I want to. I don't need connections for that."

"You have to think beyond the end of your self-centered little world to hear what I'm saying to you."

He let the sarcasm pass. It was no use fighting. He waited for her to continue. Pankie became serious and intense.

"There's a lot of unrest. We've never seen things happen like they are now. We thought nuclear fear was the greatest threat to psychological stability. All that has changed. It's only one of many threats. People don't understand these disasters, the economic collapses, wars, or government's inability to do anything about any of it."

She studied Moe to be sure he was understanding. "Do you know the new suicide statistics?"

"I saw some information . . ."

"More people killed themselves during the past six months than during the previous eighteen months."

Moe blanched. "Voters and taxpayers," he said morosely.

"People!" Pankie retorted.

"Right, right. So get to your point."

Pankie lit her last cigar, crumpled the box, and threw it disgustedly into the waste slot. "That statistic is what's happening to people on this planet. You heard the testimony last week. What no one is talking about as much as they ought to is the effect. It's overwhelming. An entire planet is frightened to death. The old rules are gone. Got a house on the beach? You thought you'd keep going there every summer. Wrong. No more beach. Want to go to the mountains? At the present rate of volcanic eruption the odds are one in fifteen that any mountain higher than eight thousand feet will be buried by hot ash within a month."

Moe gasped.

"People are more vulnerable now than ever in history. Why do you think SelfGuide is growing so fast? People are confused and frightened. They need something to hang on to. We provide it.

Moe shifted his weight and gazed out the window. The sun was up now, hidden behind a thick layer of mottled orange-gray cloud. Two airborne personnel platforms hover-droned past the tenth story SelfGuide windows, moving toward the student riot area. He could see the pilot in each, gas hose slung over his shoulder, leaning in the direction of travel as if looking forward to the confrontation a few blocks away.

"Must be getting bad down there," Moe remarked.

"It's a scene being repeated across the world."

"So, Pankie — what's your point? We seem to be a long way from Emerson Prantzer and that fellow you showed on the screen."

Pankie sat down with a hateful anger in her eyes. Her hands trembling slightly. "Another group is growing too, in case you hadn't noticed. Faster than SelfGuide. It's the non-WOEC churches, the ones who believe like Prantzer does. They're convinced we're in the so-called last days and that their leader's return is near. People are flocking to their churches like stampeding sheep. They're a threat."

"Now wait. I do have current information on that one." Moe chuckled reassuringly. "Stroke of genius, I might add, the auditing provision of all those little groups. That was my rider, you know."

Pankie was unimpressed.

"Christian groups number under five million people. Twenty years ago it was more than thirty million. WOEC, on the other hand, is nearing two hundred million. Not to worry, Pankie. They're declining. It's just a passing thing, a little dying burp."

"Moe," Pankie said with exasperation, "Christian membership doubled in the last four months! Their churches are holding services around the clock, and every one is standing room only. Simple arithmetic says that they'll equal WOEC's size in a couple of years!"

"There aren't enough unassigned people left for that to happen." Moe used his best voice of comfort. "Maximum non-WOEC potential is under twenty million, tops. Compared with total population, at that size they're only statistical noise. A little salt for the steak."

Pankie spoke with razor-edged crispness. "Can't you get beyond bureaucratic drivel? I'm talking vitality, not numbers. WOEC is a sham. And don't unload any party-line nonsense. Three hundred million frightened people in this Region alone are polarizing toward one of two camps: WOEC, and this Jesus Christ. The action is in that polarization. WOEC is like a morgue as far as energy or commitment is concerned. There's no fire there. SelfGuide draws from them. It's in SelfGuide that the philosophy catches fire. But those Christians are on fire too. They, and we, are the only groups that are alive. Everything else is dead."

"Just a minute, Pankie. As a good Pro-Method Reformed Anglican I must tell you I resent . . ."

"Shut up senator. I'm talking real and you know it." Pankie's voice softened. "Look, there's opportunity here which the world has never seen. And you're on the inside, part of it all, unlike the blundering deadwood most of your colleagues seem to be. The issue is global leadership. We're at the right place at the right time. Forget your little world. A senator today, with the World Alliance ready to take over as the governing authority, is like the local councilman a generation ago. You can become big, Moe. Very big."

Her conciliatory tone disarmed Moe Cummings quickly. He was never more mindful than now of the influence which Pankie Quille Retson indeed had, not only through SelfGuide, but through the press, TV and AV stations, and satellite networks.

"Okay. I'm listening."

"I've studied what these Christians believe."

"All WOEC is Christian, Pankie!" Moe said indignantly. "It's just those hard line types . . ."

"Those hard line types, as you so eloquently call them, may be the enemy, but they've got something those flabby idiots in WOEC never heard of! You're no more a Christian than I am."

How lumbering hypocrites like Moe Cummings ever made it to positions of influence escaped her. Choice, good or bad, not fence-sitting. Single-minded focus. Ruthless determination. That's what character is made of, not the vacillating torpidity of this semi-intelligent carcass in her office. She shuddered, and continued. "They believe that the man Jesus Christ is God, that he came back to life after being killed, went off to heaven, and now is coming back. Soon. To rule as king. They relate these natural catastrophes to signs of his return."

Moe snorted, trying to regain parity with the hard woman across from him. "Amazing how ancient legends survive. If there is a heaven and he is there he'd have to be nuts to come back to a place like this."

"Spoken like a true Christian," Pankie said sarcastically. "Most legends are innocuous. This one is different. How many adherents do you see to the cause of Jason and the Golden Fleece? These Christian groups are getting stronger fast, in spite of heavy government pressure and the obviously popular SelfGuide alternative. There's energy there and I'm worried about it. SelfGuide is on a roll. The World Alliance government is only now becoming stabilized. Those Christians could spoil a lot, senator."

"They must be under some kind of coercion. Can you imagine intelligent men and women going against everything which we, of the enlightened governments have worked so long and hard to bring to . . . ."

"Stuff the rhetoric, Moe. There are no cameras here, and I wouldn't vote for you anyhow. Even if we still voted."

"It's true," he whined. "We've worked hard . . . ."

"We're going to help them." Pankie's look was triumphant.

Moe's jaw pantomined up and down in disbelief. "What did you say?"

"We're going to help them achieve their fondest goal. Those people get stronger under pressure — unlike many of our legislators. Christians refusing to conform to the values we've built are the only real threat to SelfGuide, to the World Alliance, and to my hopes and yours. Either we or they will dominate within two years — fear will drive people to one camp or the other, unassigned or not. If we compete we balance each other, like the superpower arms races once did. But if we can co-opt them we can win it all."

"And just how do you expect to co-opt people who insist there is one God into a cause which insists that God is a fragmented myth, and that harmony comes only in aligned human potential?"

"By setting up the second coming of their leader."

Moe blinked. "By what?"

"That's what this Jesus apparently promised he would do. They've been hoping for it ever since. We're setting up a few miracles, too. Their book says miracles will happen around the time of the return. And it talks about the Antichrist, who will do many of those things, whatever they really are."

"Antichrist? And who is that supposed to be?"

"Don't know yet. But I'm sure that World Alliance does."

"Look, Pankie, where are you getting all of this?" Moe's indignation was beginning to rise. After all, he was the senator. Pankie noted the warning signs.

"I'm only a messenger, Moe. You'll be briefed by Franklin."

He was mollified.

"After a few miracles the second coming itself will be staged. That's where Ames comes in. He'll appear as the returned Christ, and herald his new kingdom by designating the World Alliance chairman as his appointed ruler. Real power will consolidate, and the single group which could derail World Alliance unity — the Christians — will have been disarmed by their own leader. Presto. A fully aligned world under our control."

Moe Cummings paled visibly. He reached for his coffee cup and drew it to his dry lips, spilling a few drops on his trousers. Pankie tore open a fresh packet of thin cigars, pleased.

"Pankie, isn't this just a little aggressive, even for you?" His voice was shaking.

"Trust me — it'll happen. Your role is very important. But — it sounds like you have some doubts . . . ."

"No, no, I'm with you!" Moe almost fell over himself assuring her of his participation. "When . . . when does all this begin? We'll need to set a lot of things up, of course — get plugged into Region and World groups much better than we are now — hmm. Two years?"

"We start next week. The appearance is scheduled for about forty days after that. The World Alliance is going to get this resistance out of the way once and for all, and get on with things."

Moe dropped the half-filled cup squarely onto his lap. Coffee splashed over his trousers and onto the cream-colored carpeting.

"Moe, are you sure you're up to this?"

"I'm sorry, really," he said, jumping up to brush the coffee off his lap. He disappeared beneath the desk, daubing the dark stains from the carpet with his handkerchief.

"Get up, Moe, for goodness sake." Pankie pressed a sensor along the edge of her desk. Her secretary's voice acknowledged through a hidden speaker.

"Yes, Ms. Retson?"

"Send the janitor in."

Flustered, Moe plopped down again in the chair, red and breathing hard from the mild exertion. Pankie watched him with amusement.

"How do we stop all these catastrophes that have been happening?" he said at length. "Maybe we can handle the other magic, Pankie, but . . ."

"We don't. The drama will underscore what we'll be doing. After that . . . it's going to stop some time. How do I know? We'll deal with it when the time comes."

"How do you deal with an earthquake?"

"That's not my problem. Your job is to get Franklin to arrange Prantzer's firing, and to get your briefing from him."

Moe Cummings did not look very convinced.

"This isn't only me talking. There are others involved, including people you, er, want in your corner." Pankie knew much less than the impression she was creating for Moe. But she did realize, from her own briefing and instructions, the importance of the role they had cast Moe Cummings into. And she was miffed that someone as inept as he would be a larger player than she would. At least she could play what she did have to the hilt with this heavy-scented creature. He was bound to slip, sooner or later, and she would find another handle on things.

"Who? Give me names, Pankie. Who besides Franklin?"

"Don't you think I would have told you if I could? I've told you all I can. But there is something more tangible . . ."

Reaching into her drawer, she pulled out a check written to Moe Cummings. It was for a very large amount of money, drafted against the Official Bank of the World Alliance and signed by the chief controller. Moe gasped.

"Moe," Pankie said in a soft, velvety tone, "I admire your courage. It takes something to make history."

Moe flushed, pleased at the compliment. The office door opened and a building custodian entered, carrying rags and a bucket. Suddenly his face registered horror. His arms came up to cover his eyes, and he staggered backwards out of the door, losing his cloth cap as he left.

Pankie blinked with surprise and pressed the intercom sensor. The sound of shrill winds crackled through the speaker, then died away.

"Fredrick, what happened? That janitor came in, then ran out like he'd seen a ghost!"

"Ms. Retson, he looks terrible, pale as chalk. He said something about a strong, terrible odor, and that it was icy cold."

"That will do, Fredrick." She looked at Moe and shrugged. "Fear. You see? It's getting to everyone. Even janitors." She tried to lighten a crawling feeling. The fright on the janitor's face had been real.

Moe seemed to be in shock. Pankie regained her composure and prepared to reinforce her control over the senator.

"You've got a big day ahead, Moe."

His attention instantly flickered back to life.

"Yes." He smiled an odd sort of smile which balanced tension, excitement, and uncertainty, and disappeared into her private washroom.

Pankie activated the telephone. Her call was answered immediately.

"Loyalty," she said.

"Prosperity," the voice responded.

"Done."

"Good."

The receiver clicked dead. Pankie sighed and got up from her desk.

Chapter 10

Michael pressed his palm against the electronic scanner and waited, watching workmen on scaffolding along the east wall of the main reception lobby. He had long ago learned how accurately the little things about a company reflect its inner excellence. Many such things about Prantzer Defense Group were impressive. This was one more. The wall had cracked and broken away near the ceiling in the last series of earth tremors. Repairs were being done despite forecasts of more severe tremors today.

Prantzer Defense Group would not tolerate a less than perfect image. Repairing the lobby wall was almost a defiant act, as if Milton Franklin was shaking his fist at the trembling ground while repairing the wounds it had caused. It summed up his style — exacting, demanding, relentless. That style had often tested Michael's skills and endurance. He hoped this meeting would, at last, win final approval on reorganization action.

A digital voice announced on both sides of twelve-foot bronze doors separating the lobby from the business side of Prantzer Defense, "Michael J. Ames entering Corridor A."

The huge doors glided silently apart. Michael began his walk down the two hundred foot corridor to the elevators, the fifth floor, and Milton Franklin's regal offices. The corridor was lit by thin glass strands stretched in the corners along their full length, outlining it like a cartoon rectangle. It seemed to be like walking through the screen of a video game. Michael stopped as he approached the elevator doors and peered at the dial of his wristwatch in the dim glow of the strands. A digital voice nearby startled him. "Keep moving forward, Michael J. Ames."

"Good morning, Mr. Ames."

"Morning, Peggy." Michael took off his overcoat and hung it in the guest closet. "Brisk today," he said, rubbing his hands.

Peggy nodded condescendingly, as if this was no place for idle chatter. "Mr. Franklin had an unscheduled meeting. He'll be with you shortly."

Michael took the briefing folio from his case and sat on the reception room divan, puzzled. Surprises, if they occurred here at all, were rare. Every movement appeared to be executed like clockwork, as if planned and rehearsed. An unscheduled meeting was completely uncharacteristic.

He did not have to wonder very long. In minutes the outer door opened and a paunchy man emerged, accompanied by Franklin who turned back through the door without acknowledging Michael's presence. The man looked directly at him, then grinned and waddled across the plush carpet.

"Mr. Ames?"

Michael stood to gain equality. "Yes?"

They shook hands. "It's a pleasure. Milton has spoken highly of you."

Michael's intuition sounded a warning. "I don't believe I know you . . ."

"Moe Cummings. Senator Moe Cummings."

Michael hoped his surprise was not noticed.

May I call you Michael?" The senator continued without a pause. "We're impressed with the work you're doing with Prantzer Defense, Michael. Very impressed." Moe put his hand on the consultant's shoulder.

Michael had many questions but was unsure how to ask them of a senator. He'd devoted so much time and self to his Prantzer Defense account that he was out of touch with world events. He would not have recognized Senator Moe Cummings, let alone known his positions on issues, subcommittee involvements, and voting records. He made a mental note to correct the error.

"Sir, I . . ."

"Call me Moe."

". . . Moe. Thank you. We're making good progress."

Moe moved conspiratorially close. "You've done more than that," he said in a low voice. "Milton showed me some of your work. It's brilliant. Brilliant!"

"Thank you, sir — Moe," Michael stammered, his intuition screeching louder warnings. He willed them into silence.

"Perhaps you would join us for lunch today? There's more to this than you know, and certain, er, conditions have forced us to accelerate other plans."

Michael blinked, confused. "That's very kind."

A familiar gruff voice broke through Peggy's nearby intercom. "Mr. Ames," she interrupted, "Mr. Franklin will see you now."

Moe pumped Michael's hand again as if on cue. "I'll look forward to seeing you, then, Michael. One o'clock, Regency Room." He smiled his warmest smile. The door into Milton Franklin's office swung open seemingly of its own accord. Moe motioned Michael toward it. Growing interest overpowered his wariness.

"Fine. Fine, sir. I'll be there."

"Sit down, Ames," Franklin growled.

Michael took the leather chair at the conference table across from the president. "Good morning, Mr. Franklin. I have the final organiz . . ." He paled, realizing he'd left his briefing folio on the divan after his chance encounter with Moe Cummings.

"It's on the couch." Franklin grinned with satisfaction. He crossed his forearms on the table, hunching challengingly toward his reorganization consultant. His craggy features were flint-hard above an ice-cold smirk, and he studied Michael with a probing gaze for which he was known and feared. Michael felt as though he could see through his eyes and straight down into his socks. He flushed with embarrassment. Highly paid consultants should not be so clumsy.

"Forget the folio. I've made my decision. We'll do it as structured now."

Michael was stunned. "Shouldn't we . . ."

"No! Why more delay? Are Security and Personnel combined under Jorgen and set up by business theater?"

"Yes."

"Good!" Milton Franklin slammed the table. "We implement Monday. Have the announcement ready tomorrow. I'm terminating the rest of this contract."

Michael stared in disbelief, crushed with disappointment. Franklin leered, watching his reaction like a boy studies a fly whose wings he is pulling off.

"Mr. Franklin," Michael said in measured tones. "This is a mistake."

Franklin waited. Michael took very small hope in what he thought was a twinkle in his eye.

"Your people will be disorganized, communications links will be disrupted, productivity will drop. Preparing for these changes requires substantial support."

"Wrong, Ames. My organization is prepared now. They may not know it, but they are. This contract is over."

Michael's heart sank. He pictured Rob Peary's certain response to this news, and envisioned his career in ruins. The one thing Peary hated more than sandbagging was premature contract termination. This was not only a bad surprise, but completely unjustified. Money was no issue with Franklin. He'd done a good job and he knew it. Something else had to have happened, and it had to be a crisis. There could be no other reason for Franklin suddenly deciding to take this action. Michael took advantage of the few seconds provided when Franklin went over to his desk for a cigar to think through a response that could salvage the contact. Silence hung in the spacious office like a green gas. Franklin sat down at the table again and drew on his cigar, watching him intently. Michael made his decision.

"Mr. Franklin . . ." Michael injected an ominous tone in his voice. Before he could continue the Prantzer Defense Group president eased back in his chair and softened his hard glare, satisfied that his consultant had backbone.

"No need to go further, Ames." Franklin waved his cigar hand through the air. "You've done what you could. You followed instructions. That's more than most of the deadwood that run loose around here can do. And don't worry about Peary. I talked with him after Cummings left. He leaned toward Michael in deadly earnest. "Ames. What's your position in all of this God business?"

Michael gulped. "I don't follow you."

"The world is crumbling before our eyes, Ames, and there are people out there raising an awful stink about it."

"Yes, of course. But . . ."

"Do you understand that those people are clamoring that we're in the last days of this planet? Ames, surely you don't spend ALL of your time on reorganization plans. I want to know where you stand. Are you one of those Christians?" His derision was thinly veiled.

"I really haven't thought much about it."

"Weak answer, Ames. I do not tolerate weakness."

The cold glare in Franklin's eyes warned Michael not to challenge him on the personal tone of his probing. The fact that Franklin had raised the subject was enough for it to be appropriate.

"I am not a Christian."

"Why not?" he snapped.

Michael stuttered, caught himself, and began again. "They are irrelevant reactionaries. Strident, uncompromising people can't accomplish anything. I don't know much about them, and don't care to. They're just another fringe group barking for attention."

"Been around a long time for a fringe group, wouldn't you say?"

"There are always fools in the world."

Franklin leaned back in his chair, peering at Michael through the rising stream of cigar smoke.

"You belong to WOEC then, I take it?" Franklin said blandly.

"No. I don't get involved in any of that."

He stared mercilessly for another long moment. Michael did not flinch. Franklin eased up, and spoke to him almost as an equal.

"I ended your contract because I want you to take on another assignment. I'm satisfied you have what it will take to handle it."

Michael drew his breath inaudibly, every nerve at attention.

"It's a million dollar assignment, Ames — for two months of your time. It starts with your meeting Cummings today at one o'clock. Moe will lay it out for you. Suffice it to say that this Christian movement is getting too strong. It's jeopardizing more than most people could understand. There are implications for Prantzer Defense Group. Be warned: this is hard ball. We'll either make a very wealthy man of you or we'll destroy you."

Michael's eyes widened.

"I'm inviting you onto the fast track. Keep up or get trampled. We're out of time. Any questions?"

Michael opened his mouth. Franklin cut him off before a word came out.

"Good. Peggy has the contract. Have it back tonight, signed." Franklin stood, cigar in mouth, squinting. "Be here tomorrow morning, six o'clock sharp. We have a good deal of material to go through."

"Mr. Franklin . . ."

"One more thing, Ames." He spoke almost too casually. "There's something I want you to handle for me personally."

"Sir?" Despite his confusion Michael easily demonstrated an eagerness to cooperate.

"Get with Emerson Prantzer and fire him."

The door of the office opened noiselessly. Franklin motioned toward it. Stunned, Michael stared at him, then left. Peggy gave him a brown sealed envelope. He took it wordlessly, gathered his briefing folio, and pulled on his overcoat.

"Have a nice day, Mr. Ames."

"Yes, thank you Peggy." He bumped against a decorative pillar near the door, then stepped out and into the waiting elevator. His mind was spinning as fast and as fruitlessly as a whirring tire in a snow bank — euphoric, fearful, and confused — first one, then the other, then all of them. He palmed the security sensor at the access door, waited for the digital voice announcement and stepped into the video-game corridor.

Outside, cold early-winter air freshened his mind, although the scope of the situation remained obscure. As he walked toward his car he felt the ground tremble. The quakes were beginning again.

Chapter 12

The Regency Room bustled with Regional bureaucrats, attorneys and business people, editors and educators. Michael stood at the top of the steps leading to the ballroom-like main dining area. The luncheon arrangement was strange — certainly preplanned, yet offered with a casualness bordering on deception.

"Sir, may we help you?" The maitre'd nodded with a deferential bow, quickly estimating Michael's importance. He was neither impressed nor unimpressed.

"Senator Cummings' table please," Michael said in a voice lower than usual.

The maitre'd brightened, pleased. "Ah, Mr. Ames! The senator and Ms. Retson are expecting you."

Michael was surprised at the name of Retson. It had to be the SelfGuide leader. He followed the maitre'd on a serpentine journey through glass-clinking islands of conversation and past the huge crystal fountain at the center of the room, spotting his host with a beautiful though hard-looking woman at a table next to windows overlooking the Mid-Continent launch site. Sixteen launch pads were less than a quarter-mile away. Between major launchings hourly shuttles lifted off, bound for space laboratories or Alpha base.

Moe Cummings shifted his chair back and rose. "Hello! You know Pankie Retson of SelfGuide, I'm sure!"

Michael turned to acknowledge Pankie, taking her offered hand. She looked at him with fascination, and with an obvious yet inoffensive appraisal. A sense of being in the center of action radiated from her.

"Ms. Retson."

"Pankie, please." She smiled, holding her grip an instant longer than necessary before releasing his hand.

"We've saved the best seat for you," Moe said, motioning to a chair facing the window. Michael sat down, watching shuttle preparations taking place outside the thick, slightly convex glass. "They'll be launching shortly. Those glare screens," he continued, pointing to the top edge of the window, "come down just before ignition."

Michael scanned the sleek shuttle poised on its pad. Pankie's eyes remained fixed on him. He shifted uncomfortably in his chair.

"I've taken the liberty of ordering for you," Moe said. "Ah, here it is now." A waiter approached followed by an automated busbot laden with steaming dishes. Noiselessly and efficiently he placed them on the table.

It was then that Michael felt a strange distancing, as if peering through the large end of a pair of binoculars. The sensation was not uncomfortable, but it separated him mysteriously from his surroundings. For an instant he was aware of both unseen beauty and intense ugliness. He breathed deeply to clear his head. The sensation faded.

". . . Michael! I said would you care for a Splint?" Pankie was holding out a small packet of thin cigars. He blinked in embarrassment, and declined. Pankie lit one and put it in the ash tray near her food.

"Michael, you've talked with Milton Franklin and understand why we're meeting?" Moe said through a mouthful of food.

"Not quite. Mr. Franklin said you would be more specific. We ran out of time."

"Always out of time," Moe said with exasperation, rolling his eyes upward.

A soft pinging, like an old department store call signal, alerted guests to the imminent launch. With a quiet whirring, flexscreens dropped over the viewing windows. A flash of power exploded outside, its brilliance reduced to that of a flashlight by the flexscreens. Slowly the shuttle lifted through the furious boiling of its launch, and in seconds was speeding up and away from the pad. The flexscreens silently rose into their carriage.

"Always an awesome sight, isn't it," Pankie said.

"Michael," Moe continued, "we are pleased by your acceptance of the new contract. Your performance at Prantzer Defense has been outstanding, as I've mentioned. We're also pleased to learn of your position on the, ah, Christians. They're a very dangerous group. They jeopardize the freedom of the Region and the World Alliance unification plans."

Michael chewed a small piece of exquisitely flavored asparagus, listening carefully. He felt a growing excitement.

"Prantzer Defense interests are adversely affected by this movement. You're aware of what they're saying?"

"Of course," Michael said with satisfaction. "They claim these are the last days of the world, before the return of Jesus Christ." He thought both of them winced although he saw no physical movement.

"Exactly," Moe said, leaning into the conversation. He wiped his mouth with his napkin. "They insist the world was created by this God of theirs just a few thousand years ago in spite of irrefutable knowledge that we live on a five billion year old planet. They hang everything on the coming back to life of . . . of their leader two millenia ago. That's hardly news in these times when medical technology routinely revives people who have been clinically dead for several hours."

Michael started to interrupt but Moe held his hand up. "Let me finish, to set the tone for you. Then we can discuss details."

Michael glanced at Pankie. She looked impatient.

"Consider their present claim," Moe continued. "They're saying, as you pointed out, that these are the last days of this earth. But these are precisely the days when for the first time in all history we're on the brink of global unity and peace! We've worked toward this for generations. Finally it's within our grasp, thanks to the emerging World Alliance. These are the great days, Michael, not the last days!"

"They could be both," Michael said, wondering where the conversation was leading. He was missing the point.

"What Moe means," Pankie said, lightly touching his arm, "is that those who believe these are the last days lose all vested interest in the great plans we're setting in motion. Their priorities change. They separate from the roles and behaviors it is our duty to expect from them. They become a drain on the rest of us."

"How does that threaten anyone?" Michael asked.

"Are you familiar with SelfGuide?"

"Yes!" he said hastily, becoming charmed by the fascinating woman who was signalling such personal interest.

"Of course, Michael, I'm not suggesting that you were uninformed . . ."

". . . and I admire SelfGuide. I confess I'm not a member, but I subscribe heartily to the principles. May I say, Pankie, what a magnificent job you've done."

Pankie suppressed her displeasure with his patronizing comment. "We're only beginning. SelfGuide distills centuries of thinking into the essence of human truth. It ends confusing mystical notions which have divided the world for thousands of years. It calls every one to the essence of our truth, which is embodied in three principles." Pankie smiled and glowed, beguiling Michael beyond the point of no return.

"I know them!" Michael said enthusiastically. "Power is vested in the will of mankind. Uh . . ."

". . . Goodness is vested in the being of mankind," she prompted.

"Yes. And, ah, destiny is vested in the intent of mankind."

Pankie's eyes burned a path into him. "Those are the basics. Power without goodness is evil. Destiny without power is meaningless. Goodness without destiny is irrelevant."

Michael grew uneasy under her hypnotic gaze. He shifted in his seat, searching for the appropriate thing to say. "It all makes sense," he finally blurted, looking to the senator, who was noisily chomping his food.

Moe hastily swallowed an oversized bite of salad, mopping a drool of creamy cheese from his chin. "It makes sense because it is sense," he said. "People are responding by the millions. But what you might not know is how this links to WOEC."

"The World Organized Ecumenical Council?" Michael said.

"Yes. Everyone, regardless of their origins, needs to believe in something. A process is required to meet that need. Throughout history there has been disunity. The planet has lived in fundamental disagreement. The most obvious manifestation is war. Why? Because these beliefs have been fruits of the divergent cultures in which people have lived. To achieve one unified belief, we must achieve one unified culture."

Michael found himself nodding. It did seem sensible.

"Now," Pankie said, pleased at his response, "we know that the bedrock of motivation is in the belief system. People can be motivated to behave contrary to their beliefs, of course. But they can't be made not to regret their breach. That target emerges in some form of negative stress — guilt, for example. We're adaptive beings, and we resolve the conflicts between belief and behavior by adjusting one or the other, or both. Each of us constantly seeks equilibrium that way. We have to. But it's never been a controlled process, has it, Michael?"

"No, I guess not."

"Why do you think that? I don't mean to put you on the spot . . ."

"Not at all!" Michael's pride responded. "I'm beginning to see your point. You're saying that without controlled unification the world is like an ever-changing kaleidoscope, intriguing but without direction."

Pankie beamed and looked at Moe. "Extraordinary insight, Senator. He's grasping subtleties that most of our members takes months to absorb!"

Manipulative, perhaps, Michael thought. But pleasant manipulation, nevertheless.

"In WOEC," Pankie continued, "the process of expressing a belief has been unified. SelfGuide principles are accurate recognitions of human nature, of our humanity and of overwhelming evidence that our humanity is supreme. SelfGuide ends the war with self. It is in a real sense the ultimate adjustment. When our nature and our belief system match, unity is achieved. And we're almost there. WOEC provides a nonthreatening format in which this can happen. Because the principles work for us all, the beliefs which emerge will be universal once the adjustment is complete.

"When we're achieved that," Moe Cummings broke in, "we'll have the basis for perpetuating world unity. Think what that can mean!"

While Michael sensed gaps in the fabric Pankie and Moe were weaving he realized that they had struck the primal chords, and he liked the sounds. There was a sensual attractiveness in the harmonics, and it resonated nicely with his own self.

"There's more to it — but let's get to your involvement." Michael watched Pankie's lips, transfixed.

"The world is on the brink of its ultimate good: Unity. But there's a disruption — those who reject WOEC, reject SelfGuide, and insist that no one can make it without God. The Christians." She spat the word out, and her eyes glittered with malice.

"They've been silent for decades, and nothing much to be concerned about. Now they're growing fast. It's essential that SelfGuide principles prevail without challenge before the World Alliance foundation can be in place. What they are politically, and WOEC is religiously, SelfGuide is socially. All three must be in harmony. As long as the Christians keep focusing people's attention on their leader, it can't be."

Michael nodded, dubious but intrigued. "And how does all of this affect Prantzer Defense — or me?"

Moe leaned across the table. Michael was startled by the business-like hardened countenance replacing what a moment before had been the stupidly grinning face of an overweight diner.

"Are you prepared for the answer?"

"I'm ready." Michael returned his stare, fascinated.

"We're dealing with matters of extraordinary scope," he said. "Pankie and I are just two of many. World power is coalescing around the World Alliance. Actions of incalculable proportion are even now being set into motion. Everything is happening as planned. Believe me, Michael, Prantzer Defense Group is affected. And so are you."

"Everything is happening as it should except for one little matter," Pankie interrupted.

"The Christians?" Michael said.

Pankie nodded.

"I see." Michael didn't see at all.

"This is where your role is." Moe spoke urgently, in hushed tones. "Their entire premise — hope, they call it — is in the return of their leader."

"Jesus' second coming," Michael said. He noticed Moe had definitely winced that time.

"Yes," Moe said smoothly. "So, he is going to come. In about forty days."

Michael looked at him in disbelief. Slowly, what they had in mind began to dawn on him.

"We can't attack them or treat them harshly, Michael. That's been tried, and we think it was the dominant reason behind their strong recovery. History shows that persecution strengthens them. But we can't ignore them. They're too vocal, too visible, and now too big."

Pankie glanced scornfully at Moe. 'That's not what you were saying in my office last weekend,' she thought to herself.

"They believe their leader will return and reign as king of a new and perfect world. If he did," Moe chuckled, "he'd be stealing the credit for a world we're about to put on-line . . . a perfect world, at last."

"And they stubbornly refuse to acknowledge that WE are about to complete that world!" Pankie interrupted vehemently.

"So," Moe continued, "we're going to facilitate their hope. After it happens, many of them will wake up to the delusion and align with SelfGuide and WOEC. Those who don't defect will end up supporting the return as real, and be forced to acknowledge the World Alliance chairman as the valid ruler. We get them by giving them what they've been looking for."

Michael leaned back slowly, as if sitting on eggs. "My role is somehow related to all of this?"

Pankie leaned toward him. "You, Michael," she said, "have been chosen as the one who is to appear, in Jerusalem, as their leader."

Michael gulped.

"Don't be concerned. It's a perfectly safe assignment."

"No concern?" Michael blurted, "You want me to commit suicide! This is high risk. Even if I get through it people will recognize me everywhere!"

"Michael," Moe said, "that obviously wouldn't do, would it. We've prepared for every contingency. You'll hear more as we go."

Unconvinced, Michael probed the logic of the plan, going as far as Pankie and Moe could — or were willing to — explain it. Slowly it began to make sense. Assuming the Christians were the barrier, the appearance ruse should work. WOEC would surely hail it as real, and the Christians would be divided. They would argue it forever, and while they argued, the World Alliance would consolidate its power.

Michael pushed his fork around the linen tablecloth, lining up grains of pepper along the fold. His mind accepted the logic. But he could not comprehend the magnitude of what he had heard. Either these people were crazy or the world was in for tremendous shock. Two things slowly became clear. First, they were not crazy. Second, he wanted no part of it.

"No thanks," Michael said at last.

"Michael, let me be as gentle as possible," Moe said, speaking in his most fatherly tone. "We know more about you than you know yourself. We have complete psychological profiles. We know your moves from childhood to the present. We know about your debts, your friends, your wife, your fears, your ambitions. You've been handpicked. And you now know of plans which would be rather awkward, don't you think, for anyone outside the team to know about. It's simple: you have no choice."

That was all Michael had to hear. He tossed his napkin on the table and stood, every nerve straining to put as much distance between them and himself as possible. His eyes glittered angrily. "I have a choice all right. And I've just made it. Thanks for lunch, senator."

"This will not please Mr. Franklin. Or Rob Peary . . ."

Pankie interrupted Moe's warning. "Michael, please stay a little longer and talk it through with us. Moe made a mistake in telling you there was no choice. Of course there is."

Moe, for all his clumsiness, did not lack a certain amount of astuteness.

"Michael, is THAT it? I'm sorry! You certainly have every option available to you, though of course we ask you to respect the confidentiality of our discussion if you do reject our offer."

Michael had tap danced enough to know the game when it was played. And he had no difficulty realizing the risks he took by not participating. Maybe he really didn't yet understand the issues. He sat back down, glaring indignantly. "I heard you say 'no choice.' Now I hear something else. Be straight with me."

"We're the ones who have no choice, Michael. We are committed. We've been working toward this for years. We know the high need for peaceful, unified government. It is a great and lofty objective, and it demands courage and integrity. You have both of those qualities. Very few do. That's what I meant. This assignment may be your destiny — not that it's for us to say — but our knowledge of you is quite complete. We have expert analysis of Michael Ames by the most eminent doctors in the world. You're famous in the power circles, Michael, even though you don't know it. They are waiting with hope and expectation that you'll make the right decision."

"How in the world can you claim to know so much about me?" Michael said, though with less steam than before.

"We did out homework. For example, all of those people you worked with on your first Prantzer Defense Group contract weren't ALL Franklin's minions."

More understanding dawned — that explained some of the strange behaviors and questions that had come up during the past few months.

Pankie looked alluringly at Michael, her eyes liquid with admiration. "We need you. The world needs you. Stand with us and be counted."

A busbot glided over. Moe Cummings took the check from it and placed his palm on the glass-covered reader in its side. "Thank you, Senator Cummings," its speaker replied. Quietly it glided away.

"Michael?" she said, waiting for his response. Her eyes burned deeper trails into his soul and strummed the call to his masculinity, his vanity, his deep-seated need to be significant.

"When I meet with Mr. Franklin tomorrow about the new contract," Michael said finally, "maybe I'll understand better what to do. You'll have my answer then."

"Michael," Moe said, "this role IS the new contract. You don't want to see Franklin with any doubts in your mind."

Michael looked at Moe and the will to resist faded. Without the contract his career was gone. Without his income he'd probably never climb out of his mounting debts. They had pegged his role to his life. The tactic was consistent with Michael's own style, and he understood. Moe was right. There really was no choice.

"Okay. I'm in."

He felt very tired. But he responded to their cheering congratulations. By the third decanter of liqueur he believed he was about to perform a consummate service for his country and the world. 'Why me?' he thought again. 'Why not.'

Chapter 12

"This stuff is bad enough hot. Lukewarm, it's terrible!" Gabe Diehl leaned back in the worn chair behind his desk, grimacing as he sipped his coffee. A storm the night before had piled fresh snow on the sill of the window across the room. Now it was clear and sunny, and the windows sparkled with life.

"Remember when we were kids, Gabe?" Em Prantzer said. "This was Christmas then. Oh, there was a lot of commercialism, of course. But the Christ child was proclaimed publicly. There was a joy then that's gone today."

"I remember."

"He's done great things through you, Gabe. Great things."

Gabe was thoughtful. "Yes, He has, Emerson. No one knows how impossible it is for me to do what I've been doing. But you're one of the few I can say that to. You understand. You've been there yourself. The hearings were just the latest in your faithfulness to our Lord. I thank Him for you, Emerson."

Em sighed. "Vessels of clay behaving like urns of gold. Still I wonder — would this have happened had it not been for my statements in those hearings?"

"I think so. I met Milton Franklin once, at a convention of the first church I was with, back when WOEC was being set up. He chaired one of the committees. A more ruthless, manipulative man I've never met." Gabe paused. "And a fallen man. His kind cannot tolerate a shred of light in the darkness in which they work and plan. You had to go. I'm sorry it's been so painful for you. But I'm also glad."

Emerson looked up at his friend, surprised.

" 'Count it all joy, my brothers, whenever you face trials . . .' " Gabe smiled. "You were obedient. Remember the times, and rejoice."

"Lucy says the same thing. And I guess I agree. I was obedient. And it felt good, so good. As for these days . . . I don't know. It's not for us to know the time of His return. We could keep on sliding like this for another thousand years."

"You haven't been listening to my sermons!" Gabe laughed. "We're not to know the time — but we are to know the approach of the time. Jesus gave us many signs. All of them are happening, even the rebuilding of the temple in Jerusalem. It's close."

Em stood up bad began pacing. "I'm tired. Right now I feel like a discouraged old man."

Gabe waited for him to continue, sensing his need to talk.

"We started with one small contract for missile silo covers. Worked three days without sleep to make the deadline for the first delivery. The government put us on their favored contractor list. That's how I met the Secretary of Defense to present the network scheme." Emerson Prantzer gazed wistfully through the window. "Talk about excitement. A year later we were working on a thirty million dollar contract."

"You've left a lot behind, haven't you."

"A lot, yes. Friends from the start-up days are still there. Tom Godrille, Jim Canyon, Pete Jorgen . . . . Pete's the personnel head now, or at least was until this reorganization. Now, I don't know. I hired Pete. Even loaned him enough to cover his wife's operation. I always liked him. But he went over to the other side, Gabe. So many have gone over to the other side."

"It's true." Gabe spun a paper clip on the tip of a pencil. It flew off and landed on the small rug by his desk.

"What hurts is the way Franklin did it," Em continued. "That, and friends who seem to be abandoning me like rats from a sinking ship."

"Did you know that's a myth, Em? Maybe some of your friends haven't really left you. They're under a lot of pressure. And a lot of confusion."

Em slumped back on the couch. "Franklin didn't have the courage to talk to me personally. Sent that reorganization consultant after me. Michael Ames, I think his name was. He gave me the news with all the style of a frightened cow.

Gabe was instantly alert. "Michael Ames?"

"I think so. Why?"

The pastor rummaged through a stack of papers on his desk. "Ah, here it is. This came yesterday from Senator Morris Cummings. He recommends Michael J. Ames for membership in our church. Isn't that strange? Here, read it."

Em glanced through the two page letter. "It's strange, all right. But so what?"

"It sounds like a recommendation for membership in a country club. The senator obviously has no idea what our church is all about."

"And a pretty inaccurate notion of where he has influence," Em added.

"Em, we have over four thousand members. We hold services every Sunday, Wednesday and Thursday. Nothing prevents Ames or anyone from just coming to one of them. Why would he try this?"

"If he did. Maybe there are other reasons."

Gabe shook his head, mystified.

"Or, maybe he did ask Cummings to intercede for him. A lot of people fear coming to a church for the first time, if that's what it is for him. Or maybe he's having second thoughts about being used the way Franklin is using him, Gabe. He certainly didn't seem to be enjoying firing me any more than I did."

Gabe walked over to the window. "Always thinking the best of the other guy . . . even one who has humiliated you. And you're right, Emerson. Cynicism is one of my traits I find hardest to yield to Him."

"Remember, Gabe, Jesus tells us to be 'wise as serpents, harmless as doves.' You may be right. I may be about as wise as a turtle in assuming good about him."

Gabe stared through the frosty window glass gleaming like diamonds in the sun, lost in thought. "It really is a walk of faith. And the walk may be nearly over. Lord, may Michael Ames truly experience that conviction of heart, and find his way home, while there is time. That's my prayer."

Cars moved along the snow-packed street below, tires crunching in the cold. A monitor hovercraft glided by, moving slowly about twenty feet above the street. Distant buildings glistened in bright winter sunlight. A block away the sound of the wrecking crane and falling rubble could be heard ever so faintly as a building partly demolished by a tremor was being razed. Two men were standing across the street talking, hunched against the wind.

"That's how it will be at the coming of our Lord," Gabe said pensively. " 'Two men will be in the field; one will be taken and the other left. Two women will be grinding with a hand mill; one will be taken and the other left.' I love them, Em. I don't always show it, but I do. Most of them are irretrievably gone. Lost. And they don't even know it." His voice was steady, but a small tear in the corner of his eye revealed the depth of his feeling.

Em joined Gabe at the window. "How does one share Jesus Christ with millions of resistant, apathetic people? Perhaps the tragedies of these days will shake some, at least, to their senses, to realize how fragile and dependent we all are. How, Em, in the remaining times . . . say!" Gabe slapped his hands together. "I know one thing we can do, now that you've got all this free time on your hands!"

Em's attention was riveted on the two men across the street. "Gabe, I think that is Michael Ames." He pointed through the glass. "There, the taller one in the gray coat."

Gabe peered through the window at the dark-haired, tall man. "Either his razor broke or he's growing a beard," Gabe observed. The two men shook hands, turned in opposite directions and walked away. The one Em had identified as Michael Ames disappeared around the corner.

"Interesting," Em muttered, moving back to the couch. "A strange coincidence, if there is such a thing."

"Em, you must join me on the crusade!"

"Me? Oh no, Gabe. I don't think so. There are some personal things to take care of, and . . . ."

"Emerson, listen to yourself! You sound like you had nothing to share and no desire to share it! Do you think the gift of knowledge our Lord has given to you is less important than tying up some personal matters?"

"Of course not. But I never thought of myself as being able to do that."

Gabe's eyes had caught on fire. "No 'buts!' For years you've shared your wealth in our work — now, you can share yourself, directly. And you have a lot to share, Em. People need you."

Em Prantzer looked at his friend with the love that only two Christians girding for battle in the name of their Lord can know. He sensed then that Gabe was right. And he was caught with a new sense of purpose.

"Tuesday morning we begin in Binzoe. Then we tour the east coast. I'll ask George to make your travel arrangements."

Em Prantzer slowly pulled his coat on and walked to the door. A smile crossed his face, the depression in the wake of his humiliating dismissal from the company he had founded all but forgotten. Excitement was filling his soul. "You're right, Gabe, you're right. This IS what I am to do!"

"Bless you, Emerson, for your encouragement to me among many."

"And you, Gabriel." The two men embraced briefly. Em Prantzer closed the door behind him with a song in his heart.

Gabriel Diehl beamed with excitement and dropped to his knees, filled with praise and thanksgiving. "This crusade is going to glorify you, Lord Jesus, abundantly." He shut his eyes tightly, almost picturing the armies of Heaven raised in mighty chorus, seeing the long wait almost at an end, the time which human wisdom and human nature rejected as preposterous about to become the world's reality.

"So many signs, Lord God. Will it be next month? Next summer?" Gabe shuddered in acknowledgement, chastised. 'It is for no man to know the time.' He uttered an inexpressible groan and rested his back against the side of the desk. Soft, musical sounds bubbled from within him and streamed out of his mouth. When he finished, the office was deep in the dusk of waning afternoon. He did not know what he had prayed. But he knew he was strengthened for all that lay ahead.

Chapter 13

If Michael was at all tentative at the Regency Room, after Saturday's early meeting with Milton Franklin he was fully committed and awed by the centrality of his role. That afternoon, he met with Eric Lindsay, an assistant pastor of the Family In Christ Church. He was to join that church the next day, and develop a friendship with their pastor Gabriel Diehl, the nationally-known Christian leader, as quickly as possible. He was also to begin studying about the one called Jesus, and why there was such extraordinary loyalty to him among his followers. It all had to happen fast, for Michael would be leaving for Jerusalem in just a few days.

Debbie sat staring at the sterling candelabra on the dinner table. She sighed wistfully, seeing in its reflection memories of happier times, times when she was the center of her husband's attention.

Michael scraped the last of the veal from his plate and washed it down with a gulp of Zinfandel. He was bone-tired. But there was much more to do before he could rest.

"That was great, Deb. Thanks."

She smiled half-heartedly, unable to ease the weight in her heart. Was it all Michael, or were there other oppressions on her? She looked at him. Preoccupied, self-centered, and often thoughtless, yes — but kind too, gentle yet strong, and sensitive when he wanted to be.

The weight began to lift. She loved him still, and that alone was no small triumph. And she knew, in the most knowing of knowings, of his utter faithfulness to her. A good man, she thought with an inward smile. There may be many competitors for his time and attention and enormous energies. But there was no distraction or competitor which bore the form of woman. In her arena, where it counted most, she wholly and completely prevailed.

Debbie glanced around the room, admiring the cornicework and the handsome formal yet warm foyer visible through the wide doorway. She could do worse than a beautiful home, a faithful and successful husband, and a blossoming photography career of her own. She leaned over to Michael and hugged him. "You're welcome, Mij."

"Mij? You haven't called me that for years!" Michael smiled, unaware of her tenseness until he felt the relief she'd given him. He knew now that telling Debbie of his new assignment wouldn't be as difficult as he had feared. He'd put it off long enough.

"Deb, we need to talk about some things."

"Speak, husband!" Debbie's spirits seemed to soar. She couldn't understand why she felt so good. But she did, and that was enough.

"Franklin cancelled our contract."

"Oh, Michael . . ."

"It's not that he wasn't satisfied with our work. In fact he gave us a new contract."

"That's wonderful!"

"Yes, I'm pleased. So was Peary. I also had lunch yesterday at the Regency Room. With Moe Cummings."

Debbie's eyes widened. "The senator?"

He nodded, smiling with pride. "And Pankie Quille Retson, the SelfGuide leader."

A shadow momentarily fluttered across Debbie's eyes.

"And? What happened?"

"They're associated with Franklin in a number of areas, including my assignment."

"Michael, this is exciting! Tell me about it!" Debbie's eyes glistened as pride in her husband swelled up in her. The years she had grown accustomed to counting as lost shrank in importance.

"I can't talk about all of it, Deb — there's still a lot I don't know. But the first step is one we need to take together."

"I like it already." She wiggled her eyebrows, to Michael's delight.

"We're going to join a church tomorrow."

Debbie's face went blank.

"The one on Townsend Avenue. I talked with their assistant pastor today."

"What on earth does that have to do with a business assignment?"

Michael framed his words carefully, remembering Franklin's fierce expression outlining what he could and what he could not, under any circumstances, reveal to anyone, even his wife.

"We need to meet certain people who are critical in this assignment." Michael wondered what he would say if he ran across Emerson Prantzer there.

"You can't meet them at their offices, Michael?" Debbie had a strong and accurate intuition. She was sensing something awry now.

"They don't work for Prantzer Defense. The new assignment deals more with the company's involvement with other groups than with anything inside. Matter of fact," Michael tried to sound non-chalant, "for part of the job I'll have to go to the Middle East."

"That's . . . nice." She began stacking salad dishes and silverware. Growing resentments picked away at her good mood.

"It's the opportunity we've been waiting for, Deb."

"Will you be gone very long?"

"Just for a short time."

"How short?"

"Uh — seven weeks. But I'll be home two or three weekends."

Debbie looked at her husband.

"I leave Monday. Be back Friday though."

She put the stack of dishes on the busbot. "Coffee?" She poured cups for them both. Michael watched her, aware of her mild disturbance, glad it was only mild. A good woman, he thought. Ever since his Binzoe beating and encounter with Ben two months before they seemed to be building on a new foundation. He did not want to jeopardize that.

Michael took his wife's hand. "It's just a few weeks, Deb, but it's very important. Maybe we can work out a trip together!" He felt a momentary prick of conscience, knowing how impossible that would be.

But Debbie was pleased. Michael sipped his coffee, looking over the rim at his wife's excited face. It was going well, much better than he'd expected.

"Michael? What are you going to be doing? Is this something that has to do with oil?"

"Nothing like that. I wish I could tell you more, but I can't." Her look of hurt was unmistakable.

"I don't know much more myself! Everything else is classified. I'm not permitted to speak about it."

"Even with your own wife?"

"Yes, even with you. I'm sorry. But the rules were spelled out clearly by Franklin himself. Most of it's a matter of law."

Michael had been involved in classified work ever since Prantzer Defense Group had been his client. Debbie didn't like it, but it rang true enough for now and she accepted it on that basis. They finished loading dishes onto the busbot, each mulling their thoughts. A push of the start button sent the machine rolling into the kitchen. Moments later they heard the click of the hose connections and the whoosh of the busbot filling with water.

"I love it," Debbie said.

Michael smiled, "Science triumphs again."

She released her disturbance and it promptly disappeared. Arm in arm they walked into the living room.

"It's dangerous over there, isn't it? I heard the news today of another attack on the construction people building that temple, or whatever, in Jerusalem."

"I'll be safe, Deb. Prantzer Defense has a lot of connections."

Her uncertainty showed. Michael hugged her. "Piece of cake. Don't worry."

They sat in separate chairs. Debbie began reviewing proofs from the day's work, a slide documentary on urban poverty. Michael took his briefing materials, snapped on the light, and opened the bulky package with "CLASSIFIED — EYES ONLY" stamped in large red letters across the front. He withdrew a smaller sealed envelope. "Open enroute — not before. M.F."

He set it aside and removed a small Bible, notebook, identification documents, a key, and a typed memo.

"Omega: Study and memorize before departure. Burn memo."

He crumpled the memo and tossed it in the fireplace. Debbie looked up over her glasses.

"What was that?"

"Just classified stuff." He lit the paper and watched it blacken into ashes, then returned to his chair and picked up the small book. "A Bible," he mused, thumbing through the pages. He'd never held a Bible before. His finger slipped, stopping the pages momentarily.

". . . Peace I leave with you; my peace I give to you. I do not give to you as the world gives . . ." His mind automatically recorded the passage into his memory.

He settled into the chair and began to read. 'A record of the genealogy of Jesus Christ, the son of David, the son of Abraham . . .' "Oh, boy," he muttered.

"What? Are you talking to me, Mij?" Debbie looked up from her photographs.

"No, no. Nothing, Deb."

"What's that little book?"

Michael felt strange. "It's a, uh, just a book."

"What book, Michael?"

"Debbie, come on. It's a Bible."

"A Bible? Aren't you taking this church joining a little too seriously?"

"Deb," he sighed, "it's what I have to read. It's part of the assignment."

"Just what is this assignment, Michael? I never heard of any such thing, reading a Bible for your work. Are they going to make you their chaplain?" Debbie laughed. "I can just picture you, Mij, pronouncing the benediction over a nuclear missile . . ."

Michael threw the chair pillow at his wife, laughing at the image she'd painted.

"Michael . ... gimme a mumble jumble or two . . ." He leaped toward her and pulled her to the floor, rolling together, embracing, happy.

"I love you." Debbie smiled through eyes wet from laughter.

"I love you, Deb. Very much."

Debbie pushed her finger against Michael's nose, flattening it.

"You know, Mij, when I think we turned around?"

They'd never discussed their worsening marriage. But they both knew that it had been. To speak of it would be to admit knowledge of the deterioration and the lack of communication about it.

'But — if she's willing, then so am I,' he thought.

"When you picked me up at Lake Shore Hospital," he said matter-of-factly. Debbie nodded, smiling, and then frowned.

"You looked so bad that night. I realized how much you really mean to me."

Michael lost himself to the memory for a moment. "I was just thinking about that, and Ben, during dinner."

"So was I!" Debbie exclaimed. "I'm glad he was there, Michael. A twinkle appeared in her eyes, the kind that heralded a good idea.

"It's almost Remembrance Day . . . let's go and see him!"

"Oh, Deb . . ."

"Michael, really! Remember how badly you felt that you had no money for him? And how he was so gracious about it just so you wouldn't feel bad?"

"Deb, it's cold and snowy out, and I have a ton of reading to do."

Debbie wriggled out from under him. "How cold do you think Ben is? Come on. You can give him something for Remembrance Day. We owe him, you know."

Michael remembered the crisp autumn air, the tall, impoverished derelict standing by his shanty, and his words . . . "There is one who did much more for me than I have for you. It was for him that I helped you." And he remembered the peacefulness in Ben's face. He considered himself at peace — he and Debbie were happier now, he had a new contract, and all that he counted as important was going well. Situational. But he'd seen Ben at peace in circumstances which would have depressed him beyond recovery. Non-situational. Something clicked. His peace depended on his situation — Ben's did not. Where did Ben's kind of peace come from? Michael suddenly no longer felt happy at all. He longed for Ben's kind of peace. Next to it, his life seemed merely a series of cease-fires. Where did it come from?

'Peace I leave with you; my peace I give you. I do not give to you as the world gives . . .' "He must be!" Michael shouted. The chance to help his learning assignment, and to find out more about this strange peace, overtook him.

"What?"

Michael scrambled to his feet and tucked his shirttails in. "You're right Deb. Let's go!"

By the time they reached the Binzoe District Michael's mind was full of bad memories.

"Lock those doors, honey."

"Michael, that's the third time you've said that."

"We should have taken the van. This car will attract those animals . . ."

Debbie's own worry surfaced. "They can't be out on the street in ten degree weather waiting for fancy cars. Can they?"

She had a point, Michael mused. The frigid temperature could be an ally. The streets were empty.

"It's right around the corner, Deb." Michael spotted the vacant lot. And there it was — Ben's shanty, nestled against the brick wall. Dim light glowed from within.

"That's it."

Debbie stared, suddenly near tears. "Oh, Michael, look. Look at that . . ."

The Jaguar purred to a stop by the crumbled curb. They looked at the shanty. Its roof was frosted where snow had blown off. It sparkled in the yellow street lamp glow. Frozen stumps of summer's weeds poked up from the lot like whiskers of icy stubble, casting countless slanted shadows.

"Huh?" Michael said.

"What? I didn't say anything."

"Someone said 'Go in' and no one else is in the car!" For just a moment Michael experienced the same sensation he'd had at the Regency Room.

"Well, then, I think we should go in, Michael. There, now you heard me say it. That's why we came down here."

"I know, I know!" He said irritably. "Sorry. I'm just a little nervous, I guess." He gently rubbed the scar on his right arm.

Suddenly Debbie's fears took over and her resolve melted away. "Michael, maybe this wasn't such a good idea after all. We can mail the money to him."

But he was drawn now, and boldness filled him.

"No, we're here and it'll be fine. Let's go. I owe him — remember?" He smiled and touched his hand to her cheek.

The icy stubble crunched under their feet as they approached Ben's shanty. Michael put his hand on the exhaust pipe poking out of the roof. It was cold. Of course, he realized. The plant probably only operates during the day. Warm, Ben had said. Right.

"Ben?" Michael called, softly.

The wall shook slightly, and they heard a faint sound.

"Ben? It's me, Michael Ames. You helped me last fall."

Muffled but unmistakable words sifted through the shanty wall. "Michael Ames?" The blankets over the doorway parted, and Ben's large frame poked through. The first thing Michael noticed was his peace and contentment. He'd been looking for it.

"Ah, it is you — welcome!" He turned to Debbie. "And this would be your wife. She's as lovely as I had pictured her. Come in, friends, come in!"

"We just wanted to stop by and wish you a good Remembrance Day. And give you this." Michael pulled a fifty dollar bill from his pocket and pushed it toward the large man.

Ben looked at the money. "You are so kind, so kind. Please, come in for a cup of hot tea."

"We'd like to, but . . ." He looked at his car nervously. "Those guys . .. the Crowns . . . I don't think, with my wife here and all . . ."

Debbie was watching Ben's face, drawn by its strength and peace.

" . . . I don't know how safe . . ." Michael continued. "Here, please take it. It's only a small token."

"We'd be delighted, Ben." Debbie's words caught Michael by surprise. Ben beamed and held the blanket-door open for his guests.

"Mrs. Ames, please — sit there." He pointed to a wooden box covered with a blanket. "I'll just heat up the tea." He lit a small can of flammable jelly and set it under a pot of water. Michael's nervousness seemed to fill the small room.

"Michael, how's your arm?"

"Fine. Ben, listen, we can't stay." He glowered at his wife, who sat awkwardly on the low crate, looking now every inch a woman who regretted her impetuousness.

Ben set his expression to cheerful and carefully extinguished the small purple flame. He turned to them, head bent slightly downward to avoid the slope of the roof. "I understand. Thank you for coming here."

Michael crammed the bill into Ben's overcoat pocket. He did not resist. "Thank you, Michael. You've made my Christmas very happy. Bless you."

"Christmas?" said Debbie. "You mean Remembrance Day! And you're welcome. I'm grateful to you for helping my husband." She inched toward the blanketed opening.

"No, I mean Christmas, the celebration of the birth of Jesus Christ."

Michael's face smoothed. "So, you're a Christian, Ben."

"I know Jesus Christ as my Lord and Savior. If that's what you mean by Christian, I am."

"I knew it!" Michael's worry for the car, for their safety, and his irrational urgency to escape faded away even as Debbie signalled 'Please let's go!' with her eyes.

"Thank you both for coming. Mrs. Ames, it was nice to meet you." Ben nodded courteously. Debbie felt inexplicably close to tears.

Michael was torn. The urge to leave came again like unseen forces. But he knew he could accomplish his study faster if he could talk with Ben about the man he was, in a few short weeks, to imitate. He made his decision.

"I must talk with you Ben. Will you come home with us tonight?"

Ben sat down on the low wooden box, his lanky knees poking upward like an Ichabod Crane. His steady peace, and the fact that he no longer towered over them, helped to settle Debbie's nerves.

"I appreciate the invitation but I don't think I belong where you are."

"No — please! I'm asking you as a favor. I need to talk with you!"

"We can't talk here?" Ben looked up at Debbie. "But of course not. Forgive me, this is a most uncomfortable place for you both."

"It's not that Ben," Debbie protested weakly.

Ben stood up and smiled. "My life is very different than yours, and I understand. You need not feel badly. You've been most kind to me, and . . ." Ben patted his pocket . . . "I am grateful."

"Please Ben!" Michael pleaded. "Come with us. I must talk with you about this Jesus!"

Ben's expression changed immediately. He looked at Michael but addressed Debbie. "If you're both willing, I accept your kind invitation. But I must be back tomorrow afternoon and I have no way other than to ask you to bring me."

"Of course! We'll be glad to, won't we, Deb!" Michael's gladness was entirely out of character for himself or for that which he had just gained. Had he been told two months ago that he would be pleading with a derelict to come to his home for discussion about Jesus Christ he'd have thought it utterly bizarre.

Debbie offered a wan smile of polite welcome. Michael looked forward to this shortcut to his study requirement. It should please Franklin that he was going the extra mile. By the time he got to Jerusalem he would have a handle on the role he was to play. And he would know more about this peace.

Chapter 14

"How was your flight, sir?" Bo smiled the self-confident smile he'd nervously rehearsed waiting for Milton Franklin's plane to land. He took the travel bag Franklin held out for him to carry, jostled by other arriving passengers. The small airport at Gander, Newfoundland was crowded with holiday travellers and public monitors.

"Where's Cummings?" Franklin growled.

"His flight was delayed, sir. It should be here in twenty minutes."

"Just what I need, stuck in this miserable part of the world waiting for that idiot. We'll go now. He can find his own way."

A small boy in a thin worn coat, holding a huge ice cream bar ran laughing away from his brother and bumped into Franklin. The sticky cream smeared on the lower flap of his cashmere overcoat. "Watch it!" Franklin shouted, raising his arm to strike the boy. A large man dressed in the rough clothing of a laborer glowered at him, half-rising off a plastic bench along the wall. Franklin scowled and stopped his heavy hand in mid-swing toward the frightened upstaring face. He turned and stomped toward the exit. Bo hastily scurried after him.

"It's gonna be a lousy day," Franklin muttered. "Quick briefing Sunday 10 a.m. Quick nothing — 'emergency's' more like it. I hate emergencies. Bunch of bureaucratic incompetents . . ." Grumbling, he burst through the doors and into the raw-cold, gray Newfoundland winter morning.

"Taxi, sir?"

"Get out of my way!" He pushed across the startled man's path and into his waiting limousine. The sounds of public holiday bedlam receded, and the warmth of the heated compartment gave comfort to his chilled legs. As they sped away he wiped the cream from his coat with a moist towelette, poured a hot cup of coffee from the built-in service, and settled back to read the morning's Times. Bo had made certain it was available.

The news would have been shocking a year before. Front page headlines reported three earthquakes, a small nuclear explosion in the simmering Sino-Russian border war, and a grim announcement that suicides had reached a record high in November. Tragic, no matter how familiar — but no longer shocking. Franklin snorted and turned to the business section.

The half hour ride through the Newfoundland countryside brought Franklin to the large Nexa Inn, built in the early years of the Gander Shuttle program. The Nexa was one of four World Alliance communications centers, sister to the Colonia near Lima, Peru, the Cape Grattas Centre on the east coast of Africa, and Martre Jon in northern Belgium. Its exterior blended with the simplicity of its surroundings. But inside, from the sixth floor above ground to the fourth floor underground, were all the appointments and equipment necessary to support world strategy conferences and heads of state.

Bo pushed a small plastic card into the entrance electronic scanner. The heavy iron gate swung open, and they continued along the remaining half-mile to the Nexa. As they approached Franklin noticed a commercial airborne platform hover overhead. Under the glass canopy the bulging figure of Senator Moe Cummings was unmistakable. They arrived at the front door of The Nexa almost simultaneously.

"Morning Milton," Moe puffed. "Ever been on one of those?" He motioned toward the platform, idling slightly off the ground while its pilot signed the landing forms for the Nexa guard.

"They're expensive," Franklin growled. "If you'd been here on time you could have gone with me. Safer, too. This is no time to take useless risks."

"What risk? You're in the air only four minutes," Moe said casually, chafing under the admonishment. They strode up the wide white steps and into the lobby where they were greeted immediately by the resident director and escorted down the elevators to the fourth subfloor communications conference room.

The room was enormous, with a twenty foot ceiling and walls panelled in olivewood. A large triangular oak table occupied the center area, with leather chairs along two of the three sides and an array of screens, cameras, and speakers along the third. On the table directly in front of the control console, a series of image plates glistened under waiting low voltage power. Floor-to-ceiling windows were spaced along the walls, their views holographically generated. On this bleak Sunday morning, it appeared through the east windows as though they were on a bluff overlooking the ocean, while a view of distant snow-capped mountains could be seen across the room. They handed their coats to a waiting porter. Technicians prepared the equipment for the morning meeting, and an attendant put coffee and pastries on the table. Franklin pulled a fresh cigar from his jacket pocket and poured some coffee.

"So, senator, how are things in the power group?"

Moe coughed. "Good. We met with Omega Friday . . ."

"Old news. We talked Friday night. Remember?"

"Just reviewing, Milton. As for new information, Omega went to the Binzoe District last night, picked up some derelict, and took him back to his house."

"What!" Franklin exploded. "He knows that's not . . ."

"We'll know why soon. He's scheduled to join Diehl's church this morning. We'll take the bum while he's gone."

"Cummings, we cannot afford the slightest foul-up. You'd better make absolutely sure everything is solid. If you don't . . ."

"It's solid, I assure you," Moe said, hiding the alarm he'd felt ever since receiving the report.

"I assure you," Franklin mocked sarcastically. "No surprises, Cummings. That's the rule. This emergency meeting is bad enough. Your people should have known what he was going to do and prevented that fool from deviating from plan."

"Milt, there WAS no plan until six o'clock this morning!"

"No matter!" he rasped savagely. "Any fool would know the plan wouldn't include some hare-brained trip to a ghetto!" Franklin slapped his hand on the heavy oak table to vent his irritation.

"Sir, we're ready." The technician had been watching Franklin, whose brief performance generated gratitude that he was but a simple communications specialist.

"Go."

He aligned the cameras and touched sensors on the control console. Screens flashed into light, and shapes shimmered above two of the image plates and coalesced into the heads of two men, who peered directly at Moe and at Franklin. The screens behind these images showed each in a similarly appointed conference room. The older of the two heads spoke, its beady eyes seeming to look at both men simultaneously. "Gentlemen, good morning."

Franklin and Moe Cummings responded in kind.

"It's snowing outside my windows here at Grattas — lovely, beautiful snow. How nice it must be between ocean and mountains, yes Milton?"

"Very nice sir," Franklin said.

"And you, Anton? What have you at Jon's?"

"We have mountains here sir," the other head replied. "Very nice."

The first head smiled. "Yes, very nice. All right, to business. Rooms clear? Yes, I see, you're alone. Good."

Moe Cummings and Milton Franklin sat alert and ready. The image head belonging to World Organization Ecumenical Council Visgate Dr. Anton Jedesky turned toward the World Alliance Chairman's image, waiting.

"This meeting was quickly called, but it is not an emergency. You will appreciate that, Milton."

Franklin nodded, chagrined by the chairman's perceptiveness.

"You're aware of the changes in plans and the need to implement with precision and speed over the next six weeks. We must keep in close touch during this time. I am waiving established protocol, and ask that we communicate daily via global voicecode and weekly from the conference centers."

'Ask,' Franklin snorted silently.

"You three are the key players in our little drama. And Omega of course. Congratulations, Senator. His profile appears perfect."

"Thank you sir," Moe beamed, exulting. "We worked . . ."

"Anton, you will coordinate all logistics and manage all news releases and coverage as detailed in the Omega Plan. WOEC has excellent resources for that."

"We're ready, sir."

"Yes. And senator, you are prepared to provide surveillance and reporting on Omega himself, and on every aspect of the Christian movement?"

"Yes, sir," said Moe, sensing the wisdom of a short reply.

"Status, please." His voice carried a hint of challenge. Moe Cummings opened his briefing folio, blinking to clear his eyes. He'd had only five hours of sleep since Thursday. "North American, South American, and European Regions are all deployed, sir. Asian Region is 85 percent ready and will be deployed by two o'clock today. Lower Quadrant is 75 percent ready, and the North Cap is 70 percent. Both will be fully deployed by five o'clock today. We have a total of 20,350 activaries."

"Good. That's what I like, senator. Facts. Milton, your role. You've had Omega working for you. You know him. I trust you, Milton." The chairman noted his gratification. "Ah, you are pleased. But not surprised. Properly so. Competent men are aware of their assets as well as their liabilities."

"Yes, Mr. Chairman, I quite agree."

"Good. Milton, in six days you will assume command of the World Alliance."

Franklin gasped.

"All for public consumption of course," the chairman said. "Section Eight of the Omega Plan is blank. Here is Section Eight. I will be killed next Saturday at two thirty-three in the afternoon. Of course you will not be associated with my demise in any way. You will take immediate control and initiate intense persecution on Christians throughout the world. When Omega appears as their returned leader, he will depose you."

Franklin recovered his composure. "It's brilliant, sir."

"Yes. After doing away with you, Milton, Omega will raise me back from death. He should be able to, shouldn't he. So he shall. This will consolidate our power once and for all. No one else knows of Section Eight. I have now entrusted you with very precious knowledge."

The impact of the chairman's outline stunned them. 'Megalomaniac,' Moe Cummings thought. 'Shrewd, and dangerous,' was Milton Franklin's assessment. Anton Jedesky's head disappeared from the image plate as he left his chair at the Martre Jon conference room and began to pace.

The chairman spoke sharply. "Anton — someone is in that room!"

Through Anton's screen Moe and Franklin could see an attendant who had just entered the room. Anton's brief exchange with the man revealed that the attendant did not realize the meaning of the red warning light outside the conference room door, and had just then entered with fresh coffee. Jedesky dismissed him. The chairman's head turned to Moe Cummings.

"Senator, what will you do?"

"Sir, I'll assign surveillance to him immediately."

The chairman's voice was cold, and held its listener in contempt. "You believe that is sufficient, senator?"

Moe gulped with understanding. He rose unsteadily and went to the global voicecode equipment. Soon, speaking in a low voice, he was making the necessary arrangements.

"Milton," the chairman continued, "while the senator is handling this unfortunate breach there is one more element in your role. You are to become Omega's confidante. Get close to him. Be with him frequently, and at all times during the final week."

Franklin could not avoid a scowl. This was not only a surprise, but would impede his heavy work schedule.

"Sir, that will be difficult. We . . ."

"There are no appeals, Milton. Everything hinges on these next six weeks. If you must vent your frustration, do so on the Christians when you assume control of World Alliance. After all, it is their stubbornness which threatens all that we've worked toward. We must admire them, for all of it, mustn't we?" The chairman's head leered at Franklin.

There was only one man able to intimidate Milton Franklin, only one whose ruthlessness, singlemindedness of purpose, and mental power exceeded his own. That man was the Chairman of the World Alliance. The shaken, plump senator huddled over the voicecode equipment was only one of the many evidences of the chairman's singlemindedness.

"It will be done, sir."

The chairman looked pleased.

Moe waddled back to his seat, pale and perspiring. "It's handled, sir."

"Good. Very good. Gentlemen, I remind you of the historic moment at hand. Nothing — I repeat, nothing — can be permitted to jeopardize the Omega Plan. Nothing. When it succeeds and my government is installed, you will ascend to the innermost circles of power. As we build an unhindered world government you will experience more than all you have ever worked toward or hoped for. I have chosen each of you. Now it is for you to perform.

"If, on the other hand, there is an error of even the slightest degree, whether by accident or —" the chairman's head looked stonily at each of the other three — "deliberately, I will hold you personally accountable up to and beyond the limits of law. You will wish you had never been born. This is not a threat — it's a statement of fact. You are wholly dependent upon each other. There is no middle ground. Win, and win incredible wealth, power, prestige, and elimination of any accountability whatsoever. Except to me of course. Lose, and you will lose everything in a manner of extreme anguish. You are in. You are it. Questions?"

None needed clarification.

"I am being unusually blunt. Count it as a sacrifice of image on my part to ensure the immensely important priority of the Omega Plan. The unity of the world hinges on your capabilities and discretion. It goes without saying, of course, that there are no limits to the resources you may request in accomplishing the purpose. Now, to the detailed plan . . . ."

It was mid-afternoon when the session ended. They ordered lunch, saying little until they had finished eating, each lost in his own thoughts. It was Franklin who spoke.

"Like it or not, we have a lot riding on each other," he remarked.

"We sure do," Moe said, wiping his chin.

"All right." Franklin steeled himself. "You know I haven't thought too highly of you. I'm, uh, sorry. I'm willing to work with you, heads up, no side shows. I don't want any animosity in the way." Franklin stuck his hand out. Moe shook it.

"Thanks. Thanks, Milt!"

Franklin suppressed an urge to retch. He hated the name 'Milt.' And he was more repulsed than ever by Moe Cummings' flaccid handshake, his inability to look him in the eye, his degenerate lack of discipline. 'The Chairman can't be serious about this bozo being in the Inner Circle,' he thought silently. 'But business is business. I can't afford to have him nervous and alienated now.'

Franklin forced his most comradely smile. "Okay."

They rose to go, buzzing the porter in for their coats. "Milt, I'll go back with you! I want to go over what I've been doing with the senate bill on nuclear defense dispersion . . ."

"Listen, Moe. Don't call me Milt. Understand? It's 'Milton.'"

"Sure, sure Milt . . on. Sorry." Moe grinned as he waddled next to Milton Franklin like a pet dog toward the lobby door. "Anyhow, Milt, nuclear . . ."

"Milton!"

"Sorry! Nuclear overkill ratios doubled last year . . . ."

Chapter 15

Michael was worried — Ben was not in the house. They had talked with him long into the night, and found that the man who lived under such shabby conditions was not only at peace with himself, but charming and well-educated. Michael was sure Ben had saved him days of time in research. He would be more than ready to work with the Omega team in Jerusalem. So confident was he, in fact, that he had not tried to contact Gabriel Diehl after the morning's service, feeling that next weekend would be soon enough.

As instructed by Eric Lindsay, he and Debbie had gone forward on the pastor's invitation. With no prior church affiliation, Gabe had asked them two questions. Did they believe in Jesus Christ as the risen and now living Son of God? Did they believe Jesus had died for them personally as an atonement for their sin? "Yes," they had mumbled.

Michael thought their reception into "God's family" as Gabe Diehl had called it, with all hugging welcomes, was a bit much. One can only smile just so many times at just so many happy faces when one doesn't understand what is going on.

They'd invited Ben to come along but he had declined. Michael had wondered whether to leave his house alone with Ben. But he sensed it would be safe. Now they were back, and Ben was missing.

"Michael, come down here — I found something!" Debbie called from the back hallway. He ran down the stairs two at a time.

"Look." She handed him a piece of crumpled newspaper. "Crusade — Dr. Gabriel Diehl" it announced. Ben had pulled that clipping out of his tattered pocket, inviting them to come along.

"What do you think?"

"Could be nothing. It's strange, though, that he would lose it. I remember him putting it back into his pocket."

They both were realizing how much they liked this humble, self-effacing man. "He wouldn't just leave and drop it on the floor that way!"

Debbie voiced the worry neither had yet spoken. "I'm afraid something may have happened, Michael."

He nodded. "Let's think it through. He's not here and he should be. Hitchhike back? No. Assuming he wouldn't leave on his own, then . . . Someone had to come and get him. Who?"

"Or, to take him away," Debbie interjected.

Michael paused. Sensible or not, that could be true.

"But who even knows he exists, let alone be someone worth abducting!"

Thoughts of the week ahead with all its uncertainties and unanswered questions pushed into his mind. He felt angry, too, at the inconvenience Ben was causing. He had things to do. His concern for Ben began to evaporate.

"Wherever he went he's gone, and I don't have time to keep hunting for him. I'm going to change and then study. My plane leaves at seven in the morning."

"Michael, we can't just ignore him! Shouldn't we call the monitors?"

He laughed sarcastically. "What do we say . . . 'our pet bum is missing?' Debbie, he's gone. Forget it."

"Maybe he felt he was too much trouble to be driven back, Michael, and is walking!"

"Eight miles?"

"Let's drive to Binzoe — maybe we'll see him along the way." Debbie pleaded for the gentle man whose words had touched her the evening before.

"Enough is enough! I got what I needed, and we paid him for his services. For all we know, there are probably things missing we haven't found out about yet. Did you check your jewel box?"

"Michael, how can you say that?" Her eyes shimmered with anger. "He . . . . well, he just wouldn't."

"Trust is the first deadly weakness, believe me."

"I trust you, Michael Ames!" Debbie retorted, her anger flaring. Michael muttered a response and went up the stairs to escape before a real argument began. He wanted no more of those hurtful days. But he knew the deadness of his accusations. If only there was somebody to trust. Michael was sure there wasn't — not really. He'd rejected Ben's words out of hand . . . 'the Lord Jesus is trustworthy. He's taken care of me for twelve years in Binzoe . . .' Michael hadn't had an experience. He'd been burned enough, and no one could convince him otherwise.

"Curtis!"

A burly young man slipped into the room. "Lieutenant?"

"Book him. Vagrancy. We should have instructions soon." Lieutenant Croft looked at the tall grizzled man seated silently by his desk. "Unless, that is, you want one more chance to talk in the comfort of this office. For the last time, bub, what were you doing in that house?"

Ben shifted in the straight-backed chair. "I was there as an invited guest. Mr. Ames will verify it."

"Sure." The lieutenant rubbed the back of his neck. He was already tired and the day was young. "Three times I ask a simple question. Three times you tell me that you, a rundown drifter, were invited to a home in the rich part of town. Can't you do any better?"

Ben's peaceful acquiescence infuriated the lieutenant. "Get him out of my sight, Curtis," he growled.

Ben was pushed out of the room. He did not resist. Lieutenant Croft collected his papers, looking out the window onto Sunday's traffic. "Sixty hours a week I work," he muttered, shaking his head, "and they drag me out on a Sunday for this."

Curtis returned. "He's in, sir."

Craft looked up. "Wonderful. That makes my day. It's such a thrilling shift."

Curtis chuckled politely.

"Isn't this a little strange?" Croft continued. "All this attention — we used to run over guys like him on patrol duty. Besides, he was too educated for a bum."

"A plant, maybe?" Curtis offered.

"Dunno," Croft replied. But he felt better. Maybe this was more important that it first appeared, after all — something worthy of his twenty-two years of service. He sighed, and touched the automatic dialer. The videoscreen fluttered to life. Muted ringing came through the speaker.

"Senator Cummings' office. Briggs."

"He still says he was invited."

"We know, lieutenant. That's why you picked him up. Remember?"

"We couldn't get any more from him. He said they talked for a few hours, then went to sleep. The next morning Ames and his wife went to . . ."

"What did they talk about, lieutenant?" Charlie Briggs' tone reflected thinly veiled impatience.

"Mostly about some guy named Jesus."

Briggs paused and scribbled some notes. "Anything else?"

"That's all we could get. I think he was there to rip 'em off."

"You would, lieutenant. Release him. We'll take it from here."

"That's all?"

"Take the rest of the day off." The screen blanked.

Croft clenched his hands in frustration. "Know what I hate most about this job, Curtis? They don't tell you nuthin."

"No sir."

"This World Alliance stuff stinks, Curtis. Ya know?"

Curtis fidgeted.

"Twenty-two years on the force, and I know less about what's going on now than when I was a rookie like you. Know what's gonna happen, Curtis, if you know less in twenty-two years than you do now?"

"What, sir?"

"You're gonna be a negative entity. Antimatter! You're gonna be a vacuum. You're not even gonna know your own name!"

"Yes sir."

Croft dropped his head between his hands. "Let him out."

"Sir?"

"Let him out, Curtis! Out!"

"Sir, before . . . well, they're about to deliver lunch. I thought maybe . . . he could use a meal . . ."

Croft looked at his young charge, surprised. Then he grinned.

"Why not. Let him eat. Then release him."

"Yes sir." Curtis disappeared through the door before Croft might change his mind.

"Mr. Ames?" A polite voice said.

"Yes?" Michael answered groggily, awakened from a brief nap. The thought that it might be Ben came to him at the first ring.

"This is Charlie Briggs, of Senator Cummings' office."

Michael's mind cleared quickly. "Yes?"

"I'm calling on behalf of the senator, asking you to refrain from unauthorized contact during the term of your assignment."

"What? What do you . . ."

"You and your wife were observed driving into the Binzoe District last evening. You picked up a derelict named Ben Crockett and returned to your house with him."

"Ben! Where is he?"

"We picked him up this morning."

"What? That's outrageous!" Michael sputtered with anger.

The aide's voice took on an edge. "Mr. Ames, your assignment is critical to world interests. During its term you must comply with instructions. Avoid all unauthorized contacts. You've read the notebook?"

Michael thought about the three ring binder, still unopened, judged less important in view of his discussion with Ben. "The study guide?"

"That's part of it, yes. Apparently you have not. It contains explicit instructions for your conduct. You were to have read that last evening." Briggs paused. Michael was becoming uncomfortable.

"How was your meeting with Gabriel Diehl?"

Michael reflected on his decision to forego that meeting. "I decided to see him next weekend. Mr. Briggs, I was able, in talking with Ben, the derelict as you call him, to . . ."

115

"We know you left without meeting Dr. Diehl. There are reasons for the instructions to meet with him today. Do whatever you must, but meet him."

"Listen, Mr. Briggs . . ."

"And see that you read the manual immediately, Mr. Ames. The success of the mission depends on your professionalism in all aspects. That includes doing your homework."

Michael burned from the chastisement, worsened by a shrill nasal quality of the aide's voice. No one had ever accused him of negligence. Amazed at the thorough surveillance he was obviously under he began to realize that he'd become part of something much larger than he'd thought.

"We won't alert the senator to these slips, Mr. Ames. This time. There's no need to undermine his or Mr. Franklin's confidence in you."

"What about Ben?" Michael asked, relieved.

"He's been questioned at the monitor station. We understand you talked about the man you are to portray, this Jesus. The senator will appreciate your initiative. But stick to the book, Mr. Ames. Goodbye."

The telephone clicked before Michael could respond. He lay back on the bed and drew his hands across his face. The assignment was becoming complicated, and dangerous in strange and undefinable ways. He closed his eyes for just a moment. In that moment, he dozed.

He sensed a tingling, neither unpleasant nor familiar. All seemed larger, more potent and more real, yet without physical point of reference. He floated without effort in a warm pool of light. And such a light it was — its strength should have scarred his eyes, yet it flowed through him with an exuberant power even as it held him secure in its refreshing wellbeing. He opened his arms into the loving glow which filled him as the sea fills a bucket submerged in it.

"Where am I?"

He was startled at the sound — his own voice, yes, but a voice enriched and perfected. He peered through the glow toward his feet but could not see them, yet they were there. He stretched out his arms but saw nothing to interrupt the silken, soothing ambiance. He was content to remain motionless in his realm of sustaining peace. 'This, perhaps, is the Heaven Ben talked about? Have I died? If so I don't mind . . . .'

The glow assimilated into shapes and tones, each warmer and more inviting than the others. Sounds of distant music touched him, soaring choirs of selfless, uninhibited joy. The gladness was overwhelming. He continued filling, strengthening, and increasing, made able to hold to the heavy joy without effort. Fragrances suffused his space, cleansing aromas of freedom which opened him further to goodness he did not know could be. Then a being took shape from the gathering glow, and spoke.

"Michael, rejoice and enter!"

He was awed by the magnificence before him — distinctly human yet alive with great power and wellness and perfect in every detail.

"My dearest friend!" Michael exclaimed, not knowing the being at all yet knowing him all his life.

"I am Henri. Be glad, for God loves you well beyond what you would think. Yet he loves no one any less. You shall see and bear witness of that. The days of fulfillment are coming. We prepare now. Behold, Michael."

Henri spread his arms apart. The glow diffused, revealing a misty panorama of Heavenly beauty in marvelous glory. The power of pure and perfect love came upon Michael immediately. He fell to his knees in adoration, yet without sense of movement or floor to kneel upon.

Henri touched his bowed head. "You do well to be in worship, for you are in the presence of creation as created. But turn yourself away from me. See now the majesty of eternal places and receive the beginnings of understanding."

Michael lifted his eyes, sustained by Henri's supporting nearness, and looked, and absorbed.

There was a city of light which exuded a matchless joy. Columned mansions rose in majesty to great heights and shone with warm and enduring welcome. Broad avenues serpentined like great silken designs in perfect harmony one to the other. Bushes and vines lined the avenues and surrounded the columned mansions. Wide rolling grounds lushly overflowed with every manner of tree and flower. Great and small creatures, familiar and unfamiliar, teemed in satisfying balance with all else.

At the center there was a great golden dome bathed in brilliant white light from which all life seemed to emanate; indeed, all that he was as well. All glowed with life not merely as Michael knew it, but joy-filled and perfect. All moved in harmony. And from each one flowed worship and praise toward the center which passed along the appearance of silver cords, one for each, which would never break.

"You must speak," said Henri, "and tell me what is in your heart."

"I cannot speak," Michael whispered.

"Yet are there not matters weighing upon you?"

Michael realized then that he'd lost consciousness of himself. But Henri's question spurred him back into self-awareness. A lessening of the precious ecstasy crept over him as thoughts of his own devising returned. Michael found poverty in the best of himself against the wealth and splendor of the Kingdom into Whose seeing presence he had been brought. All he counted as riches was as if nothing compared with even a glimpse of this wonderful place. He began to understand, then, and he wept.

"You weep now because you taste the consequence of the fall. What you have seen you might join at your appointed time. You have received the first understanding. There are more before you can hope in this. But now you must pass to the other side. The Spirit of God be with you, Michael."

The warm glow reenveloped him and Henri faded into it. Darkness came. Michael heard his name pronounced in a banal tone. A dark and dirty alleyway appeared. Strange buildings hunched close to the ground as if fearing to rise upward. Gloom filled the heavy air.

Michael was startled by the sound of pounding hoofbeats. Horses galloped around a bend in the alley and into view, pulling a wooden cart which bounced crazily along the rough cobblestones. Dust flew, and shrieks and coarse shouts pierced the air. He tried to scramble out of the way as horses and cart sped past, spewing an oily foul-smelling mud. The wheel grazed his hip as it careened by and shoved him against the alley fence. Dazed, he watched in horror as two hooded figures atop the cart threw a body onto the grimy stones. It landed with a dull thud not far from him. Cart and horses disappeared in the gloom.

The body stirred, then rose to its hands and knees and stared at Michael. Yellow eyes gleamed from a disheveled face. Michael felt cold fingers grip his heart. A baleful wind moaned its way between the hump-backed buildings, swirling the dust of the alley. Micahel shivered, frozen in lonely misery. His body throbbed with pain.

"You don't belong here." The raspy gargling voice was full of venom and hatred. Michael was horrified.

"Where am I?" He forced the question from his lips.

"The chief's world. Where else, idiot. Are you blind?"

A rooster crowed in the distance. It sounded twice, and then screeched the laugh of a madman. The body got to its feet and commanded Michael to do the same. Michael winced, shivering in the cold wind. He was filled with dread and would have run had he known where to go.

"Aw, is you scared?" it mocked. Suddenly it stiffened and peered down the alley. The stench of garbage seeped from it. A large black-robed figure was coming toward them. Its face contorted in anguish; it stood rigid and trembling. Suddenly it pushed Michael down and ran with a loud wail toward the approaching figure. It dropped to its knees on the cobblestones, wailing and pleading.

"Help me, help me!" The raspy cry was desperate. "I repent, I believe . . . help me . . . ."

The figure took no notice, but continued toward Michael. It grabbed at the hem of his robe but was repelled as if by anti-magnetic force.

Michael's own horror eased as the figure drew closer. Neither fear nor malice was present, and he walked with confidence and power. Then Michael recognized the features under the hood. A flood of relief washed over him and he sank to the cobblestones, drained of strength. Henri stopped next to him and stood quietly. The tattered defeated body shuffled off into the murk, and the mad rooster crowed again in the distance.

"Be protected, Michael." Henri stretched out his hand. Michael grasped it eagerly. It was warm and strong, and pulsed with energy. Henri helped him to his feet.

"By the power of the Creator you are here for this moment. This is the edge of His absence. You shall see and understand." He placed his hands on Michael's shoulders. Immediately pain left him and strength returned. Henri turned to walk away.

"Don't go!" Michael pleaded. "What shall I do?"

Henri smiled. "Consider what you have seen. Be ready."

The air darkened, and Michael passed through a wave of dizziness. Then his eyes popped open. Debbie was standing over him.

". . . Michael! I said, who was on the phone? Are you all right?"

He shook his head to clear it.

"What time is it, Deb?"

"It's . . . two twenty. Michael, what's wrong?"

"Nothing." He sat up on the bed and swung his feet to the floor. "How long was I asleep?"

"Asleep? You just hung up the phone a minute ago! You lay back on the bed just as I came into the room, and wouldn't answer me!"

"I . . . Deb, I just had an incredible dream. It feels like I've been gone for hours."

Debbie sat down next to him, somewhat concerned. But he was overtaken with things he had to do, and the vivid remembrances were fading. He patted her hand. "I have to study. And I have to get over to see Diehl today. A guy from Cummings' office called." He sighed and got up from the bed. There wasn't much time left to set right his mistakes before leaving for Jerusalem.

Chapter 16

The afternoon sky was like old lead, heavy with snow just beginning to fall. Michael pulled his collar around his neck as he backed the Jaguar out of the driveway for a 4:00 appointment with Gabe Diehl. He'd been cordial enough on the phone but the thought that he may know something of his real motivations nagged at him.

Michael was a person who demanded answers to the questions he came upon. It was part of a deeper need to be in control, and to stay his own course on the basis of knowledge he worked hard to possess. The mechanics of life bored him. The substance of his questions lay in the Why of life and all it contained. Michael sought not just answers, but real answers.

In some mysterious way he had been vaulted from anonymity into the fulcrum of history. Why? He recounted his experiences, from the unlikely and unseemly Binzoe attack to being thrust into a working relationship with national and powerful leaders. His marriage had recently turned for the better. He had received help from a derelict who was not a derelict at all, and for whom he had developed a surprising affection. He had received, in a most unusual way, an amazing assignment, one of mystery and secrecy, and enormous ego gratification. All this had happened within a few weeks and in a world retching with calamity and tearing its social fabric apart thread by thread.

Then there were his dreams. Another question occurred to him: how could he go blithely about in the wake of such dreams? He could because doing so fit his definition of life on planet earth. But if Ben had spoken truth, then everything he had based his life upon was wrong. Indeed, his life was doomed.

Doomed? Michael mused, feeling the solid power of the XJ-12, stroking the soft, reassuringly elegant cloth of his cashmere overcoat. If this is doom, I'll take it. Deception. The things Ben told me must be deceptions. Michael felt like one who, told the house is on fire, continues to read the paper. Either it isn't true or its consequences are so far beyond his control that he may as well ignore it.

His thoughts turned to the opportunities ahead. He savored the stimulation of his central role in the Omega drama, anticipating great personal gain from his associations with high people. He pictured himself circulating in the gatherings of the known and the important, receiving their acknowledgements, entering into the privileged vectors of their special lives. He, Michael Jeremy Ames, was about to become one very important person.

He arrived at the church in an ebullient frame of mind. Snow was falling steadily now, and the streets were slippery and white. As he stepped out of the car, Gabriel Diehl opened the front entrance door and waved. Michael patted his jacket pocket, assuring himself that the envelope he'd put there before leaving was still in place.

"Good of you to see me on such short notice, Dr. Diehl."

" 'Gabe' is fine, Michael." He shook his hand warmly, looking him in the eye. "We'll talk in my study. Right up these stairs."

They entered a warm room lined with bookshelves. It felt like a sanctuary from the cold air and the stress of life.

"We're glad to have you and Mrs. Ames as member candidates, Michael. Coffee?" Gabe motioned to the pot simmering on a small electric stove.

"Please, with cream only."

"Powdered milk — I hope you don't mind," Gabe said cheerily, handing Michael a steaming mug. They sat on the large couch.

"You mentioned you were leaving on a business trip tomorrow and needed to see me. How can I help?"

Michael wondered about the word 'candidate.' Was he not yet a member? He decided to drop it and keep to his agenda.

"Yes I did," he said. "Not for counselling, though — I have a good job, a good marriage, and no personal problems." Michael was surprised at his outburst.

"I wish it could be so for all of our people. There are increasing hardships these days, Michael. Many are on the edge of financial collapse, or in poor health. But we have the Lord Jesus, don't we? 'My grace is sufficient for you,' He said. How true it is, Michael, how true." Gabe's matter-of-fact confidence unsettled his visitor.

"That's why I called. I want to help. Frankly," Michael paused thoughtfully, "I don't think there are many days left before . . . well, I just want to do what I can before it's too late."

Gabe's eyes narrowed slightly. "A number of us believe the time is near for Jesus' return. And there are many opportunities for you to help. But Michael, first tell me your story."

Michael looked blank. "My story?"

"Yes. How did you come to know Jesus? It's always a great joy for me to hear how people are led back home." Gabe leaned toward Michael, eager and expectant.

In business Michael would recognize this as a set-up. He'd practiced the art himself more times than he could remember. The signals of the game were not so much in the words used as in tones and expressions. These revealed the truth of intention to one skilled in such interpretation.

But this was different — or else Gabriel Diehl was so skillful himself that Michael could detect no sign of hidden motive. *He actually thinks I know someone who's been dead for centuries*, Michael thought, amazed. He thumbed quickly through the mental pages of his previous night's reading, trying to create a story that would do.

"It wasn't much, really," he began, remembering to be humble. "Last week I had a personal crisis in my job. Not that I haven't had them before," he added hastily. "But this triggered a lot of thoughts that had been with me for years." He stopped to think. Gabe sipped his coffee and waited.

"I realized that there would be many more of them, no matter what I did or didn't do. It finally occurred to me that it all wasn't very dependable. Do you know what I mean?"

His mind hunted for the next words. It tweaked his conscience, this weaving of a deliberate lie to a man who was being altogether kind and hospitable. On the other hand, it was for the good of the world.

"Yes I do," Gabe said with what for Michael was an alarming degree of encouragement. Michael remembered something Ben had said about a sinner's prayer. Apparently Christians believe that people are trapped by sin — an ugly word, he thought — and therefore, need forgiveness.

"So I prayed for forgiveness from my sins."

The minister waited, silent.

"And here I am!" Michael laughed awkwardly, shrugging as if the whole thing was clearly inevitable.

Gabe slowly set his coffee cup on the table. Michael sensed he wasn't buying a word he'd said.

Gabe walked over to the window and looked down through the gloom of waning winter light at Michael's shiny expensive car. He remembered seeing him standing there talking with another man, and Em Prantzer's finger pointing through the snow-laced panes of glass to identify him. He thought about Eric's impression of his brief meeting with Michael — ill at ease and preoccupied, but otherwise a nice fellow. "Michael," he began, softly and with compassion, "the Lord Jesus knew you when he hung on that cross. He died for you personally so you wouldn't have to bear the consequences for your sin nature. If you'd been the only man alive He would have done the same. Do you understand?"

Michael nodded blankly.

"He is the Savior and the Lord of all of us. You acknowledged this morning that you believe He is Who He says He is."

Michael knew, then, the doubt in Gabe Diehl's mind. But maybe it could still work. Perhaps he could save face with the kindly pastor, and still forge the relationship he was there to establish.

"I want to believe that. If I'm not there yet, I want to be." Michael paused, stunned to realize that what he had intended as relational manipulation had come out as something he really meant. It was a sudden and unexpected twist away from accustomed control.

Gabe understood the battle. He had mopped the brows and held the weapons of hundreds of people over the years as they wrestled against their adversary. He focused intently on his guest and spoke with the authority of accurate perception. Warmth and caring was etched on every line of his face. "You are not ready to join our church. Not yet. But you're on the right road. There's a mighty spark in you Michael, although you haven't recognized it. I can't welcome you into membership yet, but I certainly welcome your friendship." Gabe smiled and extended his hand.

"Thank you. Thank you Gabe." Michael's emotion was strong, and he struggled to contain it.

"As for your desire to help, we have many needs. Among them are the food and shelter programs we're doing with other churches in the city. Can I count on you?"

"Gabe, I don't think I have much to offer in that line. I mean, the skills I have might better be used in something like working with your executive committee, or board of — what are they called here — financial advisors?"

"Trustees. I'm sure you have many talents, Michael, and I thank you for your enthusiasm."

"Then I'll help there, with the Trustees?"

"If you really wish to help, our need is for volunteers to take food to people who are hungry, running errands for our older people, and spending some time with many deserted or orphaned children."

"But you just need arms and legs and heavy coats, or people with plenty of time for that," Michael protested. "Surely you use your less capable people to pass out the food!"

Gabe reached for a Bible and turned to Mark 9. "Listen to this. 'If anyone would be first, he must be last of all and a servant of all.' "

Michael stared at him. "Why that makes no sense at all!" he exclaimed. "You have to work hard to be first at anything! Who said that?" He already knew, of course.

"Jesus."

"What kind of a teaching is that?" Michael had no desire to waste his time swilling soup. But he had his job to do. If he was to get close to Gabriel Diehl he'd have to work on his terms.

"All right," he sighed. "Sign me up."

"Good!" Gabe beamed. "We're opening a crusade the day after tomorrow in the Binzoe District. Those in need will be there. Can you . . . oh, but I forgot, you'll be out of town."

"I'll be gone until Friday."

"Friday we'll be in Washington. When you return contact Eric, the man you spoke with yesterday. He's leading the relief program. He'll get you involved. Thank you Michael. And bless you for your willingness to help."

Michael was on his feet before Gabe had finished, suddenly anxious to leave.

"Okay. Say, perhaps we can have dinner together next weekend — wives too?"

Gabe was startled. "I'm not married, and . . ."

"Then allow us to take you . . ."

"But I'll be in Washington."

Michael thought quickly. "Fine. We'll meet you there."

It was one of the few times Gabe had ever found himself at a loss for words. His guest seemed extremely insistent.

"All right then. But isn't that rather expensive for you?"

Michael had almost forgotten the envelope. "No, no, it's nothing! I'll stop in Washington on my way back. My company will fly my wife in to meet us."

'To meet with a pastor?' Gabe noted silently.
Michael reached into his pocket. "Here, Gabe. This is a contribution. My first of, I hope, many."
Gabe accepted the envelope and opened it. "Five thousand dollars, Michael? You can't buy your way in here, you know!" Gabe smiled in amazement. His church operated on a very large budget thanks to the sharing spirit of its members. Money had not been a problem, and the financial abundance had made possible a wide range of services. Gabe knew now without a doubt that something else was driving Michael Ames, but had no idea what it might be.
Michael relaxed. Money had such a superb way of dealing with difficult situations. If his story hadn't aroused Gabe's attention, the check certainly would. And Franklin wouldn't say a word about it when it appeared on the next expense report.
"It's a token of our appreciation. We look forward to a long and mutually rewarding relationship." It was a poor choice of words, but Gabe showed no negative reaction.
"I must go," Michael said, moving toward the door. "I'll see you in Washington. Where shall I contact you?"
"We're staying at the Bethel Inn . . ." Michael shook his hand and eased out the door before Gabe had finished.

Chapter 17

The Prantzer Defense jet climbed steeply. Early morning sunlight pierced the cabin with brilliance as the plane poked through the clouds. Michael was impressed with the cabin's walnut trim, leather couches, and battery of communications equipment neatly built into the bulkhead. It all reflected the kind of wealth and power which was his consuming goal.
"Like it?" Milton Franklin smiled as he leaned back against his seat and pulled on a freshly lit cigar.

Michael nodded, still wondering at the strange and sudden turnabout in Franklin's attitude. His call the night before, arranging to meet him personally with the company limousine and accompany him to Jerusalem, was enough of a surprise. But his cordiality was most untypical. Michael suspected there was more to the situation than met the eye, but he easily convinced himself that most of the reason lay in the simple fact that he was earning the friendship and respect of one of the wealthiest and most powerful men in business. It was strong tonic.

"Look there." Franklin pointed out the window, sighting the ground below through an opening in the thinning clouds.

It was the meteorite crater. Six months before, the Pocono Mountains had been hit by a massive meteorite. The weathered spine of the eastern mountain chain had been split in two by the three mile wide crater produced by the impact. Camelback was gone, splattered across fifty miles of once-wooded terrain. The impact had been felt a hundred miles away, and the casualty count was in the thousands.

"Unbelievable," Michael breathed.

"With everything else happening on this planet it seems almost normal," Franklin said non-chalantly. "A good time for your return, Omega."

Michael thought about Ben's description of the last days of the earth before the return of Jesus. "Yes it is. From what I've read, Jesus told his followers there would be increasing wars and natural disasters all over the earth just before he returns."

Franklin snorted. "Fools. Since fish first crawled on land anyone could have predicted wars and disasters and be right."

"It's certainly gotten worse, though," Michael said.

"Maybe. But it'll pass, like it always does. All that counts is power among men. Remember that."

They sat for a time in silence.

"Shouldn't you be studying? We've got a lot to do when we get there, and we expect you to pull this off without a hitch." Franklin grinned.

Michael nodded and extracted his copy of the Omega Plan along with the sealed envelope from his briefcase.

Franklin rang for coffee and the airphone, and broke open a fresh package of cigars. Becky appeared carrying a silver tray with a coffee pot and two china cups. As she poured coffee for them both, she smiled at Michael. Michael mumbled a "thank you" sufficient to the occasion, though he was quite distracted by her scant uniform. He turned to his papers and soon was absorbed by the intriguing and complex macchinations of the Omega scenario.

He would spend the first week studying and memorizing, and in briefings with World Alliance officials and those identified as the Omega Team. A special expert in Middle Eastern drama, Professor Bertrum Schmidt of the University of Bergenstrassen, would be his personal coach.

Michael noted with dismay that he would not, as previously promised, be returning home most weekends. In fact only one trip was scheduled — next weekend. More briefings, intense study and role playing, and meetings filled the second and third week. Rehearsals would occupy the remaining weeks.

And there it was, one innocuous line on the last page of the schedule for Friday, February 3. "14:52 — OMEGA'S RETURN."

He closed the cover over the thin set of papers. "There doesn't seem to be very much here, Mr. Franklin, considering the impact it's going to have."

Franklin looked up from his note pad, peering over his glasses.

"First of all, it's 'Milton,' not 'Mr. Franklin.' " He grinned. Michael was having difficulty adjusting to that smile. It seemed as unnatural as an elbow bent backwards.

"Milton. Sorry."

"Forget it. The full Omega Plan is much larger. Took six weeks to prepare, although parts had been in development for months. Not bad for a stodgy bureaucracy, eh Mr. Consultant?"

Franklin laughed, and Michael with him, picking up on the reference to his frequent statements during his first contract referenced to the Prantzer bureaucracy.

Michael settled in to his study. 'Profile of the man Jesus' the guide began, listing several Biblical references. He went through them all, checking each one off as he read.

> "He was despised and rejected by men; a man of sorrows, and acquainted with grief; and as one from whom men hide their faces he was despised, and we esteemed him not . . ." "And Jesus increased in wisdom and stature, and in favor with God and man . . ."

He looked to the study guide.

> "Note in these two passages, from Isaiah and Luke, the contradiction. How does one who is despised increase in favor? The Christians' answer is based on the same book in which this and other contradictions appear. Their answers must therefore be wrong. Yet they believe them."

'What answers?' he wondered. 'Some study guide.' His host interrupted him.

"I'm going to, ah, disappear for a while." As he spoke the aft curtains parted slightly. Michael could see Becky's hand through the opening.

"See you," Franklin said, winking.

"Right," said Michael, surprised and embarrassed, but interested in this glimpse of the humanness behind all the man's power and pomp. Franklin disappeared behind the curtains and the door latch clicked. Michael went back to his studies. The Prantzer CEO seemed a good deal less awesome.

Forty-five minutes outside of Jerusalem the communications equipment burst into activity and a red alarm light flashed, accompanied by an urgent "pong" sound. The mid-cabin door burst open, and a disheveled Milton Franklin tumbled through the cutains, tucking his shirt into his trousers. The co-pilot ran into the cabin at the same time, a sheet of paper from the cockpit communications console in his hand. He was obviously alarmed. Franklin's expression turned to steel.

"What is it?" he snapped.

"Jerusalem's under attack. Syria and Iraq, possibly Egypt."

Michael was stunned. Franklin leaped to the bulkhead video screen and punched a sequence of numbers into the console keyboard.

"What else?" As Franklin spoke a voice came over the speakers. It was an interrupt newscast bulletin.

'... just learned of a concentrated attack on Jerusalem by combined Arabian forces. The attack includes use of small arms nuclear weaponry ...'

"This has been brewing for two years. Why NOW, of all times," Franklin muttered angrily. "Get COM-34. Fast."

The co-pilot reached inside his shirt and pulled out a lanyard with several small keys attached. Franklin scrambled hastily back through the curtains, returning a moment later clutching his lanyard, breathing heavily. They inserted their matching keys. A blank panel on the bulkhead slid upward, revealing a much larger screen. Lightflecks crackled, then yielded to the image of a man seated at a desk. Michael immediately disliked the small, closely set beady eyes.

"That's all, Jeff," Franklin said tersely.

"Sir." The co-pilot nodded and disappeared through the forward curtains.

"What's going on?" Franklin demanded, glaring into the screen. Michael was beginning to realize the situation. Attack! Nuclear weapons! If this had happened an hour later, after we'd landed .... He shuddered.

"Milton, how nice to hear from you," the beady-eyed man said smoothly. "Omega is with you, I take it?"

Michael was instantly attentive.

"Yes, of course he's here, Mr. Chairman. Did you know that Arabs have just attacked Jerusalem . . ."

"I know you detest surprises, Milton, but I had to do it this way. Hmmm . . ." the man looked at his wristwatch . . . . "they were twenty minutes behind schedule. Not good."

"YOU set this up?"

"Do you really think it would have happened otherwise?"

Michael gaped in amazement. He was watching the World Alliance Chairman himself.

Milton Franklin calmed down. "I guess it couldn't. But it was not in my copy of the plan, sir."

"You had no need to know."

"And now what? We're due to land soon."

"Actually you'll be landing in Alexandria. It's safe there, at least for awhile. The schedule remains intact, incidentally. On Wednesday this skirmish will be over. You'll go to Jerusalem then."

"But they're using nuclear weapons!"

"Don't believe everything you hear, Milton." The face smiled disconcertingly. "You of all people should know pseudo weaponry. After all, your company helped develop them."

Franklin accepted the rebuff. The faint whir of a servo-motor sounded. "Milton, step away, will you? There. Good, very good."

The chairman was manipulating a small lever on his desk. Michael noticed a lens attached to the cabin wall move and focus its eerie stare on him.

"And you are Omega. Welcome to our team."

Michael looked at the lens, then at the video screen, unable to summon a response.

"You find all of this interesting I take it?"

"Very, sir. Very interesting." Michael's throat was dry, and his tongue felt swollen. He was looking at a man who apparently had just sentenced thousands of people to death as if he were ordering a steak sandwich. Power again.' Is there such a thing as too much power? 'Michael wondered.

The chairman interrupted his thoughts. "Please stand up, Omega." Michael complied.

"Yes. Good. Tall and slender. Very good." Omega, the course of history is vested in your competence. Our world has existed for more than two thousand years under the scourge of this movement called Christianity. During that time there have been six hundred and thirty-two wars. One-fourth of all people have been chronically undernourished. One-sixth have never learned to read a word."

"Yes, sir," Michael responded. The chairman's voice was hypnotic, and his gaze compelled attention.

"Yours is an heroic role. Many are involved. But you alone will stand before the peoples of the world thirty-nine days from today and end two millenia of confusion and fantasy. In so doing, you will be enabling the peace of the world through, for the first time, a united world government."

The chairman paused, assessing the reaction. Michael trembled with anticipation and tension.

"Your deeds will not go unrewarded. You are a man of destiny, Omega, the instrument of closure to an era of chaos. We salute you. Do what you're chosen to do with style and pride."

Suddenly Michael pictured himself and Debbie on the tiny back porch of the apartment they had when they were first married, sipping wine and laughing together with the carefree, youthful abandon of no responsibility and high hope. A surging desire to get out of all of this gripped him. But under the chairman's gaze his resolve crumbled like a dry leaf underfoot.

"Yes sir. I'll do my best."

"I know you will, Omega. You are irrevocably committed."

A chill shot up Michael's spine. The chairman manipulated the small lever again. The small lens pivoted toward Milton Franklin.

"Carry on, Milton."

"One question sir, before you go. Why the attack?"

"We've initiated what the Christians will, soon enough, come to regard as a brief preview of Armageddon, Milton. Enjoy."

The video screen fizzed into static, and then blanked. Its wooden panel slid downward. Franklin dropped wearily back into his seat, rubbing his eyes.

"We'll be landing in ten minutes, gentlemen, in Alexandria," the pilot announced over the intercom.

Milton Franklin looked at Michael, motioning with his thumb to the now-covered videoscreen. "Powerful man. Doesn't miss a thing."

Becky glided through the aisle, her uniform fresh and her perfume tantalizing.

"Buckle up, gentlemen." She smiled as she gathered up the coffee service and glided through the curtains. Minutes later the plane touched down on the runway. They were in Egypt.

Chapter 18

It was a large tent, and crowded. Some came to escape the bitter late December cold, or for their own personal and perhaps peculiar reasons. But most came to hear Gabe Diehl speak about a person who, they had heard, could answer every need, heal any life, and restore peace and stability to a world which seemed close to the edge of insanity. They were fearful, tired, and hungry, yearning for refuge from hopelessness. They came from all walks of life. Residents of the Binzoe District were not all veterans of years on the street — many were recent arrivals, anonymous victims of the stress and politics of a newly emerging world order and of the horrible uncertainties which seemed to be the only certainty. They were all there, waiting to hear Gabe Diehl. Expensive coats rubbed against tattered rags and educated conversation blended with coarse banter. An air of expectancy filled the tent and seemed to bond them all together.

Gabe often held his meetings in the poorer sections of cities. The affluent could make their way there if they wished to — they had the means. But those who had been pushed to humanity's scrap heap, vacant lot and door stoop residents well acquainted with grief and despair, were Gabe Diehl's primary concern. Such as these could find hope, love, and the saving Word right in their back yard.

The press would come of course. Gabe could count on that. They seemed to have singled him out as their favorite target, and lost no opportunity to salt the next day's news with mockeries of the meetings and of the forlorn flocks who gathered there.

Tonight was no exception. Banks of floodlights loomed along the inside walls of the tent, generating, along with nearly a thousand people crowded inside, more than enough warmth. Several hundred more huddled outside against the cold, watching through glassine sections in the canvas. Dust stirred and swirled in the glare of the floodlights and hymns flowed from large speakers at each side of the slightly raised platform, sounding greetings to any who would hear.

In a small trailer nearby Gabe, Em, and others prayed that people would hear and find comfort. An impatient knock on the door interrupted the quiet. Gabe answered. A woman in a thick fur coat hunched against the cold glared at him. Several others stood with her.

"I am Pankie Retson Quille of SelfGuide. Under Section 17A of the Public Meeting Act I ask you either to close this meeting immediately or provide equal time for myself."

A police monitor stepped through the tiny knot of people and handed Gabe a complaint filed by SelfGuide which authorized Pankie's action.

Pankie spotted Emerson Prantzer inside the trailer. "Dr. Prantzer," she said. "I'm surprised to find you here. Associations such as these have already cost you your company and your reputation."

Gabe interrupted. "Miss Retson, please come inside, out of the cold. He opened the door wider, beckoning to her.

"No. What is your answer?"

He was unsure what to do. "Miss Retson," he began, "this is hardly a setting advocated by your movement."

"You people have been spreading poison long enough without direct challenge. SelfGuide has always supported responsible personal involvement. I won't allow you to emotionalize one more person into your pathetic little club without their hearing the truth of life as it really is. Do I speak? Or will the monitor here . . ." Pankie motioned to the helmeted official . . . "make your tent-razing an 11:00 news item?"

Gabe knew she wanted the news coverage. He knew her approach. It was clever and seductive, appealing to universal, ego-centered instincts with every form of sensory apparatus and illusion available. She would use her charisma and stage presence to call people into the freedom of their own minds, drives, and wants. Her "Power — Goodness — Destiny" message had been borne on primal rhythms and hypnotic light shows to millions. And she had, as a result, become the champion for all that the flesh longed for. Would the Lord have him engaged in public battle?

Pankie waited impatiently as Gabe searched for his answer. The passage in Luke came to him: 'Do not be anxious how or what you are to answer or what you are to say; for the Holy Spirit will teach you in that very hour what you ought to say.' He smiled and knew what to do.

"Miss Retson, we welcome you to the program. May the grace of God touch you this evening."

Gabe knew her intent was to drive the crowd into self-centered frenzy. "We yield equal time to you because it's the law. You may speak after seeing how much time you need to equal ours."

Pankie scowled but did not press the issue. She turned away and stalked toward the tent. Her entourage stepped briskly to keep up with her, moving like a flock of carrion crows startled in the cornfield. Pops of light flashed as several of the media captured the brief confrontation on film.

Gabe shut the trailer door and turned to his crusade team. "It had to happen, sooner or later."

"I don't know if we should . . . ."

"Wait," Gabe interrupted. "Pankie Retson and the others are not the real enemy — they're only tools. 'We are not fighting against people made of flesh and blood, but against persons without bodies, the evil rulers of the unseen world, those mighty satanic beings and great evil princes who rule this world, and against huge numbers of wicked spirits in the spirit world,' " he quoted. "Have we forgotten there's really a battle going on? Let's go. Lord Jesus, be with us in power this evening. It's your show."

They went into the tent and up on the platform before the waiting crowd. Gabe lifted his hands. "Greetings, and welcome in the name of the Lord Jesus Christ!" His voice boomed through the speakers. "How Great Thou Art, O God, How Great Thou Art!"

A projector switched on. Words and music to the hymn appeared on a large screen above the platform. The tape turned, and Bert stepped to the microstalk and began to sing, encouraging people to join in. Half the crowd did so. By the end of the first verse, all were singing. By the third, they were singing in strength, forgetting the cold, their concerns, their worries. By the end of the last verse many sang with arms stretched high in the air.

Gabe watched the excitement building so quickly, and knew something very special was being worked this night. Among Christians he'd seen this before. But among people drawn from diverse, tragic backgrounds, with the enemy glaring across the crowd and pawing the earth as they awaited their time to speak, this was not how it usually began.

"Then sings my soul, my Savior God, to Thee: How great Thou art, How great Thou art!" Em Prantzer sang with gusto, looking far beyond the tent roof, his eyes filled. God's Spirit presided. The crowd cheered at the end of the hymn, themselves overcome with their own response of release.

"Can you believe it?" Pankie whispered to Ing Hammock.

"We'll have our turn." His eyes burned like coals.

Em Prantzer spoke with eloquent simplicity about the common need which unites — the need to be loved, forgiven, and empowered. When he finished, only the sound of a passing car interrupted the silence.

As Gabe approached the microstalk, one in the crowd looked intently at Emerson Prantzer. "He looks so familiar . . ." Ben's thoughts wandered to times years ago, to sunny summers on the Atlantic shore during med school when he was young and strong and all the world seemed waiting to be captured. And then there was the accident, and trial and prison and parole. And the months of unemployment until, finally, one man trusted a job to him . . .

Recognition came. Em Prantzer was the man who'd given him that job, the one man willing to trust an ex-con. Meg tugged on his sleeve. "Why no noise, Ben? I like sing better."

He patted her hand. "We'll sing soon again. Look, here's Gabriel Diehl now!" Meg grinned her crooked drooling grin and turned as a little child back to the floodlit platform.

"He handsum, Ben!"

"Shhh, Meg." Ben took her hand and patted it again.

Gabe felt the power of God's Spirit hovering throughout the tent. He began to speak.

"God created us with the power of choice," Gabe began. "He commanded us to use that power to respond to Him. But knowing we would choose our own ways instead, He sent Jesus to redeem us. My friends, outside this tent is the suffering proof of just how right our own ways have been!"

"I speak to you with urgency tonight," he continued, perspiring now. "Soon I must yield this platform to representatives of the SelfGuide movement. For all of us the time is short. Do you see the signs? Do you feel the tension, the battle, the climaxing of evil on the prowl? The earth trembles. Nations fight and fall. Some of you are here because you have nowhere else to turn. You hurt. You're confused and frightened. But some day there will be a mighty shout like a trumpet call. The

Lord Jesus Christ will appear in the heavens above, and 'when He appears we shall be like Him, for we will see Him as He is!' "

All eyes were on him, waiting expectantly.

"Do you know what the response to this message of hope has been, by millions of people?" Gabe paused waiting, then thundered. "So what. 'So what' is our response."

"We are sinners, my friends. Sinners! An ugly word, sin. 'Why, we're not sinful!' some say. 'Look at my clothes; they're clean, and nice! And look at the job I have, and the generous things I do. Look at my nice house. Sin is just an ancient fable! There's no sin here; I'm proud of what I do and of who I am!' "

"Some of you here tonight may still be saying that. Look around, then — what of the rest of you? Do you feel good? How are your jobs? When was your last meal? Oh, friends, so many of you are victims of greed and insensitivity. The innermost nature of the human being is still absolutely and utterly lost beyond the shadow of any hope. Two thousand years for man, in all his shrivelled wisdom, to go it on his own, first contesting, then ignoring, and now, in these times, blaspheming the sovereign Creator God, the only Source of love, joy, peace, patience, kindness, goodness, faithfulness, gentleness, and self-control."

"I watched you as we sang that great hymn of praise. The light of Heaven itself was in your faces and in your voices. For just a moment you experienced the power of a Loving God. That momentary joy is a mere passing shadow of the richness which Christ Jesus, your Savior, your Lord, your God, has for you. He suffered humiliation for you. He understands. He suffered agony for you! Some of you have, too. Jesus understands. He's been there. He suffered a terrible death for you! You there with the tan coat . . . Jesus Christ did it for YOU!"

He took the microstalk from its holder and stepped into the aisle, stopping by a shabbily clad girl in her early teens.

He put his hand on her shoulder and looked upon her with the Love of His Lord coursing through Him.

"Jesus Christ allowed people like us to nail iron spikes through his hands and feet, for you, Jessica."

Gabe was as surprised as she was that he'd spoken her name. She burst into tears of Spirit-given recognition that Jesus' sacrifice was made for her personally.

Further down the aisle an arm reached toward him. He clasped the outstretched hand and looked into the desperate face of a well-dressed man.

"And for you too, my friend. Jesus knew you when He hung on that cross. Jesus knows you now, just as you are, and calls you to Him. He knows the ache in your heart, and offers you His victory and forgiveness." The man burst into sobs of conviction and sank to his knees. Gabe returned to the platform.

"Why did Jesus suffer so much for you? Because He loves you. He knows the terrible penalties of sin. He knows sin is real. He knows sin eats away at you like maggots. Jesus took those penalties Himself, in your place. That's why He suffered! That's why He came to us in bodies like these!" Gabe pulled at the skin of his hand to emphasize his point.

"But of course there are those who call it something different, aren't there." He looked toward the shadows where Pankie Retson had been standing. "Some tell you to follow your own instincts, to lift yourselves to the peak of your potential, to do what feels good. Every day you walk this planet without that personal, precious oneness with the Lord you travel alone, without that relationship He bought for you with His own blood. If you've been following your own instincts, doing what feels good or would have felt good — where are your shouts of joy? They're buried under the fears and greeds and animosities and all the bitterness and anger which festers in those who reject God."

" 'The desires of the flesh are against the Spirit and the desires of the Spirit are against the flesh; they are opposed to each other, to prevent you from doing what you would.' If ritual worship and deceit and lying and cruelties and insane lunges toward perverted sensualities of every kind could make us content, the people of this planet should by now be euphoric."

"There is no mystery except the barriers you throw in your own way. 'Do not be deceived; God is not mocked. Whatever you sow, you'll reap.' Whatever you give, you'll get. Whatever you determine in your heart, that you will become. Jesus Christ defeated the power of your sin with His blood. He is your salvation from darkness and bitterness. You need Him, for you are on the edge of Hell this very evening. Do you say 'So what?' Come home to peace, and joy, and life. Jesus calls you. As you are moved, come forward. Receive His free gift of Love, His gift to you of salvation, safety, and eternal life. Come."

The tape turned and the strains of Amazing Grace filled the tent. Gabe closed his eyes in prayer, asking God to enable these precious people to receive the call. When he looked up, throngs were gathered by the platform, many crying. He jumped off the platform into their midst, hugging whoever was nearby. Before long everyone was hugging everyone else. And the unspeakable joy and power of the risen Christ was in evidence.

Finally, exhausted and exultant, Gabe lifted his hands in a parting blessing. " 'And in the last days it shall be, God declares, that I will pour out my Spirit among all flesh . . . and I will show wonders in the heavens above and signs on the earth beneath, blood, and fire, and vapor of smoke; the sun shall be turned into darkness and the moon into blood, before the great day of the Lord comes, the great and manifest day. And it shall be that whoever calls on the name of the Lord shall be saved.' Welcome home to Jesus. Go in peace."

Gradually the crowds thinned. Men and women who came alone walked out in twos and threes, their conversation exuberant, released, triumphant. For many, life would be no easier in the coming days and weeks. But those lives would no longer be lived in vain.

With a start, Gabe remembered the SelfGuide demand for equal time. He looked around the tent. Pankie Retson was nowhere in sight. Then a rough hand grabbed his arm, and he turned to face the sneering monitor.

"Nice little show. Too bad you blew it." He shoved a paper into Gabe's hands. "You're shut down, pal."

Gabe looked at the document. "We'll see, friend."

The monitor snorted. "Sure." He turned and stalked off.

Gabe felt neither anger nor concern. It was all God's show. The whole thing.

Em Prantzer heard a voice behind him. He turned and saw a tall aging man, evidently a Binzoe resident. Then he looked more intently at him — the man seemed familiar. "Say, don't I know you?"

Ben broke into a broad smile. "Ben Crockett. You gave me a job and a chance many years ago back in New Jersey."

"I remember! Ben Crockett!" Em smiled and pumped Ben's hand in greeting. "You were our best driver. I still remember!"

Ben blushed, unaccustomed to praise. Em glanced at his shabby clothing and wondered how hard life must have been since he had left his then-fledgling company.

"What brings you here?"

He beamed. "I received God soon after leaving your company. I came here to Binzoe and started working at the Peace Garden Mission. You influenced me, sir. You helped me recognize Jesus by the way you lived."

Em's eyes gleamed with joy. "Will you come home with me tonight? Meet my wife Lucy and catch up on the last twenty-five years?"

A short, bedraggled woman watched the reunion with wide eyes and gaping jaw. Now she tugged at Ben's sleeve. "You gonna leave Meg, Ben?" Her face filled with concern.

Ben put his arm around her. "No, Meg. I'm not going to leave." He turned to Em. "Meg is one of my friends. I think she understood more of our Lord this evening than ever before. It was the hugging. I think Meg got more hugging tonight than she's had in her whole, starved life. I can't leave her now."

"I understand. Tomorrow, then. I'll pick you up. Any time — nine o'clock?"

"I'll look forward to it."

"I'll meet you right here, Ben."

Spontaneously, Ben wrapped his arms around Meg and Em in a huge bear hug.

"The Lord is good, Em!" Gabe said, coming up to him. "I feel terrific!" Suddenly the tent shook, and one sidewall fell inward.

"What?" Em said, startled.

"We're out of business. Pankie Retson shut us down. I can't wait to see what happens next!"

"Come to think of it, she didn't demand her time! Wonder Who stopped her?"

They laughed, and walked out of the tent with Meg between them.

Chapter 19

Smoke from Pankie's thin cigar serpentined upward into a pouting haze above her desk. Most of her group had left. But two others, Ing Hammock and Ted Shriver, remained to review the films. They were stinging from a heated argument as they returned to SelfGuide headquarters. Pankie insisted she'd told Ing to take over the platform. He said that she never said a word. Shriver said he'd urged Pankie to interrupt. Pankie said he'd been mumbling incoherently. Tempers flared, each suspicious of the other, each more confused as their stories unfolded.

Now they waited for the film to be delivered. Pankie began to pace behind her desk. "Something was going on there, I'll tell you that," she said. "Six perfectly sane human beings don't suddenly start hallucinating. Especially with what's at stake."

We'll see the films. Then we'll decide." Ing Hammock's tone was as cold as his eyes. Pankie respected his abilities perhaps above all the others. Since the World Alliance had assigned him to work with SelfGuide he had almost single-handedly built its now-huge seminar network. The network had become an influential and lucrative tool. He was working now to implement the same structure in the European Region, a task which Pankie had no doubt would be accomplished with the same calculating ruthless dispatch which drove the North American Region program into high gear. But she did not trust him, not that she trusted anyone. Ing Hammock was like a vulture. She knew, in the end, they would fight to the death.

"Where is he?" Ted slapped his fist on the arm of the chair.

Ing looked at him coolly. "You must learn patience, Tedrick. Patience." He smiled unpleasantly, the unspoken "gotcha" blooming across his ruddy face.

At the knock Pankie yanked the door open. A breathless man, the collar of his jacket pulled around his neck, stood in the doorway clutching a film cartridge. "Sorry it's so late, Miss Retson. They just finished about twenty minutes ago."

Pankie forced a smile and a brief thank you.

"I had to get clearance from my boss," he said, relaxing. "When you told me to bring the film to your office right after it was over I just couldn't . . ."

"I know," Pankie said. She sighed impatiently. "Ing, do you have money?"

Ing scowled as he reached into his pocket. He peeled a hundred dollar bill from a packet of notes. Pankie took it and handed it through the door, then slammed it shut.

"Time for answers. We have to keep Cummings off our back." She inserted the cartridge into the video player. The crowd appeared on the screen, hands raised high, singing. Gabe was on the platform leading them, his voice a resonant baritone.

"Too bad he's not with us," Ted remarked sourly.

"He will be, whether he knows it or not, if Ames does his part right."

"Ted, fast forward it a little." Irritated, Ted went to the control panel and advanced the film. It restarted during Gabe's message. Then the film began to lighten, as if the floodlights were aiming into the camera lens. Soon the screen was all white.

"What a time for a camera screw-up."

"Those lights didn't just get brighter by themselves."

They watched in silence for another twenty minutes. Static suddenly filled the screen. The tape finished.

Pankie switched the lamp on by her desk and sighed with disgust. "Better call Cummings. It's a mystery, I'll tell you that. What do you think, Ing?" Her associate shook his head.

A nasal voice answered Pankie's call. "Senator Cummings' office; Charlie Briggs. May I help you?"

"Pankie Retson. Charlie, we're on the speakerphone."

"Where have you been? The senator is pacing in his office waiting for your call. You're behind schedule."

"Be nice, Charles, or I'll cut off your allowance. Put him on."

"Pankie? What happened?" Moes' voice was tense.

"We shut them down."

"You were suposed to discredit Diehl, not close them! Why?"

Pankie hated being unable to explain anything to anyone. But there was no explanation to offer. She sighed with resignation. "Something went wrong. We don't know what happened."

"How could anything go wrong?"

"It just did!" she shouted.

"What am I going to tell Franklin and the chairman?"

"Look, something went wrong with the lighting right when we were to go on. We reviewed the tape. Most of it's blank. It would have been a waste."

"Tomorrow night then. Get it right this time. We're a day behind schedule now."

"Moe. I shut the them down I told you. There is no tomorrow night." Moe, safe in his own office, began an ostentatious tirade.

Ing interrupted. "Senator Cummings? Can you hear me?"

"Yes?" Cummings stopped his discourse in mid-sentence.

"Pankie is being modest. That crowd was so whipped up it would have been a black eye for SelfGuide to interrupt. Realizing the importance of this to you, she arranged a news conference tomorrow at the Charlemagne Hotel. That's a more appropriate setting than a carnival tent, don't you think?" Ing said smoothly.

"Well, yes, of course."

"The newscast tonight — if they air it at all — will show a few people shouting in a tent. Our session tomorrow will present SelfGuide in one of its finest hours. Be assured, senator. Everything is under control."

Cummings hesitated. He knew of Ing's association with the World Alliance and suspected he was familiar with parts of the Omega Plan. But he did not know how well he was plugged in. Better at this point, he reasoned, to go along with him.

"Hammock, I like what you've said. Makes me feel a good deal more confident. Pankie?"

"What?" Pankie answered, staring at Ing.

"Why didn't you tell me that at the beginning? I buy it. Either I, or Charlie, will be at the Charlemagne tomorrow. What time?"

Ing flashed ten fingers, then one more.

"Eleven o'clock," she said.

Moe checked his Omega schedule. "Looks like that will work. Diehl must be discredited by tomorrow night's newscast. But we need the publicity for several days to drive his little problem home to people. You'd better get that crusade reopened."

Pankie groaned, knowing he was right. "Right. We'll take care of it. Don't worry."

Moe grunted with satisfaction. "Well, then, good night."

"Good bye, senator — it was nice talking with you," Ing said loudly. He had easily picked up on Pankie's error, and relished the chance to add to her discomfort. The phone line clicked dead.

Pankie was boiling. "What are you talking about, Hammock? Are you insane?"

"Pankie, you underestimate the power of your own organization," Ing replied. "I'll set it up." He disappeared into the hall.

"I'd like to wring his neck," Pankie steamed. "Ted, call Gabe Diehl and get that crusade back on track. Tell him whatever you have to."

Ted grinned. "Never thought I'd hear those words from you!"

"Out! Get to it! And forget this evening. It never happened. Understand?"

"Sure." He paused, uncertain. "Shall I come back when I've handled it?"

Pankie's eyes softened just a trace. "I must deal with Ing, for a while, to prepare for this conference idea of his. That won't take long." She looked at Ted, her eyes warmer now. "An hour."

Ted went down the hall to his office. The call to the monitor station was time-consuming but not difficult, especially when he used Moe Cummings' name. A reinstatement order would be served to Gabe Diehl the next morning. Ted looked at his watch — too late to contact him? No. He dialed the evangelist's home number. The conversation lasted barely four minutes. Gabe accepted the reopening but rejected any money from SelfGuide.

Ted leaned back in his chair. Through the wall he could hear the muffled voice of Ing Hammock, shouting. Apparently he was having difficulty setting up the conference on such short notice. I wonder what really DID happen tonight,' he mused. Maybe there really is something to all this. He remembered how he'd felt drawn by Gabe's message, and struggled to hide any evidence of that feeling from the others. Would I have gone to the front with the rest of those people if Ing hadn't been in my way? he wondered. 'Come!' Gabe's rich voice rang in Ted's mind. Preposterous, he thought, rejecting again. He propped his feet on the desk. Before long he dozed.

"I'm waiting, Tedrick."

His eyes popped open. Pankie was leaning in his office doorway with that look he knew so well. He looked at his watch — two-twenty in the morning. Pankie disappeared into her suite, laughing. Ted followed.

"Milton?" The phone crackled. Moe hated these static-filled decoding circuits with their maddening delays as each transmission was scrambled, sent, and unscrambled.

"You're calling late. It's nine-thirty in the morning here."

"Is it going well?"

"Omega is doing better than expected. His memory is excellent."

"What? I didn't catch that last . . ."

"Forget it. What's your report?"

"Slight change, nothing serious. Diehl's crusade was shut down tonight. Lighting problem. They're setting up a news conference tomorrow."

"What about tomorrow night?" Franklin's voice crackled through the phone.

"As scheduled. Only change is tonight."

"Diehl has to be in trouble by tomorrow to have time to set him up."

"I know. Don't worry, we'll handle it."

"You sure about Retson? Sometimes she's a flake."

"Don't worry, Milt. I . . ."

"Milton!"

Moe flinched. "Sorry. It's under control. We can step in any time if necessary."

"Sure. So why didn't you step in tonight and keep on schedule? We lost a day because of your slight change."

Moe took an extra breath before responding. "I'll call the chairman. Just wanted to give you the report first."

"Get them back on schedule without fail. Understand? After next weekend, Omega's here for good. By then it'll be too late."

"Milton, any new developments on the attack?"

"Attack? Oh. They're mopping up now. We fly in later today."

"I heard that the New Soviets are building something up in Afganistan. Tanks and armor."

Moe heard the Franklin snort of disgust reflect from the satellite network and crawl through his telephone. 'Amazing,' he thought to himself. They can even scramble and unscramble that. "Just thought you'd be interested. It's not all that far from where you are."

"Yeah. Talk to you tomorrow."

Moe dialed the chairman's special access number, wondering whether the man ever slept. The call was terse and to the point. When it was over, Moe Cummings vowed not to allow one slip from the plan again, ever again.

The ivory-cased clock on the marble mantel of his office chimed. He pulled on his overcoat, exhausted, and left for his home.

At four fifty-one that morning, the earth shook with violence. Tremors had become common in recent months. Vibrations would last between one and three minutes before fading. Occasionally an after-shock would touch the earth's surface, as if to warn her inhabitants that it was mercy and not terrestrial exhaustion which returned stillness to the land.

But rarely was damage worse than an occasional cracked wall or buckled street. In fact, earthquakes were among the least of the strange stream of calamities in these days. Tremors deep under the earth's surface had become just one more thing to live with. People adapt, after all. No one can live in a state of constant panic.

Awakened by the strength of the shaking, Moe Cummings watched the crystal chandelier in his bedroom swing back and forth. Five minutes passed. The tremors continued, punctuated more frequently by powerful staccato bursts like a bowling ball bouncing down a staircase. They were not fading away. He got out of bed and went to the window. Lights in the northward suburbs winked on across the distance, signalling through the cold night darkness that he was not the only one awake.

Pankie eased silently off the sofabed and tiptoed to her window. The new moon's sliver cast no light. Steam from buildings' heating plants billowed into the air and disappeared into the coldness. Ted watched her, caught between admiration of her willowy figure and terror at the strengthening tremors. He got up and started toward her. Half-way across the room he froze, immobilized in panic. Pankie's jaw dropped, and she screamed.

Across the city, Moe Cummings' heartbeat sped up dangerously.

Deeper than deep, slower than slow, the roar built and accelerated like the engine of a shuttlecraft at full throttle. A fearsome violence shook the earth. An orange glow rose on the northern horizon like a gigantic eye. It throbbed higher and brighter, dancing madly upward to the accompaniment of a hellish symphony of background tremors and staccato foreground shocks. The glowing mass became yellow-hot, breathing fire on the city like a great dragon clawing skyward from the depths of the earth. White and red heat disgorged from its power fountain, rolling away and downward, and the molten mass became a mountain.

A volcano?" Pankie whispered, twitching with terror. "Here?"

The roar of a hundred locomotives and the ear-splitting thunderclaps collided until all thought was crushed. Primal fear ruled. Sun-bright lava spewed upward. Immense clouds of ash and steam replaced the evening sky. Rivulets of glowing molten rock coursed from thirty miles away in all directions. And still the volcano grew. The window imploded with gunshot suddenness. Pankie shrieked, hit by flying glass, and was knocked backward against the sofabed. Ted felt the heat from the blast of inrushing air before tumbling against the wall like a thrown rag doll.

Moe's bedroom window was angled to the line of shock, and no breakage occurred. He watched, held by horror, as the great molten mountain expanded into the night and filled the land with an eerie glow. The large elm tree just outside, lightly snow-glazed half an hour before, was now wet bark glistening in the orange light.

"Must call Franklin," he said aloud, though he couldn't hear himself. He felt sick. His pulse was much too fast. In the drawer by his bed — the pills. He dumped the bottle into shaking hands, swallowing two without water. Gradually his pounding heart quieted.

Snow flashed into steam shrouded the eruption in a foggy sheen. It had been half an hour since the earth had parted and pushed its anger through the surface. North and to the east, the gravest damage was occurring as land caved in. But the main stream of lava was directly south. University scientists, some with pajama legs poking out from under hastily-donned trousers, gathered to plot its course and rate of flow, determining that active lava would reach the city's edge by eight o'clock. Emergency broadcasts began. Residents were ordered to evacuate.

Curled up in shock under a blanket, Pankie sobbed convulsively. Salty tears ran over glass-flecked facial wounds, stinging like angry wasps. She heard a soft pelting noise and peeked through the blanket folds. Through the broken window she could see the volcano raging. The air was filling with warm acidic dust and hot pebble-sized rock fragments. It looked like slow gray rain, angling in and covering the cream-colored carpet with ash. A dull "ping" snapped her to attention as a cherry-red stone fragment struck the iron window railing and bounced onto her carpet hissing and burning. The building trembled, and a gargantuan explosion broke through the volcano's crest. Thousands of tons of molten matter broke upward. Pankie heard a voice above the chaos, and realized it was her own screaming.

By eight o'clock the eruption had eased. The sides of the new mountain glowed dull red. The lava flow, case-hardened in its tracks, had stopped less than a hundred yards from the city limits, its leading boundary solidified into a pillow of steaming rock twenty feet high and a half a mile wide. Swirling ash and dust made unprotected breathing impossible. If the sun rose it was not evident. The temperature on this midwestern January morning was seventy-eight degrees. It dropped only slightly throughout the day.

Chapter 20

Michael Ames and Milton Franklin, dressed in open-collared light khaki and sunglasses against the hot Egyptian sun, strode briskly across the tarmac toward the Prantzer jet. Michael looked forward to this respite from incessant study and briefings of the last three days. Already, he probably knew more about the man Jesus Christ than most of the WOEC world, and possible more than some who called themselves Christians. He smiled wryly at the irony.

They'd reached the boarding steps of the gleaming light blue aircraft when tires squealed and a limousine lurched to a stop just behind them. World Alliance escorts pushed them to the ground and stood in front of them, automatic rifles at the ready. Uniformed officers jumped out of the car waving papers and shouting in Arabic. The rifles lowered. After a terse exchange the officers were motioned toward the plane.

"Mr. Franklin. We have very bad news." A general saluted and addressed him with an accent. The Prantzer executive and his consultant got up from the pavement. The officer handed him a bulletin. They scanned it with horror. Not only had a major volcanic eruption broken through the flat mid-section of America, but a second had occurred along the Gulf of Mexico, and a third five hundred miles north of Lake Huron.

All had inflicted massive damage and casualties. All were still highly active.

"Debbie," Michael whispered, in shock.

Franklin spoke sharply. "General, what's the status of Prantzer Defense Group Headquarters?"

"We are sorry but we do not yet know. It is being checked."

"My wife?" Michael said pleadingly. "Do you have . . ."

"We'll check that," Franklin interrupted. He could not risk divulging Michael's real name to anyone. "Transmit further bulletins to us en route, General."

"Sir." The General and his aides saluted, spun on their heels, and marched back to their car.

"Let's go," Franklin said tersely. "Nothing can be done for the moment."

Michael turned on him angrily. "But Debbie — thousands of people — your company! We just keep going as if nothing happened?"

Debbie's probably safe. Get control of yourself."

Michael glared, but realized his anger was misplaced. Franklin was right. He shivered and despondently boarded the plane, his mind filled with fearful imaginings.

The whine of jet engines increased as the plane eased toward the runway. Michael saw their bodyguards saluting on the sunny tarmac as the plane turned. Then they were in the air, bound for Jerusalem.

Tense and drawn, the co-pilot handed Franklin several cockpit bulletins, and activated the communications equipment. World channel information crackling through the speakers seemed to ease their tension. At least they would hear what news there was.

Micahel noticed a tear in the co-pilot's eye, and realized that he too probably had family and friends in the disaster area. His own heaviness of heart increased.

"Michael." Franklin, feeling no less burdened himself but more seasoned by the years, had been watching his younger charge. "If this had happened when I was a boy it would have

153

been impossible. But there is precedent. Mexico City, for example. Or Columbia, or Sicily just two years ago. And we can respond much more efficiently to disaster now than we could then. It'll work out." It was one of the few times he'd ever offered a compassionate word. It released Michael's turbulent emotions, and he waged an inner war to prevent their showing. All he had worked for, all that had meaning to him, was in jeopardy, and perhaps gone forever. Debbie, his home, his car, his company . . . . gone. Tommy Thompson, gone. Michael pictured his good friend pointing up to a red moon that late summer evening on the golf course, and sank more deeply into grief. Other thoughts too slipped past Michael's guard and stung his consciousness. Chief among these was vulnerability. Apparently man is not master of his own destiny after all. This disturbed him more than he realized at the time.

A wooden panel slid upward, revealing the private channel videoscreen. Crackling spots of light resolved into the aging lined face of the World Alliance chairman. The small camera in the corner of the cabin whirred as it turned toward them.

"Gentlemen," the chairman began. Michael noticed tension in his voice. "Doubtless you've heard of the American Regions' volcanic eruptions early this morning."

"We have, sir," Franklin said evenly.

"Prantzer Defense Headquarters was in the path of the lava flow from what is now being called 'Mt. Kruger.' We will have to change some plans."

Had Michael's attention not been riveted to the chairman, awaiting possible news of his own world, he would have noticed the twitch in Franklin's eye and the slight shaking of his hands.

The camera pivoted until it focused on Michael. "As for you, Omega . . ."

Michael sat without breath, waiting.

". . . the news is not so bad. Your residence is covered with ash, but otherwise intact."

"And . . . my wife?"

"It took some effort to find her."

"Michael's heart leaped in relief. "Sir?"

"We of course sought her out as soon as the disaster hit." Not such a bad sort, Michael thought gratefully. "We found her in the Binzoe District helping the man with whom you made unauthorized contact four days ago. Ben Crockett."

Michael fell back against the seat. A warmth toward Debbie filled him. The chairman watched Michael but found no evidence of emotion other than the expected relief. He was satisfied.

"Carry on. We'll notify you if we cancel your trip back on Friday."

Michael jumped up but was held back by the seat belt. "I must return sir, especially now!"

The chairman's eyes narrowed. "It may not be necessary for you to go back until the Omega Plan has been accomplished."

"I must see my wife. Don't you understand?"

The chairman's features darkened. Franklin hastily intervened. "Sir, we'll work it through here. We understand."

The chairman's stony gaze held Michael for long moments before easing. "That is appropriate, Milton. I remind you both of the absolute importance of this mission. I encourage you to put this situation out of your mind and renew your commitment. Are you prepared to do this?"

"Absolutely sir," Franklin said quickly.

"Omega will speak for himself, Milton."

Michael thought furiously. As before, the desire to escape circumstances he knew were far over his head, and which he sensed to be dark and evil, enveloped him. But he had no choice — not now.

"I'm ready."

"Good. Very good. Carry on, then." He smiled coldly, and in that instant before the screen went blank Michael saw his madness.

The chairman had not revealed that Emerson Prantzer and Gabriel Diehl were also seen with Ben and Debbie. By tomorrow he would know what changes in the Omega Plan would be required. In the meantime, the situation required further investigation.

Franklin looked nervous and haggard, and spoke little for the remainder of the flight. Headquarters was the last bit of conversation for the remainder of the brief flight. Prantzer Defense Group had eight major facilities in North America, but he'd lost his main research center, and with it, invaluable data, prototypes, and possibly, scientists. His power base was weakened.

They were taken to their hotel in Jerusalem by World Alliance officials. On the way they learned more about the Three Day War, as the media had dubbed the brief but ferocious Pan-Arabic assault. They saw that it was not quite over as they raced along the boulevards. But Israeli forces were clearly in control. The target, they were told, was the capture of Old Jerusalem along with its mosques. As Arabs, it was a matter of honor to destroy Israel. And as Moslems it was a moral imperative to recapture the seat of a holy site of their faith. Old Jerusalem suffered only minor damage. Nor was New Jerusalem damaged badly, thanks not to a lack of aggressiveness by allied Syrian, Iraqi, Jordanian, Egyptian and Lebanese forces, but to superb defense and counterattack by the Israelis. Most of the damage of battle occurred in surrounding areas. Haifa and Tel-Aviv suffered severely.

Israel would not allow the aggression to go unavenged. At the emergency directive of World Alliance leadership and their promise of massive support, the Pan-Arabic armies had taken their best and final shot. As it turned out they attacked alone. Diplomatic channels burned with outrage. But the chairman had not underestimated Israeli strength or courage.

What damage had occurred was far in excess of the physical. The complex balance of international relationships had been endangered by the manipulations of an emerging world government. In the wake of the World Alliance deliberate failure to meet its pledge of support that balance began to snap in the closed back rooms of the world. Protection became a greater motivation than contribution. Opportunistic aggression became more palatable than tentative next-step diplomacy by which the World Alliance had consolidated its fragile power.

Soviet forces were not only gathering in Afganistan at Hormuz, the crucial oil link between the Persian Gulf and the Gulf of Oman, but also in the Black Sea. Reports of Chinese and Indian forces massing within their borders had also reached World Alliance Headquarters. And the European Region itself, only recently confederated into one military-economic-political entity, was preparing to challenge a one-government world.

Franklin grasped the implications. The World Alliance — to which he had committed his life — may not be what it seemed to be. Private conversation with the chairman was essential prior to implementing Section Eight of the Omega Plan, his staged take-over.

However confusing the panorama of unfolding catastrophe and confrontation may have been, Michael Ames was aware of his role and its meaning. "Once and for all . . ." the words repeated in his mind as he stared out the window of the car. In five weeks all this would be over. He would have made his appearance. A man he'd never met, backed by military and economic forces of which he had no knowledge, would by his own cooperation be put into the seat of ultimate power. The World Alliance would be consolidated, the Christians neutralized, the ages-old struggle with morality and beliefs resolved. The time of enlightened consistency would be here. Peace would come. Or would it? And would volcanoes and earthquakes suddenly stop? Would the desolation of the great African plague suddenly lift, or acid-poisoned forests suddenly spring back to life? Would the increases in crime, in suicides, in terrorism, simply evaporate? Fearful of the obvious answers, he had not dared ask the obvious questions. But peace must come — how could it not, with all under one government? It would take time. But surely it would come. It just had to.

Michael allowed himself to dream of the happier days ahead, as a wealthy, influential man known to the inner circles of power, sought and honored when the time came to reveal the role he had played in these pivotal days. He tried to relax. But something deep within his soul would not release him.

"Are you all right Debbie?" Ben looked up at her, rivulets of perspiration running down his face through caked ash and beard stubble, dampening the kerchief tied around his nose and mouth. He held a canteen for a young man who had been trapped under a collapsed roof. She nodded, her own face streaked and chalky, and continued wiping the wounded man's forehead with a wet towel.

"Ben, over here!" Em Prantzer scampered over the rubble, spotting a young child under a collapsed wall. Ben turned again to Debbie. "Finish him?"

She nodded again, and took the canteen. Ben stood up, wincing at the pain in his back, and made his way over loose bricks and cooling rock fragments.

Throughout the day it was difficult to see even after powerful floodlights had been set up. Swarms of volunteers combed debris at the north edge of the city, where damage had been worst. Many had been killed there, and many more injured by hot rocks and molten globules which had rained down upon homes and shops. Fires burned, and wails and shouts drifted through the smoky ash-filled air. Barely a quarter mile away a rolled edge of rock as high as a single-story building, still so hot that approach within fifty feet was not possible, stood sentinel. Charred trees, smoldering foundations, and steaming ground formed a ghastly boulevard along the front of the hissing magma.

Ben knelt down to the trapped child and felt her temple, then looked up sadly, shaking his head. Em plunged a thin metal pole into the ash near the tiny body. It would signal the stretcher bearers. The two men stood, surveying the incredible damage. They had been searching for survivors all day without a break.

Gloom increased as the sun set behind the miles-high cloud of ash. The volcanic carcass belched debris and steam impatiently. Gabe joined them, dirty and exhausted. They stood together for a time, bone-weary, feeling it now in the pause from their saddening labors.

"She's a trooper," Ben remarked, motioning toward Debbie. "Came down to see if I was okay. There she was, coming through all that ash and smoke like an angel. Amazing that she'd bother."

"Her husband came to see me last Sunday," Gabe said, watching her gently helping medics transfer a man onto a stretcher. "They came forward during the service. There was something about it . . . too rushed . . . something."

"Michael Ames seems to be connected with each of us," Em Prantzer mused. "He fired me. And you, Ben, said you'd found him unconscious in Binzoe a couple of months ago."

They squinted through the ash-laden air at the new mountain looming in the haze.

Debbie came over and they stood, bonded by common experience, watching the volcano but not yet quite able to believe it. Ben wrapped his huge arm around her. She buried her face in her hands and began to cry.

"There, it's been mighty rough. Bless you, child."

Her sobbing intensified. "I . . . I think Michael's involved in all of this somehow . . . I don't know what it is. But I'm so afraid . . . ."

Gabe's voice was kind. "Do you want to talk it through?"

She wanted to desperately. What was different? She'd wondered over and over again as they struggled together in the ruins. Hundreds of volunteers combed the rubble, helping, cleaning, feeding, searching. What was it about these three men, that she would confide such feelings and fears? But she was prompted to trust, and in trusting she found kindness and surety.

"Yes, I do." Her voice wavered but her resolve was steady. Gabe's eyes told her she was safe. They turned and walked through ankle-deep ash toward the distant street.

Pankie managed to get to the Charlemagne on time for the SelfGuide news conference. Her mind had all but blocked the events of the past few hours. She was in shock and suspected as much. But she had to be at this meeting — the World Alliance had a very limited tolerance. Moe Cummings' haughty words came to her . . . "either I or Charlie will be there . . ." She smiled grimly. "Neither of those bozos will show up, not today. But I will be."

Her car coughed and sputtered a block away, its filtering system choked with ash dust. She left it in the street and walked, breathing through a silk scarf.

The once-elegant Charlemagne Hotel was dust-filled and shattered. An awning over the carpeted approach to the main entry hung in charred perforated tatters. As she pushed the door open two looters shoved past her with what they could carry from the ornate lobby. Pankie was shoved to the sidewalk, cursing with abandon. The looters disappeared into the dirty haze.

She made her way to the elevators, waiting impatiently while trying to brush ash from her clothes. It took several minutes for her to realize the power was off. The great marble staircase was her only choice. She ran up the two flights to the meeting room level, disturbed that the debris cluttering the steps was ruining her shoes. She coughed, tasting the dry acidic bitterness in her mouth and throat. Powdery ash filled the air even inside the Charlemagne. The high wooden doors of the Empire Room stood ajar. She hurried inside. It was dark, and empty.

"Ma'am?" A deep voice from behind startled her. Pankie whirled around.

"Yes! The press conference . . . where is everyone? Why aren't they here? And why are you so . . . so filthy?"

The man wiped the back of his hand across his streaked, perspiring forehead. "Uh, ma'am, we're closed today . . ."

"Are you the manager? I want to see the manager. Immediately!"

"I am the manager."

"Then do something! I have a meeting here at eleven. Don't you check your schedule?" Her voice was more shrill with each word.

"I am Pankie Quille Retson!"

Recognition crept into the manager's eyes.

"Well?" she shouted. "Get going . . . get the people in here. This must be the wrong room. You've moved the meeting — that's it. Where is it?" She pushed past him and through the doorway.

"Miss Retson, there's a slight problem, I'm afraid. We've had a volcanic eruption and . . ."

"I know that!" she shrieked bitterly. Then, abruptly, she wheeled and stalked away. At the top of the staircase she turned again and shouted. "No more business here! Not after this!" She stormed down the stairs, her footsteps muffled in the thick ash. "It's not fair! It's just not fair!" Her words echoed up te stairs. The manager shook his head and went back down the hall.

"Senator, the mayor insists on talking with you. This is the third time he's called."

"The lines are to be kept open, Briggs. Try Jerusalem again. Keep trying. I must talk with Franklin. And check the surveillance on Debbie Ames. I want data on every move she makes."

"But sir . . ."

"That's final! Handle it."

Moe Cummings turned his back and looked out the large window of his office. Charlie Briggs shrugged helplessly, returning to his desk in the outer section. Still shaken, Moe viewed the scene of desolation. He knew of the extensive damage to Prantzer Defense Headquarters complex and how significant a loss it was. He had already determined that certain Omega Plan preparations had already been completed and shipped from the main Prantzer research center before the volcano erupted. But without that center Prantzer Defense was just one more big electronics and airframe manufacturer, and Milton Franklin was far less formidable an ally. Even less than twenty-four hours ago.

'Perhaps I should make a few adjustments,' he mused. But he thought the better of it. Too much was in motion. The chairman would generate alternatives. He'd wait and see what happened before making any moves.

"Charlie!" Moe called. His aide jumped from his desk and hurried into the office.

"Get some lunch. Cheeseburger, salad, milk."

Charlie stopped in mid-step. "Uh . . . where, senator?"

"Handle it, Charlie. Just handle it."

Chapter 21

"Just got the word, Omega." Milton Franklin slipped back into his chair and poured some of the dark tepid hotel coffee into his cup. Thursday morning had come early after an exhausting evening tour of Old Jerusalem followed by more study and a meeting with the Omega team leader, Major O'Keefe. The hotel coffee shop was small and dingy, pushed off to the side of the main lobby. Franklin had been gone for over half an hour to take a priority call in his room.

"And?" Michael was irritable. The tiring pace of the last few days and frustration that he had not been able to contact Debbie had drained him. Sixteen-hour work days, gunfire in the streets, and new volcanoes appearing in major cities were taking their toll.

"You're not going to like it," Franklin said, looking hard at him. But here's how it is. The schedule's been changed. You go on a week from Sunday."

Michael slammed his hand on the table and began to protest. Franklin cut him off sharply. "It's a lousy break — so what? This is important. Quit your complaining and get to it. When it's over you can run back to your other concerns. Not now."

Michael threw his napkin on the table. "You guys are crazy. I don't know what's going on, but I've had enough. Shove your contract. Sir." He stormed through the doorway and around the corner.

Franklin waited. Minutes later two large men appeared with Michael held firmly between them, his feet dangling inches off the floor.

"Hello Omega." Franklin said, smiling pleasantly. He motioned to Michael's empty chair. "Join me for breakfast?"

Michael pulled away from his escorts and dropped to his feet. He remembered his intuition when he first met Moe Cummings and Pankie Retson and wished fervently that he'd heeded its signals. The men silently disappeared through the coffee shop door. Michael slouched in his chair, despondent. He'd tried to call Debbie from the lobby phone. Before the connection could be made his 'escorts' appeared.

"Let's review," Franklin said. Michael glared petulantly.

"You wanted to play hard ball, Omega . . ."

"Will you stop using that ridiculous name!"

". . . I could see it in your face. The big leagues, Omega. I thought you were tougher. Anyhow, it doesn't matter. You're in whether you like it or not. Either act more professionally or you'll have those gorillas for constant companions."

Michael's cheeks burned in embarrassment.

"Eat while we talk. You have a heavy day ahead."

Michael scowled, more from wounded pride than from anger. Franklin's words and his own increasing understanding had dealt with his anger quite effectively. He picked up a slice of black bread and dabbed jam over it.

"I'm leaving later to meet with the chairman. You will go to the Tower of the Ascension to work out the precise methods for your return with Professor Schmidt. This afternoon you are to prepare a draft of what you will say. You know, just like you used to do for all those little folks you were reorganizing back at Prantzer Defense." Franklin's eyes gleamed. Sarcasm perhaps? Michael wasn't sure.

"You'll submit it to Professor Schmidt. He'll refine it and organize it into a script. Tonight, more study. Where are you in the book?"

"I finished John last night."

"Good — a day ahead of schedule. What do you think?" Michael snorted. 'A myth, since you ask."

Franklin grinned slyly, "Perhaps, then, you just skimmed it?"

"I've got it word for word, right up here," Michael retorted, tapping his finger to his head.

"We'll see." Franklin pulled some notes from his pocket. "What did Jesus say to Nicodemus?"

Michael's mental camera flashed through the Book of John, and he found what he needed. " 'Truly I say to you, unless one is born anew, he cannot see the Kingdom of God.' "

Franklin smiled. "Excellent." Michael felt better.

"We're dropping the rest of the New Testament because of the schedule change," Franklin continued, "except Revelation. That you'll do tonight. Tomorrow, Daniel. Saturday and Sunday, Isaiah. Monday and Tuesday, Psalms. Got it?"

"Yeah."

"After that, study time is over. So learn it well. You'll spend the next four days rehearsing your return. On Sunday it happens."

"And after that?"

Franklin sighed. "Then, Omega, you'll reign in power for a while. That script is being prepared now. But don't worry. The world will only see you three or four times." He paused, eyeing a stranger who had walked into the coffee shop. The stranger went to a table at the far end of the long narrow room.

"It's time to give you more background, Omega." Michael's anger ebbed as the drama of the next eleven days began to unfold.

"You do not understand the scope of this mission or the resources behind it. You've been exposed strictly on a need to know basis. Despite your tendency to let your emotions rule,'' Franklin looked pointedly at him . . . ''you're a man of extraordinary intelligence, and you have a very unique gift. We recognize that you need the more complete picture if you're to be as successful as is necessary. You are not a soldier, but a future leader. The only question remaining, Omega, is your emotional stability. Can you be trusted?''

Franklin sat back and poured more coffee, watching Michael closely. The answer was, by definition, Yes. Franklin would continue working with Michael, pleasantly or otherwise, until it came out correctly. He had bent stronger men than Michael to his purposes. If the man in Michael had any doubts, his ego and pride in him did not. Franklin's positive strokes were all the sweeter on the heels of his chastisements. The opportunity for redemption into the circle reached out for him. He hesitated only enough to frame the words he knew by instinct were necessary to bring closure to the gap he'd created.

"I did let it get out of hand, I admit. The chairman said Debbie was safe. That should have been enough. You don't have to question my commitment. It's there.''

Franklin saw it all once again. Give a man something that's already his, link it to something worthy, and he's in. It seemed too easy. But there he was, all lined up. 'When this is over I don't want that man anywhere near me,' Franklin thought to himself. I'd have thrown the table over and fought my way back to the States to see my wife if I were him. He would have done nothing of the kind. But he'd prostituted himself so often over so many years that he now had the passing luxury of thinking whatever he wished about himself. His sense of truth had long since died. He held his hand out. "All right." Michael shook it vigorously.

"Listen carefully. I'm only going to say this once." Franklin looked around, satisfied that he would not be heard.

"The chairman is not an old man playing out a science fiction dream. He is incredibly powerful. He owns two of the largest companies in the world and controls many others. His advisors include some of the most capable and influential people alive. They're extremely loyal, and they realize the Alliance is the only way to the next step in human history. They're not motivated by money or power — they have more than they'll ever use. They're motivated by the dream, the legacy, the eternal impact they can have."

"These people — just so you have the right perspective — control half the world's military and economic power. That beady-eyed old man, Omega, could destroy this planet at the touch of a button, or transform it by the fulfillment of the Global Unification Plan. That plan is his. He created it. He spent thirty years cultivating the right people and influencing the course of events until a foundation had been laid. We've created a visible, highly idealistic World Government apparatus for public consumption. We've been consolidating power and resources behind the scenes for the actual emergence of World Alliance governing authority. You've noticed, perhaps, certain laws passed and policies set over the last several years by national and regional governments in the Americans, Europe, parts of Asia, and the South Pacific. All synchronized, all preplanned."

Franklin sat back, speaking proudly. "When the Alliance takes over the world won't miss a beat. The separate governments are already aligned. In fact, the Alliance has been functioning for a year. The only difference is that we haven't gone public. That will come as a result of the Omega Plan, the last piece of the equation."

Michael was astonished. These were things he'd thought of only in fictional terms. He recalled occasional news articles or cocktail conversations speculating on the existence of a consolidating power group. But real?

"The Omega Plan was not part of the original text of Global Unification. It was developed because of recent increases in the influence of the Christians. Flexibility, you know, is one of the hallmarks of great leadership."

"From what I've heard so far, all this great leadership is hardly a democratic process," Michael commented, instantly regretting his observation. Franklin's eyes lit with sudden intensity.

"You think Christians believe in a myth? Democracy is the real myth!"

He seemed insane, Michael thought, just for that instant. "History has proven that the only real freedom democracy offers is the freedom to fail. Democracy is the ultimate corruption. It's slow, inefficient, self-serving, exploitative, and degenerative. Give people a voice in government and they speak with their groin and their stomach. Decline is inevitable."

"Seems to me a lot of Chinese wouldn't mind trying it," Michael said.

"Neither would I, were I in their shoes."

"Then what difference is there between the World Alliance and a totalitarian government telling people what to do?"

"Omega, you're naive. And so resisting . . ."

"Not at all!" Michael protested. "In fact I'm fascinated. I only want to understand."

Franklin lifted his coffee cup and took a sip. His hands were shaking very slightly. "We're getting off the track. Suffice it to say that the journals of the world's best thinkers and the lessons of history herself reveal that an enlightened, serving autocracy is the only form of government capable of generating consensus. And peace comes only with consensus."

Michael deferred from further questions. But very basic issues were disturbing to him, issues he would have to deal with.

Franklin checked his watch. "We haven't much more time, Omega. As you obviously know, a problem developed even as final preparations for public installation of the World Alliance were being finalized. The loyalty of man toward a cause is dependent on his value system being in harmony with that cause. Total loyalty to the World Alliance is a prerequisite for successful installation. With peace as our goal, the war we had to fight was not with our mission, but with its credibility. After all, every charlatan who comes along promises to work toward peace. That's where WOEC, SelfGuide, and others come in. These groups have been working for years with World Alliance people, structuring subtle but basic changes in the values of diverse societies throughout the world, and moving them closer together.

"Men cannot have two leaders, Omega." Franklin's statement triggered the text stored in Michael's memory. ". . . no man can serve two masters. For either he will hate the one and love the other . . ."

"Jesus spoke those words," Michael said.

"Perhaps. Anyhow, the principle is essential. We knew we could not do away with the God of the people. We're not fully rational beings, Omega. There is an emotional component that is real, and needs to be dealt with. The only master outside of government as we envision it is the God of the people. For thousands of years we've tried to kill that God. It hasn't worked. So, through WOEC we are acknowledging his — its, whatever — existence, and encouraging people to unite in that acknowledgement. We're just adjusting the rules a bit. So you see how important WOEC and SelfGuide, as well as Life Mystic Society and Huang Ki, are to the World Alliance plan. These are the refuges of the people. Think about it. The same person will cheat on his income tax and then give twice as much to some cause. The same one who will weasel out of a year's military duty will work eighty hours a week for a pittance helping SelfGuide promote its values. Why?"

Michael didn't know why. He'd never given it much thought.

"Because that's where their loyalty is." Franklin shifted back in his chair. "All right, there's the background. WOEC's god and SelfGuide's values are fully synchronized, not only with each other but with the World Alliance. When the World Alliance goes public . . ." Franklin paused with drama . . . "the people will see their God in the flesh."

Michael was not a religious man, but he was not unmindful of the implications of what Franklin had said.

"No more looking into the sky or fearing the underground, Omega. It's the beginning of a world focused on its own reality, its potential, its tremendous possibilities."

Michael sipped his coffee, now acrid and cold. It eased the dryness in his throat.

"Unfortunately, a few outspoken Christians began to rant against us. They attracted a lot of people. Their clamoring to return to the 'one true God' is now jeopardizing the entire World Alliance plan. It just goes to show you, doesn't it?"

Michael looked at Franklin, puzzled. "What?"

"That the value system of man is more powerful than all the armies and resources the world can muster."

"Oh. I suppose so," Michael said, not understanding.

"Omega, on Saturday I will take over the World Alliance."

Michael twitched visibly.

Franklin looked around. The room was empty now, except for a heavy-set waitress behind the counter cleaning metal napkin holders.

"It's in the plan. The chairman will appear to be killed. There will be worldwide mourning for the great man of peace. As soon as I take control I will bring a semblance of the World Alliance public, and initiate a persecution of the Christian movement."

Michael had never seen Milton Franklin appear more ruthless or determined as he did at that moment. A shiver went up his spine.

"This will only make the Christians stronger and more resolute, if somewhat fewer in number," Franklin continued. "World sympathies will be with them. WOEC itself will vigorously denounce our actions. Then on Sunday you will appear as the returned Christ. You will end that persecution."

"How?"

"You'll simply command it, Omega. Aren't you supposed to be able to do that? The Christians will rally around you, of course . . ."

"But Jesus warned his followers about false Christs . . ."

"We know, we know," Franklin interrupted impatiently. "It's all been researched. In fact, Professor Schmidt is one of the architects of your return scenario. Fine scholar, he is, and a respected member of the WOEC European Region High Council. You will do your return in a convincing way."

Michael skimmed more mental pages, interpreting as he read. Suddenly he stopped, surprised.

"I'm going to come down like lightning?"

Franklin grinned. "Don't underestimate modern technology."

Michael felt a tug of fear. "I'd like to know a little more about that . . ."

"You'll be safe. It would hardly fit to have the returned Christ limping around, now, would it?"

Michael felt better. "So I'm here, like lightning. Then what?"

"You'll name the designated world administrator. That person is our chairman."

"Our then-dead chairman," Michael reminded him.

"Not after you bring him back to life. That will be the unifying act," Franklin explained. "He will reascend the throne of the World Alliance. I will be disposed of — again, I hasten to add, for the public consumption."

"What about the non-Christian, non-WOEC people? The Chinese, for example. Or atheists, or Buddists? I don't see much unity there."

"You don't know the clout of our peripheral organizations. SelfGuide, for example, has millions of members. Polls show that eighty-plus percent of the population is sympathetic to their principles. Huang Ki embraces every living Chinese. You probably know it better by the name 'National Socialist Party.' "

"The official government of China!" Michael exclaimed.

"You're getting it. Government where government is their religion. Idealism where idealism is their religion. Lusts of the flesh, as the Christians say, where that is their religion. Wherever the handle is, there, too, are we."

"And what happens to me? And to you?"

"I'll continue as a member of the World Alliance Inner Circle."

"You . . . you're one of them?" Michael said, awed.

"I am." Michael looked at Franklin with renewed admiration. It never occured to him how dangerous it was to know such things.

"As for you," Franklin continued, "according to Professor Schmidt you need to live for about a thousand years. We have other Omegas in training. One will take your place soon after you raise the chairman back to power."

"I'm beginning to see it," said Michael. "He'll be made to look like me. Plastic surgery?"

Franklin's eyes gleamed strangely. "Actually you'll be adjusted to look like the returned Christ. But don't worry — the change will be small. There's already a great deal of resemblance."

"Now wait, Milton. No way are you going to . . ."

He hadn't been aware of the return of his two burly escorts who had silently approached from behind him. As he pushed his chair back they gripped his arms. Fear bubbled in the pit of his stomach.

"You'll heal," Franklin said matter-of-factly. "You must leave now, very quietly. The operation will take an hour. You'll be in the field with the rest of us by noon. A little pain perhaps, but nothing severe. Ignore it."

His escorts turned him toward the doorway, their grip tightening until he walked between them without struggle. Milton Franklin threw a bill on the table, gathered his bags and took the waiting limousine to the airport. It would be a long flight to World Alliance Headquarters in Geneva.

Chapter 22

Gabe's church, located in the southern suburbs, was hardly affected by the volcano. But ash deposits were heavy. Members had spent the day cleaning and scrubbing. By the time the three men and Debbie arrived they could see their own footprints tracking ash across the freshly waxed tile floor.

They'd found an open delicatessen on the way back and managed to pick from what was left a box of crackers, cheese, pickles, and two nearly-black bananas. It would have to do.

"Would someone mind making coffee? It's there, in that cabinet." Gabe pointed, then left, returning shortly with four choir robes. "Not exactly form-fitting, but clean. Put these on if you like. There's a washroom down the hall."

Debbie sat in a soft chair, surrounded by an aura of loneliness. Her feet were curled under her, and her hair, quickly washed before donning a robe, hung damp and auburn, naturally curled, to her shoulders.

"How can you look so sad in the company of a balding preacher, an ex-scientist and an old man?" Ben said, laughing.

She smiled. "I was just . . . thinking about Michael. It's about six in the morning over there. He always gets up early." Then tears brimmed her voice became husky. "Does he know I'm all right? Maybe he doesn't even know about the volcano!" Her tears spilled over. "I hope he's safe . . ."

"I'm sure he's fine," Gabe said gently. "He probably can't get a connection. Many of the lines are out of service here."

"Maybe." She hesitated. "I didn't feel right about that assignment from the start. It's all backwards, sort of. Everything about it is strange."

"You wanted to talk," Gabe prompted.

A thousand thoughts pushing at Debbie's mind now disguised themselves, and a thousand things she wanted to say slipped just beyond the pale of her grasp. So much had happened, and so fast.

"Had you and Michael both decided to come forward last Sunday?"

"No. He said it was part of his assignment." Though Michael had never warned her, she knew she was telling these men things he might not want anyone to hear. But the outpouring, now begun, would not be quenched. She felt newly drawn to them as if they were dear and long-lost friends, not new acquaintances.

"Assignments to join a church?" Em said, surprised.

"Yes. He was studying a Bible, too, to prepare."

Gabe was intrigued more than he revealed.

"I'm worried to death by this assignment. I'm afraid he's in trouble of some kind . . . I can almost feel it!" Debbie told them all she knew about the strange circumstances, his meeting with Senator Cummings and Pankie Retson, his being picked up personally by Franklin himself to fly to Jerusalem, the calls from Rob Peary updating her on Michael's location and condition. Only by those calls did she know that her husband was out of danger during the Three Day War. But Peary had to be a middleman relaying messages from someone else because she couldn't get answers to her questions. Peary could offer only repeated assurances that Michael was safe but unable to be in touch.

They listened intently as Debbie talked, taking a special interest in Michael's assignment to Jerusalem and the lofty connections he seemed to have. When she finished their concern was unmistakable. She felt the despair of fears confirmed. She sighed, emotionally exhausted. "If only it was over with. He is so driven, so ambitious."

Em Prantzer looked up, his brow furrowed with thought. "I know the people you mentioned, Debbie. Milton Franklin is a ruthless shrewd man well connected all over the world. Pankie Retson is brilliant — and a she-devil. I know Cummings only superficially. But from what I've seen he has the morals of a toad and a backbone to match. These people do not waste their time on small issues. Whatever Michael's into, it's big. And — sorry, Debbie — probably dangerous. I think we need to understand what's going on."

Em Prantzer reminded her of her much-loved grandfather. She nodded.

"Debbie," Gabe said, "we'd like to pray. Would you mind . . ."

"Not at all!" she responded quickly. "I'll just . . ."

"No no!" Gabe said. "You don't have to leave the room, dear!"

"But I thought . . . I don't know what you do. If you're really talking to someone I don't want to be in the way." She looked at Ben, remembering their long conversation at her home. She'd seen that there was nothing false in his faith — whatever he had, it was real. She waited, tensely, expectantly. The room was quiet and peaceful.

"Lord God," Gabe said. "Thank you for today, a day that You have made. We don't understand but we trust in You. We thank you for Debbie Ames, Lord, for her compassion and help, her thoughtfulness, her love for her husband. Lord, we ask your healing for those who are suffering in all that is touching us. And we ask for your insight now, about Michael's assignment. Lift the veil from our eyes, Father, and guide us. This we pray because we can, thanks to Jesus."

"All right," Em Prantzer began, "as soon as I was fired Franklin ended Michael's contract and sent him to Jerusalem. Michael also met with Cummings and Retson. So. It's international, and it involves government. Probably the World Alliance."

"Meanwhile there are world-wide disasters of all kinds, events the Lord said would occur near the time of His return," Gabe added.

"Is there a link?"

"Maybe we should focus on Jerusalem."

"Right. Jesus' death and resurrection. Israel's statehood. The attack again last Monday by her enemies . . ."

"Interesting, that one," Em interrupted. "With Michael sent over at the same time."

"I think you're on to something. Daniel, the Psalms, Revelation all reveal a concerted Arabic attack before . . ."

" . . . the king of the North — Russia. Or maybe China. There's talk of a buildup in Afganistan and the Black Sea."

"What else — the Temple! It's nearly finished!"

"What are you talking about?" Debbie said, unable to contain herself.

"The Bible says certain things will happen just before Jesus Christ returns. Most of these were fulfilled in the first century or two after His resurrection. But . . ."

"His what? Like coming alive after being dead?"

Gabe looked earnestly at her. "Yes. Jesus was killed by crucifixion. But after three days God raised Him up, alive again."

"That's impossible! A few hours maybe, but not three days!"

"Impossible for men. Possible with God. Jesus Himself said that."

"Ben," Debbie said, "that's what you told us last week! I didn't think you meant that it actually happened."

"I assure you, my dear, that what you've heard abut Jesus is quite true, quite true indeed."

Debbie wondered how he knew, how he could be so sure. She turned back to Gabe. "So this Jesus rose from the dead?"

"Yes. He is man, and more than man. He is God."

"And God is God, and the Holy Spirit is God." Em's eyes twinkled.

"Look," he continued, holding up his empty coffee mug. "The silhouette is rectangular."

Debbie nodded.

He turned the opening toward her. "And now what's the shape?"

"It's a circle."

"And . . ." He tilted the mug at an angle.

"It's an oval."

"The three shapes are all of the same thing, a coffee cup. So the Father, the Son, and the Holy Spirit are God."

Debbie paused, thinking. Gabe became intense. "The Temple is almost done. That's an important prophesy for Jerusalem. Where Michael is."

"Suppose there's more to the World Alliance than we know," Ben interjected, shifting his position on the couch. "I have a hunch there is, the more I think on it. The regional governments, for example. And all this WOEC hype about

A 'world-wide God of unity.' Now take the earthquakes, volcanoes, plagues — all of it. Folks are scared. It's times like these when they turn to whoever they think can make them feel safe again."

"If I was a politician who wanted to run the world," Gabe mused, "I'd say just about everything was in place to do it. Except, that is, for the Christians. We're the discordant note. Everybody else has aligned with WOEC, SelfGuide, Regional government, Twenty-Ninth Amendment, except us! Even the Moslems are affiliated with WOEC!"

"Oh, my Lord. It fits." Em stood up, pacing. "Remember where it says 'And I will pour out my Spirit on all flesh' — Corinthians?"

"Acts," Gabe corrected.

"With all these catastrophes people are turning to Jesus Christ by the thousands. These calamities, as we think of them, seem to be the only force awakening people to their reality . . . anything man has ever done pales by comparison."

"A new generation of outspoken Christians has been raised, too, Gabe," Em said. "You, Amy Greene, and others — we haven't had such leadership since Billy Graham."

"The Christian revival has to be a direct threat to any world-based move. They have to get rid of us."

"How? Persecution never has and never will work."

Gabe trembled ever so slightly and closed his eyes, suddenly and irrevocably certain. The other men sensed the familiar presence of the Spirit. Gabe almost glowed. Debbie sensed energy and felt she was witnessing something terribly important.

"They're going to counterfeit His return. Look — if we reject their charade we risk wholesale slaughter — WOEC, SelfGuide and others will have turned to the counterfeit Christ. If we accept it we merely become one of them. Either way, the world is 'united.' Under them. And Michael Ames is to be that counterfeit Christ."

Debbie shivered from a rush of shock, and a brief gasp escaped.

"I don't know why I didn't notice the resemblance before! Debbie, have you ever seen a picture of Jesus?"

"No, I don't think so. But surely you . . ."

Gabe reached into his drawer and pulled out a small rendering. "Except for images on the linen burial shroud and some brief descriptions in the Scripture, we don't know what He looked like. But over the centuries His portrait has become more or less standardized by artists' conceptions. If the World Alliance uses any model at all they'll use this one. Look."

He handed the small painting to Debbie. She gasped. With shorter hair and a slightly smaller nose, it was her husband. Debbie broke into hysterical sobs.

Chapter 24

Michael's escorts said nothing on the way to the clinic. He was panicky at the thought of his face coming under the knife. At a checkpoint Israeli soldiers peered inside the car and checked their papers. Michael wanted to shout for help, to escape what had become a nightmare. One glance at the man beside him ended his fantasy.

The glass front door of the clinic opened as they arrived. A short, thin woman in a white smock ushered them inside. "Everything ready," she said.

One of his escorts motioned to Michael to go with the woman. There was no malice — only business-like attention to duty. The escorts sat on a torn plastic couch along the wall in the tiny reception room to wait.

Michael's tension heightened as they walked down a dim corridor and into a large brightly lit room. A surgeon and a nurse stood by an operating table. "You will take your shirts off and use these." She pulled a paper gown and cap from a shelf. "Also please to recite your studies."

Michael felt disoriented. He removed his shirt, as she had instructed, unduly fumbling with the buttons on his sleeve.

"Recite please!" she barked.

"Don't worry," the surgeon interrupted. "This will be simple and painless. You must recite so we know when the anesthesia has taken effect."

The first mental page that came to his mind was near the end of the Book of Matthew. " 'As He sat on the Mount of Olives, the disciples came to him privately, saying . . .' "

"Good," the surgeon said. "Keep talking, and put on your gown."

Michael pulled on the paper gown and cap. ". . . 'Tell us when this will be, and what will be the sign of your coming and of the close of the age?' And Jesus answered them . . ."

The nurse helped him lay down on the white-papered surface of the operating table.

" '. . . take heed that no one leads you astray. For many will come in my name . . .' "

A respirator mask covered his face, and the surgeon's eyes loomed above him. He could hear his breath stream noisily through the respirator.

" . . .'saying, 'I am the Christ,' and they will lead . . . many astray . . . And hear . . . wars . . . . an' . . . rumorzz . . .'

"Pencil." The surgeon took the marking instrument the nurse deftly slapped into his hand and began sketching lines on Michael's face, glancing frequently at a large photograph.

Michael expanded into a warm suffused glow. Tension fell away, and peace entered. A form coalesced — radiant, strong, smiling. It was Henri.

"Michael, beloved of God, greetings." His voice was rich and deep, and Michael sensed a powerful love. They moved effortlessly into the glow. Soon Michael found himself on a crystal veranda. Brilliant sunlight streamed through a deep azure sky and reflected from distant golden hills. Flowers waved in gentle-breezed salutes of joy, and grasspatches and hedgerows parted here and there for silvered brooks and mirrored ponds. Fragrance and song danced in the air. Beyond the hills, mountains rose with majestic silver-streaked splendor.

Everything spoke of exquisite richness and life. "Henri, I cannot imagine anything more wonderful than this."

"You stand on holy ground. Come now. We must go to the Window."

Henri turned, and Michael was compelled to follow. Through an enormous crystal arch he saw pure white marble inlaid with paths of gold spreading in all directions. Shafts of jewels sprang upward like glades of fountains, lifting far above to an immense dome which glistened with light. The jewelled shafts radiated their own light, and there were no shadows anywhere. Each wondrous javelin of brilliance was intricately carved, each unique like different snowflakes, refracting light into everchanging rainbow dances. There was such crispness and purity that even the smallest detail far across the marble surface could be appreciated with no less a sense of awe than the delicate praiseforms nearby.

They stepped onto the marble and found new and beautiful aromas. Faint driftings of delightful music offered welcome and love. Henri smiled. "This was created for you Michael, and for now."

Michael stared with disbelief.

"Such is His Love. Now, look."

A circular opening developed, as if the marble surface melted away. "The Window," Henri said softly. As they approached the sweet fragrances weakened and the sounds of joy became impeded and more distant.

Through the Window Michael found a clear view of life on earth in all of its infinite detail. In the Window's miraculous clarity he found he could see every face even to the hairs on people's heads. All was familiar, yet in some undefinable way very different, as if all was caricatured in light and color, in form, in aroma, and feeling.

"Look there." Henri had not moved, but Michael knew exactly where.

"Debbie!" he exclaimed. She was a flickering light which wavered from a dull grayish hue to a moderate white glow. Surrounding her were three very bright lights. He recognized them with great surprise.

The panorama of the world was dark, as if only moments remained before the final setting of the sun. Pockets of light spread across the continents, millions of dots of infinitely varying intensities casting warmth within the lightpockets and beyond their perimeters. But there were many more pockets of blackness, so black as if to absorb the feeble glows surrounding them.

Henri pointed silently. Michael turned his attention to the inside of a prison cell. A brilliant glow knelt beside a faint flicker. "Watch — this is his time. You will witness either birth or death."

He watched, moved to cheer and encourage the dimly flickering light. It wavered, disappeared, and wavered again. "Come on, you can make it — come on!" The flickering steadied slightly. Then the bright light began to pray, and his light became a beacon aimed directly at Michael's eyes.

"Come on — come on!" The brilliant beacon ebbed, the prayer finished. The dim spot fluttered, then winked into blackness and became nothing where something used to be. Michael felt as though part of himself had died.

Henri's expression was inscrutable. "Now you must view the passage of time since the birth of the one you will counterfeit." His tone was matter-of-fact, but Michael felt as if a dark secret had been found out and exposed. Henri drew his hand across the Window. A single brightness shone from the Middle East geography like a master beacon of incalculable power. Its halo glowed over the surface of the world, bringing warmth into even the dark recesses of all the continents. In that glow countless spots of blackness throughout the dawn-gray tapestry were revealed, as if it had been infested by smallpox only now discovered.

The beacon seemed to be reproducing itself, and lights began to spread across the world's surface, brightening, darkening, increasing and decreasing. Suddenly the brilliant master beacon was extinguished. For a moment the world darkened and had few lights at all. Then in splendidly indescribable radiance the glow began to build and multiply throughout the lands. As time continued the light began to diminish. Fewer and fewer appeared, and darkness, ever seeking opportunity to encroach into lighted areas, oozed across the surface like black tar in a furnace. Michael saw Debbie again, flickering. A deep sadness gripped him. Blackness spread, overpowering the dim glows. Brightness, scattered like salt, decreased.

Then their number dropped with chilling suddenness. From the deepening gloom of the world Michael sensed an unleashed arrogance wafting upward through the Window, and tasted unpleasant odors of decay and fear. Though repulsed, he could not turn away. He felt trapped inside a sealed closet. His heart sank into deep depression. The last things — he realized he'd been urging them on, cheering as he had before — were gone. The chill became a paralyzing cold, and the stench of the world was overpowering.

"Where are they?" Michael gasped, alarmed. "The lights are all we have! He wailed with remorse, leaning far over the Window's edge despite the cold and the stench, searching. A sickening lost feeling came over him and he screamed again and again as he tumbled over the edge into the blackness. The Window dimmed, and then disappeared.

He did not know how long he fell. But gradually he became more accustomed to the chill and the odor. His terror diminished. Was he falling toward the earth? Perhaps. He knew only that he was falling very, very far.

The air seemed now more like a blotchy dark soup. His sense of downward movement disappeared and he felt suspended like a living fossil interred in the dark history of his planet. No thought could form in his mind. His single consciousness was that he was conscious.

"It's about time."

Michael jumped at the gutteral rasping words. A hooded, scowling visage appeared. "Get over here — I don't have much time."

Michael stood, wobbling, abandoned into a hopeless horror. The visage glowed like burning phosphorus, but not as bright. It laughed maliciously and moved away. Michael was compelled to follow.

They came to a balconied terrace overlooking a huge polished cavern. Michael knotted up in sheer terror as something unhuman approached from out of the blackness, a half-body larger than he, naked and covered with matted hair, and very thin. Its bones showed through a mottled covering of infested skin. Michael was overcome by the stench of its breath as it spoke to the visage in clipped precise words. The visage shrank away without glance or word. The creature turned its head slowly toward Michael and grinned horribly.

"You're about to become a hero, young Michael. You are here to receive powers you will need to complete your mission. But — my appearance must be offensive. Permit me . . ." The creature's withered limbs and torso filled out, and it shrank until it was slightly shorter than Michael. Neatly combed hair replaced the wisps of wool-like residue which had clung to its head. Expensive, well-tailored clothing covered its body. The face became human. Michael found himself with one of his own kind.

"You may call me Milt."

"Milton Franklin?" Michael blurted, astonished.

"That one is far too oafish to talk or think as I do. But you've named one of our best. He is learned and experienced for all his oafishness, and his influence is important."

"I want out of here."

Milt looked hurt. "You don't like this place? You do want power, do you not?" The creature leered. "Watch!" He waved his hand and the visage reappeared, suspended in mid-air just beyond the terrace railing, cowering.

"You battled often with this one, young Michael. You were superior in every way, but weakened by those morals and ethics which you keep stumbling over up there. You haven't learned that morals and ethics are manipulative tools, not behavioral standards."

"Without that we're just animals!" Michael protested, resisting the corruption.

"You're animal anyhow. Don't think you're something special — you're not. What did Milton Franklin tell you?

'Power is everything!' Don't argue with me. Just watch. I'll show you power."

Milt crooked his finger and the pitiful visage crawled through the dank air like a dog prepared for a whipping. Milt grabbed its arm and broke it off with a quick jerk of his wrist. Jewelry poured out of the stump. Its shriek of agony echoed in the cavern.

"Have some, young Michael," Milt grinned.

Michael was aghast. His breath seemed unwilling to come. Milt sneered. "Last chance, fool."

Horrified, Michael reached toward the agony-wracked arm stump and held his trembling hands beneath the flow of treasure. Soon he could not hold all the gold, silver and precious stones.

Milt leered. "How'd you like to do that one up top?"

Michael stared at the handful of treasure. Although it sickened him, he felt a glimmer of interest.

Milt flicked his hand. As if a cord had been cut, the visage dropped downward with a wailing lost scream and out of sight.

"He's one of them, Michael. You're one of us, we who deserve power and know how to get it and use it. Come along."

They walked along the terrace corridor, presently coming to a door which Milt commanded Michael to enter. They stepped inside. Blinding spotlights focused on Michael, and he heard a wild chanting. He found himself on an ornate dais overlooking a huge crowd of cheering people.

"Wave to them idiot," Milt hissed. "They're worshipping you!"

He blinked and stared at the crowd. "Mi-kal, Mi-kal" they chanted. Banners waved, and the beat of drums sounded in the distance. Michael waved in tentative acknowledgement. The cheers multiplied. He waved again, then brought both hands up and clasped them together. The crowd went into a deafening frenzy of adulation. 'Mi-kal! Mi-kal!' Michael began to enjoy himself. The more he waved, the more they cheered. Perspiration dripped down his forehead and the burn of excitement was in his face. Milt leaned close, his voice piercing through the noise of the crowd.

"Do what we ask of you and all of this, and more, is yours." Michael trembled with excitement. "I will — count on it!" He waved his arms wildly above his head, fingers of both hands in a "V."

"Mi-kal! Mi-kal! Mi-kal!"

A different stream of light streaked across his vision as if he were film accidentally exposed to a glimpse of sunlight while still in the camera.

"Bye," Milt said suddenly. "Remember. Power is reality."

Another streak of strange light shot across Michael's view.

"Mi-kal! Mi-chal! Michael. Michael!"

He blinked. A masked face loomed over him. "Michael," it said. "Wake up!

"Wher . . where are the crowds?" Michael stammered, lifting his hand to his face. It was wrapped in gauze. He sat up. Nausea flowed through him, then eased. The short thin woman peered at him through thick glasses. "All right? You get up now, can you?"

He groaned and slowly pushed his legs over the edge of the table. Recollections of his vision faded.

"Better. Yes," the woman said. "Stay one moment. I help you put shirts on." A moment later Michael was wriggling into his clothes, now more or less fully conscious. A man appeared in the doorway. "Isn't he ready yet? We're late. Let's go."

Michael groaned and eased himself off the table. "Help him!" the woman commanded. The man pulled Michael's arm over his shoulder. They disappeared down the narrow corridor. Soon they were back in the car, speeding toward the Tower of the Ascension.

Chapter 24

The World Alliance headquarters was more utilitarian than opulent. Expensive panelling and plush furniture was rare, but the offices were filled with electronics, briefing screens and communications equipment. The chairman conducted his affairs surrounded by bullet-proof one-way glass walls, secure yet able to see the activity and on-line updates from contact points throughout the world. Milton Franklin was ushered through the familiar bustle of technicians, specialists and administrators in the outer work area and into the chairman's personal office.

"You're looking well sir."

"And you, Milton. You have ten minutes. Proceed."

"I appreciate your making this time available. I know . . ."

"Issues, Milton."

"Sir, I need instructions on my actions while in temporary control of World Alliance."

The chairman smiled blandly. "And?"

"That's it, sir."

"The Minister of Interior Affairs will brief you. Time does not permit me the pleasure of reviewing it personally."

"I understand, sir."

"But I do appreciate your visit. A briefing in person is more efficient than it is over those things." He motioned through the heavy glass wall to the huge bank of videoscreens. "Two questions, Milton. "First, what is Omega's psychological status? Second, are you aware that Omega's wife Deborah, along with Gabriel Diehl, Benjamin Crockett and Emerson Prantzer, purchased tickets for a flight to Jerusalem?"

Franklin trembled slightly. He hated surprises. "Omega's transformation was completed this morning. He's in the field now with Schmidt and the others. He's subdued and a little preoccupied, but otherwise cooperating."

"Shall we use one of the other Omegas?"

"Neither could learn the background in time."

"They're progressing well, Milton. But I'll rely on your judgment."

Franklin was relieved. It was a moment by moment thing with the chairman. He could win a point yesterday, with all due commendation from this most ruthless and powerful man, and be shot today for failure to have the answer to a question. It had happened to others. But he'd passed through that wicket, it seemed — until the next one.

Milton Franklin idolized the chairman so much that he was blinded to truth. The chairman had lied boldly about the Russian buildup. Indeed, the World Alliance was powerless to stop it — and deep inside, Franklin knew it. But to admit that would be to lose everything.

"Milton," the chairman prompted, "about Omega's wife and the others?"

"I have no information. That's Cummings' purview."

"And Cummings is your purview."

"Yes sir — I only meant to . . ."

The chairman waved him to silence. "Why would they do that? There can be only one reason — they know of our plans. I want to know how. And I want you to stop them. There must be no distractions. Is that understood?"

"Yes sir. I'll handle it."

The chairman smiled shrewdly. "Very good. See that you do. Now, we have one minute left. Here is your copy of the detailed plan on my demise — Section Eight. Follow standard usage and disposal procedures." He pulled a thin black folder from his desk and handed it to Franklin.

"The Inner Circle, as you well know, meets Saturday. They are not aware of my temporary disappearance — except, of course, the Minister of Internal Affairs. There are two recalcitrant members whom I cannot trust with the foreknowledge of Section Eight. You must therefore act appropriately when the news is announced. You'll be meeting then."

"They don't know I will take over? Without that established, we'll have a major fight on our hands!"

"Your hands, Milton. Not mine."

"Do you really think it will go smoothly without prearrangements?"

"Not at all!" The chairman grinned in triumph. "It will be chaos."

Franklin looked at him blankly, wondering how he was to wade into the middle of that pack of wolves which comprised the Inner Circle and take control in the short amount of time available.

"Milton, no damage can be done to the World Alliance without an organized attempt. Chaos is the best protection during my absence — and incidentally a nice springboard for my return."

"Surely you don't think that I . . ."

"No, Milton. I know of your loyalty. If I didn't I would have had you killed." Franklin knew he meant it. The chairman hunched over his desk, leaning closer. "All that really matters is the Christian persecution. They are the last stumbling block. I'm issuing a directive appointing you Acting Minister of Peace. It will go out at midnight. All military cooperatives will come under your authority in my absence. What more do you need?"

It was dark when Milton Franklin emerged from the World Alliance Headquarters following his briefing with the Internal Affairs Minister. All seemed ready. He'd been assured of adequate support. The lighted clock tower far down the Rue d'Emissaire stared balefully across the city. 'Less than three hours to find out what Ames' wife and those others are up to. Crisis makes strange bedfellows.' He walked three blocks down the wet street, the collar of his overcoat hunched up against the damp cold, and disappeared through the Alliance Club's massive carved wood main entrance. The doorman acknowledged him by name.

"Yah Omenka, dat iss better!"

Professor Schmidt had constant difficulty with Michael's code name. Michael touched his gauze bandages, pressing slightly in another fruitless attempt to alleviate the itching which, more than any pain, was his major discomfort. They had 'adjusted' his nose, chin, and ears. He wore a phonics booster to hear through the gauze and modified tissue. As he had read through his draft script for the professor his voice sounded to him as if he were speaking through a long tube.

"But Omenka, you must change last part. All else iss goot but last part. "Here, I show you." The professor rocked forward on his chair and pushed it closer to the table. Holding a pen over the last page of Michael's outline, he touched it to the paper about half-way down. "There. Now you have arrived, no? You are here — here at last!" He rolled his r's melodramatically, with a guttural swallow. "Der vorld iss stunned! Dis hass been folkentale for two thousand years — und suddently, Poink! You are here! Dis part where you say 'Blessed are ye who vaited mit patience, and voe to ye who doubted.' And den you go on to der details of der plans. No no, Omenka, you must build der drama! You must bring der volkspipple to frenzy, you must fill der cups mit biggenpowers!" The professor gestured broadly, speaking with excitement. "Dis part, Omenka . . ." he poked at the script with a stubby finger . . . "dis part iss der . . . der, uh biggensprechen!"

Michael looked at him, puzzled.

"Der sellemspielen! How you . . ."

"Oh, the pitch!"

Professor Schmidt jumped off his chair and danced around the table. "Ya ya. Der pitch!" Then he dropped his voice and spoke with gravity. "Iss very important here to set in place your autority. Not so big what you say but dat you talk mit power! Tink back . . . vat he say? Matthew chapter twenty-five, Omenka . . ."

Michael scanned his imaged memory bank. " 'When the Son of Man comes in his glory, and all the angels with him, then he will sit on his glorious throne.' That?"

"Ya ya! Kip goink, Omenka, kip goink!"

". . . 'Before him will be gathered all the nations, and he will separate them one from another as a shepherd separates the sheep from the goats, and he will . . . .' "

"Ya, dat's it. You see? Der is power! So, Omenka, build up it good. Ve do again, ya?"

Michael was exhausted. It was late in the evening and his face ached. But more than that, he could not escape the ominous foreboding which had come over him that afternoon. The four books about the man Jesus Christ, who he was scheduled to counterfeit in ten short days, had begun to seep from the storage banks of his mind and into the inner places of his soul, places into which he permitted no entry. It was not so much that he was experiencing an acceptance, but rather that he was having to expend energy to resist and reject. Contradictions loomed without satisfactory resolution. Jesus obviously had power, more than Michael had dreamt could be. Yet he behaved exactly contrary to the ways men used in order to acquire power. And that horrible suffering he had endured — for what? 'For me? Impossible! I wasn't there; I'm here now. Nobody knew me two thousand years ago, And' — his thoughts became tinged with honest sadness — 'I'm not worth that price.'

His dreams added to his turmoil. For a time they were forgotten. But after the vivid operating table experience all the others had been reawakened. Henri . . . Michael remembered the name and yearned for another time with him in those magnificent places. And the other, those cheering crowds, tugged with an eerie sirenic luring. Could those crowds be mine, right here? he wondered. Yes, just maybe, yes, he found himself answering.

"Omenka, listen to me, ya? Iss too early to be dreamink yet."

Michael pulled his attention back to his coach. The professor clapped his pudgy, nail-polished hand on Michael's shoulder. "You go now to your room to practice. I see you in hour, ya?"

"Hokay professor. See ya." Michael gathered his papers and left. The professor stood gazing through the window, finger pressed against his pale lips in thought. "Iss goink to be hokay," he mused, slowly nodding his head. "I can create him, ya." He slapped his fist into his hand, smiling, remembering golden times years ago at the university where he had done similar creations with the theater company. "Iss going to be finest performance ever, ya!" His brow furrowed, bushy eyebrows twitching. "Ya, it must be finest performance. Ya."

A fresh snowfall had left a clean white covering on the horrible afterbirth of Mt. Kruger, now looming benignly to the north. Winds had cleared the air. But where the ravages of nature ended, the ravages of men began. It was not evident which was worse. Pillaging and looting became normal daylight activity as police monitors, exhausted by twenty-hour shifts, fell off the pace of their vigilance.

For many years, following a landmark ruling by the World Court, laws pertaining to "victimless" crime had been liberalized until all criteria of behavior had been eliminated. Numerous groups practiced perversions and committed atrocities enabled by the "legislative and judicial enlightenment" of two decades ago. The single restriction which the Court had upheld with regard to "the freedom to practice, individually or severally, those acts of physical, mental, or emotional substance deemed satisfactory and suitable to the parties consenting to such acts," was that such practices be prohibited in public.

The extensive volcanic destruction had destroyed many of the sites used by such groups. But this did not deter their practice. Some took over abandoned buildings and warehouses. But most took to the streets, the thrill of exposing their sick practices publicly more than compensation for the coldness of the season. In those days many a parent was forced to hurry children past shouting, steaming-breathed mobs engaging in satanic ritual, mass orgies, drug trips, and carousing and brawling. These practices seemed for a time to have become the only law the city had. They played their fantasies out to exhaustion. If resisted, they maimed or killed. The power to stop them seemed non-existent.

In Binzoe people who had long since forgotten what it meant to be human took over. It was open warfare for a short time. But the Crowns were stronger and better organized. Once established, they looked for other ways to satisfy insatiable appetites. The helpless were the first victims of their wanton liberation, atrocities committed in the shadows of steel drum bonfires, behind crumbling brick walls of dilapidated buildings, up and down fetid alleys of the city known as a "center of human dignity." Day by day, more and more joined the Crowns in their abandonments. And growing numbers of hopeless people demonstrated over and over that there is no limit to the degeneration which the human soul is capable of.

Pankie Quille Retson did her best to stop the spread. She had no particular judgment about it, having long ago given herself over to the fullest pursuit of whatever pushed in her to be exercised. Indeed, the so-called liberty to do so was a part of the founding impetus of SelfGuide. But she also knew human nature and knew people had to be led into new levels of degradation. If it happened too fast their sense of shock could return, and resistance could build.

The bursting of this infection in the wake of catastrophe threatened the apathy for which SelfGuide represented itself as the answer. The filling of pleasures far in excess even of the free-falling social climate of these days would, she feared, shock too many people into action. That would bring, at the very least, substantial distraction away from the polarizing role SelfGuide was playing in the lives of millions. Worse, some among them might begin to see the linkages, or understand the subtleties of what had been happening. The last thing Pankie wanted was the abrupt emergence of morality, especially on the eve of the consummate event in human history now taking final shape in the city of Jerusalem.

To suggest she was less than successful would be an understatement. Like caged animals suddenly set loose, the frustrations and lusts and greeds of those in whom such inclinations lurked raged forth from what had been their confinement. Fire touched dry grass, and there was no force on earth that could stop it. Pankie was helpless among her own kind. She alone, it seemed, had the discipline of mind set high enough to see the selfish danger. The insight had done her no good.

Her last defeat before retreating to her shattered offices came in a strange twist of irony. It was at the orgy for the elite that Senator Moe Cummings met his end.

She and Ted Shriver had charged into the Charlemagne ballroom, coincidentally adjacent to the room in which

Pankie's aborted press conference was to have been — to try to convince them to disperse. They stepped among writhing bodies strewn across the mattress-covered ballroom floor as if tiptoeing through the rubble of the volcanic eruption. Ted was nervous. The laser pen inside his overcoat pocket was clasped in his hidden, sweating palm. For all his own liberality he'd never seen anything like it before.

Suddenly Pankie was pulled onto the mattressed-floor, and a flaccid, pasty body rolled over, leering.

"Nice legs, there — c'mon down here and. . . Pankie!"

It was Moe Cummings.

The incident triggered Ted's nervousness into action. He pointed the laser pen and pushed the clip. Its brief "pffft" was lost in the noise. A tiny round dot appeared on the senator's forehead and began to bleed.

Pankie knew with sinking certainty that it was all over for Moe Cummings. She shouted hysterically — he was her only controllable contact into the World Alliance. And he was, in a strange and kinky way, important to her. His skin was already greying, and a thin stream of blood drooled past the bridge of his nose. Two inches further in, the tip of the beam had cooked a section of his mind the size of a golf ball to medium-well done. "I can't see," he said, glassy-eyed. Then he slumped over, dead.

They checked the room. No one noticed them. "Let's go Tedrick," she hissed. They worked their way back through a sea of squirming bodies. Ted Shriver had no words. It was just as well as far as Pankie was concerned. She had much more weighty matters on her mind now.

Chapter 25

Early on Saturday an ebony jet with a golden falcon wreathed in purple emblazoned on its fuselage glided down the runway at the Geneva airport. Eight fighter planes were its escorts. The jet lifted quickly through the overcast of the gray European winter sky. Above the clouds, moving at Mach 2, the escorts surrounded the big jet as if each was the corner of a cube.

The World Alliance chairman worked during the first part of the trip to Whistler Air Defense Base in the United States. Of the five aides travelling with him only one knew the real plan. The others, in a separate section of the aircraft, continued confirming arrangements for the speech at the Unification Symposium and for official state meetings and receptions. These four were not aware that a new personal aide accompanied the chairman in his office quarters.

Pankie Quille Retson came to be that aide through a series of events which began shortly after she and Ted Shriver had returned, tense and shocked by Moe Cummings' death, to the SelfGuide office. Charlie Briggs had called, asking if the senator was there. His mistake had been to mention why he was calling. Pankie's mind had been racing to figure out other avenues into the World Alliance since Cummings was no longer available. She always thought big, ignoring the hill in order to climb the mountain. Why not the chairman himself! The thought came and she seized the opportunity.

'I'm so glad you called!" Pankie had said, instantly charming him. "Moe left just a few minutes ago on an urgent call to Geneva. He told me to contact you and give you some very specific instructions. I have them right here." She shuffled some papers on her desk, close enough to the phone that it could be heard.

"This is highly irregular, ma'am. The senator . . ."

"I know, Charlie. Moe often boasts of your loyalty and flexibility. He assured me we could count on you now."

Charlie Briggs sat up a little straighter in his chair. "Now listen. His people have uncovered possible grounds for treason against the chairman's personal aide . . ."

Pankie thought quickly. "Oh — Pat? — the new one Moe mentioned . . ."

"Basilia Aretha?"

"Yes, that's it."

"Treason — I can't believe it!"

"Especially with her connections to the New Soviets. You can't trust anyone these days."

"The New Soviets!" Charlie repeated, obviously shocked.

"Moe wants you to contact the chairman immediately, by code of course, and have her quarantined. He asked that I take her place until a permanent aide can be named. That's why he was here. Can you handle that?"

"Of course I can, but . . ."

"I leave for Geneva in the morning and won't have time to get my security papers together. Would you be a dear and draw up duplicates for me tonight?"

"That would be like forgery! I don't think I can . . ."

"Charlie, come now. We don't have time for formalities, and the senator is counting on you. Excuse me . . ." Pankie put her hand over the telephone and made sounds of muffled conversation. ". . . Sorry. Just got a communique from the president — I have to run. Please, don't embarrass the senator — there's too much at stake. You can confirm all this in the morning."

He sighed. "Very well, Ms. Retson. I'll draw up your papers and have them to you by courier within the hour."

"Thanks, Charlie. You've done a great service. I'm sure Moe will be proud of you."

The ruse worked beyond her expectations. She not only had top clearance papers in her hands by midnight — a clearance for which she had never qualified — but by two in the morning Charlie Briggs had called to confirm that the World Alliance had quarantined Basilia Aretha and extended a formal appointment to Pankie Quille Retson as acting special aide, along with the thanks and congratulations of the chairman himself. Charlie Briggs may have been a dullard, but he knew how to manipulate the levers of bureaucracy.

Pankie, of course, attributed the success to her own cleverness. She did not know of the extraordinary pressures on the

World Alliance organization from the combination of a yearlong seige of natural catastrophe, an increasingly intransigent New Soviet bloc, and the hastily finalized Omega Plan. These together had outstripped World Alliance resources and capabilities and caused fatal breakdowns in bureaucratic communications and security.

Pankie, now working within the chairman's private suite at the center of the aircraft, maintained continous contact with Ing Hammock, site contact for plan execution. The chairman would frequently interrupt to probe the arrangements. There was no margin for error — everything had to fit precisely. And it appeared that everything did. Ing's responses to Pankie's checklist were terse, factual, and complete. The two may as well have been reviewing routine shuttle launch preparations, except for the content of their discussion. A time signal tone beeped softly. Pankie glanced at the chairman and logged off with Ing.

"They're ready, sir."

The chairman smiled. "Good. Very good. You may begin."

Pankie began to feel the tension. The chairman looked utterly calm. "Good luck, sir." Her comment was more for herself than for him.

"It is not a matter of luck, Miss Retson. But thank you."

She opened the airlock door. Inside was a large wooden crate on rollers. She pulled it over the thick carpeting into the office and pried the front panel off.

"Unstrap him gently."

"Yes sir. I'll be careful." She loosened the canvas straps holding a drugged and hypnotized man securely inside the crate. He moaned. Had the chairman himself not been present Pankie would have sworn the man she was unstrapping was he.

"Distance?"

She checked the instruments. "Eight minutes, sir."

"Altitude?"

"Three hundred feet."

"Good. Very good."

They moved the chairman's double into the chair and pushed him up to the desk. Pankie took a hypodermic needle from her kit and jabbed it into his arm. The chairman watched closely, still not fully confident in his new aide. They carefully reset the front panel into position and pushed the crate back into the rear compartment, following it through the door and locking it. A video monitor mounted inside allowed them to see the office clearly.

"Five minutes, sir."

At the rear of their compartment a spherical vehicle eight feet in diameter rested on the floor like a huge ball bearing. Pankie pulled a flush-mounted handle down, opening the door to two cramped seats surrounded by equipment and gear. They each took a plastic oversuit from inside the sphere and pulled it over their clothing. The chairman stooped down and climbed through the opening, taking one of the seats. Pankie followed, pulling the tiny door shut behind her. They drifted back and forth in the seats, which were mounted on plastic springs. A small light popped on. Each pulled an oxygen unit over their heads and flipped the switch. Their voices were muted through the speaker system in the helmets.

"Time?"

"Three minutes twelve seconds."

"Good. Execute at exactly two minutes." He handed her a small key.

Pankie watched the digital clock count down to the mark. As double zeroes flicked on the tiny display she unlocked a small box mounted in the chamber wall. The chairman was pleased with her steadiness. Pankie pushed a button inside the box. Small motors whirred, and plastic foam flowed into the air space and expanded, holding their bodies secure and immobile. As the filling completed, a solenoid closed the tiny air vent. Other solenoids released pins holding the vehicle in place. They waited in the darkness.

Precisely on schedule, a small plane entered the ebony jet's flight path. Immediate evasive action was ordered by the escort commander. The pilot veered quickly to starboard, then back to port, decelerating and dropping to within fifty feet of the ocean surface. The maneuver took the jet out of the cube-like pattern formed by the escort guard.

Suddenly the small plane exploded, and for a few seconds the attention of all eight escort pilots was riveted on the unfurling orange and black fireball. Aft cargo bay doors on the jet swooshed open under the spherical vehicle. Fifty feet below, the icy Atlantic skimmed by at 340 knots. A burst of compressed air pushed the sphere through the opening and into the sea. It was visible less than one second. Flaming debris from the explosion peppered the rolling waters and camaflouged the sphere's splash. The waters closed over it and the jet's cargo doors slid together.

The sphere sank to a depth of thirty meters and then stablizied. Jet pumps activated and propelled them in a southwesterly direction at twenty knots. Inside, a nozzle sprayed chemicals which dissolved much of their foam prison. Pankie reached over and removed the last of the foam from the chairman's arms, very glad to have that part of the trip behind her. A small light winked on. The chairman blinked, and looked toward his aide.

"We have several hours until arrival, Miss Retson. I'm going to take a nap. I suggest you do the same."

It was bedlam on board the jet. Jack Trammel, the chairman's news secretary, had been sitting by the port window putting final touches on the chairman's Unification Symposium speech when he saw the small aircraft boring in on them. Max Crane leaned over Jack's small desk, peering through the window in amazement. Warning sirens hooted with a nerve-jarring shrillness which left no room for thought or speech. As the jet dove, Max fell over the desk and broke it. The other two aides were thrown against the compartment wall. As the plane veered to port, the scramble was repeated, and all four tumbeld across the compartment along with briefing books, notes, cups of coffee, and tape recorders.

"The chairman!" Jack shouted. He was on the floor against the starboard wall, his shirt torn and soaked with spilled coffee. Another aide lay heaped across his legs, unconscious. He pushed him away and struggled to his feet. Max jumped up at the same time, shoving a section of broken desk board from him. They rushed for the chairman's suite and burst into the office. They found him on the floor sprawled against the sofa. He looked up, dazed, and had difficulty focusing his eyes. They sprang to his side and helped him to his feet.

"Are you all right, sir?" Jack asked.

"The chairman stared at him vacantly, then spoke. "Help me to my desk."

Jack looked at Max. Something was definitely wrong.

"Help me, you idiots! Good, very good!"

They shrugged, and helped him to the chair.

Just then a flash burst outside the window followed by a loud "whump." The aides dropped to the floor, stunned at the sight of the fireball.

The chairman saw it too. He opened the desk drawer and pulled out a pistol, pointing it at his temple.

"This is the sign of my departure. There can be no world peace as long as there is resistance."

His aides looked at him, briefly immobilized. Then Jack sprang toward him, arm extended to grab the pistol as if reaching for a high pass ten years before on the university's football team. The gun fired a fraction of a second before he could grab it. The impact pushed the man's body over the side of the chair. Most of his head was gone. Jack fell, clutching the gun. Max watched in disbelief.

". . . . in spite of your objection we must go forward with the program. It's senseless to wait!"

"So you say, Milton, so you say," Bartholomew Ringgold countered.

The issue was funding for WOEC, an organization against which the head of the Zi'Hra Oil Complex had been staunchly opposed since its inception.

Milton Franklin looked to the Minister of Internal Affairs. "Mr. Acting Chairman, we've been at this for twenty minutes.

Dr. Ringgold, as usual, has yet to say anything of substance. I insist on a vote. Now!"

"Absolutely!" Luis Obiscon said impatiently, strongly supporting Franklin's demand. He had been one of the architects of WOEC, and intended that nothing should impede its development as a tool to consolidate and unify world values. Increased funding was, as far as he was concerned, essential. The Internal Affairs Minister looked toward Dr. Ringgold. The doctor shrugged.

"What can I say? It's a waste of money. But yes, let us vote. I have little time left before I must leave."

Ringgold had accomplished what he'd intended, which was to make it difficult to do anything in the Inner Circle which might benefit WOEC. It was a matter of personal honor. He knew each of the others' positions, and knew they would not change. The vote was taken — eight to one in favor. The acting chairman gavelled. "Passed, and recommended for action to the Cabinet." He took a sheaf of papers from the stack before him and passed them behind his chair to his clerk.

A red-faced page burst through the meeting room door and scrambled, breathless and frightened, behind the row of chairs to the Minister of Internal Affairs and acting chairman. Color drained from his face, and he trembled visibly. Smooth, Franklin thought. Absolutely smooth. The Minister touched his gavel to the table.

"Gentlemen," he began, struggling to overcome feigned shock. "Our chairman is dead."

The Inner Circle, stunned for just a moment, began clamoring for more information. The Minister gavelled order. "I'll read the bulletin, gentlemen." The members quieted.

> "At 02:36 Eastern Standard Time, the Chairman of the World Alliance was found shot to death in his jet en route to the Unification Symposium. Two of his aides have called it suicide. The jet was approached by a light aircraft which exploded shortly before an apparent collision. The plane is now on

the ground at Whistler AFB. Region and United States officials are investigating. -end-"

There was little grief. The chairman had led the organization since its founding. A consummate statesman and master politician, he had used his considerable power with a skill sufficient to emerge in the early days as the undisputed authority. But it was a role maintained by shifting coalition power, subtle intimidation, and ruthless action. Such a man is born into the world perhaps once a generation. When this one died, whatever mourning took place told of the vacuum his departure had created and of the disruptions surely to come. Little thought was given to the man himself.

The chaos predicted by the late chairman developed quickly. Circle members came and went from the conference room, checking with aides, issuing emergency directives, redrawing lines of defense and parochial alliances which had been diminished only by years of relentless work toward world consensus.

The World Alliance constitution called for election of a new chairman by the Inner Circle and from the Inner Circle, with ratification by the Cabinet. When the Circle finally reconvened the acting chairman had had corridor discussions with five of the members, working to cement Milton Franklin's ascendency to power. Three agreed, and two hedged. With Franklin, they had four of nine votes. Each member voted electronically. When the last ballot was cast, results flashed immediately on the videoscreen. Three were for Anton Jedesky, WOEC Chairman. Four were for Milton Franklin. One was for Bartholemew Ringgold, and there was one abstention.

"We have two candidates. Statements, please."

"There are three of us, not two," Ringgold interrupted.

"Thre are two, Dr. Ringgold. One vote does not make a candidate." The acting chairman's voice was cold.

"That is not true! Any vote . . ." But Ringgold was shouted down.

Statements were made and issues debated until well into the evening, finally recessing until the next morning. None of them slept. It was a night of negotiation, power bartering, and coalition-forming. By midnight over two hundred advisors, executives and beholden officials had joined them, and the process of ascension to and descension from power was well underway. Loyalties of armies were traded that night like tokens on a gigantic game board. Vested interests in billions of dollars shifted, new national and regional government structures were created, selected leaders were marked for elimination and loyal underlings were negotiated into critical new roles. Friends were found, enemies made, leverages discovered and applied. When they reconvened at eleven o'clock the next morning news networks from all over the world ringed the World Alliance headquarters complex, Lilliputians capturing their Gulliver with thousands of strands of electronic cable. Two squadrons of police monitors were needed to maintain order.

They met again, swollen-eyed and exhausted, with new global rules and relationships forged and steaming in the residual heat of their creation. In the adjoining meeting hall the Cabinet awaited the Inner Circle vote.

Most of Milton Franklin's power came through his acting cabinet post and his alliance with the Minister of the Interior. They had four of the six votes required before they began ... a fact used often throughout the long and intense night. The balloting was quick and decisive. Negotiations were over, and it was time to get on with it. Each had gained most of what they'd wanted and given up what they believed they could afford. Already the leadership of the late chairman was a relic of the past, a matter to be relegated to a portrait to hang in the Great Lobby of World Alliance Headquarters.

Milton Franklin won with seven votes. He'd given up much more to gain victory than he might have had he really believed the chairman was dead.

Chapter 26

"The city seems almost normal," Em said, driving with Gabe along Northern Boulevard. They turned the corner into Binzoe, soon arriving at the vacant lot by the dry-cleaning plant. Ben came up as they pulled alongside the curb and climbed quickly into the car, glad to be out of the bitter cold air.

"The adventure continues," he said, shaking Em's hand and patting Gabe on the shoulder. "Where's Debbie?"

"We're meeting her at the airport."

"Delightful woman, isn't she," Gabe remarked.

"Not only that — I think she's opening up a little more to God." Ben spoke hopefully, his arms hanging over the front seat to better talk with Gabe and Em. "Hope there's enough time left."

At the autotrack entrance Gabe paid the toll and glided into the access lane. He released the wheel and they accelerated smoothly to 110 miles an hour, guided along the arrow-straight roadway by imbedded cables. Ben's eyes widened, never having been on the track before, as the countryside flew past them. At the airport turnoff they eased into the exit lane and back into manual control. Minutes later they had parked and were inside, walking through the huge domed terminal to the Quintair ticket counter.

"There she is." Gabe pointed toward a woman talking with two men. They saw that she was distressed, and quickened their pace.

Debbie saw them approach and was astonished. The men with her paled, and walked quickly away. Halfway across the polished terminal floor, looking back over their shoulders, they broke into a trot, and then into a dead run. One tumbled over a potted tree and fell. The other disappeared down an escalator ramp. His companion scrambled to his feet and limped after him.

Debbie stared at her friends as they joined her. "How — how did you do that?" she stammered, looking as if a miracle had happened. "Those two huge men just behind you — where are they?"

"Debbie, what did those fellows want from you?" Gabe asked, seeming to ignore her amazement.

"They said they were doing a routine check. They looked at my passport and told me it was invalid! And . . . oh no! They still have it!"

Ben realized what had happened. 'He shall give his angels charge over thee . . .' The passage settled gently into his thoughts, as it had often since that day many years ago when he was new to the Binzoe District. God had shown him just how true His promises are. He'd been surrounded by a street gang like an antelope surrounded by jackals. As they'd approached with knives in hand, they'd suddenly froze, stunned and frightened, staring above Ben's head. They dropped their weapons and ran. Astonished, Ben turned around. There were two huge beings towering over him. Each was massively formed, barechested, and wore a short jewel-studded garment and sandals. They exuded enormous power. He was so overcome that he fell to the ground. "Do not be afraid, Benjamin," one of them had rumbled. "God has revealed us so you may walk in peace and serve in glory." They disappeared then, leaving in their place the faintest trace of a sweet and pure aroma. Ben sensed that same sweet aroma now. As he savored what had happened, he felt prompted to speak.

"Debbie, your passport may be in your purse."

"Ben, it isn't! I distinctly remember handing it to . . ."

"Look in your purse."

"Do you think I'm losing my mind?"

Ben waited, serene and confident.

"I'll show you!" She popped her purse open and rummaged impatiently through its contents. Suddenly she stopped, and slowly pulled her passport out.

"How did you know?" Her question was soft and insistent. Gabe and Em were as amazed as she was.

"The Lord told me," he said simply.

"Oh Ben," she said, with friendly disdain. But she was mystified, somehow, knowing Ben's answer was true.

"The ways of men must be understood to be believed — the ways of God must be believed to be understood. Pascal." Ben smiled as he quoted. Debbie's eyes widened even more. "I do a lot of reading," he said, shrugging.

Their flight was announced and they hurried to the departure gate, passing by the potted tree one of the men had tumbled over. A small amount of dirt circled the pot on the polished floor. That part was real, anyhow, Debbie thought. She determined to find out more.

" 'In the last days I will pour out my Spirit . . .' " Gabe whispered. Em nodded, trying to keep his shorter legs moving with the rest of them. Ben moved with strong even strides, smiling in joy, looking far, far beyond the distant end of the corridor.

They landed with the sun high in a cloudless Middle Eastern sky, baking the clay of the old city and the concrete of the new as it had for millenia. They felt a strange tension as they cleared customs. Baggage in hand, they made their way through the heavy crowds of the New Jerusalem airport and out to the taxi stand.

"Mrs. Ames?" A uniformed chauffeur approached and nodded courteously. "Welcome to Jerusalem. I will take you to your hotel."

Debbie smiled, pleased, and certain now that Michael had received her cable.

"Who are you?" Gabe asked. Debbie noticed his concern.

The chauffeur bowed, but asked, "You, sir, are?"

"My name is Gabriel Diehl. These two gentlemen and I are travelling with Mrs. Ames."

The chauffeur seemed distressed. "Ah. I am so sorry. I was instructed to pick only Mrs. Ames up."

"Who instructed you?" Em demanded, piqued.

The chauffeur thrust his chest out with pride, gesturing toward a black limousine parked nearby. The World Alliance insignia, a golden hooded falcon within a wreath of purple, was emblazoned on the door.

"Thanks anyhow, friend," Ben snorted. "We'll take a taxi."

"Of course, sir." The chauffeur reached for Debbie's bag. Ben's large hand gripped the chauffeur's arm. "You don't understand, friend. We're together."

The chauffeur looked at him with resignation. "Very well, sir." He pulled a small whistle from his pocket and blew it. Police materialized and surrounded them. Though they spoke in Hebrew, Gabe understood. This had been prearranged. The police sergeant turned to Gabe. "The three of you are under arrest. Accompany me please."

"Wait!" Debbie pleaded. "There must be a misunderstanding!"

"If you please, Mrs. Ames . . . . now?" The chauffeur and one of the police escorted her forcefully to the limousine. The others were taken to a van waiting at the other end of the terminal building. They knew they were in trouble — it all had happened too easily. Gabe had an idea. "You want to be Paul or Silas, Em?" he said. Em's worried frown eased. Ben clapped his hands on their shoulders and smiled. "Great idea!"

They began to sing, and their harmony drifted through the crowded arrival area. The police watched in disbelief. They were marked men who had been under surveillance since their attempt to stop them from boarding had been thwarted.

"Do you think it is only by interfering with the limousine that they were arrested?" one of the police walking alongside Gabe whispered to another. The other shrugged. " I wouldn't want to be arrested by order of the World Alliance, I'll tell you," the first one whispered again. Gabe heard and understood. He sang louder.

The limo weaved in and out of lanes flowing with cars, buses, and trucks, pre-empting all vehicles and traffic signals as it sped toward the El Shar Resort Hotel. Debbie was worried, but she was also fascinated at the bustling sights of New Jerusalem. The honking traffic, people thronging the sidewalk marts, and noises and smells of the busy city consumed her attention. Before long they were out of the congestion and speeding along a narrow country road.

"I thought the hotel was in Jerusalem!" Debbie shouted.

The driver nudged the wheel to swerve around several sheep grazing next to the road. He did not reply. Debbie sat back into the plush rear seat, folding her arms in irritation.

"There, Mrs. Ames. El Shar." He pointed as they approached a beautiful series of villas set into the Judean hillside. They stopped under billowing multicolored canvas canopies which shielded the main entrance from the bright sun. A tanned man in a white suit waited, opening the door as the limousine glided to a stop. He bowed and offered his hand.

"Welcome, Mrs. Ames. We hope your stay will be pleasant."

Debbie looked uncertainly at her unknown host. He held her hand and looked deeply into her eyes until she pulled her arm away, somewhat flustered.

"I am Ingomar Hammock." He snapped his fingers. Nearby porters took her suitcases into the lobby. Ing touched her arm lightly, motioning her to follow.

Debbie was dazzled by the splendid lobby interior. Fountains and waterfalls circled a cavernous open area and continued up and along the hills, connecting each villa to the others with sparkling waters and lush plant growth. Soft music — a lute, she thought — floated mysteriously in the air.

"The tram will take you to your suite. Please join us for dinner at . . ."

"Mr. Hammock," she said, shaking off his hypnotic gaze. "Why am I here, and where is my husband?"

Ing flashed his most charming smile. "Perhaps you would join me for a cocktail? I'll be delighted to explain everything."

Debbie's anger erupted, and she was about to unravel the mystery right then and there when a distant rumbling drumroll, like thunder, sounded. Ing looked up, and seemed surprised.

"What was that?"

"Thunder, perhaps? I don't know."

Another drumroll reverberated, and then another. Debbie's eyes widened. "That's gunfire, Mr. Hammock!"

"Please. 'Ing,' if you don't mind."

"That is gunfire! Look, I want answers and I want them now!"

Ing reached for her arm again. Debbie pulled away. "Forgive me, Mrs. Ames. We mean no offense. Let us not disturb the other guests, shall we? You must have many questions..."

"You've got that right, mister!" Her eyes sparked with anger.

"Of course. Please, come with me. I'll explain everything." Ing made his way toward the lobby bar. She had no choice but to follow. The frequency of the distant gunfire increased. Ing motioned for a waiter. Debbie sat down, miffed and confused. Two cream-colored drinks were set on the glass table between them, each with a pineapple slice perched on the rim of the goblet.

"May I call you Debbie?" he asked soothingly.

She nodded impatiently.

"Debbie, I can assure you that your husband is quite safe."

"Why am I not permitted to see him? And why am I apparently expected to take the word of a perfect stranger?" She spoke coldly, as frustrated as she was angry.

Ing pulled an envelope from the inside pocket of his jacket. "Here. This will help you understand." Debbie tore it open and pulled a sheet of linen stationery out. It bore the insignia of the World Alliance, and was in Michael's handwriting.

Deb —
I'm involved in much more than I'd first realized. It's all Secret Priority so couldn't contact you. I'm okay. What we're doing is important. I love you and I miss you. We'll celebrate soon.
Mij

"Is everything all right?"

Debbie sensed that he was studying her. She forced a sigh of relief. Two explosions came in quick succession. They sounded closer. She jumped. "What is going on, Mr. Hammock?" Her words were tinged with fear.

"You're here for your safety as well as for reasons of security, as you might surmise from your husband's note."

"Oh, so you've read it too." Her eyes flashed her indignation.

"Please," Ing said sheepishly. "All secret materials must be screened. It's nothing personal. There has been considerable unrest along sections of the Russian border. We learned that an attack on Israel was likely."

Debbie remembered speculation in the news about such a possibility during the last few days. She held her silence.

"As for who I am," Ing continued, 'I am with the World Alliance, a special liaison to your husband's assignment. We learned of your plans to see him. Please understand our position. His work cannot be interrupted or distracted in any way, particularly by his beautiful wife. We tried to prevent your having to make the trip."

"You mean those . . . those gorillas were yours? Phony passenger checks — you'd better come up with an explanation of that little antic, Mr. Hammock!"

Ing accepted the chastisement. "You're right. Our people were instructed to act with courtesy and honesty. We blew it, and I apologize."

Debbie was mollified.

"In any event, having failed there, we had to bring you here. The least we can do is make your stay comfortable. If you wish to return home we'll drive you back to the airport tomorrow. If you decide to stay —" Ing gestured to reinforce the plush comfort of El Shar — "we'll be honored to accommodate you as our guest. Your husband is engaged in an assignment which will bring you a lifetime of pride. Bear with us until it is completed."

Debbie's hostility drained away under his smooth words. Weariness replaced tension. A smile crossed her lips, and she felt guilty about her moments of resentment at Michael's lack of contact. At least, judging by his note, he'd wanted to.

"All right, Mr. Hammock. I'll cooperate. But I'm certainly not convinced." She sipped her drink, a delightfully exotic fruit-like concoction with a faint taste of almond.

"I'm sure you won't be disappointed."

Debbie's eyes narrowed. "Now, why were my three friends arrested? Would you please get them out of whatever mess you've gotten them into?"

Ing's eyes widened in surprise. "Friends? You didn't travel alone?"

"Stop it, Mr. Hammock."

Ing looked hurt. In spite of the obvious logic of her conclusion, she felt badly. 'Could he really not know?' she wondered.

"Debbie, give me their names. We'll look into it immediately."

The distant gunfire erupted with new ferocity.

"Ben . . . I don't know his last name." She felt foolish. "And Gabriel Diehl, and Emerson Prantzer."

Ing wrote the names in a pocket notebook. "Don't worry. We'll find out what happened." He smiled confidently.

She felt extremely tired, and somewhat woozy. Ing was looking for the signs. "You must be exhausted. May I help you to your suite?"

She stood, holding the back of the divan for support, and steadied herself. "No, thank you. I'll find my own way. Goodbye."

"For now, Debbie. Rest well."

"Yes." She took a few wobbling steps, then turned back. "Where's my room?" Ing took her arm. "Come with me to the tram. It will take you there." Minutes later Debbie was inside her room, sprawled on the huge round bed in a sound, lightly drugged sleep.

Chapter 27

The Russian attack on that fateful Monday centered on Haifa, the important coastal city on the western shores of Isarel, and on the Gulf of Hormuz to the east, through which vital supplies of oil moved daily on tankers and through the Trans Eastern pipeline. Differing opinions and heated debate over the reasons behind the attack raged in the offices and the halls of governments throughout the world. Some believed Russia had acted as part of a long range World Alliance strategic plan. These paid no great attention to the armed aggression, expecting a quick end and few casualties. Others believed Russia had acted unilaterally, and that the unprovoked offensive signalled the end of an unstable relationship with World Alliance unification policies, and the precursor of more aggressions against other nations. These officials advocated massive counter-attack.

Isarel was well-prepared. Although they had incurred damage from the recent three day Pan-Arabic attack, they nevertheless readied themselves for a probable imminent assault from the north, and their defense against the aggression was formidable.

During these years war was the rule, not the exception. Military actions which once might have prompted powerful outcries now resulted in little more tham empty threats of retaliation. An entire generation were strangers to military peace. Priorities had shifted from determination to avoid global holocaust to a twisted sort of gratitude that hostilities were not any worse. The Russian attack on Israel was deplored, of course. But so many other military actions were in progress that it failed to be front-page headlines in most of the North American Region's newspapers.

As far as Milton Franklin was concerned the timing could not have been worse. At World Alliance Headquarters the truth of the invasion was known — and feared. New Russia was part of the World Alliance in name only, encouraging its unification efforts to consolidate the enemies of their purposes into one global force which they would then deal with in one massive initiative.

As pride is the strongest self-worship, so sophistry is the greatest naivete. The World Alliance had convinced itself by its own propaganda that it was as powerful as it needed to be, that the ability to conquer rabbits at will meant the fox was also easy prey. The truth was quite different.

In Geneva, Franklin had been working around the clock finalizing plans for Christian persecution in accordance with the "late" chairman's orders. The persecution would be no series of hastily conceived actions, but the rapid execution of programs carefully laid out months before. As an Inner Circle member, that annoying realization shook his confidence. He wondered what else might be in the works of the inscrutably complicated world bureaucracy for which he now had responsibility.

The strain of his schedule, the need to consolidate his power, and the lack of sleep and sustinence were starting to affect the new chairman. Judgment began to lose its honed edge, gruffness yielded to rancor, and emotional release became the easier pathway to action than rationality and discipline. It had never crossed his mind to retain his hold on power. But that opportunity was a major flaw in the Omega Plan. The real chairman was, during these crucial six days, wholly dependent upon others to carry out the plan as prescribed. If Michael Ames did not bring him back into life and world leadership when he appeared as the returned Christ, it would be the end of him. Of course the chairman-in-hiding had people who would go to any length to insure that this gap was not exploited. But there were those with other persuasions, and the risk was large. Now, in the daze of a moment's rest, the thought did occur to Milton Franklin. It seemed far too easy, far too simplistic, to be possible. The chairman was bound to have the bases covered. Still . . . . Franklin felt new energy. He drained his coffee cup, and stored the possibility in the back of his mind.

The Middle Eastern sector force commander entered silently and waited for the signal to speak. Franklin nodded.

"They just landed, sir."

"Good. See that Mrs. Ames is comfortable. Be sure Hammock is ready. Arrest the others. I don't care what you do — just get that statement signed. Keep them alive. They're going to be examples, and their fate will encourage their kind to give up this stupid resistance without more bloodshed. Understand?"

"Sir!" The commander turned quickly and left.

Aides, advisors, and cabinet members streamed into the office for the next meeting. Franklin sighed, rubbing his eyes, and lit a fresh cigar. He hoped this one would resolve the last issue of the persecution. It would begin Tuesday morning.

The chairman sat in his private office at the Nexa Inn, working at his ornately inlaid Louis XIV desk. It was late at night. The glow of the fireplace and the small tortoise shell desk lamp focused on the papers before him, cast dim flickering light over the walnut wall panels and silk tapestries. Communications equipment had been humming ever since his arrival late that afternoon. He and Pankie had endured their strange voyage without mishap, other than a faulty heater. Their journey ended when they were pulled through underwater doors in the hull of the converted whaling vessel and flown by helicopter to the Nexa. A steaming shower and hot meal eased the strains and tensions of his aging body. Bulletins and video reports indicating the success of the ruse had lifted his spirits. It was all working according to plan. "Good, very good," he finally said, handing the latest bulletin back to Pankie. She poured a snifter of brandy for him.

"Will there be anything else, sir?"

"Not tonight, Miss Retson."

"Good night then, sir." Pankie glided through the long, darkened room, her gown flowing like gossamer, and disappeared into the bedrooms. The chairman adjusted the reading lamp and resumed his work.

An hour later he heard the muffled clacking of the bedroom communications printer, and Pankie burst into the study clutching a bulletin. He looked up with a discomforting adrenalin, instantly alert. She handed him the news of the attack on Israel. His eyes scanned the document. Beyond a slight sag of his shoulders he made no visible response. It was a long time before he spoke.

"Thank you, Miss Retson. That will be all."

Pankie was startled when he looked up. He seemed to have aged years in these few motionless moments, and his voice had the tone of defeat. She nodded and left, closing the door softly behind her. Few knew how deeply he felt the hatred which Soviet intransigence and dissension against the World Alliance had created in him over the years. He feared no other man on earth — but he greatly feared the possibility of disruption of the delicate fabric he had woven. He did not expect the attack with the Soviets spread so thin already across several fronts. They had more to gain by holding at least to the form of unification. He'd seen it in Kossovsky's eyes again and again, a greedy man whose appetite had been whetted by the spoils of World Alliance cooperation. Too much was at stake to allow the slightest risk to exist. But in this case, the chairman could only seek to contain and understand the subtleties of the risks involved. Given the tradition of Soviet unpredictability, the risks could not go away. Rational evaluation yielded only one answer: they would not attack. But what if something irrational happened — something which upset the sensitive balance of interests and power upon which the World Alliance strategy was based?

He stared through the paper in his hand and suddenly saw his vision, his dreams, and his work crumble. To the world it was one more invasion. For the chairman it was the end. He was convinced now that they would not stop at the coast but would push into Jerusalem and take it apart brick by brick. Omega was doomed. With that, he was out of power — in fact, out of life. The realization that he, the most powerful man on earth, now faced the likelihood of being powerless weighed on him like a millstone. He'd planned foolishly because he had planned risk without adequate containment. That knowledge hammered against him and defeated him. He had made a fatal miscalculation.

He poured another brandy, feeling strangely lightheaded. His legs wobbled and he slumped back in his chair. He tried to call out but could barely hear his own words. Thumping pain exploded in his chest. The light darkened and fragmented into tiny pieces. The room spun, and then he was looking at the ceiling far, far away. Finally it turned black.

Em Prantzer leaned in a corner of the fetid cell rubbing his knee, clenching his teeth against the pain. He'd been thrown into the cell by two guards, twisting his legs as he tumbled to the dirt floor. The air was cold, and evil-smelling vapors hung about the walls, seeming to deny even the simple freedom to breathe.

A wooden stick clanged along the steel bars of the cell. Em shrank back into the corner as the two guards reappeared. While one continued to beat the bars, the other, a huge man with large-muscled arms, held Gabe Diehl off the ground by the back of his shirt. He hung limply as if in a sling, and his face was covered with blood and bruises. They opened the rusting iron door and pushed the unconscious preacher inside.

"Slap 'im a little, old man. He'll wake up." They slammed the cell door, laughing as they disappeared down the hallway.

Em shuffled over to Gabe, every move accompanied by stabs of pain, and felt the pulse in his neck. He looked around the cell. The only water lay yellowish and stagnant in a dented metal bowl, a film of oily dirt on the surface. He propped Gabe's head on his lap, praying over him, barely able to stand the pain in his knee. A guard appeared again, now bending the arm of a very conscious Ben Crockett in a tight hammerlock. Ben looked steadfastly ahead, expressionless.

The door clanged open and he was shoved inside. His large frame lessened the force of the guard's heavy hand, and he was able to hold his balance and avoid stumbling into the others.

Ben examined Gabe quickly. "He'll be fine. The Lord gave him a hard head."

"Yes." Em winced.

"You okay?"

"Twisted my knee when they shoved me in here."

Ben's jaw stiffened.

Gabe moaned, and his eyes fluttered open. He sat up slowly and peered around the dark cell. "Lousy hotel. We could have done better."

"Not on a pastor's wages," Em said, chuckling with relief.

They sat in silence, each with his own thoughts. They were alive and together — that was a start. A small opening in the wall about twelve feet above the floor offered the only light. Plaster and grime hung in cobwebbed straggles, and a small bench and the metal water bowl were the only two objects in the cell.

"What happened, Gabe?" Ben asked the question softly.

"They wanted me to sign a statement." He saw their concern. "Now is the pastor of the Lord Jesus going to sign something endorsing WOEC? Is that a seemly thing to do?"

They were aware enough of what Gabe had been through. Now they both hugged him in support. "God keep you strong, brother," Em said hoarsely.

"There'll be another round," Gabe said simply. "They won't stop until they get it. They're in an awful hurry though."

Ben's statement was simple and straightforward: "We need to pray." They knelt down on the straw-strewn dirt and put their hands on each other's shoulders as if forming a football huddle. The pains of their injuries were ignored. After a time, Gabe was moved to speak.

"Great and glorious God, You are true and perfect to your word. By Your word the devil will cast some of us into prison. And by Your word in all things we can rejoice because of You. Now we do so. We ask for wisdom to recognize Your will and strength to follow Your lead. Protect Debbie and Michael. Guide us to them."

Distant rumblings of heavy gunfire echoed outside. They continued. "We await Your perfect timing for our release from this cell, believing it is to be so. Even so, Lord, we ask by the power of Jesus for speedy deliverance. There are things to be done."

The cell had not changed and their bodies ached. But in their hearts a lifting spirit of victorious joy crushed the fears and worries which had been seeping into them like water invading a leaky bucket. They began to sing a hymn. The gunfire seemed to increase in intensity. They sang louder. Soon heavy footsteps thumped down the hallway. The guard rapped his nightstick on the cell bars. He was livid.

"No noise! What'sa matter with you?" he roared, banging his club in a deafening metallic din. "I'm gonna break your arms!" He fumbled with his keys, then shoved one into the lock.

The squeak of rusting hinges and the shrill whine of something far overhead came at the same time. The angry guard lunged toward them, his club raised. In the next moment the cell exploded in dust and debris, and an earsplitting explosion hurled them against the wall.

Quietness gradually returned. Huddled against the wall, they opened their eyes and tried to see through the swirling smoke. It seemed much lighter. They looked up and saw only open, early evening sky above the smoke and dust. Panicky shouts and roaring automobiles squealing through the street just outside signalled pandemonium from the close impact of the shell. Slanted shafts of fading light made bluish-grey streaks in the smoke.

The guard lay spread-eagle on the floor of the cell with a large piece of concrete resting on his still chest. A pool of blood leaked out from under him and made a dark widening stain in the dirt. Carefully they stepped over the knee-high remnant of the cell wall and into the street.

"Passports!" Gabe said, suddenly remembering. He stumbled back through the cell and into the jail office. He pushed debris off the desk and pulled the drawer open. All three passports were there, along with their precious envelope of cash. He was surprised to find the envelope intact — then realized he should not have been. He grabbed their belongings up and ran back to the street to join the others. Alive, free and anonymous in the fear-crazed crowds, they made their way toward the outskirts of Jerusalem. No words were necessary.

Chapter 28

The Omega team was lodged in a small inn on the northwest edge of Old Jerusalem. Hotel Mischa was chosen not only because it faced the Tower of the Ascension square but because it was secure against possible danger. The walls were constructed of rock and clay, ten feet thick at the base and six feet thick at first floor level. There were several accesses from the first floor down into underground passageways which networked beneath the hills of the city, passageways for ancient aqueducts, catacombs, and more recently carved escape routes and connecting tunnels. Major O'Keefe, the Omega team leader, estimated that the Mischa could withstand many direct hits from most non-nuclear artillery before crumbling. It would, if necessary, provide a vital margin of time to escape underground until any possible danger had run its course.

Tuesday morning, the entire team gathered in the briefing room for their first review of the Omega Plan final section. Distant explosions of shells turning the Judean soil between Jerusalem and the seacoast into a vast dusty crater field seemed to be a constant companion.

Michael's bandages were removed just before the briefing. Physically the surgery had been successful. Psychologically there was a casualty — Michael's self-identity. It was a casualty the World Alliance had counted on. The more their counterfeit Christ could be separated from himself, the less likely his personal values, habits, and practices would impede the fulfillment of his role. Intensive psychological pressure, a mentally exhausting work pace, and the trauma of physical change were the tools used to maximize Michael's utility to the World Alliance cause.

In a small room down the hall he inspected his new appearance. Much resembled the Michael of old. But much did not. He had an eerie, lost feeling deep inside as he studied the man in the mirror. He passed the fingers of his familiar hand over the contours of a strange face. Though he was recognizable, it was not really himself upon whom he looked. It was someone else.

The surgeon was prepared for the crisis. Before the inevitable depression came, Michael was escorted down the corridor and into the briefing room. The Omega Team applauded and cheered, long and in earnest, as soon as he entered. Michael slowly responded. It required but half an hour of attention and adulation to restabilize and shake off the onset of immobilizing psychological shock. When he began to joke with some of them the doctor gave a brief signal to Major O'Keefe and left the room. The crisis was past. Michael was theirs.

Even the major was impressed with the lean, handsome man in the front row of chairs, tanned from the Middle Eastern sun, brown hair long enough to take on more the look of tousled countryside strength and freedom than the mid-city businessman's trim. So that is to be the man, Jesus Christ. The major stared at him, amazed with the change.

He rapped his swagger stick on the podium. "Tomorrow it begins. Four days of world-shaking events. Sunday at one o'clock —" he pointed the stick at Michael — "the Christ returns."

The room was silent now as the best the World Alliance could find in their fields concentrated on the mission.

"We'll review the miracles now. After lunch we'll rehearse the return scene, step by step. Be ready. We've had the entire section surrounding the square evacuated and cordoned off.

Hawk informed me at breakfast that the area was secure. You could run around out there today stark naked and nobody would know. Kris, you're on."

The special effects director, George Kristofer, came to the front of the room and took the swagger stick from the major. "As you know, the point of these miracles is to focus world attention here, and qualify Omega's return as valid in the minds of the target group, the Christians. There'll be a few spectaculars, but most of the events will be mind games. Mass psychology applied on a global scale. Tomorrow you'll hear a Voice from the sky speaking an unknown language. It will be audible all over the globe. The WOEC Visgate, Anton Jedesky, will publicly interpret this Global Voice. By nightfall the Voice and Jedesky's translation will be front-page headline material. Thursday, the Voice will return and confirm the intepretation. That will hit prime news time for most of the day."

"Tell us how this will happen!" Becker Simpson interrupted. Her eyes sparkled with excitement. She knew very well how the mechanics would work. As the Omega Team's chief psychoanalyst and lieutenant commander, she had been its architect. But she wanted the others to hear it.

Kristofer grinned. "It's based on the common dish antenna. Under proper conditions those dishes can reflect audible sounds as well as high frequency audio/video signals. We'll broadcast the Voice simultaneously from all five primary communications satellites. There are eighty million of those little dishes around the world. The signal will turn each dish into a giant speaker. No matter where you are, you'll hear these words three times: PELEM THRASHA ZIM BILDRAYAN."

"What does it mean?" Michael asked, fascinated.

Kristofer pointed at him, peering directly into his eyes. "It's gibberish. But Jedesky will interpret this: 'Make Ready The Way Of The Lord.' " Michael looked down, unaccountably shivering.

"Keep going," the major growled, checking his watch. Kristofer nodded.

"The Bible provides a good road map. Fortunately. It says that four horses will come in the end times, each bringing a different disaster to the earth. So, white horses will ride into every battle zone on the globe. That's sixty-six wars at last count, folks, including the one the Russians started up yesterday. Those horses will stand on the side designated as the conqueror."

Several hands shot up. 'At least they're listening,' Kristopher thought grimly. "I know, you're going to ask me how we know. The fact is, folks, that all but two of these wars are scripted and controlled by the World Alliance. Studio wrestling on a larger scale." He looked pointedly at one of the team members who showed shock at the revelation. "I needn't say it of course — but just for the record you never heard that. And if I find out anyone in this rooms leaks that information I'll have you skinned alive. Literally."

"Talk, Kris," O'Keefe prompted. "We haven't got all day."

"The enemy armies will capitulate within hours of the horses' arrival," Kris continued. "The battle count will drop to almost zero. Watch the front pages on that one. But the peace will only last a day. On Thursday red horses will appear. Wars ended on Wednesday will be rekindled, more fiercely than before. As soon as world hopes soar, the red horse will crush them."

There were no questions.

"Black horses will strike the world economy on Friday. Hundreds of them will swarm through every financial trading center. Simultaneously certain of the wealthy nations will withdraw their funds from countries which have been resistant or disruptive to World Alliance objectives. The world economy is tottering as it is. That action alone will force most of our detractors into insolvency. And there's more, which I won't detail now."

The Omega team was silent, realizing even more the magnitude and deadly nature of their mission. Kristofer ticked off quick descriptions of events to be deliberately unleashed on a scarred and unsuspecting population. The initial excitement had yielded to a grave and somber feeling.

Michael had been listening, absorbing, thinking. The more he heard the more trapped he felt and the more he yearned for a way of escape. It was a helpless, terrifying sensation. "That brings us to Saturday. Let's see . . ." Kristofer scanned his notes . . . "meteor and fire showers, locust swarms, mountain shift . . . yes, this one is especially good." He grinned in an odd way and his eyes seemed to sparkle with insane mischief. "Mount Etna will be lost on Saturday. It will be blown up, and will slide into the ocean."

They stared at the special effects director, stunned at the awesomeness of what he'd said.

"The whole mountain? You can actually blow up a whole mountain?" The electronics specialist spoke as if dazed.

"The whole mountain, yes. We'll be using nuclear for this one. Fifty microblasts around the base and seventy from inside. Absorption shields are in place now and will activate with the blast. Danger from radiation is zilch."

Major O'Keefe stepped forward, holding his hand up. "We'll break for lunch — we've got a video conference with the new World Alliance chairman in an hour. Be in the communications room in forty minutes."

The team shuffled left in twos and threes, buzzing with discussion. Michael sat alone, deeply disturbed. This was the first time he'd heard specifics outside of his own direct involvement and was convinced that his associates were stark crazy. His head ached. Professor Schmidt squeezed into the next desk chair and leaned over to him, speaking in a conspiratorial whisper. "Iss vunderbar, huh Omenka?"

Michael looked at him, expressionless. "It's madness, Professor."

"Shhh!" The professor arched his eyebrows and held his finger over his lips. "Omenka, do not say dos tings! Not to worry, nien! It vill vork! I feel it here." He thumped his chest. "Omenka, listen. You know der new chairenstassen . . . presidentske, ya? Vatever. He iss Herr Franklin, ya, who you know goot?"

Michael nodded. "Ya. Vell now he iss der chairenstassen. Ven you see him on der blinkenscreen you must not say his namen, understand? Nien! Never ever say der namen of der chairenstassen in public. Okay Omenka?" The professor's expression was deadly earnest.

Michael did not understand why, but he understood what. "Hokay boss. I no speak der namenschlisselgravensportung."

"Ach, you mock me. Vait till your name iss in lightzenglimmer. Den ve see who it iss you tank very much."

Michael smiled. Of all the team, he liked the professor best. "Okay, I tank you now, professor. Let's eatenheimer."

"Ya, ya, goot, Omenka." They walked out of the room and down the hall to the cafeteria.

Chapter 29

Gray early light streamed in through the leaded glass windows. The six o'clock wake-up call seemed to come only moments after Pankie had tumbled exhausted onto the bed. The chairman's video conference with Milton Franklin was the only communication he had planned while in hiding. Preparation for the highly secret call were complex but effective. It would be impossible to detect, let alone trace.

She rolled out of bed and took a cold, brisk shower. As she dressed, a soft knock sounded at the door. A waiter rolled two breakfast settings into the bedroom, silver covers steaming and hot cinnamon coffee enlivening the stale bedroom air. He sampled each dish and beverage. It was standard security procedure. Satisfied, she dismissed him.

"Mr. Chairman?" Pankie called, rapping on the door between their bedrooms. There was no sound. She rapped again without response, then punched the unlock code into the key pad and peeked inside. Clean white sheets and a beige blanket bearing the Nexa coat of arms were stretched smoothly over the mattress, unused. A twinge of anxiety pulsed through her. "Mr. Chairman?" She stepped across the plush carpet, checking the bathroom and closet, then paused at the door to his private office, remembering his instructions to bring breakfast at exactly 6:05. She glanced at her watch — it read 6:08. She pushed the door open and walked in. Legs flat on the floor poked out beyond the Louis XIV desk. The small tortoise shell lamp was still on. She rushed over with a surge of panic. The chairman's lifeless robed body sprawled on the Basque carpet, one arm bent awkwardly under him. The bulletin she'd delivered to him the night before lay on the floor nearby.

Pankie thought rapidly. 'How do I contact Franklin before the eight o'clock video conference — the Nexa manager! No. Oh what will this do the plans — Briggs!' She ran to the phone, intent on getting the news of the chairman's death to someone. Charlie was as good as anyone to get her off the hook. The receiver was halfway to her ear when her thinking cleared. She hung up quickly. In the Nexa communications room the 'In Use' light on the chairman's private line blinked on. The two duty technicians were busy disputing the outcome of next Sunday's Superbowl. The light blinked off again, unnoticed.

It dawned on Pankie that she was the only one who knew of the chairman's actual death. No one else expected to see him before Sunday afternoon except Milton Franklin, on the videoscreen, in an hour and a half. Her pulse pounded with new excitement. She evaluated the situation carefully, examining every possibility. Ames appears on Sunday. Then he calls the chairman back to life. Nothing happens — he's dead. Nothing happens! Pankie laughed at the immense absurdity. Franklin calls in 90 minutes. I can't be here with a dead chairman . . . She slapped her hand against her leg, the course of action suddenly clear. Assuming she could trick Franklin during the video conference she could act as surrogate chairman of the World Alliance for a few days. The opportunity, even if temporary, overcame her sense of risk. She grabbed a note pad and began working out the details.

An hour later the body was in its bed, caked with Pankie's make-up to mask the hue of death. Thin cords cut from the draperies were attached to his arms and legs, running under the covers and bedframe and along the rug to the chair she would use during the videoconference. Though "fevered and asleep," the chairman would stir for the cameras. Pankie had disguised herself as much as she could. Her hair was black, streaked in white, and oiled, thanks to shoe polish. She made herself to appear as old as possible, and added warts across her face and hands.

It was time. She lifted the receiver.

"Manager?" Her voice was lower and slower than normal, a soft southern drawl flavoring her words. "This is Aretha. We're . . Basilia Aretha. Who? Retson?" Her tone sharpened. "Are you saying your records are not current? I don't know anything about a Retson. Get your records in order quickly. The chairman would be most distressed at your breach of security."

She paused, satisfied with the flustered apologies of the weak-kneed Nexa manager. She'd estimated his character correctly.

"All right. We're ready. After the video conference see that we're not disturbed for the rest of the day. You may send lunch at twelve and supper at six." Pankie hung the phone up, exhaling tension.

At precisely eight o'clock the haggard face of Milton Franklin appeared on the communications screen.

In spite of muted bursts of distant artillery, Debbie slept soundly. The El Shar had provided for her every comfort, from an enormous, soft round bed to a private stock of wines and liqueurs. She awoke refreshed, and languished in bed for awhile, luxuriating in that peaceful haven between freedom of slumber and chains of wakefulness.

Her peace was short-lived. Thoughts of her three friends focused her concerns. She still wasn't sure why they decided to come to Jerusalem with her. Her motivation was simple —

she knew intuitively that Michael was in trouble and she had to find him. It was an insistent inner urging which impelled her decision to make the trip. But the others — it was puzzling.

She pulled the curtains open, admiring the morning-shadowed countryside through the window's ornate grillwork. Other villas rambled down the hillside toward the main buildings of the El Shar, waiting for the day to begin. A gardener knelt in one of the gardens, clipping branches from a dense cluster of blooming bushes and placing them into a basket. A porter rolled a breakfast cart piled high with covered dishes across the flagstoned terrace walk.

Dressing quickly, eager now to explore, she took her camera and several rolls of film from her bag. With a final glance in the mirror, she went to the door and grasped the handle. It was locked. The image of the ornate iron window grillwork popped into her mind. She rushed to the bathroom. Grillwork covered its window too. But, she noted with both anger and panic, the windows of the villas further down the hill had no ornamental coverings. She grabbed the phone.

"I'm sorry, Mrs. Ames." The concierge was polite. "Telephone lines are out of service, probably due to the bombings."

"I seem to be talking to you!" she shouted angrily.

"Yes ma'am. Within the hotel the lines are all right."

"Then I want Mr. Hammock's room!"

After fifteen rings — Debbie counted them — she slammed the receiver back into its cradle. Suddenly a key scraped in her door, followed by a knock. She lunged from the bed and twisted the knob. This time the door opened. Ing Hammock stood in the entrance. The porter she'd seen with the breakfast cart waited behind him.

"Good morning — did you sleep well?" He greeted her with his most charming smile.

"What do you mean by locking me into my room!" Debbie exploded.

Ing motioned to the porter, who pushed the cart into the room and left quickly.

"It's for your own safety. Shall we eat — and talk?" Debbie glared. Ing pulled a chair up to the table for her. She soon found it difficult to keep an edge to her anger. And the orange juice tasted sweet and delicious.

They were just beyond Jerusalem, three miles from their prison. Now, after a night's sleep in the protection of a small grove of wild olive trees, they sat together in a field of scrub bush and high grass, warming under the rising morning sun. No one had followed them after their miraculous escape the evening before. They had picked up a newspaper, two loaves of bread, and some fruit from a delicatessen. Ben tore a piece of bread from the remaining loaf.

"I think, Gabe, from what you read for us, that the time may be near for the Master to return to His house. Perhaps even in the next moment . . ." Ben's light blue eyes gazed toward the sky. His browned, crinkly skin was wreathed in longing anticipation. He looked like a young boy who'd just realized the father he loved dearly, and who had been away for a long time, would appear around the corner any minute.

Gabe's knowledge of Hebrew was adequate for most of the news items. The Russian attack was much more damaging than they'd realized. Invading by land, sea, and air, their forces had hit Israel at many points. Except for minor damage from stray shells — one of which had become their instrument of freedom — no harm had yet come to Jerusalem. But the Strait of Hormuz had been under fierce assault and the vital flow of oil through the Persian Gulf had been stopped. Other articles reported on hastily-called World Alliance meetings and diplomatic missions as intensive efforts escalated to try to end the ill-timed attack.

They were most shocked, however, by the death of the World Alliance chairman and Milton Franklin's election as the new head of the emerging world-wide government. And Michael Ames had been working directly with him. More and more, they were realizing the implications. Em had read aloud from Daniel in his small pocket Bible. The "King of the North" had been interpreted for centuries as referring to Russia. Gabe was of the same mind, particularly now that the New Russian Federation, forged after the collapse of Soviet communism, had become a major military power.

"I'm convinced. There was the three-day war, then the Russian attack. The temple was just finished." He looked over the rolling countryside toward Jerusalem, rising in the mid-morning mist three miles away like a light on top of the hills. The new dome of the temple gleamed, beckoning them to it.

"And of course, the catastrophes." Em picked up where Gabe had stopped. "Including a new volcano right in our own back yard."

"I'll say it this way, friends," Ben said quietly. "If the Lord isn't coming soon, this world's got an awful mess on its hands."

They were silent, thinking. Ben's comment seemed terribly understated. No other period of history came close. It appeared impossible to recover from the chaos the planet seemed to have been plunged into.

"What was that?" Gabe cocked his head like a robin listening for the worm. "There . . ."

"I hear it!" Em said, looking up into the sky. "It sounded like a — drum!"

Another bark of thunder tumbled out of the heavens. They looked at each other in disbelief. "Boooom." Louder yet. And then another, each one about ten seconds apart.

At a factory in Germany which produced large dish antennas, two workers sat on the surface of a large diameter model drinking their morning coffee. The first drum-boom upset their thermos bottle as the big dish vibrated. One of them set it upright. The second time the thermos capsized they heard the boom. The third one knocked them off the dish. They scrambled to their feet, frightened. By the sixth they were running like lemmings in uncomprehending panic through the factory with throngs of their fellow workers.

Gabe gasped as the Voice uttered its message. It was very deep and slow, and it seemed to roll across the hills like liquid thunder, splashing and then disappearing into the ridges behind them.

"PELEM-THRASHA-ZIM-BILDRAYAN"

The last syllable echoed and ebbed into the morning stillness. They looked at each other, eyes wide and mouths gaping. Half a minute passed. Then the booms and strange word-like sounds were repeated. All three dropped to their knees, Em grunted from the pain. Faint shouts from Jerusalem floated across the countryside. Then the mysterious syllables were repeated a final time.

They waited, aware of the eerie silence. A bird sang a tentative note nearby and Ben realized even they, which had been twittering cheerfully earlier, had been silent. The bird's cheerfully renewed song broke the trance. Faint shouts rose again from the direction of the city.

"You don't look radiant with expectation, my dear pastor," Em said to Gabe, noting his furrowed brow. Em, too, had sensed something other than rapture.

Gabe nodded. "I know. What do you think, Ben?"

Ben did not hesitate. "I think the devil's been loosed."

Em slapped the ground with the palm of his hand. "Right."

"Something's terribly wrong," Gabe said, drawing designs in the dust with a stick. "I've known Jesus for many years and so have you. I don't sense His presence and I don't sense His peace. But I can sense His suffering. He drew another figure in the dust, then looked at his friends. "If that — whatever it was that we just heard — was of the Lord, wouldn't we know it? Somehow?"

Ben nodded. "Feels bad, Gabe. Like when street gangs back in Binzoe would beat up one of our people. But even worse."

Em stood up, rubbing his knee. "If it wasn't of God . . . It's certainly not in Scripture, is it?"

"Not anywhere," Gabe said matter-of-factly.

"What were those words? 'Pelem, Tarsa . . .' "

"Thrasha," Ben corrected. " 'Pelem, Thrasha, Zim, Bildrayan.' "

Gabe thought on the strange words. He knew no Hebrew, Greek or Aramaic equivalents. He stood up. "I don't know what it is, but it's not good. Pray as you walk, brothers. I believe we're here in this place for a reason. Michael Ames is connected in some way. And we don't know what happened to Debbie. We've got to find them. Fast."

A surprising sense of cheerfulness seemed to fall upon them. "Which way?" Em said. Gabe pointed toward Old Jerusalem, higher in the hills than the modern city, and behind it to the stone spire rising majestically above the Old Jerusalem skyline.

"There." They began to walk toward the Tower of the Ascension.

Chapter 30

Exhaustion forced Milton Franklin into a restless sleep. Even so it was for less than two hours. His security aide awakened him as he snored on the couch of his inner office to speak with the Russian premier, Alex Kossovsky, on the priority communications channel.

Since the Soviet attack against Israel, World Alliance diplomats had been bringing whatever pressure they could to bear upon their Soviet counterparts to withdraw. Unable to discuss the real reason for their request, they only aroused suspicions and irritated them beyond even Soviet patience. The hostile tone of the powerful Russian leader rang in the sleep-fuzzed mind of the beleaguered new chairman. "You are wasting our time," Kossovsky said with regal sarcasm. "We will continue military action until our rightful claim to the Middle East has been established. We reject your empty ravings and denounce the empty World Alliance. This is the year we will destroy you and establish Soviet supremacy and peace." The premier broke the connection in the middle of Franklin's response. The ultimate challenge had been uttered.

Franklin sat on the couch, hands over his face, his swollen, bloodshot eyes staring blanky through his fingers. He sighed wearily, then turned to his aide standing quietly, awaiting instructions. Milton Franklin was never one to run from challenge, even when exhausted. He stood, clenching his fists, a rising thirst for vengeance driving sleepiness way. "We're going to crush them. Get the Cabinet and the European Region President and his military people. I want a meeting in one hour." The aide hurried away to comply. Franklin washed and changed his shirt.

The hastily convened meeting ended just ten minutes before the scheduled video conference with the chairman-in-hiding. The World Alliance had voted to put attack plans against the New Soviet forces in motion. If the strategy worked the Russian army would be crushed within forty-eight hours and Omega's return would be secure. But the cooperation of the Chinese military and its enormous army was essential, and that cooperation was not at all assured.

As the conferencing equipment was activated Franklin wondered how he would position the situation to the chairman. Ideas seemed blocked by his tense fatigued mind. The videoscreen filled with the bedroom at the Nexa Inn, the chairman asleep in his bed, and a rather ugly woman seated nearby. He did not know the aide who accompanied the chairman on his planned disappearance, but he knew the sour-looking woman peering back at him was not the type the chairman normally chose for his closer associates. The motionless form in the bed further aroused his suspicions.

"Who are you?" he growled.
"Basilia Aretha, Mr. Chairman. Good morning."
"Why is he on that bed?"
"He had an attack of food poisoning last night, sir."
Franklin waited. "And?" he said, impatiently.
"Sir?"

"Idiot! How is he? Never mind. Wake him and get out."

"The doctor gave him a sedative. I was warned not to disturb him." Franklin's fatigue was affecting him. Pankie watched, wary of every movement. When she saw his anger she knew she could make the ruse work. She shifted in her chair, tightening the cord tied around her ankle. She moved her leg, hidden under a blanket over her lap. The cord pulled, and under the covers the chairman's leg moved.

"Listen, Arthur or whoever you are . . ."

"Aretha, sir. I am the chairman's personal aide." Pankie pulled the cord under her lap blanket again.

"He's stirring. Wake him!"

"As you wish. But I do not want the responsibility if it is damaging to him. The doctor said he was too old to take the shock of premature release from the sedative." Pankie rose as she spoke and leaned over the bed. "He gave me a list of issues to review with you, sir, before the doctor administered the shot." She began to shake the chairman's body gently. Franklin watched morosely.

"I'm going to get some water." Out of camera range she pulled another cord. The body rolled over onto its side and a leg bent under the covers. 'He's out cold,' Franklin thought, watching. But something didn't seem right. The woman returned with a wet cloth and began applying it to the chairman's forehead.

"Forget it," Franklin interrupted. "I don't have time to watch you play nurse."

Pankie hoped he could not hear her exhalation of relief.

"The issues. Let's have them."

Pankie sat down and opened a folder laying on the table just behind her. "First, he said 'Christian persecution is behind schedule. Get to it.' "

Franklin's stomach churned with acidic frustration.

"Second, he asked me to write down your summary status report. I'm ready, sir." She poised a pen over her tablet, looking innocently into the videoscreen at the scowling, agitated man.

'I'm supposed to report status to a ninety-year-old crone,' Franklin thought grimly. The sense that something was amiss faded under exhaustion and tension. "Get it right the first time, hag."

Pankie felt one of her warts coming loose and held her head very steady. But Franklin had started to give his report and was no longer paying attention to her.

"One. Omega's wife, Ben Crockett, Gabriel Diehl, and Emerson Prantzer flew to Jerusalem. Debbie Ames in custody at El Shar. Hammock's got her. The others were jailed, but escaped when a Russian shell hit the wall of their cell. We're hunting them down."

Pankie wrote quickly, hardly daring to breathe.

"Two. Soviet attack did not damage Jerusalem. Omega Plan is intact. Initial announcement successful. Omega doing well."

"Three. Russians pulled out of World Alliance. We're —" Franklin paused, framing his words — "preparing corrective action." He knew that wouldn't be enough. And he didn't want another video conference with the chairman jabbing at him because of incomplete information. "Add to number three — European Region and China joining forces for counterassault against Soviets."

Pankie almost choked as she wrote.

"Four. Christian initiative begins today. Primary target is American Region. Leaders to be arrested."

Pankie finished writing and looked up.

"Send a message as soon as he wakes. Understand?"

"Yes sir."

The screen blanked. Pankie was flooded with relief. She'd done it. Her ambitions, and the cause of SelfGuide, could be enhanced nicely during the next few days. Perspiring from the heat of the lap blanket and the tension, she stripped her clothes off, tossing them into the air with gleeful abandon. Her sweater landed on the dead chairman's face. She danced across the carpet and into the marble shower, revelling in the delightful sting of hot steaming spray. Her tension melted away.

Milton Franklin absently fingered the handle on his coffee mug. He did not like what he'd just seen. There had been enough surprises in the past two days to last a lifetime. This was one too many. It didn't fit. 'So stiff,' he thought, mulling over the possibilities. They were there. "Aide!" he bellowed. Faces looked up through the one-way glass of the inner office wall. An aide came running in. "Go to Gander. Now. Go to the Nexa and check . . ." He stopped suddenly. With a flash of insight the truth dawned on him. 'Fool!' he thought to himself. 'No one knows. I almost blew it.' "Forget it. Send Hammock in here."

"We're behind schedule — go!" Major O'keefe shouted through the megaphone. The narrow streets surrounding the tower square were deserted, cordoned off by World Alliance special militia. "Set," voices responded from positions around the square.

"We'll do it all except Omega's descent from the tower. For now just climb up on the fountain." O'Keefe looked at the white-robed man leaning against the tower wall. Michael waved acknowledgement.

"Do it right. Go!"

Michael's hands were cold and clammy despite the sunshine. He went toward the center of the square where the fountain, built during the reign of Constantine, had been dismantled stone by stone and a large image plate installed under its foundation. Then it had been carefully rebuilt over the plate. As he came near, large generators pumped high voltage power into the plate, and holographic equipment was activated. A shimmering developed above the fountain. As it strengthened, the 'townspeople' feigned surprise, gawking and jostling as they looked on the forming image. Michael mounted the rim of the fountain and, using its yawning gargoyles as a foothold, stepped up into the image. A crackling energy surrounded him like St. Elmo's Fire. Through it he could see faint silhouettes pointing at him and shouting with excitement. He assumed the pose which Professor Schmidt had coached him on. The image began to shrink and Michael felt the surrounding energy decrease. As it approached his own size he shifted his left arm slightly to match the hologram. Then the energy field dropped away, and only a residual static charge clung to him. Ultraviolet lamps in the fountain created a visible aura shimmering in the static charge. Michael lifted his arms up in a pose of annunciation.

"Peace be with you," he intoned. His voice was transmitted through a tiny microstalk under his tunic into speakers hidden in the fountain. It boomed with authority. Some of the 'townspeople' ran. Others fell to their knees.

"You who worship me . . . you do well, for you have recognized your Lord. I am come as I have promised!" As Michael spoke he steeled himself for the most difficult part of the scene, being lifted off the fountain and transported to the cobblestoned square. A magnetic girdle was strapped under his tunic for this event. The force developed by twin macro-electron guns which would focus on the girdle and manipulate his position had caused severe pain in previous rehearsals. Team engineers thought they'd solved the problem. Michael hoped they were right. Powerful unseen forces lifted him. His feet left the fountain rim and he was pulled through the air, coming to rest on the pavement exactly as planned. There was no pain.

Becker Simpson, hunched over as if her back had been broken years ago and healed crookedly, watched Michael with feigned awe. She'd spent several days in the square before the team arrived so she would be a familiar sight when the public would be allowed back in just before Omega's appearance. Cries of surprise, and later words of testimony, from the locals were important to the illusion's effectiveness. Now Michael turned to her. "Child, you are deformed. What would you have of me?"

Becker trembled, and tears came to her eyes. "Master," she quavered, "I would have you heal me. But it is not possible . . I've been deformed since birth."

"Child, do you believe I can heal what the world cannot heal?"

Becker looked up with radiant hope. "I want to believe!" "Your hope is sufficient. Go your way, woman. You are healed." Michael grasped her robe and pulled it up, revealing her ugly misshapen back. No one who would see the poor woman could doubt her misery. He moved his hands through the air, producing a gossamer-like gown lodged under the ample sleeves of his linen tunic. Gently pulling it over Becker's body, he punctured the thin rubbery sac which created the hunch on her back. Slowly she straightened. Liquid oozed down her legs as the sac flattened, dripping onto the cobblestones. She raised her arms, shouting with happiness, and ran off into the crowd.

Professor Schmidt watched frowning from a window midway up the Tower, then shook his head. "Tackytacky," he muttered. "Schlockenschtik."

After rehearsing his other healings Michael turned to the ceremonial table where the WOEC Visgate and the others would be on Sunday, and addressed the man standing in for Anton Jedesky. "Your trials are at an end. Well done, my servant."

The stand-ins behaved as the dignitaries were expected to behave based on extensive psychological analysis of their personalities. The chief priest would watch the Israeli prime minister and follow his lead. The Visgate would respond immediately to the Christ figure's endorsement. The prime minister would be skeptical. Michael now turned to the prime minister's stand-in. "I am your Messiah. You are the leader of my people. Would you deny me again?" The prime minister could respond in one of two ways according to his psychological profile. This rehearsal was set to practice the more difficult option.

"I do not recognize you as the Messiah!" he cried defiantly.

Michael gazed at him sadly. "Even demons recognize me. Who, then, are you? Be gone."

A blindfolded and gagged man was dragged into the stand-in's place. Horrified, Michael suddenly realized they were going to execute this part of the plan. Generators surged, and antivoltage charged the metal plate buried under the cobblestones where the wretched man stood. A duplicate of the ceremonial metal crown to be worn by the prime minister was shoved on his head. A switch was thrown, and the crown collapsed. His cheeks sucked inward, his eyes squeezed shut, and the man shivered and twitched as a electronically-induced vacuum collapsed every cell in his body. With suction-like noise he imploded. His clothing dropped to the ground, hot and soaking from separated body fluids, and a lump of hardened, condensed steaming tissue lay on the cobblestones.

Michael stared, aghast in shock and rage. O'Keefe was at his side in a moment. "You're doing fine, Omega. Don't weaken now!"

"Murderer! My God, do you know what you've done?"

"He was a criminal sentenced to death. And you had to see this in case . . ."

"Murderer!"

Security guards came at O'Keefe's signal and held Michael still. "Steady, Omega," one of them said, his tone tinged with warning.

"Imagine," the major said conversationally, "if you'd seen this on Sunday for the first time. It may have to happen, you know." He looked directly at Michael, his eyes flint-hard. In many ways O'Keefe was like Milton Franklin. Michael turned and leaned over the fountain, his strained sensitivities exploding out of him and clouding the quiet waters. O'Keefe rolled his eyes at the guards. "Take him in to rest. Keep an eye on him." They took the arms of the heaving robed figure. Michael walked submissively between them toward the Mischa.

From the darkened window in the Tower, Professor Schmidt watched with interest, arms folded across his barrel-like chest. "Ya, much better," he nodded. "Omenka goot when he believe his part. No actor though. I tink better have talk mit him or he blitzmessen real ting. Ya, I talk mit Omeka tonight."

"They're probably hunting for us, you know," Gabe observed. They'd been walking slowly and resting often, trying not to strain Em's knee any more than necessary. Now they were back in the outskirts of Jerusalem. "If we split up, the chances of finding them are better."

"Let's stay together," Ben suggested. "We might need a helping hand. Besides . . ." he clenched his fist and shook it . . . "I may be old, but I think I can handle some of the smaller problems if any come along." Gabe and Em smiled.

They came to a low building with portions of its walls blown out. A crater several yards across was carved into the ground, and part of the concrete road running along the front of the building had caved in. Judging by the crates and boxes strewn over the floor it appeared to be an old warehouse.

"Car!" Ben shouted.

Down the road a cloud of dust appeared, and the sun reflected off an approaching vehicle. They scrambled through the crumbled opening in the wall and crouched. The car slowed as it neared the collapsed section of road, eased past the crater and sped away in a cloud of dust.

"I'm glad the Lord knows how we're going to get through this because I don't," Gabe remarked.

They decided to rest for awhile. Ben began to explore as they talked. He kicked absently at a flat crate laying on the floor. It didn't move. Curious, he kicked it again.

"Something strange here," he called. They studied the crate. "Doesn't seem it should be held to the floor like that."

"Maybe it's just heavy."

They tried to shove it aside. It didn't move, but a piece of the wood broke off.

Ben found a length of rusting pipe and pried the crate apart. A wooden door set into the concrete floor saw its first light in years. It took awhile to loosen it but at last it creaked open. Steps descended into a tunnel, and cool air wafted upward.

"I'm going in."

"It's pitch dark, Gabe," Em objected.

"I'll just go a short distance." He stepped onto the log steps and eased himself down into the hole.

"Careful," Ben said. "Remember, you've got the food."

Gabe smiled in the darkness, feeling the remnant of the loaf of bread tucked into his jacket pocket. He worked his way slowly down the steps until the bottom of his foot touched ground. He could stand with ample headroom. "Okay so far," he called. His voice sounded like a hollow echo.

At length he reappeared, his head popping up through the opening like a prairie dog. "There's no end to it. A short way in I saw a shaft of light ahead. I walked that far, passing several side tunnels on the way. The light came from a crevice up on the surface. The sign of the fish was carved into the stone just under the light shaft."

They were excited. This evidence of their first-century brothers eased the sense of alienation in what for them had become a hostile land.

"Catacombs and tunnels are networked all over this area," Gabe said. "It was the only way many of the early Christians escaped persecution. I'll bet this is part of that network. A little further on I think there was a much larger cavern. That's when I came back."

"It was about time," Em said, irritated. "You could have gotten lost."

"No, I didn't make any turns. But we need something to see with if we go in. And we should — down there we won't risk capture. It has to lead into Old Jerusalem. All we have to do is pick the right passageways."

"It won't work, Gabe!" Em became agitated. "We've got enough trouble — now you want to go down there without water or food? We're bound to get lost."

"I don't think so . . ."

"You can't just go traipsing off down there without thinking it through, Gabe! Do you know what the chances are of ever getting out?" Em limped a few steps away, his hands on his hips. "We're not young men you know, and we've been through enough. This is ridiculous — airport hoodlums, jails, bombs —"

"You've been in tougher spots than this, my friend," Gabe said, gently but with determination. "If the Lord leads us in, He'll lead us out."

Em's rheumy eyes blazed. "How do you know the Lord wants us down there?"

"How did you know you were to speak out at the hearings?"

The reminder hit its mark. He dragged his fears into submission with a sigh and a shrug.

"All right, all right. It's hard to understand . . ."

"Amen to that," Ben acknowledged.

"Sorry. The strain must be getting to me."

"Forget it," Gabe said. "You just said what we're all thinking. Whether we stay up here or go down there, we've got a big problem. Sometimes the Lord guides us by giving no other choice." He looked down into the blackness of the cavern opening. "But I do wish we had a light of some kind."

"Yeah," Ben said, kicking an old box nearby. Its side splintered open and cellophane-wrapped candles tumbled out. They stared, amazed. A slow and knowing smile spread across their faces. "Guess we're on a roll," Gabe said, his spirits soaring.

They took what they could carry and went down the log steps. Ben followed last and pulled the heavy wooden door back over the opening. Before long they'd passed the light shaft and entered the cavern Gabe had mentioned. The flickering glow of the candles revealed several openings around its walls. They selected one directly across from them and continued on.

Chapter 31

Widespread suffering from natural disasters, crime, wars, and terrorism, and ruined economies had softened the mettle of self-sufficiency. Chronic exposure to airborne chemicals, contaminated food, epidemics of disease, and spurious radiation claimed a further toll on the world's deteriorating sense of well-being. People began taking to the streets, there to exhaust pent-up hostility, lusts, and fears. In many ways the planet was becoming an asylum, and those who remained stable and hopeful were outnumbered. The Global Voice proved to be a significant factor in separating people further from the familiarities of reason, order and sanity.

In some areas life staggered on almost as usual. Crowded, impoverished ghettos of Pakistan and Brazil, and starving millions perishing in the parched desertlands of central Africa merely continued in their cycle of suffering and dying, unaware that the rest of the world was moving toward the same destitute and hopeless condition. Not all of these people had heard the Voice that Wednesday, for there were not too many dish antennas in these parts of the world. But World Alliance planners had determined that it didn't matter. They were the expendables, the non-influentials, the useless.

In the more advanced countries, no longer could the daily business of industry, education and government provide its ointment of separation from the personal worries and cares of life. Dates were set with hesitation, the unspoken 'Will we be here then?' a constant and fearsome attendant. Limping and uncertain, the world tiptoed through the days one at a time, hoping the chaos would begin to recede, fearful that chaos would continue unabated.

Yet some had a real hope, understanding as Paul wrote to Timothy, "the creation was subjected to futility, not of its own will but by the will of him who subjected it in hope; because the creation itself will be set free from its bondage to decay and obtain the glorious liberty of the children of God." These looked beyond the menace of the earthquake and the firestorm, and saw the hopelessness of a prideful response. Under stress we steal from one another. Under suffering it's everyone for himself. These disasters do not create human misery, but mirror it. Without the earthquake we're free to return to our own arrogance, and without the firestorm we have time to plot again against our neighbors. The year just passed had made such things clear to all who had ears to hear and eyes to see. The grotesqueness of human nature had been dragged into the light from its technicolored hiding places and revealed. The world had proven its deceit. Those very few who had set their minds on the Savior Jesus Christ and His unwavering Lordship found a sure place to stand even as monumental tragedies and difficulties prowled to confuse and damage them all.

Then the Global Voice came.

Some thought it was indeed the voice of God. The World Alliance would have been pleased. Others were not so quick to judge, mindful of God's warning:

> "See to it that no one makes a prey of you by philosophy and empty deceit, according to human tradition, according to the elemental spirits of the universe, and not according to Christ:
>
> ... beware lest you be carried away with the error of lawless men and lose your own stability ... Many are the plans in the mind of a man, but it is the purpose of the Lord that will be established ... False Christs and false prophets will arise and show great signs and wonders, so as to lead astray, if possible, even the elect."

Those with a more technical bent developed theories. Some hypothesized that satellite broadcasts to dish antennas, which covered the globe like mushrooms, could have been used. But these were droplets of speculation lost in oceans of hysteria and political dogma. The Voice pushed many people past the edge of familiar rationality. The world had been made vunerable to the days ahead.

Christian leadership spoke out boldly. Warren R. Heath stood on the steps of the capitol of the United States that afternoon, labelling the Voice a "treacherous deceit generated by pawns of Satan." Amy Greene took to the air, and asked, "Is this God's call to His beloved creation and for which He gave His Son, our Lord Jesus, that He would terrorize a frightened and vulnerable world through cheap carnival trickery? That is not God's way. He allows us to have our own ways. He forces no way upon us."

God's elect knew the truth. That truth was despised and rejected by most. What the World Alliance had counted on was Christian leaders speaking out against the opening global miracle of the Omega Plan. This they did, and set the stage for their persecution.

That evening, television networks broadcast a message from Dr. Anton Jedesky, the WOEC Visgate. His office was sparsely furnished for the broadcast. The WOEC symbol, an ornate gold cross on a six-sided olivewood base with figures of a man and woman standing, each extending their hands toward the other, was carefully positioned on his desk.

"My friends and fellow worshippers in unity and peace, I bring you good news," the Visgate began. His words were swiftly translated into hundreds of languages. Conversation stopped in pubs and households across the world.

"We have forged a global community of peace and harmony. You have courageously laid aside your prejudices and fears, and united with a common heart and mind. Fringe groups have worked to dissuade you. Hostile nations have sought to undermine you, fearful of a world united against war, hunger and deprivation. We have come together in this common spirit. Today we heard a voice and sought its meaning. Our courage was gathered from yours, and our willingness to seek the mysteries of creation was sustained by your strength. We come now to you who are in the factories and fields, the places of business and government, the halls of our universities and schools and the homes of our nations, to share with you this revelation."

The filming director clasped both hands together over his head, mouthing "Bravo!" Jedesky cleared his throat.

"We've heard the majestic call to peace and stability. The one whom we worship, known according to the supreme dictates of your own conscience, has pronounced benediction upon our turbulence, 'Pelem Thrasha Zim Bildrayan . . . . Make Ready The Way Of The Lord.' A new era of peace and stability will be heralded with mighty signs and wonders the world over. We to whom this interpretation has been entrusted have been weighed in the balances and found sufficient. You who have valiantly and steadfastly served in the founding travail of the World Organization Ecumenical Council may look forward to a sweet repast in the ages to come. Worship therefore this office, the office of your Visgate. One among you will succeed me, and then another. Together, across time, across boundaries, across cultures, we have been vindicated. 'Pelem, Thrasha, Zim, Bildrayan.' Make Ready The Way Of The Lord. May the part of you that is creator sustain the part of you that is created. Amen.''

A world sat on tavern stools and living room sofas, in auditoriums and offices, stunned. Regular programming returned. A game show was in progress on one channel. Two young women, stripped and covered with shaving foam, ran in circles around a small plastic wading pool while a clock ticked off thousand-dollar seconds. On another channel a commercial heralded a deodorant bar as the answer to all social problems.

In a room of the Mischa Hotel a tall slender man turned and twisted restlessly, unable to sleep. He had watched the broadcast with the rest of the Omega team after another long and exhausting day. It affected him more than he knew. Cumulative pressures pushed him to his own boundaries. Though the desire to escape with sleep weighed heavily, he could not close his eyes without seeing the fleeting traces of ugly creatures, the cruel murder of the poor soul in the square, the leering, too-bright stare of Major O'Keefe. His restlessness matured into writhing suffering. Parts of Jesus' words, etched into his memory, coalesced into sword-wielding warriors engaging the Visgate's pronouncements in a battle to the death. And Michael Ames found himself in the crossfire, trapped under the clashing of weapons, fearful of crawling away in the darkness lest a lance or an arrow find its mark. Sensing the separation from himself which his altered physical identity called him to experience, he clung tenaciously to what he once had been, refusing to think of himself as another person as

Professor Schmidt had counselled. They had words about that earlier, and on that account Michael was disappointed in himself and in the man he'd thought was the most real and sincere of all. "You must beliefen, Omenka, in what you are doink!" he'd said. Michael relived his surprisingly vehement reaction, pounding his fist on the table as he shouted that he resented being used, and that he did not believe in it at all.

He shut off his recollections, pained by the implications. It was confusing that the professor would make such a fuss about this matter of belief, and that it bothered him so much. Years before, he'd tried to believe in what he was doing. But something in him had rejected it as surely as his body would reject a turnip if that rather than a heart had been transplanted into the chest cavity. 'Others seem able to believe in something,' he thought. 'Ben, for one. I want that kind of peace and strength. Or Pankie Retson, totally believing in SelfGuide. I know its principles well enough. I agree with them. But I can't believe in them. I can't believe in anything!'

He got up from his rumpled bed and walked across the thin carpet to the window. The moon was high and full, shining brightly in the night sky. A shell exploded in the distance as if serving notice that morning, and renewed hostility, was only a few hours away. Below in the courtyard a rooster frightened by the echoing rumbles squawked and hopped with thrashing wings across the paving stones.

Thirsty, he went into the bathroom. His white linen robe hung over the straight-backed chair. The man called Jesus, he thought. He downed a small paper cupful of water, then crumpled it angrily and threw it against the wall, cursing in frustration. "I'm supposed to act out a role a bunch of crazies put together and I don't even know the man," he muttered. "Henri, where are you when I need you?" Scriptures scrolled through his mind. "Peter began to curse and swear. 'I don't even know the man,' he said. And immediately the cock crowed. Then . . ." Michael froze with the sound in the courtyard, faint through windows closed against the chill. The rooster was crowing.

He sagged down on the edge of his bed, staring out the window. That peculiar sensation fell upon him, lightheaded without being lightheaded, energized and beckoned forward. He gasped. In the corner of his room a golden glow appeared. He recognized it immediately. Henri stood before him.

"Michael, I bid you greeting!"

"Shhh!" Michael jumped off the bed with alarm. "You'll wake them!"

"They will not hear me. You have been given a special gift of discernment, but that only for a little while."

Michael reached out, wishing desperately to touch Henri, to shake his hand, to feel the reassuring hold on his shoulder.

"Stay your distance, my friend. It is not within this narrow realm that the desires of your heart are fulfilled."

Disappointed, Michael sat back on the bed, watching his strange and wonderful companion. Henri held his hand up. "You called for me. I came. But you call in error. What is my appearance to you? Your friends could duplicate what you see."

"They are not my friends!"

Henri exuded confidence and peace. Michael wanted to share in that more than he could describe. "You have arrived at your crossroad, Michael. Evil forces are gathered in the air, and the battle is near. Much depends upon your decision. You see what you need to see. You know what you need to know. The struggle is within you. Who do you say He is?"

Michael looked blank. "Who?" But he knew the answer. "Jesus? Who do I say Jesus is?"

Henri nodded ever so slightly.

Michael's lip quivered. His mind had embraced the truth of the gospels, and the edge of his soul had been stirred from a slumbering death. The forces of deception swirled in among the powers of truth, mingling in his thoughts like a marble cake. The battle was evident, but there was too much dust and smoke to see the warriors' colors. He stood on the edge of the sword, unable to balance yet not knowing which way to jump to safety. The rooster crowed again, its cry piercing into his soul. Demands for simple, clear Answers of fact clashed with mysterious and deep Questions of faith. He could neither conquer nor set aside the tensions of contradiction between the way he insisted upon and the way which beckoned him. Confused and vulnerable, Michael lashed out. "Henri, this has gone far enough. For all I know you're just one more hologram!" With sudden rage he lunged toward him but was diverted as if by magnetic replusion, unable to touch even the edge of Henri's shimmering robe. He tumbled backwards and fell, fully angered now.

"What right do you have to put me in the middle of this? I was having a decent life. I didn't ask for any of it! If you're from this God of yours, and if this Jesus I'm here to play is really God and really cares about me, he's got a foul way of showing it. Why have I been dragged halfway around the world into things I don't understand? What right does he have, Henri? What about everybody else? I'm not as bad as a lot of other people — why me?"

His anger peaked and disappeared like a bursting bubble. He blinked sheepishly, fearful that his outburst might have been heard outside the room. Henri's warm, accepting glow was even stronger. "Your strength is your weakness, Michael. By God's great mercy, you are where you are because you could not hear His call in any other way. As for others — many will hear more easily. You would do well to receive and worship Him. No man perishes without first having heard." Henri stroked his arm through the air, acknowledging Michael's presence in Jerusalem, the Omega Plan, and all that had accompanied his circumstances in a single angelic gesture. "This is your way home. It is up to you to accept or reject."

Suddenly Henri was no longer there. Michael's sense of largeness and energy faded. Faint light appeared through the window beyond the southeastern horizon. Another day would begin soon. He paced, disturbed, overwhelmed, confused. Had he hallucinated? He remembered tumbling back on the carpet. That was no hallucination. "What then?"

"You're talking to yourself."

"Am I mad?"
"Of course not."
"I have to get out of here."
"You got that right."
He pulled his trousers on, trembling, driven to escape. Shoes, sweater . . . He lunged for the bureau, nearly stumbling over the chair, and scooped coins and a half-eaten chocolate bar into his pocket. There was his linen tunic slung over the backslat. 'I can say I had an early rehearsal' . . . He pulled the floor-length garment over his sweater and opened the door carefully, fearing the least noise. Apparently his shouting was not as loud as he'd thought, for The Mischa echoed in sleeping silence. He tiptoed along the edge of the hallway, mindful of creaky boards under the worn carpet runner. At the bottom of the stairs a guard dozing in his chair shifted and snorted. Michael ducked behind the bannister and waited. Step by step he eased down to the first floor. The staircase creaked. The guard didn't move. His eyes were riveted to the main door as his foot touched the stone of the lobby floor and he moved stealthily toward the door. Suddenly a hand seized his arm. His heart jumped into this throat. "Where're you goin'?" The guard mumbled, half-asleep.

'God, if you're really up there, show your stuff.' The thought came and went in a wink. "Shhh . . . idiot!" Michael hissed. "You want to go on report?"

"What report . . ."

Michael leaned over the guard, a finger held over his pursed lips. "Early rehearsal, you ox. It's on your schedule. And get your fat hand off me." He pulled his arm away and grabbed the guard roughly under the chin, puckering his mouth from the force. "Listen bozo," he whispered harshly. "You wake anyone and the major will hang you from the Tower!" He shook the guard's head back and forth like a rawhide bone in the jaws of a puppy, then pushed his head back. "Keep awake. Understand?" He glared for what seemed to be a long time. The guard scowled and looked away.

Michael walked boldly to the front door, convinced his acting was better than Professor Schmidt thought. But another guard paced outside in the faint dawn light. He turned nonchalantly and went across the hall into the dining room, moving through a forest of shadowy upended chairs perched on their tables, searching for a way out. In the kitchen a faint light leaked out from under the pantry door. He went in, his heart racing. Lined up neatly along the alley fence, garbage cans stared back at him through the pantry window. He locked the door softly behind him, feeling better even with that small protection against forces he was now convinced were incomprehensibly malevolent.

The windows were forever sealed by layers of paint. Panicky, he looked around the narrow room. Bags of biscuits were on one of the shelves. He took several and stuffed them under his sweater. Suddenly there was a sound in the kitchen. Lights clicked on and streaked underneath the door. The cook! he thought, thoroughly frightened now. 'God, you did it once. Let's see it again. Please please please . . .' Nearly hidden under sacks of potatoes, Michael spotted a wooden cover set into the floor. Seizing on the hope, he quietly moved the sacks and pulled on the hatch. It opened, exposing stairs leading down into darkness. He stepping quickly into the opening and pulled the cover back in place just as the lock on the pantry door turned.

Chapter 32

Debbie did not sleep well on her second night at the El Shar. Forced confinement alone would have prevented it. But she'd heard the Voice that morning, too. Though suspicious and unwilling to ascribe to it any extraterrestrial power, it affected her. Later she'd watched the WOEC Visgate's broadcast. That helped a little. The Visgate was not, after all, just anybody.

The products of her subconscious were more influential on her state of mind than those thoughts processed consciously. Over the years, her intuition had proven to be remarkably accurate. She knew her husband was in trouble, and Gabe, Em, and Ben, too. Ing had assured her they would be out of prison, with formal apologies from the Israeli government, by early afternoon. But she'd heard nothing, and he would not respond to her phone messages.

She got up from her bed and went over to the window. The night was clear and the moon gave enough light to see the outlines of the hotel buildings and grounds. Jerusalem spread out on the distant horizon, the old section set higher on the hills like an elder keeping watch over the younger. The Tower of the Ascension rose above the low skyline like a lonely sentinel. Debbie remembered from a travel book she'd read during the flight that it stood on the traditional spot where he who was the subject of so much controversy, Jesus Christ, stood as he "ascended into the heavens." The tower seemed to call out, inviting her to approach it.

Much of her lonely afternoon had been spent conjuring up various escape plans. She'd thought to break the flower vase on the bureau over the porter's head when he brought dinner and run through the maze of flagstoned walks into freedom. Somehow, the plan didn't seem practical when the porter's knock sounded earlier that evening. Later she planned to feign illness, hoping to be taken to a hospital where the chances of escape might be better. But she lost the courage to try. Now, well past midnight, she stared at the beautiful moonlit Israeli countryside and faced the fact that she could be held here a very long time. "Until Michael finishes his work," she remembered Ing saying. Her intuition told her his promise was worthless.

She lay back down on the bed, looking around the room. Shafts of moonlight pierced through the ornate window grillework, etching intricate patterns on the carpet. A dim blinking behind an air duct cover caught her eye. She stared at the rectangular opening. There it was again, and again. Fifteen second intervals. Suspicious, she rose from the bed as if to go into the bathroom, and pulled a chair under the air duct. On tiptoe she could see into the louvers. She heard a faint whirring, and something moved. Then she saw the dim outline of a camera. She climbed off the chair and went back to the bed casually, pulling the covers over her as if, at last, going to sleep. Gradually the plan developed.

Pankie spent the afternoon with the only complete copy of the Omega Plan in existence. The chairman's meticulous notes were printed along the margins. She was stunned by its scope and by the intricate checks and balances. Had the video conference with Milton Franklin not happened elaborate bureaucratic machinery would have been activated which would have brought swarms of officials to the Nexa Inn. Now she knew every step that was to come until Omega's call to resurrect the chairman and reestablish him into governing power on Sunday afternoon. It was with a heady sense of opportunity that she wrote and rewrote strategies to take maximum advantage of the next few days.

The sun had set when she finished, and the office was gloomy. She patted her scratch pad. Her own plans were now set. SelfGuide would be designated as head of all six of the world's major social movements. Pankie would be appointed Visgate of Cultural Responsibility, a new World Alliance cabinet post. She loved the title, and could sense the day when she would be able to influence a merger with WOEC, and her own ascendency to its combined leadership.

It was past time for the Nexa porter to set the fire and bring supper. She intended to be in the bedroom with the chairman's body, guarding the door, when he came with the firewood and food. Pankie felt a twinge of concern. She went to the door and noiselessly opened the lockbolt. Then she shed her clothes, took a fresh sheet from the closet, and tucked it up under her arms.

The knock seemed loud. Pankie tousled her hair until it looked like she'd just gotten out of bed, then poked her head out into the chairman's office, looking toward the outer door. "Come in." The door opened slowly and a white-jacketed porter wearing the Nexa plaid beret wheeled a tray of steaming dishes into the room. His back was toward her as he went over to a marble table. She wanted him to see her and make the proper inferences. They would be quite discreet about such things. Pity the loutish employee who might talk a little too much of the chairman's relationship with his personal aide. He would not just be fired . . .

"There on that table is fine." Her thin smooth arm stretched out from behind the door, pointing to the table. "Did you bring firewood?"

"Yes ma'am," he said, keeping his back toward her.

An alarm rang in Pankie's mind. There was something familiar about that voice. He finished setting the hot silver dishes on the table and wheeled the cart to the fireplace. "Will the chairman be joining you?" he asked, opening the screen and piling wood on the andirons.

"No. Later perhaps."

"You sound nervous, ma'am," he said, lighting the kindling.

Pankie pulled the sheet tightly around her, now suspecting the worst. "And you are impudent, servant." She tried to make her voice disdainful, but it came out filled with dread.

The porter closed the fire screen. "May I see the chairman, ma'am?"

"Of course not! He's asleep . . . ."

Pankie jumped, her fears confirmed. She grabbed the door to steady herself. The sheet slid away and fell to the floor. The porter who had turned to face her was Ing Hammock.

"Well my goodness! Pankie Retson of all people. And in uniform!"

She retrieved the sheet and wrapped it around her, glaring in helpless frustration. Ing came toward her.

"Stop! You can not come in! He's resting. We . . ."

Ing pushed past her and went into the bedroom, studying the still body under the bedcovers in the darkened room. "I thought so," he said softly. His anger rose like a volcano and he tore the sheet from Pankie, shaking her violently.

"How'd you do it? Suffocation? Injection?" He threw her onto the bed. Her head bumped against the chairman's. Ing pulled her by the ankles onto the carpet at his feet. Pankie shrieked, knowing this man was capable of anything.

"I didn't kill him! He had a heart attack!" She shrank back under his malevolent glare. The muscles in his jaw twiched in frenzy and his breath pushed through tightly clenched teeth. Without warning his fist swooped through the air and landed flush against Pankie's cheek. The impact tumbled her backward. Then he dropped heavily onto the bed, sighing with defeat.

Pankie lay on the floor, holding her bruised face. "You look disgusting," he hissed. "Put some clothes on."

She scrambled to her feet and escaped to her room. Her mind calmed quickly, and plans began to form. She looked around the room. Maybe the window . . . she thought, hastily buttoning her blouse. Ing appeared in the doorway, leaning against the jamb with arms folded across his chest.

"He was the greatest leader in two centuries. But that would never occur to you."

Pankie was silent.

"That conference was quite a performance." He clapped his hands in mock applause. "Bravo, Miss Retson, bravo."

"Ing," Pankie pleaded, "I didn't kill him! He died working at his desk. The Russian attack was too much of a shock."

"Oh, now I understand. And you were going to get around to mentioning his death one of these days, hmm? Your intentions are obviously honorable. How unfair to assume that that idiotic costume you had on was to deceive anyone!" Ing's sarcasm pushed beyond Pankie's tolerance. It was impossible to withstand.

"Please Miss Retson," he continued, smirking, "accept our humble apologies. Carry on, please." He bowed low, accentuating his contempt. Time froze in that instant Ing's head was bent down before her. In an unthinking explosion Pankie brought the heel of her hand crashing against his temple in a quick karate chop. Stunned, he slumped to his knees. Her eyes fastened on the alarm clock on the table. She clutched it frantically and swung her arm full circle, cracking it hard against Ing's skull. He fell to the floor, motionless.

Pankie trembled, her body weak with escaping tension, and flopped on the bed. Gradually the nausea passed and her thoughts came into focus. A course of action formed and her panic drained away. Soon her disguise was back on, and she was kneading a shallow wound self-inflicted with a razor blade until bloodstains on her blouse were obvious. Then she screamed, and screamed again. In less than a minute the short, bespectacled Nexa manager was pounding furiously at her door. Sobbing, she fumbled with the lock, then opened the door and hurled herself into the startled manager's arms. Blood from her wound stained his Nexa plaid tie.

Sometime later at World Alliance headquarters an aide rushed into Milton Franklin's office to announce a transmission from the Nexa. Franklin looked up through swollen, heavy eyes and waved resigned acceptance. The Nexa's panic-stricken face appeared on the screen. Franklin was roused to attention. "What's the matter? Where's Hammock?"

The manager stammered incoherently.

"Settle down!" Franklin commanded. He was anxious now. After reviewing the tape of the morning's conference, he and the Interior Secretary were convinced something was wrong. Basilia Aretha, for one, was incarcerated in Geneva, the former personal aide under suspicion of grand treason, and Pankie Retson had been appointed acting aide through Moe Cummings' recommendation. The crone in the videoscreen was definitely not Pankie, Franklin had noted.

His biting command had the intended impact on the Nexa manager, and the story was quickly told. The chairman had contracted food poisoning. Ing Hammock arrived and went to the chairman's suite. Later, screams were heard. The manager ran to the suite, and the chairman's aide had staggered out, wounded and bleeding. Ing Hammock was on the floor, dead. The chairman lay in his bed, also dead, a pillow over his face. Ing had murdered the chairman. The aide tried to stop him with the only weapon she could find — her alarm clock — and did, but not before the chairman had suffocated and she had been stabbed.

Franklin stared glassy-eyed at the videoscreen. Decisions which should have been issued like a burst of automatic weapons fire trickled instead through ruptures in the circuitry of his exhausted mind. Faltering questions only added to his confusion. Even the obvious scam over the identity of the aide seemed blurred. Listlessly, he manipulated the camera across the chairman's bed, and looked at the man who had arranged his controlling interest in Prantzer Defense laying cold and lifeless. Through the door he could see the aide laying on her bed, her shoulder dressed with gauze bandages, her eyes closed. Can't be Retson, he murmured, staring at the sloppy shapeless figure. He turned the camera back to the Nexa manager, too tired to be suspicious, too exhausted even to scowl at the forlorn shaken figure. His only thought was that he wanted desperately to sleep. "Send a complete report." Franklin clicked the communication off and sat, remembering and forgetting.

"Sir?" The quiet voice interrupted his reverie. His head snapped up, struggling for alertness. His young aide looked alarmed. "I thought the chairman was already dead, sir. Didn't he — I mean, wasn't he . . ."

Adrenalin pumped its last supplies into Franklin's bloodstream. "Sit down and close the door."

Ten minutes later he was satisfied that no one other than that aide could have seen the transmission. The tape had been destroyed as he watched, and the young man had confirmed very clear understanding of the penalties awaiting the slightest breach of confidentiality. "Now go away," Franklin mumbled, sinking into incoherent exhaustion. "Cancel everything for a few hours and see that I'm not disturbed." He half-stood out of his high leather chair and tumbled onto the long couch, falling almost immediately into a deep sleep. His aide switched the lights off and left, locking the door behind him. 'No way will anyone hear about this,' he vowed to himself, still shaking.

Chapter 33

The chimes of the El Shar tower clock rolled through the villas nestled in the hills. Debbie stood trembling in the bathtub behind the shower curtain, counting. Nine tones sounded. She bit her lip anxiously. As if on cue, a key turned softly in the bedroom door and the maid entered to perform her ritual chores. 'Close it, close it . . .' Debbie pushed the thought toward the unseen maid. The door tapped against the jamb but did not latch. She clutched the towel bar tightly in her perspiring hand, fearful of dropping the metal rod into the tub, dreading the moment she would have to strike the maid. To hurt an innocent woman by her own hand seemed unbearable, even in its planning.

Humming, the maid came into the bathroom and began to wipe off the basin. Through the slit in the shower curtain Debbie could see her back, very close. She had to act now — the maid would pull the curtain open any second to clean the tub.

"I'm sorry, I'm so sorry," she wailed, pushing the curtain away, towel bar raised over her head. The maid turned around, wide-eyed. Debbie swung the towel bar — it clanged against the overhead metal curtain runner and stopped in its arc. The maid fainted. Debbie watched her sink to the floor, grateful she had not had to hurt the poor woman.

She stripped her quickly, pulling the blue and white uniform on and fitting the small starched cap on her head. The cord cut from the bedroom lamp was quickly tied around the maid's hands and feet. She got her into the tub with some difficulty, gagged her and pulled the shower curtain closed.

Adjusting the starched cap, she gathered up the cleaning materials and went to the door, keeping close against the wall to avoid the hidden camera. The most dangerous part was just ahead. She took a deep breath, and then shuffled casually through the door.

The maid's supply cart stood on the walkway. Debbie grabbed the handles, noting two men who undoubtedly were her guards talking a few yards away. Trying to appear calm, she pushed the cart past them. She felt too hurried, stopped and scratched her rump with exaggerated gestures, moving her jaw as if chewing a wad of gum like the maid had done the day before. She continued on, the cart rumbling over the flagstones. Then she was around the corner and out of view. She realized she'd been holding her breath.

Another maid appeared in front of the villa up the hill and waved a greeting. Debbie responded casually as she pushed the cart to the end of the flagstone walk. Without breaking stride, she left it and kept going. The better part of the previous day had been used to study this section of villas from her window, piecing together with logic what the limited view prevented her from seeing. She felt she knew the way to freedom. She turned another corner and came to a stone staircase. It was almost as she had pictured it. Up the stairs, along the path, turn left . . . "I'm coming, Mij," she breathed. Her eyes moistened. She blinked the tears away and forced herself to concentrate. Turn right here, then left again . . . She paced her way toward freedom, not daring to look back.

Finally she reached the most remote villa, the highest in the El Shar complex. Grassland punctuated by small clusters of laurel and scrub bush, and patches of hyacinth and iris, stretched out beyond the crest of the last hill opening to the brief warmth of the February middle-East sunshine. She stopped to catch her breath and peeked around the sun-baked clay wall. El Shar villas rambled down the hillside. Far below a gardener knelt beside a flowering myrtle, his basket of clippings resting nearby. To her left, in the distant haze, the city of Jerusalem offered hope. 'Michael is in there somewhere,' she thought. 'Probably Ben and the others too.'

"What do you want missy?" The shrill voice terrorized her. "Why are you just standing there?"

Debbie spun around and looked up to face a woman leaning out through a window just above the clay wall. Her condescending haughtiness was accentuated by a carefully coiffed black hair bun and garish sunglasses.

"Sorry, ma'am." Debbie tried to inflect her voice with an accent.

"Hmmph!"

She squeezed her eyes shut, hoping this unpleasant guest would not call the front desk to complain. A mere quarter mile across the open grassland separated her from the crest of the hill, and freedom. Maximum exposure — ninety seconds, she had estimated.

"Well?" the woman snorted. "For what they charge here I should think the help would not be . . . Hey!"

Debbie sprang from the villa wall like an olympic sprinter at the sound of the gun. Run faster, expose less . . . She raced up the long hill like the wind, directing every ounce of energy toward the rhythmic pumping of her legs, adrenalin adding an afterburner surge. The crest drew closer. Pump, pump, pump . . . soft crunching of her feet in the grass echoed in her ears. Faster, faster . . . . Spots danced in her eyes, and her legs became rubbery. She stumbled, then caught her balance. Terrain beyond the crest popped into view, and her heart leaped as she spotted a stand of trees, precious protection, perhaps another half mile away. Pumping furiously, she staggered the last fifty yards in what seemed like an eternity. Flying over the crest, she sensed the downward slope under her feet as she collapsed, gasping for air. Above her the blue and cloudless sky welcomed her into freedom.

"God — if you're there?" She gasped for breath. "Thank you."

Only one person had witnessed the escape.

"Harry, that impudent little tripe just ran away while I was speaking to her!"

"I don't blame her, Myrna," a laconic voice replied.

"I'm going to report her! The nerve!"

"Mind your own business," Harry said, resigned for many years to his fate.

"Mind your own business" her shrill voice mocked. "Can't you ever be pleasant? And tuck your shirt in. You look like a slob, Harry. Do you know how you humiliate me? My friends always talk about your shirt tails . . . I could have married Alvin, you know . . ."

As strength returned Debbie thought she could jog the distance to the stand of trees. She was loping toward the protective cover when a deep voice filled the air. She broke into a desperate run.

"MAKE-READY-THE-WAY-OF-THE-LORD"

She reached the grove during the third repetition, crumpling to the ground against a large willow. Then she fainted, and missed the last words of the Global Voice.

"WOEC-IS-MY-CHURCH."

"WORSHIP-YOUR-VISGATE."

Her absence was not noticed until lunch was delivered more than three hours later. The guards questioned the frightened maid at length, rightly fearing reprisal. By the time they were in the jeeps to begin searching, nearly two more hours had passed.

They searched in vain, having no idea where to look. She might have headed toward Jerusalem to the left or toward the coast to the right. They returned to the El Shar at dusk and radioed Jerusalem police for an air search. Two mobile platforms were dispatched into the early evening sky, bobbing and weaving over a four hundred square mile area of rolling wooded and scrub bush terrain. Searchlight beams poked down through the treetops, but revealed nothing. They quit at about ten o'clock.

Debbie worked her way through the wooded patches and over scrub bush hills toward Jerusalem with no idea of what most of the world was experiencing. Soon after the Voice had spoken, shimmering riders on huge thickly muscled white horses rose a hundred feet into the tired dusts of conflict in battle zones and pocket wars around the world. The illusion depended on psychological disorientation developed during the last two days and on the obedience of the field commanders. The victors were to attack, charging in the protection of the immense images. Those who were to be defeated were not to resist.

In most zones, attacking armies devastated disorganized opponents abandoned by military leaders called from the battlefield by governments who saw greater long term gain in temporary loss. The World Allaince had traded much for their acquiescence. Little thought had been given to their straggling forces, now pursued, decimated, and dying in the shimmering mists of huge, sword-wielding horsemen on angry white horses which neither bullet nor shell could affect. Most who perished had never heard of holography. Their terror immoblized what little will to resist might have remained. These were the wars of greed, and the armies were political tools of larger purposes of state, as always. The World Alliance had satiated the greeds of the defeated nations with promises of largesse to come. Even as the dusts of contrived battle settled, leaders from both sides had gathered in gilded rooms of state, signing truce accords and celebrating a new era of peace. That day, the political balance of the world shifted extensively.

But there were other wars in which the combatants were not so compliant. These were the wars of cause, the resistances of conquered people struggling for freedom, the coups against harsh and hated dictators. In these battles, the ploy was unsuccessful. Leaders kept their field commanders in position. Commanders refused to leave their posts, and fierce assaults were met with fiercer counterattack. In these battlefields there was no resolution of conflict. The holographic white horse had hardly brought its peace to the planet.

Debbie, mindful only of escape and of finding Michael and her friends, saw no image. Neither did her tired and discouraged husband now feeling his way along the dark passages of subterranean catacombs, fearful of being followed. Nor did

Ben, Gabe and Em, also in those same catacombs, as they rested and prayed barely two hundred yards from the spot were Michael was.

The disintegration of world orderliness was consummated in the stream of World Alliance trickery. Like a boil slowly developed over decades of hedonism and power misused, it had irreversibly weakened the fabric of social relationships. The boil burst with the psychological pressure of overwhelming and inexplicable events now happening too fast to comprehend. Poisons spewed out, infecting, invading, and filling those regions of the soul which had been protected from absolute dissolution since before the fall in the Garden.

It was not immediately noticeable. Those who were starving were hungry after the Voice came as well as before, and those with the comforts of abundance sat down to their evening meal on the Day Of The Horseman just as they'd always done. But an eerie spiritual tension settled upon people everywhere. The pressure and torment of security lost, severe enough individually, infected hundreds of millions at once. There were few left who were able to give comfort. There was no hope, no will to survive, no reason to receive or offer encouragement. And there was real doubt whether there would be a tomorrow. The Voice had spoken and the Horse had come. Strange signs and wonders spread panic in their wake, and unlinked people across the planet from everything they thought they could count on.

Many, convinced it was the end, dropped the veneer of civilized behavior like a torn shirt and acted out fantasies of lust and revenge. Others, equally convinced it was not the end, stalked those who had shed all semblance of control as a lion stalks its prey, and gathered the spoils of destruction for themselves.

Across the villages of the lands, bands of thugs were joined or challenged by average citizens, marauding and terrorizing in the vomit of accumulated corruption. Buildings were burned and bombed at random. Armies mutinied. Communications systems were destroyed. Families were torn apart by frenzied argument. Throughout the night the sweeping hot fires of panic built, kindled by its own fuel. What people did to one another dwarfed by comparison the aggregated damage of natural disasters. The mountains and the valleys, the skies and the seas, with all their instabilities and unpredictabilities, were no match for the cruelties of human nature released to its own devices. The World Alliance had totally underestimated this terrifying turn of events. Disruption, yes — but disruption controlled by the iron hand of power — that was their premise and their foundation. Milton Franklin, seated with the Inner Circle and the Cabinet in joint session late into the night receiving communiques from around the world, slowly realized it had become every man for himself. It was clear in the furtive looks around the polished conference table that human nature among the privileged and powerful was no different than in the homes of the working man or the tents of desert dwellers. The World Alliance disintegrated like a clump of dried sand, and plotted against one another.

But in one respect their expectations had been exceeded. The subtle work of preparation and the ricocheting impacts of a world gone amok had coalesced into focused hatred toward Christians throughout the world. It was their God, it was said, who was responsible. The WOEC camp suffered somewhat by association — the differences were not as clear to most people as those who had architected the WOEC sophistries thought. But it was the Christians who took the brunt of incredibly cruel vengeance that night. Plans for their persecution, initiated in this same day, were embraced by mobs like hungry animals tearing chunks of raw meat from the hands of their trainers. Armed with official encouragement, fear-crazed people sought Christians with the cry of blood in their throats. Amy Greene was dragged from her home, stripped, and tied to a street light. The mob threw gasoline on her. The fuel would not ignite. Enraged, the crowds attacked and pummeled her into the presence of her God. Warren Heath crumbled under the pressure of threatened harm to members of his congregation. He elected to recant his beliefs rather than expose his people to more jeopardy. It was a naive sacrifice. After taping his recantation he was killed by dismemberment. Mobs spent the rest of the night hunting down his parishioners.

Because Gabriel Diehl couldn't be found, it was with special and flagrant ruthlessness that the staff of his church were stalked. Four were captured. After being beaten and tortured they were chained and crated like animals for shipment to Jerusalem. The World Alliance intended them to be examples of the consequences of failure to step in line with WOEC and the World Alliance.

In the wake of the real chairman's death Milton Franklin lost little time trying to consolidate his power. He had issued a formal change to the Omega Plan just prior to the Inner Circle — Cabinet session. Omega was to denounce the Christian community as heretics, condemn Franklin's political opponents to death, commend the WOEC Visgate for his faithfulness, and place himself in the seat of world power.

But Omega was missing. Major O'Keefe, unwilling to expose the escape and confident they would find him, did not notify the World Alliance that he was gone. O'Keefe accepted the revision in plan without comment. It was a foolish thing to do. He could not activate a back-up Omega without raising suspicion. Everything was vested in finding Michael Ames. Increasingly nervous and angry, they searched more frantically as the day passed.

Saturday morning dawned over a world exhausted and spent in dissipation, fear, and cruelty. Debbie awoke, curled in the tall grass near a grove of olive trees just outside Old Jerusalem. Foraging for olives to stave off her hunger, she noticed an unusual dark shadow near a large boulder and investigated it. It proved to be a hole in the ground. Unaccountably, she thrust her hand into it. There was no bottom.

Chapter 34

They'd travelled for what seemed like an eternity under the Jerusalem hills, guided by shards of light lancing in through surface cracks and fissures. All of Friday was spent in the underground gloom. Em's knee had become swollen and painful. Though he wanted to keep going, the others insisted on resting for a while.

They were in a large chamber with sand and pebbles strewn over the ground. High above, a fissure in the rock opened to the daylight. Its glow revealed three tunnels radiating out from the chamber — three new choices to make when again they resumed their search.

"I've kept track," Em said, stretching his aching leg on the sandy cavern floor. "We've had to choose from two or more possible directions twenty-two times." He sighed. "So far the odds against us are about four million to one."

"But we're going uphill," said Ben, ignoring the estimate of probabilities. His entire life had been lived against the odds and he knew Who had led him through. The fact that they didn't know where they were going was irrelevant.

Gabe stood and moved his arms around in circles to ease the stiffness seeping into his joints from the chilly dampness. "I wonder where we are," he said, hands on his hips, looking up at the light. His mouth was dry as cotton. They'd rationed the bread carefully but its last crumbs had been eaten. None had had water for more than a day. The felt need to get up to the surface was strong.

The parallel between their journey through the catacombs and the Christian walk of faith had not escaped them. Only the Light can guide, Gabe thought, and foolish is he who walks otherwise. He looked up at the fissure.

"It's pretty high," Ben said, watching him.

"Yeah. But maybe . . ." Gabe ran his hands along the wall, feeling for chinks in the surface. His finger touched a looseness between two large stones. "Help me here. Feels like loose mortar or fill." They pried as much material away as they could.

"I don't think they used mortar then," Em said. "It's all sandstone. They would have shaped the stones to fit flush with each other."

Gabe looked at Ben. "So we can dig footholes!" He peered through the dimness. "If we had something to pick with . . ."

"Try these." Em held his car keys out. Gabe took them and dug away at the stone. Sandy material dropped away and before long a small crevice had been shaped, enough for a toehold.

"Gabe, stand on my shoulders. That'll get you part way up."

Grunting, Gabe managed to get on the large man's shoulders. Shaking and pressing against the wall for support, Ben stood slowly, and Gabe reached up. There were still more than two feet from the tip of his outstretched fingers to the opening.

"Can you get through?" Ben puffed, holding Gabe's ankles with his hands.

"It's wide enough, but too high."

Em felt his stiff knee. 'Lord, You'd better hold this knee steady because I can't.' Then he spoke. "If I was on your shoulders, Gabe, I could get through."

Ben eased down to a crouch, his back wound feeling like it was on fire. Gabe jumped off his shoulders.

"I don't know. Your knee is pretty bad. Ben, can you hold us both?"

"We've got to try, friends."

Michael awoke with a start. It was pitch black, and for a moment he panicked. Then, feeling the sandy floor and rocky walls, he remembered. The breathless wait under the pantry opening, the slow step by step progress without light, the desire to doze for just a moment . . . He wondered despairingly how far he'd walked. He remembered coming to the end of a tunnel wall and a faint glow of light beyond. Then exhausting tension and a sleepless night had overtaken him, and he'd retraced his steps back into the security of darkness and slept.

He felt a spot of dried blood where he'd hit his head on an outcropping of rock. Suddenly hungry, he tore one of the biscuit bags open and ate slowly, thinking. They had to be hunting for him with a vengeance. He had no idea where he was or how to get back even if he wished to. He shuddered, thinking of the guard at the foot of the stairs he'd mysteriously neutralized. The biscuits filled his stomach but dried his mouth. He knew he must not panic, and had often given that advice to others. But there was a difference, now that panic was coming after him. The battle was suddenly real.

"There must be a way out. Henri! Where are you?" Michael's voice echoed in the chamber. He waited expectantly in the dark. Nothing happened.

"Henri!" Just one more time. Please!!"

'Shhh!" Gabe said, puffing for breath on his hands and knees. The second try at their human ladder had just failed. "I heard something!"

The others were instantly motionless. "Came from over there I think," Em whispered, pointing to his left.

"Maybe a stone tumbled out of the wall nearby," Ben said. Em looked at him with surprise.

"They have to fall some time," the large man said, shrugging.

"Let's try again. We've got to make it."

Ben and Gabe got on their hands and knees side by side. Em painfully climbed onto their shoulders.

Michael listened to his echoes die away. He snatched up the bags of biscuits, shivering in the chill, and stuffed them under his shirt. He brushed off his tunic and ran his hands through his lengthening hair, shaking out the sand. The openings in the walls of his cavern forced a choice. It had felt like he was going downhill before stopping to sleep. He selected the rightmost tunnel, which seemed to be higher than the others. He walked for perhaps fifty yards in the blackness. Then the tunnel curved to the right and a faint glow reflected from the wall. Dead ahead the end of the tunnel segment opened into a larger cavern. It didn't take long to reach it. He stepped out into the cavern and paused until his eyes grew accustomed to the light coming through a high crevice no more than twenty yards away.

Ignoring the stabbing pain in his knee, Em balanced on Gabe's shoulders, ready to stand up. He had relied on God many times — but never in the simple basic survival mission which now consumed him.

"Oh my . . . Lord!" Ben stared at the far wall of the chamber, suddenly oblivious to Em's weight.

"Huh?" Gabe puffed, following the direction of Ben's wide-eyed stare. Then he saw it. His body swayed and Em clawed at the wall for support. Then he too saw the figure twenty yards away. "Jesus," he breathed.

They had seen a man with tousled hair and flowing white robe, and the identical features attributed to Jesus Christ. It was as if the portrait on the office wall of Gabe's church had come to life.

Michael saw them at the same time, perched on each other's shoulders like an acrobatic pyramid. He froze, unable to believe what his sight insisted was there.

Em eased off Gabe's shoulders to the sand of the cavern floor. The others stood up slowly, their eyes squinting in the dim light. Even as they'd seen him they knew it could not be so. The passages of scripture revealing how Jesus would return in power were well settled in their spirits. Suddenly the figure disappeared. Michael had recognized them and had stepped back into the tunnel, fighting the battle of the eyes beholding a fact which the mind insisted was impossible. The eyes won. If it really was Gabe Diehl, Emerson Prantzer and Ben, he had not seen enemies but allies. He remembered his haughty treatment of the gentle scientist when he'd carried out Franklin's instruction to fire him, and regretted it deeply. With a deep breath, he returned into the chamber.

"Dr. Prantzer. And Ben. And Dr. Diehl. Michael Ames here."

They stared. It was his voice, yes. His features were similar, yet — different. Michael wondered why they hadn't acknowledged him. Then the plastic surgery came to his mind. He touched his hands to his face.

"They . . . changed me," he said.

"Michael Ames," Gabe said, astonished. "Yes, it is you." Michael composed himself and turned toward Em. "Dr. Prantzer, if there was any way to retract the way I treated you . . ." He extended his hand. "I apologize."

Em looked at Michael's offered hand, then shook it tentatively, almost absent-mindedly. Sure enough, it was real. He smiled. No words were available.

Michael reached inside his shirt. "I've got biscuits if you're hungry." They watched him pull four bags of bread rolls out, and quietly celebrated another miracle. Michael watched and heard, but could not understand. He felt estranged, yet their eyes and their tones were those of friends. He knew what he had escaped from — but what had he escaped to? His life and all he had worked for suddenly felt arid and lifeless. Bits and pieces of scripture beamed like tiny floodlamps on his dark vanity. He recoiled from the light and embraced himself more by stubbornness and habit than by genuine attraction.

Michael found himself grappling with a dissonance he could not will into silence. The more he defended the goodness of his intentions the more they revealed their malice. Visions of fat diners, journeys through galaxies, adulating crowds, and winking lightspots across the grey lands of time rushed through his thoughts and collided with his conceptions. He found a ledge on the wall of his identity partly sheltered from the sudden storm of spiritual conflict, and scrambled onto it. The storm abated then, and in its stead came not peace, but truce.

They sat on the sand, leaning against the cavern wall, and talked. Michael's story flowed out like poison leeching from a wound. Astounded, shocked, amazed, saddened, they listened. When he finished, night had fallen. Gabe fished a candle out of his pocket. He lit it and stuck its end into the sand. They silently watched the flickering flame, realizing their underground home had become a sanctuary from the horrors of hell descending upon the face of the earth. It was more than they could comprehend.

"Michael," Gabe said, "may I suggest something?" Michael nodded, somehow knowing what he would say. "Think on the words you've memorized. Feast on them. They give you the real Christ. You need Him not because of what you've done or think you've done but because you're just like us, and we need Jesus constantly. Don't fight it. There doesn't seem to be much time left." Gabe's tone had no judgment or animosity. He spoke gently, urgently. It was his sincerity which touched Michael. Before he could willfully block it he found himself inwardly acknowledging that he wanted to believe. He wished desperately that he could. Michael stared at the candle flame and thought.

The others separated around the cavern to bed down for the night. Gabe dropped to his knees in the sand along the far wall. "Lord God, I trust your prompting, that Michael not be told Debbie is here, and missing. Lord, protect her. For those of your church, Lord —" He continued to pray long into the night. From time to time, soft musical utterings drifted through the cavern. As the last moments of life flickered in the small remaining puddle of wax, the first gleams of dawn reached gently down through the fissure. Michael looked up at the strengthening sliver of light and thought of O'Keefe searching for him, angry enough to kill. There were, after all, other Omegas.

He heard a stirring in the sand and found Ben sitting next to him. A few minutes later Em joined them, excited.

"He even answers prayer that hasn't been prayed!" Em whispered, his face wreathed in a smile.

"Say what?" Ben said, a gleam in his eyes.

"My knee — a little while ago I felt a warmth, and when I moved it there was no pain or stiffness."

Ben laughed. "It was prayed, brother. But I didn't ask that the knobbiness would go away, you'll notice."

Just as Gabe rejoined them the puddle of wax flickered a last time and went out. He, too, Michael noted, seemed at peace. 'The world is ripping apart, these guys are lost underground, and they act like it was just another day.' His irritation reawakened. The contrast with his companions was disheartening.

Ben looked up at the light-filled fissure. "You know, with Michael's help I think we could get up there now." The idea was a tonic. They studied the fissure, discussing the way to climb out. Suddenly a woman's hand poked through.

Chapter 35

Even through his exhausted mind Milton Franklin saw that the World Alliance had become an empty shell. Legend and bluff had become its chief weapons of influence. Its resources had been dissipated on the trappings of new power without adequately building its substance. And all that remained had been vested in the Omega Plan.

Blunt discussion among the Cabinet had finally yielded to shouting, threats, and stormy departures of leaders and their delegations. The political balance had shifted away from a delicate network of coalitions wrought over decades of work. In its stead the equilibrium of military and economic power returned, and member nations sought their advantages without regard for precedent.

Franklin was not without allies when Saturday's cabinet session crumbled. But neither did he lack for enemies. If he could, he would have cancelled the Omega Plan. But he could not — the actions already taken were irreversible. He could not erase the terror of white horses or mysterious voices from the sky. But neither could he make good the pledges to those nations who cooperated with their manipulations. And he could not prevent stronger governments from exploiting their advantage independent of the shattered forum in Geneva.

He sat at his desk brooding, head held between his hands. His body was stiff and aching, and his eyes burned. A dull throbbing deep inside his chest had become a constant companion.

"They've gone mad."

"Sir?" The ever-present aide looked up questioningly.

"Nothing. Go away. I want to sleep."

"Sir, you depart for Jerusalem today at twelve noon."

He remembered the arrangements he made with Jedesky when he had changed the Omega Plan to have himself named to power. "You must come with me to Jerusalem, Milton," the Visgate had said, "to receive your anointing. The Alliance is dead. Omega is the only hope."

Franklin spoke with more customary brusqueness. "Prepare my luggage. Have something sent up to eat in an hour. Wake me then."

The aide stepped out quickly and closed the door. Franklin put his head down on the desk. He was asleep immediately.

"Over there!" Major O'Keefe barked, pointing to a doorway. "Check in there, idiot! Check everything!" The guard, clinging to the leash of a straining bloodhound, pushed through the doorway of the ancient clay building, returned only to signal that it was empty.

O'Keefe cursed and stomped down the dirt road, slapping his swagger stick against his thigh. Professor Schmidt hurried after him, short legs stirring up dust, stubby arms pumping back and forth. "Herr O'Keepf, I tink I got hidea," he puffed.

"Your 'hideas' haven't been too 'goot,' " O'Keefe called over his shoulder. "We're out of time. I'm calling in the alternate." He stopped and spun around. The professor almost bumped into him.

"But ve MUST find der real Omenka! Da other iss dumpkoffen . . he cannot DO vat must be done!"

"That's your problem. Just make it work." O'Keefe turned and strode angrily toward the Tower square. The professor stood in the street, palms up, still pleading.

"It von't vork, major! He iss thikenskul!"

O'Keefe stopped and wheeled around again, waving his swagger stick menacingly. "It better go like clockwork, professor, or there'll be little carved up pieces of your fat stumpy body all over this city!" He turned and stalked away.

Professor Schmidt mopped his perspiring brow with a large blue kerchief. "Ach mien," he muttered. "Omenka, Omenka, vhy haff you deserted me?" Shaking his head sadly he waddled toward the Mischa, talking himself into the possibility. "Vell, I see vat to do mit der other Omenka. I get him goink, ya — den pooph! I dischappearen. Blitz-like. Oh mama, I be in Bavaria dis time tomorrow. Enough mit der folderolschen."

He entered the lobby door, shuddering at the blood smears where the hapless guard had been stationed. When Omega's escape was discovered O'Keefe had assembled the team and instructed the guard to show everyone where he had been when Omega got by him. When the uncertain guard sat in his chair O'Keefe had taken his pistol and unceremoniously shot him.

'Maybe not tomorrow, mama,' the professor mused, rethinking his intentions. He shut the door of his room. It almost blocked the sounds of the major's shouting outside in the Tower square.

Twenty minutes later there was a knock at his door. The professor opened it carefully, peering through into the hall. Outside stood a tall, slender man clad in a white tunic. "Omenka!" he gasped, throwing the door open.

The man sauntered in, chewing a piece of gum. "Okay prof, where do we start?"

"Ho, boy," the professor mouthed, throwing his hands up in defeat. "Maybe today in Bavaria, mama, after all. Phizzelbrassen!" Sighing, he sat down beside the new Omega and opened the script book.

Satisfied that the loose ends had been tied and that the Nexa manager understood the priorities, Pankie pulled her coat on. Although she did not know the extent of deterioration within the World Alliance, she suspected from news reports that there was more than enough turmoil to meet her needs. She was confident that she could at the very least get through the days following the chairman's death unscathed and blameless. And if a few things worked out, she may even be able to carve out a bigger piece of the power pie. She remembered echoes of her past . . . 'You must become hard. You must get more than you give. They will yield control into those hands which belong to kindred spirits and to no others. For their control will be yielded only to those who are wise enough and hard enough to take it from them.'

"Steady yourself Pankie," she commanded, throwing a scarf around her neck. "Just do it right."

The Nexa manager mopped his forehead and forced a nervous smile, remembering with unwelcome vividness the time they'd spent crating two bodies into wooden boxes and hauling them down to the Nexa's storage room. His assignment was to get rid of them. He wasn't sure just how he would do it, but he already knew he would move mountains to accomplish his task rather than face the fury of this harsh and angry woman.

"I'll handle it, Miss Aretha. Really I will."

"I know." Pankie looked at him with all the malice she could muster, and confirmed his worst fears. Then she walked quickly down the wide wooden front steps and into a waiting airborne platform. The platform lifted off the frozen Newfoundland ground, leaning forward and accelerating toward the airport thirty miles away. Ten minutes later she was in a wash room near the boarding gate wiping pancake make-up from her face and dye from her hair. She was sure the Nexa manager had suspected her disguise, but more sure that he was sufficiently intimidated to neutralize his suspicions.

Pankie's plan was designed to insure her survival and capitalize on present chaos. Milton Franklin was the only one, besides herself and the Nexa manager, who knew of the chairman's death. She knew Omega was to have named him as the world's ruler, and it was elementary enough to deduce who now would be called on the coming Sunday. She could control the manager by fear. But she knew of no way to control Franklin other than by eliminating him. Within ninety minutes of her arrival in Geneva there would be no Milton Franklin. All she needed was the element of surprise, another disguise, and ten minutes alone with him. With that accomplished, survival would be assured. No other connection could threaten her. But Pankie also saw the opportunity to move SelfGuide into the void which the first part of her plan would create. When Omega appeared on Sunday he might not know of Franklin's demise and would call him to power. When Franklin would not appear, Omega would be discredited and the opportunity offered by his appearance would be lost. She had to get to him before the appearance and give him new instructions from the office of the World Alliance chairman.

Pankie had decided she did not want the post herself. Better to be the power behind the scenes and allow others over the next several years to take the brunt of the present turmoil. Later, perhaps, she would move into the open.

Unknown to Pankie as she boarded her flight, Milton Franklin took off from Geneva, bound for Jerusalem in the sleek World Alliance jet. They were thousands of feet above the ground for a part of that Saturday when contrived signs and wonders battered a reeling world.

Huge red horses billowed upward in the battle zones, reigniting wars quenched the day before. In many zones, military commanders ignored the images rising almost foolishly into the sky. They had new instructions and more important issues to deal with.

Two military detonations officers huddled behind a small rise in the rolling landscape two miles from Mt. Etna. Its seaward side had been loaded with nuclear microcharges. According to World Alliance geologists the detonation would collapse its western flank, hurling trillions of tons of mother earth into the sea. Its peak would collapse inward and its height would drop by several thousand feet.

Two minutes before automatic detonation a convoy of ships hydrofoiled into view beyond the mountain, southward bound for the coast of Africa. The lead vessel was golden, with a red emblem on its side. Escort destroyers moved alongside and behind her, foiling in criss-crossing patterns like a school of playful porpoises. The captain pressed his binoculars to his eyes, stunned at the sight.

"Who are they, sir?"

"Russian ships! I don't believe this . . . the premier's flagship! You know what that means?"

"Trouble, sir?"

The captain scrambled over the top of the rise. "We've gotta stop that timer — now!"

"All right sir — we'll just sprint two miles in — let's see —" The sergeant checked his watch.

The captain glared, piqued by the insubordination. The convoy disappeared behind the mountain. He jumped up and down on the ridge, shouting and frantically waving his arms. The sargeant watched the second hand sweep along the dial of his watch. "Eight seconds sir. Shouldn't you come down now? Four . . . three . ." The captain scrambled back down to safety.

The explosion was felt before it was heard. Then the sky darkened, and roaring conflagration erupted. Many minutes later it quieted. They peeked slowly over the rise. The sea was still boiling with the crashing of part of the mountainside into its waters. The ships were nowhere in sight. Mt. Etna smoldered in mortally wounded rage. The sergeant shook his head and lit a cigarette. "The chairman ain't gonna like this at all, sir."

"We followed instructions. It's his problem, not ours."

Suddenly a second explosion dwarfed the first like trees against toothpicks. The men were hurled off their feet by its shock waves. Etna, her thick inner crust ruptured, was erupting. Dust, steam, and molten lava drove with fury thousands of feet into the air. The men ran, stumbled, fell, and were pelted alive and buried.

Trains rumbled to a stop near New Delhi, in the central plains of the United States, in the mountains of Ecuador, and at the central Johannesburg freight station. Each had fifty freight cars and several coaches. Wearing thick clothing and helmets sealed against the atmosphere, World Alliance monitors disembarked and stationed themselves along the train's length. Freight car doors were opened. The noise of the locusts was deafening as they poured out and swarmed in huge dark clouds of whirring destruction.

"Glad to be rid of those little devils, eh?" a monitor remarked.

"Can't believe they actually did it," another said, shaking his head. "Who'da thought that . . ."

"You tryin' to welch? Pay up — you set the odds."

"Never thought they'd do it," the other said as he reached into his pocket.

A week earlier a rocket had lifted from the mid-continent launch pad, its destination an asteroid whose orbit would take it relatively close to Earth. The asteroid was five miles in diameter. World Alliance scientists had chosen it based on its iron content, which was enough to enable magnetic clap down. When the ship was firmly attached to the asteroid's rough surface, holes were laser-drilled deep into its core and nuclear charges implanted. The crew would fire the main engine while still clamped to the iron hulk in order to push it into a collision course with earth.

The command came, and the main engine fired. Thirty-seven minutes later the ship separated from the asteroid and glided away. For the next two days the asteroid accelerated in the earth's gravitational pull. At the right moment the charges were detonated, and a brilliant flash in the northern sky was seen by half of a world already reeling from explosions, locusts, poisoned air, and panic. The terrifying firestorm raged for almost an hour. Larger chunks of the asteroid slammed into the ground, devastating surrounding areas by their white-hot impacts.

The parade of contrived disasters was, by and large, successful. But persecution of the Christians on a scale envisioned by World Alliance planners did not develop. Tragedy enough it was, for those remaining, that many had been martyred the night before that terrible Black Friday, when the panic of a traumatized population ran unchecked and released the people of the world into an evil night of mindless revenge. But such intensity could not continue. Trauma and anger yielded to exhaustion. Greater forces than all the World Alliance had counted on were operating to restabilize the people. While grief and suffering and shamefulness would continue to burn the souls of a generation, the hot edge of panic had been dulled. Realization poked into immobilized thought like new shoots of green rising from charred wastes of the forest fire. Suspicions of hoax arose, and with it a new kind of anger. Rubble began to be swept up and carted away. And the wailings of a lost world given over to itself were loud and excruciating.

Chapter 36

Newly encouraged, they worked enthusiastically to build their human pyramid and climb up through the fissure. "Whoever that was would have no idea anyone's down here," Gabe remarked, positioned on his hands and knees on the sandy floor next to Ben. Michael balanced on their backs while Em held precariously onto Michael's shoulders, horseback-style, and steadied himself. Straining under Em's weight Michael stood slowly, holding the rough cavern wall for support. He could touch both sides of the vee-shaped covelet which poked through into the open air. Em managed to get his feet positioned on Michael's shoulders and wriggled his back up along the wall.

"I'm through!" he called. Ben grunted under the weight.

Em blinked in the morning light. A large boulder was inches away. To his left through the tall grass, Jerusalem stood in the haze. To his right olive trees waved gently in a slight breeze. A sudden movement behind one of the trees startled him.

Michael shifted, and in the movement Em's head bumped against the boulder. He yelped in pain. "Can't hold much longer . . ." Ben's voice floated up through the opening.

"You there!" Em shouted suddenly, deciding on boldness. "Show yourself!"

A woman peeked from behind the tree, a look of sheer astonishment flooding her face.

"Yieeee . . .!" Ben could take no more, and collapsed. Em dropped out of sight like a prairie dog, scraping his nose on the way down. They tumbled down onto the sand. Em jumped to his feet, oblivious to a slight nosebleed. "That was Debbie! Debbie's up there!" His eyebrows bobbed up and down in gleeful laughter. Gabe and Ben did a high-five and cheered. Michael watched in disbelief. "Debbie?" He looked up. And there she was, framed in the fissure's opening, looking down at the scene of celebration. A shaft of light beamed over her shoulder and illuminated Michael's face. He laughed excitedly. "Debbie! It's you!"

She stared as if he were a stranger.

Gabe looked up. "It's Michael, Debbie. And he's all right."

Her eyes were large and unblinking. "Oh, Mij, what have they done to you . . . what have they done?"

"Deb. This can be fixed." He pointed to his face.

Debbie reached down through the hole toward him. "Oh Michael I've been so worried. So much has happened . . ." Suddenly she screamed and disappeared as if being dragged away. Her hands clutched at the rim of the fissure, then were wrenched away. A few pebbles tumbled to the sand by his feet. The leering face of Major O'Keefe appeared in the opening.

"Hello Omega. Out for a little stroll?" The major's head shook as he kept his hold against Debbie's struggles. She pulled her foot around, and managed to strike a glancing blow against O'Keefe's head. He cursed.

"Excuse me Omega," he said sarcastically, disappearing from the opening. Michael could hear them scuffle, and inside him a helpless fury raged. Then the leering face reappeared.

"Somebody you know? Maybe you met her in Jerusalem last night," he said, winking with exaggeration. Michael jumped up again and again like a mad dog leaping at an assailant out of reach. O'Keefe grinned, enjoying the pathetic spectacle.

But he hadn't seen the others. Out of view in the shadows, they watched their young anger-crazed friend, and the taunting face above, with outrage. Ben was moved to action.

"I'm going to try something," he whispered, rubbing his shoulder. "It may be the only shot we've got." The fire of his own anger burned in his hushed tones. Gabe and Em looked at him, puzzled.

"Meet David," he said softly, pointing to himself. "And Goliath." He turned his finger to the face of the opening. "Em, give me that elastic belt you're wearing. And pray, both of you. May the Lord guide the stone now as He did then." He ran his hands over the sand of the cavern floor and found two pebbles, each about the size of a quarter. Setting one of the stones in the belt-sling behind his back, he got up and sauntered toward Michael, counting on surprise. He grabbed him roughly and shoved him out of the way. The major stopped in the middle of his threats, gaping with surprise. Ben looked at him sternly.

"I am Omega's special assistant, fool. Who are you?"

"You — what?" O'Keefe sputtered.

Ben readied the stone behind his back and snarled at the major. "Where's your discipline, you slob! I'll have my men up there burn you to an ash!" His voice echoed with authority. The major peered down into the hole not altogether sure what was happening. The belt-sling whirred and the stone was released before he ever saw it hurtle upward and crush into his mouth. He slumped over the edge of the hole, unconscious.

Gabe and Em cheered and clapped Ben on the shoulders. Michael stammered his gratitude, amazed. A drop of blood dripped from the major's jaw and splashed on Ben's balding head.

With Debbie's help they pulled the unconscious man through the opening and into the cavern, handing him down their pyramid formation with strength born of victory. Debbie quickly followed. With O'Keefe safely bound and gagged, they rested. Debbie, a large bruise on her cheek and an eye swollen, was cradled in Michael's arms.

"Lunch time, folks," Gabe said cheerily, passing along a bag of biscuits. They chewed the hard bread slowly, coaxing what moisture they could into their parched mouths. Michael studied his friends and thought about their handling of the major. Admiration and confusion mingled until he could not stay silent.

"Don't misunderstand — I'm grateful for your putting O'Keefe out of commission. But I thought you weren't supposed to — you know —"

Gabe chuckled. "You mean you think to be Christian is to be passive, no matter what the issue?"

Michael reddened, although no one could tell in the cavern's dimness. Gabe had snatched the words right out of his mind.

"Sort of."

"Dig into that memory of yours. Check Mark Chapter 11."

Michael mentally scrolled the pages of scripture. "The moneychangers?" He read the pictured text.

> "When they arrived back to Jerusalem he went to the temple and began to drive out the merchants and their customers, and knocked over the tables of the moneychangers and the stalls of those selling doves, and stopped everyone from bringing in loads of merchandise. He told them, 'It is written in the Scriptures that My Temple is to be a place of prayer for all nations, but you have turned it into a den of robbers.''

"Does that sound like a cowardly man, Michael, single-handedly driving away well-connected merchants and con artists, or overturning a table piled with coin and currency?" Gabe saw the realization glint in Michael's eyes. "He was angrier that day than you were an hour ago. Jesus never taught against anger, but against anger of the wrong kind. Vengeful, self-indulging anger and anger prolonged beyond its purpose is evil. Anger at injustice is a call to legitimate action."

Michael sat staring at the sandy floor, stroking Debbie's hair, deep in thought. The major groaned and moved, then slumped over unconscious again. Gabe pointed at him. "Anger filled its purpose, Michael — his intentions were obvious. Now the Lord would have you be forgiving of him."

"What?" Michael blurted. His flesh crawled with desire to damage O'Keefe thirty times over for striking his wife. It demanded revenge, and he'd already vowed that he would make him pay dearly, sooner or later. "No way," said Michael bitterly, glaring at the unconscious form on the sand.

"If God said that about us we'd all be in trouble," Em remarked. "Letting go of the right to revenge takes courage. None of us can do it without His strength."

"Okay, okay, enough preaching!" Michael smoldered, resenting their words even while suspecting they were right, and hating the thought.

Ben eyed the fissure as he stuffed the last bag of biscuits under his shirt. "We'd better get on up there and have a look around. And find some water."

The change of subject was welcome relief for Michael. He was starting to grasp the magnitude of the Omega hoax with new insight, and a new kind of anger was building and pressing for release. He knew then that he would do whatever he could to thwart the Omega Plan. If he'd never seen evil before, he saw it now in this incredibly deceitful hoax. O'Keefe had merely personalized it for him. As he passed through that crucial doorway of recognition his views of himself, his values, and his world began to crumble. An outlet for action was, perhaps, all he would have to balance the pull toward emotional collapse.

"You okay Deb?"

She nodded and sat up, understanding. "Let's do it."

Debbie was first up the pyramid and out to the fresh air. The olive grove was quiet and peaceful, the sky overcast now and threatening rain. There was no indication that calamity ravaged the world that day. Em scrambled up, puffing and red-faced. Moments later Gabe emerged and wrestled himself onto the ground.

"What about him?" Still in the cavern, Michael motioned toward O'Keefe who was now conscious and glaring with unveiled malice.

Ben waved him off. "He'll be okay for a day or two if he's as tough as half the folks in Binzoe."

Michael nodded. "Okay, get on my shoulders."

"You're kidding, friend. You think you can hold me?"

"Come on," Gabe called to them. "Make a rope out of your tunic. We'll pull you up."

Michael tore the thick linen tunic into several strips, tied them, and threw the makeshift rope up through the opening. At Ben's insistence he tied the other end around his own chest. Slowly he was lifted out of the cavern. It felt wonderful to stretch out on the cool grass. He untied the linen rope and dropped it down to Ben.

O'Keefe chose that moment to make his move. The belt that bound him had been worked loose without much trouble, and his burning revenge outweighed the intense pain in his jaw. With a small knife from his boot sheath in one hand and a rock in the other, he was on his feet. Ben turned around just as O'Keefe thrust the knife straight forward into Ben's stomach. Both fell to the sand from the impact.

Michael, galvanized into action, pushed through the fissure and dropped to the sandy floor, rolling with the fall. O'Keefe pulled himself off Ben and cocked his arm to throw the rock. Michael kicked upward, catching his wrist and knocking the rock out of his hand. He grabbed O'Keefe and pulled him to his feet in one smooth movement, crashing him against the jagged stone wall. An uppercut crunched into his jaw, and then another. O'Keefe shrieked with pain and slumped to the sand. Michael wheeled around to face Ben, expecting the worst.

He was leaning on an elbow, grinning. In one hand he held up a hard biscuit, a small knife buried in it up to the hilt. They laughed with relief and amazement. Suddenly Michael leaned over and bear-hugged the big man, crying with relief. "Thanks for staying alive you big bozo . . ." Ben smiled and patted Michael's back. "Thank the Lord Jesus, my friend."

They rested in the grove, filled with olives, thirst slaked from a small stream nearby. The Tower of the Ascension rose in the afternoon haze a mile away. Michael had described in detail what was to happen. Even Ben in his years among the downtrodden, the outcasts, and the street gangs had never confronted such absolute corruption. They discussed the options calmly. But inside, their tension mounted. It was more than the deceit set to be consummated. Something was wrong in the air, too — it had a deadness to it, a depression, an unheard scream and an unseen leer. Like that certain feeling that someone is staring at you, they could sense hidden abominations leering at them with loathing.

Occasional traffic passed by the road down the slope, threading through the Kidron Valley along the outskirts of Jerusalem. The road disappeared around a curve, and an access road futher on led up to Old Jerusalem's East Gate.

Wailing sirens broke the silence. Then a caravan of limousines appeared, moving slowly along the road. A fearfully familiar emblem adorned their doors and hoods. "World Alliance," Michael said. "Coming for the Temple consecration ceremony. The final chapter is beginning."

A tractor-drawn wagon followed the limousines, its sides made of open steel bars. It was a cage on wheels. Four men hung from wrist shackles chained to the roof. They watched, horrified. Sudden recognition drained Gabe of color. "Oh my Lord, no . . . no!"

Em Prantzer strained to see, then sagged against a tree, weak with shock. "Eric and Paul. And the Dugin twins."

Michael looked down at the passing cage and recognized Eric Linday, the assistant pastor of Gabe's church with whom he had once met.

It took time to work through the acid edge of their first grief. Finally Gabe spoke with a quiet determination. "We will wait on the Lord," he said simply.

Michael stared, disbelieving. "Aren't you carrying this is a little too far? Isn't it time to do something, Gabe?" He pushed the point, his ire rising. "Your friends are being hauled around like animals and you want to wait on some figment of your imagination?"

Ben held the biscuit up, the knife still imbedded in it, without a word. Michael exploded.

"You put that biscuit in your shirt! No magic hand from the sky put it there! It was a lucky break, Ben!" Michael jumped to his feet. It was dusk, and the lights of Jerusalem glowed. Faint sounds of the city drifted into their hearing. "You can sit there, but if you want anything done you've got to do it. I'm going to get those men out with or without you. And I'll kill any World Alliance guy I find." He turned and stomped down the slope toward the road, then stopped and faced them. "When push comes to shove you haven't got it. I knew there was nothing to all this stuff." A hot rush of awareness that he had spoken things he would regret burned inside him. But he'd taken his stand. So be it.

"Mij?"

"What?" He spat the word out with disgust.

"I think they're right."

Michael glared, surprised. Her eyes pleaded for him to stay. Debbie knew Michael well, and feared his stubbornness would prevail and put him in grave danger. "It's too big Mij. Whatever it is, we can't understand it. None of us. Something will develop. Please."

He was most angry because he knew she was right. The others held their silence, not wishing to aggravate Michael and increase the risk that he would stalk away into jeopardy. Gabe had seen it again and again, the natural man rebelling against the Christian's obedience. He'd seen it most often in himself, where his own "old nature" sought every opportunity to accuse and condemn the Spirit-led command to walk true to

God's Word whether it seemed to make sense or not. He'd never found a good, rational answer to the issue. It was only when he acknowledged the true reason for his decision — "because I believe to the best of my ability to understand that that's what God would have me do," that he found the necessary peace and courage to persevere. Michael's problem, Gabe knew only too well, was that he had no new nature to argue with. Naturally he had to strike out in his own strength — he had no other strength to draw on.

Michael wavered. "Do you really think, Gabe, that this Jesus of yours is going to do something? Your friends are out there hanging by their thumbs, they imprisoned my wife and the three of you, they tried to kill Ben — all while you've apparently been trusting in this . . . . this imaginary tradition? Is that the kind of life a Christian lives?"

Unknown to Michael, his words kindled new hope in the hearts of the three men. Some of their prayers were being answered — and it couldn't have happened without Gabe's statement of obedience, strong enough to invade the natural state of mind.

" 'Vengeance is mine — I will repay, said the Lord.' " Gabe spoke the words slowly, clearly, looking directly at Michael. "I understand your feelings. And —" Gabe paused, sadness reflected in his expression — "you're right. There've been many times when I haven't had whatever it takes."

"Me too, brother," Ben said softly, only he knowing the deep truth of his remark.

At their submission to his unjust accusation Michael felt pangs of regret. His desire to lash out evaporated like a puff of mist in a fresh breeze.

"Go if you must, friend. We'll hold you in prayer."

Their faces were nearly obscured by the approaching darkness. Debbie went to Michael and took his hand and led him back. He followed without resistance. He would not admit it, but he was glad that Debbie had pulled him back.

They waited and thought. Ben hummed a hymn softly, peace and strength filling his features. Em passed out some ripe olives he'd picked. Michael lay on the ground, his head on Debbie's lap, and wrestled with himself. He began to discover that the words of his memorized scriptures were the only effective weapons against the spirit-like screams and attacks launched against him from very deep inside.

Finally he got up. "I'm not going to go out and play heroics, Gabe," he said, smiling now. "But while we're waiting for whatever we're waiting for, I'm going to go up to the Gate and look around. Maybe I can find something out."

Gabe looked up, then suddenly stood and dusted off his trousers. "Mind if I go along?" There was purpose in his eyes. "You guys keep watch, now." he added.

"This is probably the safest place in the Middle East," Em said. "We'll be fine. You watch for yourselves."

Michael's watched showed 6:45. "Okay. Back by nine forty-five."

"Bring some beef sandwiches," Ben said. "Heavy on the catsup."

Chuckling, they went down the slope to the road.

Chapter 37

Pankie remembered the way to the chairman's office from her visit four years earlier when the World Alliance was wooing SelfGuide. The headquarters complex had deteriorated, judging from the littered desks and tired, listless faces of those she passed in the corridor. The laxity of security was encouraging. Her plan for Milton Franklin was as simple as a good Shakespearean plot. Instead of hemlock she would use modified cyanide. She would distract him sexually — sure to be a shock given her ugly disguise — and put the poison into his ever-present cup of coffee. She would be in Jerusalem before the fatal dose would take effect, and he would have met with many others before ending his day. He might even die in his sleep. No suffering, no noise, no traceability or suspicion.

She approached the private office suite. The paste-on warts felt tight on her face, and she was pleased by her cold steadiness. "Basilia Aretha to see Mr. Franklin," she said, smiling mysteriously.

"Do you have an appointment, Ms. Aretha?" An aide asked condescendingly as he scanned the chairman's schedule.

"I don't need one, young man. I was in Geneva, and Milton is an old friend . . . I was his personal aide once."

The aide pushed his glasses up higher on the bridge of his noise, suddenly suspicious. "I'm sorry, but the chairman is not taking visitors."

She touched his necktie and winked. "I don't think you understand . . . Milton and I are very . . . good . . . friends." She tugged the necktie gently and moved toward the office door. The aide jumped in front of her.

"I'm sorry Miss Aretha."

Pankie glared angrily. The aide was young, but not naive. "Very well," she said curtly. "Book me for tomorrow. And tell him I'm staying at the Maquard."

The aide held his patience. "As I said, the chairman's schedule is completely filled. And if I may say so —" he took her arm and lowered his voice to a conspiratorial hush — "he is the Chairman. He does not just appear in hotels or take personal calls." While he was whispering close to her he confirmed his suspicion. The warts were not real.

"He'll find a way," Pankie retorted, with just the right touch of sarcasm. "Thank you for all your help." She turned abruptly and walked away, her mind racing to find an alternative course of action. Her intuition told her that Franklin may not be there. She approached the security desk. "Good afternoon," she said, stopping. It was a risky move, but under the circumstances, worth it. "Did the chairman depart on time?"

The guard scowled.

"Please . . . I'm late for a briefing." She smiled enticingly and held out a hundred dollar bill. The scowl turned to short-lived suspicion. Why not, he thought. He touched the keyboard of his monitor screen. "Yes, he left on time."

"And that was to — Gander?" She offered a helpless grin.

"Are you nuts? He and about twenty of 'em went to Jerusalem."

Her heart pounded. "Thanks," she said, turning and disappearing quickly down the corridor. Hours later she was on the Saturday evening flight to Jerusalem.

"Get O'Keefe. And send Grennoble and Ames' wife to my suite immediately. This news blackout of theirs is going to be over once and for all." Since Hammock's accident at the Nexa Franklin had assigned his chief of security, Hans Grennoble, to supervise Debbie's house arrest.

"Tell me when Jedesky arrives."

"Yes sir." The aide went to the door. "And have coffee sent up here!" Franklin added as the aide disappeared.

Franklin sighed, unable to remember when he had been as tired or discouraged. He fingered the dark baggy flesh hanging under his eyes. 'One more night, just one more night . . .' He sat on the couch and pulled his briefing folio onto his lap, lighting a fresh cigar. "Sunday Schedule — Chairman. 10:00 — depart El Shar for Tower ceremony. 10:35 — debrief at Mischa . . ."

"Sir!" His aide skidded through the door, agitated. Franklin looked up over the top of his glasses.

"Grennoble — hasn't been seen since this afternoon. And . . ."

"What! Where is he then?"

"N-no one seems to know, sir."

"Find him. Now! Got it?"

The aide turned pale and gulped. "What, what!" Franklin raged. "Get going!"

"Mrs. Ames . . . uh, escaped. Sir."

Franklin set the folio down on the coffee table, straining against his screaming nerves. With blood in his eyes and menace in his voice, he spoke softly and very slowly. "Get O'Keefe in here as fast as you can. Immediately. Now. Now!"

Terrorized, the aide ran from the room. Franklin swooped his hand and caught the large china vase filled with fresh gladiolas flush on its side. It tumbled through the air and crashed against the wall.

The aide and a guard attached to the chairman's contingent collided as they rounded the same corner from opposite directions.

"Bad news," the guard puffed, bending over to retrieve his hat. "They can't find O'Keefe."

The aide groaned. "Three people missing. Three out of three. Mrs. Ames escaped. And no one can find Grennoble or O'Keefe."

The guard mopped his forehead, breathing more easily, his mind unable to carry him further. He looked dully at the aide, awaiting instructions.

"You tell Franklin," the aide commanded. "I have some things to check out."

"Yeah, sure. Which way?"

The aide pointed up to the floodlit villa. The guard's eyes followed. "Right."

A few minutes later Milton Franklin's raged-filled bellowing echoed throughout the El Shar complex. The aide shuddered and headed for the lobby bar.

As Michael and Gabe crossed the road they heard a squeal of tires, and tumbled into the bushes just before headlights caught them. A taxi sped by. Michael's brief glimpse was enough to see the passenger. There was no doubt who it was.

"That was Pankie Retson!"

Gabe's eyebrows lifted in surprise. They hurried through the cover of rolling scrub bush land toward the Gate, and Old Jerusalem. They could hear cries and shouts from within the city's walls more clearly now.

"We've been out of touch for almost two days," Gabe said. "With their plans for tomorrow they probably pulled out all the stops today."

"Why would this God of yours let so many people get hurt?" Michael asked the question suddenly, with a trace of anger.

"There are answers in the Bible, but none that I could or would accept on my own terms. Suffering, fair or not, has always been here. Jesus suffered, and most unfairly. We suffer with or without volcanoes and earthquakes. Maybe it's the calamity that gets our attention. I don't know why. But I do know that without trusting God there are no answers at all."

Michael continued walking, his head down. He felt an obligation to be angry, even incensed and offended, not at Gabe Diehl but at a God who would allow — or cause — calamity and suffering to affect so many. But his anger would not kindle. He felt like an engine fueled with water.

"What about you? You're a believer."

"By God's grace."

Michael waited. "So, what's your answer? There must be more to it than trusting some concept, Gabe."

The moon had risen over the horizon. Gabe marvelled at the similarity between Michael's appearance and the portrait of Jesus Christ on the wall of his church. It seemed so far away now, and the time that had gone by seemed more like six years than six days. He sighed. Michael thought of Henri. It was as if Gabe was his new guide and mentor. 'He even looks like a little like him,' he mused.

"God is above all a God of reality. It's a mystery why He allows suffering, especially when it seems unfair. For me, my times of suffering were important times of growth in faith of my life. A muscle grows with exercise and nourishment. And there is pain in real exercise."

"I can buy that," Michael said. "But I can't buy little kids being molested or innocent people being burned and buried in volcanoes. Or random accidents. It feels like a shotgun is pointed at us. If the scatter pattern misses, great. If it hits, that's tough."

"So it seems, my friend," Gabe said earnestly. "Does it surprise you to know that I agree?"

Michael looked at him strangely. "It certainly does."

"That's what I meant. There are no answers without the Bible. To us it not only looks like random kindness and cruelty — it is. We aren't capable of seeing it any differently."

"But there are religions that seem a lot more sensible than yours. Take the reincarnationists — at least with them you get another chance if you're blown away this time around."

"We've created some great rationales, haven't we?"

"How do you know it's rationalization, Gabe? It's no more or less valid than your Jesus, or Buddha, or even atheistic thinking!"

"Many say so. Can you agree that in the end there is only one truth?" Gabe held up his hands, motioning for patience as Michael began to protest. "I'm not insisting — yet — that any one 'religion' as you've called them is totally right and the others all wrong. Assume if you like that the truth may be some combination of all of them. Think about truth, not about religion. Wouldn't you agree that there cannot be contradition within a body of ideas or thought which is fully true?"

"On that basis it's impossible to disagree."

"Isn't it odd that the finest minds working across the centuries haven't been able to identify and agree on that truth? Today more than ever there is intense disagreement. We have no real truth by our own efforts at all."

"If you're talking about unity I couldn't agree more," Michael said ruefully, picturing the Tower square. "But individually a lot of people are very certain. You, for example. Or Pankie Retson."

"What about you, Michael? Are you certain of your position?"

Michael stopped in his tracks and faced the question he had turned from many times before.

"No I'm not. I try to act like it and feel like it, but I don't have the faintest idea why I'm here or what I'm doing. It seems futile. If I make it big, I make it big. Then I die. If I foul up and go bankrupt and ruin everything, I fail. Then I die. So what?"

Gabe nodded, understanding. "You're right about me though, Michael. I am utterly certain."

"I know! You don't have to hold it over me!" He paused, ashamed. "Sorry." Gabe smiled, and brushed it off.

"I know you're certain. How can you be certain, and I cannot? I want to know that answer."

"All right," Gabe said. "The difference is in the Person Who you were about to counterfeit. He is the Lord Jesus Christ, your Lord and mine. The difference is that I have accepted that and you have not."

"But how do you accept that? How do you know it's true?"

"We agreed, Michael, that there is only one truth. Jesus Christ said that that's Who He is . . . 'I am the Way, the Truth, and the Life . . .' How did I accept the truth? By deciding to trust Him in what He said. Then I discovered I had the real Truth indeed."

"But," Michael sputtered, frustrated. "What if I decided that Buddhism is the truth, and trusted that?"

"You wouldn't find the Truth. You would find pieces of the Truth, Michael — many of their teachings are true and strike harmonious chords deep inside. But their teaching misses the core, and so does every teaching which doesn't center on Jesus Christ as Savior and Lord. He is the core, the Author and Finisher of our faith."

"Easy for you to say, pastor. You've obviously committed to Jesus. I'll bet if I'd committed to Buddha I'd be just as defensive on his account."

"Perhaps. Many are. You could also commit to a grapefruit or an elm tree and be equally defensive."

"Maybe I will! It looks like just committing to something is the key, and that it makes no difference what it is! You happen to hit on Jesus Christ. Great. I'll take the grapefruit. Equally great."

"Go ahead, then. Commit!"

Michael looked at him with surprise. "You consider me a lost soul doomed to Hell, yet you say I should commit to a grapefruit? Meaning, I take it, anything other than Christ?"

"You hit a nugget of gold a moment ago, Michael. You said that committing to something is more preferable than committing to nothing. Jesus said 'I know you well — you are neither hot nor cold; I wish you were one or the other! But since you are merely lukewarm, I will spit you out of my mouth!' Those who commit to nothing have no anchor, no identity, and no hope. By default they go in whatever direction they're pulled, like jellyfish in the tide. They have no substance. Yes — commit to something! You'll find whether it's worthy to be trusted soon enough if you can be open to its reality. But you cannot play games. You must commit for real."

Michael listened hopefully, suspecting a great misunderstanding of his was about to be cleared up. "So you would commend me if I commit to Buddha. Right?"

"I would commend you for committing something to something rather than committing nothing to anything. And I would be confident that you wouldn't be satisfied unless it was the Truth."

"Are you saying I don't have to be right the first time?"

Gabe looked at him with compassion. "My friend," he said, putting his arm over Michael's shoulder as they walked, "who of anyone has been 'right the first time?' This is your ten thousandth time! Growth is in the searching, and truth is in the finding. Jesus' teachings are filled with words like 'seek' and 'learn,' words which mean a process, a lifelong experience. There is no final examination in life. Every breath you draw is a new opportunity to test and try. The final exam comes at death and only then. And when that time comes it is swift and sure, and utterly just, because you will have seen and heard all you need to make your decision."

They walked in silence for a distance, nearing now the walls of Old Jerusalem glowing balefully in the moonlight.

"Did you try anything else before committing to Jesus?"

"Yes I did. I was fanatically committed to sports cars, for instance, as a lad."

"That's as stupid as committing to a grapefruit!" Michael exclaimed, exasperated.

"True."

The scriptures in his memory scrolled of their own accord —

> "Before anything else existed, there was Christ, with God. He has always been alive and is Himself God.

He created everything there is . . . and Christ became a human being and lived here on earth among us and was full of loving forgiveness and truth . . . for God loved the world so much that He gave his only begotten Son so that anyone who believes in him shall not perish but have eternal life . . . there is no eternal doom awaiting those who trust Him to save them. But those who don't trust Him have already been tried and condemned for not believing in the only Son of God. Their sentence is based on this fact — that the Light from Heaven came into the world, but they loved the darkness more than the Light, for their deeds were evil. They hated the heavenly Light because they wanted to sin in the darkness. They stayed away from that Light for fear their sins would be exposed and they would be punished . . ."

Gabe dropped to his knees suddenly and crouched behind a bush, pulling Michael down with him. He pointed to the Gate just a hundred yards ahead. Sentries spaced every two or three hundred yards apart stood atop the wall. The Gate seemed to beckon to them. "What do you think?" Gabe whispered.

Michael studied the situation. "You're the one who wanted to wait for Jesus to do something, Dr. Diehl," he said, smiling. "I'm willing to wait too." He was more surprised by what he had said than was his companion.

Gabe nodded and bowed his head, his lips moving silently. 'Praying again,' Michael noted. 'Always praying.' He pulled his arms across his knees and watched the sentries pace slowly back and forth along the top of the wall. And he began to think about Gabe's friends and where they might be held, and why Pankie Retson was here, and how this incredible nightmare got started. The anguished cries which drifted over the wall sent greater chills through him than did the brisk night air.

Chapter 38

Every hotel room seemed booked as dignitaries and guests thronged to Jerusalem to commemorate the signing of the Document of Consecration for the Temple, now completely restored. Hospitality suites throughout the city buzzed with discussion of the amazing series of recent events. Most of it was not idle chatter. The destruction of the Soviet convoy and their premier when the seaward side of Mount Etna was blown apart had produced serious threats of retaliation. Publicly of course the World Alliance disassociated itself from any connection with the event, citing "an act of God" as the obvious cause of the volcano's explosion and subsequent eruption. WOEC backed the statement immediately. But behind the scenes the Soviets angrily confronted World Alliance officials, rejecting out of hand any notion of innocence.

Milton Franklin escaped the initial confrontation by coincidence of his trip to Jerusalem. But once arrived at the El Shar, he'd barely vented his anger over O'Keefe's disappearance and Debbie's escape before a Soviet delegation descended on him. It was to be an exhausting night for the chairman.

Pankie finally found a small room in a run-down motel on the outskirts of the city. The Star Hostel was not the kind of accomodation she was used to. But there was enough to occupy her attention without adding to it complaints of the neon sign glaring through her window or the noises in the next room.

The taxi driver fingered the large tip Pankie had given him to wait. She unpacked quickly, washed and changed, and stuffed money and the World Alliance stationery she'd taken in Geneva into her walking pouch. She knew where Milton Franklin was, as did everyone who saw the caravan of limousines leave the airport with military escort. Her driver had given her all the information she needed.

"Let's go," she said impatiently, jumping back into the taxi and slamming the door. "I need a typewriter first — a good one."

The driver grinned. "Yes yes, I know where!" Wheels spun in the gravel as they lunged into the road and accelerated down the highway.

"Let's go in."

"Are you sure you want to take the risk? If they find you it means trouble."

"There's some other guy in there who is supposed to look just like me. If I'm caught I'll just be him. And I know a way out if it gets bad — through the hotel and into the catacombs."

"The men in there are my responsibility, not yours, Michael. And their captors are ruthless."

"Tell me about it. We can't help them from out here. And judging from the uproar inside, we probably won't even be noticed."

Gabe noted his determination and was grateful to him. They both knew why Gabe had casually joined Michael on his walk to the wall. Once he understood his leading, he could not sit by while his brothers were in the condition he'd glimpsed of them earlier on the road.

For Michael, pride drove his decision to take the risk. He couldn't let Gabe go alone after his outburst back in the grove. And he burned from the feeling of being no more than a pawn in a terrible game. It had sunk in at last. He was a part of the Omega plan because of the set of his cheekbones and his photographic memory, and for no other reason. Deeper forces influenced him as well. Since the Omega Plan first put a Bible into his hands and its words into his mind, the light and life of Jesus Christ reached out to him. While he continued to resist the pull, he had to acknowledge that the pull was indeed there to be resisted. Prolonged resistance could eventually kill that pull — it had in many people — but it was still new for Michael. There was something in it which beckoned him through the Gate.

The events at work in these days were not at all the final triumphs of a rational world government, but the results of deranged madmen acting out the lessons of history on a well-worn stage. He saw the truth of the corruption which their kind of power had generated, not only in the ugliness of the lie about to be sprung upon the world, but in himself as a willing and even enthusiastic conspirator. 'Gabe says commit to something,' he thought. 'I committed to this, but then broke it. What, then, is commitment?' It was the sensation of an evil sickness which propelled him to action. He hoped that might purge his stains of involvement. He studied the sentries. "I've been watching them. Every two minutes they make a quarter turn left. See? There they go now," he whispered.

Gabe watched the line of sentries turn like tiny toy soldiers on a carved clock.

"We can get close enough to the Gate under cover of the scrub bush. When that one turns toward the city we'll go in."

Staying low, they moved through the brush to within a few yards of the Gate. A small parking area with several automobiles shielded them from view. Just through the Gate they could see a canopied bazaar with people thronging around endless booths and tables, and heard merchants hawking their wares. Two sentries guarded the Gate, one in each lane of the road leading in. Michael whispered his idea as they watched the sentries. It seemed like ten minutes until they moved. But then the nearest one pivoted a quarter-turn, looking down now on the city, his back toward them.

They crept between the cars up to the wall, then eased toward the edge of the Gate. Michael tossed a stone in a high arc. It thudded in the bushes on the other side of the road. Both sentries instantly brought their rifles up and stepped out to investigate the noise. For just an instant their backs were toward them. They dashed around the corner and through the Gate, Michael shoving the nearest guard hard as they went. The guard sprawled onto the road, his weapon clattering on the pavement. Michael and Gabe disappeared into the bazaar crowds and made their way toward the Tower square, stopping to buy fresh fruit from a stand along the way. They chomped it hungrily as they walked.

They approached the cage with that reverential awe one experiences in the presence of innocent suffering. Gabe's eyes filled with tears at the sight of four good friends hanging silently from wrist straps, their bodies outlined in the faint moonlight drifting in through the dirty windows. "Eric!" Gabe whispered. "Eric!"

A head lifted, slowly, and eyes looked up dully. Astonishment slowly worked across Eric Linday's features.

Michael opened the cab door of the tractor which had pulled the cage. A ring of keys hung from a knob on the dashboard. "Incredible," he breathed, fumbling through them and trying each in the cage lock. The third one worked, and they jumped up onto the cage floor. Gabe held Eric up, trying to ease the weight on this wrists. Eric smiled imperceptibly. As Michael unlocked the wrist bands Eric sagged into Gabe's arms. He eased him down onto the cage floor. They quickly released the others, Gabe checking each for signs of life.

Michael jumped back to the concrete, his adrenalin pumping. Twenty feet away a World Alliance limousine stood in the gloom, waiting. "If they left keys in the tractor . . ." He ran over and pulled the door open. The key was in the ignition. They loaded the four unconscious men into the back seat. Michael climbed in to drive while Gabe went to open the large door. Suddenly there were voices just outside. He ran back to the limo and jumped in. "They're coming. Several of them!"

"Hang on," Michael said grimly.

The door shook as the men outside pushed. Then it flew open. Michael turned the key and the engine coughed into life. He pulled the headlight knob and pressed the accelerator to the floor as he slammed the car into gear. Tires squealed and the limo hurtled forward. The men, two of whom carried small black medical bags, dove out of the way as the car charged through them to the cobblestones outside. They heard two gunshots. Both slugs hit the back window and caromed away.

"Bulletproof. Quaint," Michael said tensely.

"Which way?" Gabe's voice was tight.

"Anywhere downhill . . ." Michael wheeled to the right and accelerated through the narrow alley. They hurtled out the other end and skidded around the corner. The limo roared through the bumpy streets, scattering pedestrians. Panicked chickens flapped their wings, madly pumping spindly feet to escape. Bouncing against the stone walls of curbside buildings, they spun left at the bottom of a hill and found themselves on the main bazaar thoroughfare. "Yee-ha!" Michael shouted. They swerved their way through tourists and merchant's booths like a metal reaper. Silk scarves leaped into the air, one grabbing around the hood ornament. A fruit stand was splattered by the left headlight. The right fender glanced off a table piled with clay jugs and pots and shattered them into thousands of pieces.

Then in the distance the Gate appeared, gleaming under yellow floodlights, inviting them toward freedom and safety. Sentries stood under the arch, rifles raised and aimed directly toward them.

"Keep your head low," Michael commanded. Gabe hunched down. The crack of a rifle sounded, then another. Two bullets thudded against the windshield and caromed away. "Quality stuff!" Michael shouted.

The sentries rushed to pull the steel fence across the Gate. Michael floored the accelerator. Tires squealed on the flat paving stones and the engine roared. Bullets peppered the limousine from sentry posts along the wall. The limo burst through the sheet metal gate as if it was a paper-covered hoop, and the wooden road barriers exploded in splinters. They were through.

The narrow access road dropped off down the hillside. They sped to the intersection and swerved to the right onto the highway without slowing. Seconds later two black cars roared through the Gate in pursuit.

Alerted by the distant gunshots, Debbie stood in the grove watching tensely. Then she saw headlights break through the distant Gate, and a car sped down the hill. She gasped. Then two more cars raced through the Gate in pursuit. They could hear an engine roaring, still out of sight but coming closer.

Then headlights lanced the darkness from far down the road just below them.

"That has to be them!" Em said excitedly.

"Go! Go friends!" Ben was jumping up and down, cheering. Debbie watched with disbelief. Suddenly she squeezed her eyes tightly shut and prayed. In that instant of pure crisis she knew Someone had heard her plea.

They could see the speeding car now, and headlights of the two pursuit cars racing after them. "Okay Emerson," Ben said. "Time for action." Ben pointed to the boulder adjacent to the opening into the catacombs. They managed to upend the stone and roll it like a huge egg over the lumpy ground to the edge of the slope.

"Timing," Ben puffed. "When I shout, push hard."

Debbie ran over and wedged her feet in the ground, putting her hands on the stone next to theirs. The first car roared past just below, and in that moment they had a clear view of Michael at the wheel. They cheered spontaneously. "Get ready!" Ben shouted.

Their bodies coiled with special energy behind the waist-high stone. The whine of the pursuing cars sounded like angry banshees. Then headlights broke over the hill and knifed through the darkness along the road.

"Now!" Ben commanded.

They grunted with a mighty heave, and the stone plopped over its uneven side and onto the steeper part of the slope. It paused momentarily, shuddered, then bounced down to the road, crunching into the asphalt when the lead pursuer was only twenty feet away. The car skidded and spun, its left door slamming into the stone and crushing inward. The second car crashed into the first, and the twisted mass of metal spun around another half turn before skidding off the road and overturning in the drainage ditch.

They dashed far back into the grove, hearts pounding, and crouched down in the scrub bush. For a long time they watched and listened, alert to the slightest movement or sound. But it was all quiet. Slowly, then they carefully approached the knoll overlooking the wreckage. Glass shards glittered in the moonlight, and steam hissed from a radiator. An arm dangled out through a broken window, motionless.

Chapter 39

"We can't stay here," Em said, rubbing the back of his neck as he surveyed the wreckage. "Probably be more pursuit cars soon."

Ben scrambled back up the slope. "Doors are wedged shut. Couldn't tell, except none of 'em were moving," he said, breathing heavily.

"I hope Michael is safe," Debbie said. "And I wish this nightmare could just be over with." Ben put his arm around her shoulder. "He was doing great twenty minutes ago. They're safer than we are now. We'd best be going. Em?"

"Yes . . . back into the scrub bush would be best."

'But they won't know where to find us," Debbie protested.

Em pursed his lips, thinking. "One of us should stay here. You two get going." He pointed toward the countryside glowing under the light of the moon behind them.

"Shhh! I thought I heard something," Debbie whispered.

"There — yes. I heard it too. It sounds like somebody's digging."

"Come on," Ben said. "Let's find out."

She was exhausted, cold and hungry. But Debbie knew there was no other choice. Sighing, she fought back tears and followed Ben and Em into the scrub bush.

They'd gone about a quarter mile away from the grove when the noises of shovels scraping into the soil were very close. Ben stopped, crouching. "Over there — a light just flashed, like a reflection on metal. Through those trees."

Em pushed further forward like an advance scout and peered through a clump of low bushes.

"Praise Jesus!" he shouted.

Michael and Gabe spun around, shovels at the ready. Then tension disappeared into joy. In a moment Michael was hugging Debbie, and the men were hugging each other.

"You guys are early," Ben said, clapping Gabe on the back.

"We forgot the sandwiches," Gabe chuckled. Then he saddened. "Paul and the Dugins are gone. We're burying them. Eric's barely alive."

In a desperate effort to elude the pursuit cars they had driven off the road and into the scrub land, doubling back toward the grove. When they thought they were safe they stopped and attended to their friends. It was too late for three of them. Ben did what he could for Eric while the others buried their three friends, grieved to the quick by the torture they had endured. Their love for Paul and the Dugin brothers drove their sorrow all the more deeply. As the final shovels of dirt were tamped over their bodies, tears mingled with the good earth. They drew a cross in the dirt of each grave and placed scrub bush branches over them.

"We commend the souls of these your servants Lord, to You," Gabe prayed. "By Your promise they rest in joy. Be with each of us now and guide us safely through whatever is ahead."

They sat together by the limousine, assured that Eric was stable at least for the present. The chill night air and their grief sent shivers through them. 'What now,' Gabe wondered. 'We are so tired, Lord. So hungry, so uncertain. Do we just go to the airport and fly home?' He tried to avoid the answer he sought. But it had to come, and he knew it would. 'Okay, Lord. By Your grace and Your strength alone. I ask for Your confirming sign, for I jeopardize my faithful brothers and two who have yet to respond to Your call. Praise You and Amen.'

"I think we should stop them."

They stared, first disbelieving, then laughing. They'd each broken the silence with the same words . . . "I think we should stop them . . ." at the same moment. A sign had indeed been given. Gabe, Ben, and Em experienced again that joy of being in God's will and God's presence despite the dangers. It was a joy infinitely preferable to any other human experience, the experience that people were designed to have. They had it in abundance.

Michael and Debbie leaned against the fender of the limousine, watching with unmasked yearning. Here, away from images to maintain and with people they trusted, they had neither desire nor will to hold to any pretense. Although they had experienced simultaneous speech they neither had nor felt any ability to celebrate the occasion. Yet they saw it being celebrated, and knew the joy was real.

Michael's first instinct was to claim coincidence. But he knew it was not so. Two saying something similar, even three, maybe. But five? With the exact words? But he knew nothing else to explain it. It had happened . . . just like his "coincidental" encounter with Ben, like the incredible catacombs reunion with Debbie, like his dreams and his visions, like so many other things . . . .

Debbie was profoundly touched by the three men she had become so fond of, not in anything they were doing but in their lack of guile, their innocent trust, their steadfast kindness. And most significantly, by their inner strength and peace.

"Gabe?" Michael sighed and tossed a twig into the scrub bush with resignation. Looking straight into the pastor's eyes, he faced the truth pushing inside of him like an unborn baby squirms in the womb. "Talk to me." He looked down, his voice quavering more than he would have wished.

Gabe knew in his spirit what was happening to Michael and cut quickly through the remaining softened barriers. The two men communicated volumes in the intensity of their gazes, and spoken words revealed only small patches in the quilt of Michael's last struggle.

"What's got you?"

"I'm not sure. Pride, maybe."

"And something about time, urgency . . ."

"Yes! Too much competition, career — it's demanding — like a trap."

"What do you think about?"

"Business. Money. How to make it better, how to get more."

"Priorities."

"That's it. I've tried to fit Jesus into my scheme of things so I can have what I keep seeing you have. He won't fit. I'm afraid I can't . . ."

Gabe nodded, understanding, and waited for Michael's despondency to quiet. He rocked forward where he sat and pulled his arms around his knees. The air was crystal pure and its coolness seemed refreshing now rather than chilling. Pale moonlight bathed them in a soft glow.

"The problem," Gabe began, "is that we can't live with more than one top priority. Naturally it's ourselves. We sort and shift priorities, but one and only one remains supreme. Everything we do, deliberately or instinctively, is for our own self. As long as that natural priority stays on top nothing can separate us from it. Jesus Christ did not give us a lesser priority to work into our lifestyle. He presented in Himself a clear and very different top priority. That priority is God, not Man. When He said 'no man can serve two masters' He meant it. We can pretend to serve God while serving ourselves, but we cannot actually do it. Jesus tells us to die to self because that's the only way the top priority we were born with can be replaced."

Michael listened as if enraptured. Gabe's words seemed like gold flowing into an empty treasury.

"These two priorities are the Christian's old and new natures. The 'old man' in us is well understood. But the new Man — Jesus Christ in us — is an enigma to any who have not actually received Him. The single thing a non-believer can recognize about Jesus Christ is that He is a threat to his top priority — himself."

A splash of defensiveness gripped Michael. "Gabe, of course my top priority is me. No one else will look after me if I don't!"

"It's like being on a river in a canoe drifting toward a waterfall. Until you hit the falls that canoe looks like the best place to be. In fact it's the worst."

"But that waterfall is there for both of us! Do you really believe you're not going to die some day too?"

"This is what it means to be born again. I'll lose this body just like everyone. But I've been born spiritually. I will never lose that life, thanks to God in Jesus Christ. The birth in which we have no responsibility ends in death. The birth in which we have full responsibility never ends."

"So you say I have to be born again?"

"Your spirit already exists but needs to be born into the life of Jesus. Think of your spirit on the platform of a train station. Jesus — the train — comes, and waits. Will you climb aboard? Those who have one birth will have two deaths. Unless your spirit is born in Christ it will die like your body. Those who have two births will have only one death, that of their body. Their spirits will continue."

"So at the end I blank out — no suffering or lakes of fire at all!"

"Who says death is blankness or unconsciousness? Death, my friend, is literally the absence of life. To think that it means unconsciousness just because a corpse can't hear or see or respond is like thinking the world is flat because you can't see beyond the horizon! Yet what you say is one of the most deeply rooted hopes of the non-believer."

"Who says that death is anything else, Gabe?"

"God does."

The scriptures from Revelation scrolled through Michael's mind as if by a heavenly prompting —

> ". . . And I saw the dead, great and small, standing before the throne . . . and each person was judged according to what he had done . . . if anyone's name was not found written in the book of life he was thrown into the lake of fire."

Michael shuddered. He had scoffed at the severity, judging it too unfair to be real if there was a God and inconsequential if there wasn't. But his will to argue and rationalize seemed to be in chains, prevented from distracting him from the truth of God's judgment against sin and those who choose to love sin.

"You put a lot of faith in a book, Gabe."

"These are the written testimonies of people who lived and ate and walked with Jesus Christ Himself, Michael. The Bible is the word of God."

Michael shook his head sadly, unable to feel even a glimmer of the mystical experience he thought necessary. "I have no hope, none at all. I can't experience what I see in you, and at the end it will either be blankness or worse."

"Michael, stop focusing on our experiences and on what does or doesn't make sense. Above all, stop focusing on your natural fate. Focus on Jesus Christ. He and He alone is the hope, and He alone is sufficient. You need nothing else. Jesus is the Answer."

At those times in life where the crossroads wait it's futile to deny the presence of powers which demand a decision. These are precious moments, as varied and unique as the individuality of those confronted by the Choice which must be made. For some the times come often — for others, only once. But for all, the last occasion is the sufficient occasion of everlasting Choice. And a Choice is always made. So it came for Michael and Debbie Ames. The scriptures locked in his mind flooded his heart like the bursting of a dam, convicting and giving hope. He saw in himself the impossibility of experiencing life as his three friends did. He realized his capability and natural inclination lay in behaving as those who had tortured and killed, like Major O'Keefe. He saw that his way had no joy and that he had no virtue, and realized that for all of his ambitions and skills and earnings and future plans, he was lost. All that he had trusted ended in nothing at all. A wash of depression, an emotional downdraft he had long since learned to deal with by renewed concentration and focusing on the task at hand swept him. He instinctively began to turn from it as he always had. But a thought blinked quietly in his mind. 'This is the time of your decision — once turned away, you will stay away forever.'

He felt an accountability which seemed to be true despite the tired logic which argued against it. He knew he had The Emptiness which cried to be filled, and that he was empowered to make the Choice . . . to retreat, or to reach out to the Christ Who reached out to him.

For Debbie it was a matter of intuition, calling to her now with unique energy and urgency. She sensed an opportunity which transcended understanding and refused to be denied. It was as if she had discovered a flower so beautiful that all else paled into insignificance and she could not help but stop and touch it. Self-awareness departed and she was enabled to make the Choice to retreat, or to reach out to the Christ Who reached out to her.

Michael fought it, clinging stubbornly to what for him was the more rational course, insisting that the power he in fact experienced, the power of the Living God, was not there at all. He was neither released nor impelled. He merely wrestled within his spirit, straining to reclaim the familiar and shallow orderliness in which the nature of man finds its only solace. For a moment, his stubbornness seemed to be gaining the upper hand. Then, surprised, he realized he was clinging to the fender of the limousine. Self-conscious, he relaxed his grip and looked at the three Christians. They stood silently, watching and waiting nearby. The love and power in their faces astonished him. They almost seemed to glow.

Debbie turned to her husband, her face contorted in the anguishing choice of remaining by his side or taking another step in the direction which called to her so clearly. Then she decided, and grasped Michael's hand in her own, reaching out with the other to Gabe. "I want to know Jesus. What do I do?" She spoke softly, shyly, but clearly, and her heart leaped in the certain knowledge that she had just done something much more right and true than she could comprehend. She bubbled from within, and felt cleansed and pure, and wonderful and light. A joyous laugh of freedom and delight spilled out.

Gabe took her hand, praise in his eyes. "What must you do? Child, you've done it!"

Debbie was radiant, eyes gleaming and tear-bright. Holding fast to Michael's hand, she turned to him.

Michael was at war. He sagged even physically against the limo, his expression a turbulent blending of desire to yield to the power of the call and resistance to all it implied. He looked at his wife with fleeting contradictions of admonishment and gratitude, anger and happiness, amazement and chastisement. The enemy was most unwilling to let him go.

"Michael, the Spirit is upon you, and you wrestle as Jacob wrestled."

Michael looked at Ben, understanding only part of his meaning.

Gabe glimpsed something — someone? Milt — Milt! "In the name of Jesus Christ I bind you, Satan. By Jesus' power I command you who are defeated to leave this man. Be gone!" Gabe's command was sharp and urgent. He raised his arm up toward Michael.

Michael looked at the pastor like a wrestler twisted in a painful hammerlock might look to his trainer in the corner of the ring. He was amazed that Gabe would say such a thing. But the adversary melted away like wax in the sun, and he sensed an easing of supernatural tension.

"You must be free to make your decision yourself. Now you are. May I call you brother?" Gabe spoke matter-of-factly.

It was Debbie's expression which made the difference . . . a new Debbie, with an exquisite peace and happiness. Michael was touched as never before. As he looked at his wife it was as if she was going somewhere very special, hoping with all possible energy that he would come, but going nevertheless. She would be with him . . . but she would be new.

Weary of resisting and finding resistance no longer relevant, convicted of emptiness, he dared to hope that this time, at last, what he would choose to trust in would prove trustworthy. Michael yielded. "Yes, Gabe. Call me brother."

It was enough. Michael, of his own willingness, had opened his heart to the possibility of Truth. Possibility entered and became Christianity. Truth had been waiting for this moment. And Certainty took on the Personhood of Jesus Christ. Michael recognized Him and sank to his knees in gratitude. He felt clean. "Yes, call me brother. Call me brother!"

He jumped up and embraced his wife, lifting her up and spinning her around. Ben cried unabashedly. Gabe beamed. Em clapped Michael excitedly on his shoulders.

"Hallelujiah!" a weak voice sounded nearby. Eric was leaning out the window, pale and exhausted, but smiling with triumph, most definitely alive and conscious. "I said 'Hallelujiah!' "

The sudden burst of a gunshot and a whizzing sound through the grass cut the celebration short. Even from a quarter mile away they'd been heard by World Alliance monitors following up on the first two pursuit cars.

"The enemy doesn't waste time," Gabe said as they tumbled into the limousine. Michael had the car started and moving as the last door slammed. They bounced and swerved through the scrub bush landscape, following the path cut by the car earlier that evening. Michael veered sharply to avoid a ditch, and bounced onto the highway. In seconds they were speeding away from Old Jerusalem. The newer section of the city glittered in the distance.

"Which way?" Michael stopped at a fork in the road and peered into the rear view mirror. So far there was nothing but darkness behind them. But headlights appeared from the left, and a taxicab raced by, swirling a cloud of dust as it passed.

"I think that's the way to the El Shar!" Debbie said, pointing down the left fork.

"Taxi . . . that's what we need!" Gabe exclaimed. "We can't keep using this thing."

"We can't go to El Shar, either."

"Turn right. We'll find a taxi in the city. We can leave this by the road when we get closer, and walk in."

"Got it!" Michael pushed the pedal to the floor and spun the wheel to the right, heading for New Jerusalem.

Chapter 40

Pankie's taxi screeched to a halt at the Mischa Hotel shortly after one in the morning. The Tower square was alive with construction crews and television workers setting cameras and running cable. Since entering through the East Gate she'd noticed overturned crates and torn canopies in the bazaar area, and armed police searching the streets.

She opened her leather case and touched the precious document it contained. It was a very different paper than Pankie had first conceived it to be, and its difference reflected her ever-opportunistic approach. She reflected on her upcoming meeting with Milton Franklin. Her strategy had shifted from elimination, the expedient solution abandoned when she found that he was not in Geneva, to persuasion that her personal support within the World Alliance was critical. They needed each other, she to rally SelfGuide around his leadership and he to provide access to the power group. She would help him see both that need and its solution. Since the original chairman was dead, his loyalties would not be a barrier. It should be easy. He had to be under enormous pressure and would be overwhelmed with issues. And he would be discouraged. Pankie would come to him as a leader of a prominent movement which he himself endorsed and which she could manipulate on his behalf. The more she thought it through the more confident she became. And she liked the wording on the paper in her case — " . . . . hearby appoints Pankie Quille Retson as Executive Officer, Bureau of Internal Affairs . . ."

The most difficult part proved to be getting in to see Franklin once she arrived at the El Shar. Limousines ringed the circular drive, including several from the Soviet Embassy in Jerusalem. Only by brashness and diplomacy, and by flashing the forged Executive Order she had in her case, had she been able to pass through the legion of guards covering the main entrance.

A second barrier provided resistance at the registration desk, where the chairman had left explicit instructions not to be interrupted. The large bill she slipped to the desk clerk was ineffective, although it brought the explanation for his unavailability. The barrier disappeared when a delegation of Soviet officials marched through the lobby from a terse meeting with the World Alliance chairman. Pankie picked up the house phone and was put through. Franklin sounded tired and tense.

"Mr. Chairman?" This is Pankie Quille Retson of Self-Guide. I'm in the lobby and have a matter of urgent . . ."

"Who?" Franklin said gruffly.

"I have an offer you'll find most impressive," she retorted crisply. "I need ten minutes."

Franklin sighed, remembering the name. Pankie heard muffled conversation as he cupped his hand over the telephone, apparently talking to someone else in the room. "I'm sending my aide down to get you Miss Retson. It better be important."

Pankie hung up, concerned. Franklin's offensiveness could make her task more difficult.

The villa was surrounded by guards. Reporters hovered further away, awaiting news. One recognized Pankie and tried to question her but she pushed by brusquely and followed the aide into Franklin's suite.

"Mr. Chairman," Pankie said, extending her hand. Franklin sat on the sofa puffing a cigar, necktie pulled loosely away from his unbuttoned collar. He made her wait, then put his notes aside and looked up. "Sit down. Over there." He motioned to a chair across from the sofa.

"I'll get right to the point," Pankie said, her heart pounding.

"Good. You've come at a lousy time."

"I've come to discuss your continuance as chairman of the World Alliance."

Franklin looked sharply at her. "Go on."

She pulled the Order she had typed from her briefcase. "Omega appears tomorrow to name you the head of world government. That government is in chaos, and the Soviet situation means you are vulnerable. Nothing is more important now than to insure that you are in a secure position. I'm here on behalf of all of SelfGuide to pledge support."

She paused, watching for a reaction. There was none. Franklin waited for her to continue.

"SelfGuide has authorized me to request an appointment to the World Alliance cabinet. I agreed. Setting aside the obvious benefit to me, let me point out the value of the arrangement for you, sir." She smiled alluringly, "First . . ."

"Forget the ABCs, Miss Retson," Franklin said, controlling his temper. "You get power, I get support. I think you overestimate SelfGuide's importance. I know you underestimate a great deal about the World Alliance."

Pankie pushed forward. "SelfGuide has considerable influence over other groups. I'm talking about three or four hundred million people. As your Internal Affairs Executive you would have a strong advocate, and the support of all of those people. We've taken the liberty of drafting the Order for you to sign." She handed the paper to him.

Franklin took his glasses off and rubbed his swollen eyes, wondering if she actually thought he was such a ninny as to take her seriously. For a moment he considered tossing the brazen SelfGuide leader out of his suite. His pause provided a moment to think. One of the reasons he'd been successful was that he had never allowed his ego to get in the way of reality. Pankie's honeyed words were not credible. She was certainly not here on behalf of any members of her organization — at best she represented a special interest group, and probably just herself. Key people missing, the Russian ultimatum, O'Keefe bound and gagged in a cave no less — and now this shrew travelling half a world away to present an obviously and patently self-serving issue was all too facile, and too strange. And she looked familiar, somehow . . . he made his decision. Whatever her motives she had involved herself in matters that were much too sensitive. With World Alliance control all but gone, the only play left was his being named by Omega. That single colossal stroke would generate the support he needed.

Everything pivoted on tomorrow's success. This woman could not be trusted — she was like an unguided missile, and if she was able to wander in here like she had in the thick of a world crisis, she could do anything. No surprises, no surprises.

"Miss Retson, I appreciate the trouble you've gone to." He took the paper Pankie held out to him. "How is the senator? I haven't heard from him in a day or so."

She looked steadily at him. "I don't know. I haven't seen him for awhile."

He scanned the paper, then motioned to his aide who jumped to his side, holding a pen out for him. He scrawled his signature at the bottom. "Emboss it," he said, handing it back.

Pankie breathed a silent sigh of relief. "Thank you. SelfGuide, and I, look forward to serving you."

Franklin grinned in a sleepy, sly way. "You're welcome."

He picked up the report he'd been reading and turned his attention away from her. She was surprised by the abruptness of his dismissal. As she stood up the aide handed her the embossed paper.

"Good night, then, Mr. Chairman."

"One more thing Miss Retson. Your first assignment. Part of Internal Affairs is the Omega Plan. Get over to the Mischa Hotel and give that document to Major O'Keefe. Tell him you'll be at the ceremony tomorrow, and that he now reports to you."

"Sir, I . . ."

"Is there a problem, Miss Retson?"

"No sir. I'll go there right now."

Franklin turned back to his reading without a word. She looked sourly at the aide holding the door for her, and walked out. She had her signed document but her suspicions increased. The new appointment was off to a strange beginning. From the look of that Russian delegation, Franklin probably had much more to think about, she reasoned, rationalizing the incident.

Milton Franklin pulled his glasses off and addressed his aide. "Anything else tonight?"

"No sir."

Franklin chewed on the end of his glasses. "That woman is a snake. Whatever she's doing, it smells. Don't you think so?"

The aide looked blank. His opinion was not usually asked on anything. Franklin scowled. "See that she's arrested at the Mischa. Have her hung in the cage. I'm going to sleep. Check with Jedesky's people and confirm his arrival. Wake me at five thirty sharp."

"Yes sir."

In the taxi speeding down the dark country road toward the Mischa, Pankie began to feel better. On the way they flashed past a limousine stopped at the intersection. Pankie thought she saw the World Alliance crest on its side. They arrived at the Gate and drove into Old Jerusalem. Working its way through the narrow cobblestone streets, she grew concerned. Something was very wrong. She wanted to get this first assignment out of the way as fast as possible. She handed more money to the driver and told him to wait. The driver took the bills and waved agreement. For the kind of money she'd been handing him he'd have been happy to wait all night. As it turned out, he almost did.

"Hello, Miss Retson."

She stopped in her tracks. Just inside the front door of the Mischa a man whom she'd never seen before greeted her. Her concern soared. But it was much too late.

"I have an Order from the Chairman of the World Alliance," she said tersely. "I must see Major O'Keefe immediately."

"Right this way." The guard motioned toward the darkened doorway of the Mischa coffee shop. Pankie became aware of movements behind her, and turned around. Two other guards stood with their arms folded across their chests.

"Come, Miss Retson," the lead guard said.

"'Ms,' not 'Miss,'" Pankie said testily, following him through the coffee shop. When they entered the kitchen Pankie knew she was in trouble. "I'm here to see O'Keefe," she snapped. "Take me to him. Don't you understand? I am a member of the World Alliance Cabinet!"

The men behind her gripped her roughly. Pankie yelped in pain. The lead guard opened the door of the pantry. "In there," he commanded. Her struggles were futile. They warned her to be silent. Pankie responded with a shrill stream of curses. A heavy fist against her jaw silenced her. They locked her limp body in the pantry. Minutes later the kitchen was dark again and the phone call had been made to the chairman's aide.

On an upper floor of the Mischa the new Omega lay on his bed, mentally rehearsing the fateful role that was his to play the following day. He could hear the carpenter's hammers and the shouts of the media crews in the square. Gradually, sleep came. The two guards stationed immediately outside his door settled into a game of gin. Down the hall a haggard Professor Schmidt paced in his room, wringing his hand nervously. His bags were packed and he was ready to escape if anything went wrong. In his estimation it was likely that something would. He'd done his best but he knew it wouldn't be good enough.

In the Briefing Room members of the Omega team surrounded Major O'Keefe while a doctor treated his injured face. He'd been brought in just before Pankie had arrived, found by searchers who followed the first two pursuit cars chasing the stolen World Alliance limousine. They had come across the smashed cars by the side of the road. Scrambling up the slope and into the olive grove, they heard a strange muffled noise, as if someone was shouting from inside a long tunnel. They found the fissure nearby and beamed the spotlight down. There lay O'Keefe, weakly shouting for help as best he could. With ropes and slings they pulled him out. As they led him down the slope to their car they heard laughter and shouting, like a celebration. Two of them stalked the sounds through the bush, and soon spotted Omega, a woman, and three other men, as well as their limousine. They fired a shot, then ran back to their car to give chase. The others returned to the Mischa with the major.

With wounds cleaned and dressed and the swelling eased by drugs, O'Keefe was appraised of the events since his disappearance. Anger and frustration overruled exhaustion. Against the doctor's urgings he got up before the taping of his bandages were finished, stalking back and forth across the room. His words were still unclear but the rage in his voice was unmistakable. "I want them. I want them bad," he growled, thumping his fist into his palm.

"Major, we've tried, but . . ."

"Tried nothing!" he shouted, wincing with pain. "They're out there without weapons in our own limo and you can't even find 'em, let alone bring 'em back. I ought to shoot the lot of you! By dawn I want 'em back. Understand?"

They looked at the major, angry that now they would not get even a few hours of sleep before the 'Sunday Matinee,' as Omega's appearance had been dubbed. But they knew there was no denying the major when that look of wild anger came into his eye.

O'Keefe spat a drop of blood onto the floor, more in derision than to clear the drainage of his wounds. "They came up here, broke open the cage, stole the prisoners and escaped. They'll come back tomorrow and try to stop us — they haven't got enough sense to stay away. It's your life if this doesn't go off as scheduled. Count on it."

They knew O'Keefe was deadly serious.

"What vehicles do we have? And weapons?"

"The tractor, a jeep, and two limos," Jeff said. "A few pistols and rifles, but mostly explosives."

O'Keefe spat with disgust. "Put more men around the square. In the shadows. The work crews will be done by three. I want the area quarantined. You shoot to kill if you see any one or any thing move in that area before seven o'clock."

"Yes sir." The guard captain stood, waiting.

"Go! Get out of here!" O'Keefe shouted, waving his arms. The captain hurried out of the room.

"If I were them," he continued, looking at Jeff, "I'd get rid of that limo and get a car no one would recognize. Where would I find one? In the city."

"I'll start looking," Jeff said, anxious to get away from the major.

"You'll do more than that. Go to the taxi dispatch garages and shut down all the taxis. All of them. Understand? Use taxis to search the city. Find them. Four men and a woman. The only cabs I want running are the ones you have. If any other cab runs, bury it. Understand?"

"Yes sir."

"You know what to do when you find them?"

"Bring them back to . . ."

O'Keefe glared. "Shoot them, you useless idiot. They're a risk to the whole operation. Understand?"

"Major," Jeff said hesitantly. "We could use them in place of the ones they took from the cage. Jedesky seemed pretty hot on having someone, at least, here. It's part of the script."

The major grinned evilly. "We already have someone now, don't we Jeffrey?"

Jeff looked at him blankly.

"The shrew. Pankie Quille Retson."

"Won't that raise a lot of questions?"

O'Keefe waved him off. "What questions . . . she had a religious experience, converted, and look where it got her. That pompous WOEC buffoon will love it."

Jeff grinned. "I hadn't thought of that."

"That's obvious," O'Keefe said, stone-faced. "Get going. All of you. Come back empty and I'll personally skin you alive."

They hurried through the door, Jeff shouting instructions as they left. O'Keefe leaned back in his chair and glared at the doctor. "What're you doing?"

The doctor stopped repacking his bag, startled. "Why I'm . . ."

"You think you're special? Get out of here — you go with them!"

"But I'm not . . ."

O'Keefe stepped toward him, fists clenched. The doctor dropped his bag and ran out the door. O'Keefe picked up a desk chair and hurled it down on the floor, smashing it to pieces. He felt no better because of it. He stomped out of the room and down the stairs toward the pantry to fulfill Milton Franklin's instructions.

Chapter 41

The sun was just peeking over the eastern horizon as Milton Franklin and Anton Jedesky were ushered toward their limousines outside the El Shar. The Visgate together with the WOEC College of Prophets had landed in Jerusalem at four thirty that morning and caravaned to the El Shar along night-silent roads, escorted by World Alliance security and the more persistent members of the press.

The day was to begin with a meeting with the Chief Temple Rabbi of the newly completed world center of worship in Jerusalem. Then there would be a press conference followed by discussions with national and regional officials gathered in Jerusalem for the historic event. After a formal state luncheon the World Alliance chairman, the Visgate, and the Chief Rabbi would caravan to Old Jerusalem and arrive at the Tower of the Ascension square at one'clock. The ceremony would last for one hour and fifteen minutes. Just before its scheduled ending Omega would make his appearance.

They stood under the canopied El Shar entrance waiting while flash bulbs popped and cameras whirred. Anton Jedesky stepped up to a microstalk bundle hastily assembled for the occasion, and addressed the press and members of his and the chairman's entourage.

"On this historic occasion," he said, lifting both hands in the air, "as we gather in Jerusalem to consecrate the World Temple, may there be peace among the nations." The audience applauded. Jedesky and Franklin linked hands held high and smiled for the cameras. Milton Franklin's head was splitting — he had not been able to sleep despite his exhaustion, and wondered how he would get through the day.

Jedesky leaned into the microstalks and squeezed his eyes closed. "One to another we offer peace and companionship. One to another we pledge support in pursuit of that which drives us onward. One to another we give encouragement. Fulfill the destiny of our evolution; glorify the evolution of our destiny. One with another we stand on our rights, united in the common bond of individuality. God is in you; you are your God. Be as you wish to be. So speaks your Visgate."

Supportive applause followed he and Franklin into their limousines. Moments later a caravan of long sleek automobiles, black with the gold and purple World Alliance emblem, and light blue with the silvered man and woman which represented the World Organized Ecumenical Council, moved in stately procession down the road toward Jerusalem.

They huddled in a field, shivering in the chill pre-dawn air as the procession moved silently past. It had been a night of adventure and sadness, crowned by Michael and Debbie's joyful homecoming to the King of kings and Lord of lords. They had abandoned the limousine and walked the remaining distance into Jerusalem, resting often for Eric's sake. Exhaustion, hunger and thirst collaborated in their discomfort.

In the city they'd seen taxicabs on this eve of the temple ceremony. But the cabs had passed them by. They stopped at an all-night delicatessen and found the first inkling of new danger. Gabe had gone in to buy supplies and medicine for Eric, whose condition was steadily worsening. He came out a few minutes later and hurried them into a dark side alley.

He had noticed the night manager staring at him, and then at a piece of paper. When he picked up the telephone Gabe sensed something was wrong. He had lived his adult lifetime learning to listen to his Lord. He knew the source of the familiar signals and wasted no time in obeying this one.

As they crouched behind some trash containers a police car squealed around the corner past the alley and screeched to a halt in front of the deli. Gabe caught fragments of the excited conversation between the store manager and the police. "Big problem," he whispered. "I think we're being hunted. The cabs have been commandeered by the World Alliance. Everyone's looking for us."

They waited like sheep among wolves, knowing they faced likely capture and perhaps even death. Their lack of food or water increased their dilemma. And Eric was weakening. The wounds in his wrists were so deep that his hands were useless, and his back and chest, raw from whippings, were oozing and red. He was barely conscious.

"It's not safe here," Ben said. "Let's get out of the city."

They moved back through the alley. Michael and Ben carried Eric while Debbie scouted, checking along the darkened buildings and shadowy parked cars. It looked clear. They moved like spirits across the street, heading toward the edge of the city several blocks away. No car or taxi was seen until they were near a last row of low-rise apartments. Just on the other side a deep ditch marked the city boundary. Beyond lay scrub bush terrain, and safety. Suddenly headlights turned into the street behind them. A light glowed on top of the car.

"Taxi!" Em whispered, looking back over his shoulder. They broke into a trot, trying to cover the remaining half-block to the apartments before the cruising taxi driver realized who they were. Michael and Ben gasped as they ran, their muscles burning with the strain. Footsteps pounded on the stones, and breath came in short, steamy cloudlets in the chill air. The beams of the approaching headlights bounced up and down from the uneven street and cast their wavering shadows before them.

"Just a little more . . ." Gabe puffed, praying with fervor. Then behind them they heard what they had feared — a squeal of tires and a roar of an engine. The driver had spotted them. They crashed through the hedges along the front yard of the apartments and ran toward the back just as the taxi screeched to a stop. A coarse shout punctuated the night air.

Michael stumbled and fell. Eric's weight was too much for Ben alone, and the unconscious man tumbled to the ground. Ben spun around to face their pursuer. The driver leaped over the hedge holding a rifle high in one of his outstretched hands. Michael jumped to help Ben. Debbie, now safely through the other side of the hedgegrow, screamed.

Ben covered the distance between them in a few quick paces and grabbed for the rifle just before the driver squeezed the trigger. It deflected as it discharged, and the explosion echoed from the walls of the buildings. Michael's diving tackle sent the man crashing to the ground, and a second later Ben's huge fist crunched into their assailant's jaw with a sound like walking on fresh popcorn.

Lights came on inside the apartments. They looked at the idling taxicab, its door hanging open as if inviting them in. Gabe, Em, and Debbie were already lifting Eric up.

"Our only chance," Michael whispered urgently, pointing to the cab. "Police will be here fast."

Ben nodded and picked up the rifle. They put Eric gently into the taxi, then jumped in themselves. All except Michael, who drove, ducked down on sight. Two turns and several minutes later they were out of Jerusalem, speeding toward the fork in the road where they'd paused earlier. A mile further along they saw a dense stand of trees on the scrub land. Michael left the road and lumbered across the rough terrain and into protective cover.

Michael turned around in the seat, sighing with relief as stillness replaced the scraping and bumping against the rough ground. Eric lay across the laps of the others in the back. Gabe was stroking his forehead, his eyes streaming with tears.

"He's gone."

Anger and outrage pressed in on Michael. They'd tried so hard.

"We did all we could," Gabe said. "Lord God, we yield Eric to You, grieving. We will see him again. Thank you for his life."

A portion of scripture flashed into Michael's mind. 'For great are your rewards in Heaven . . .' "Amen," he said. His anger melted away, his new spirit crying softly in harmony with the others. Michael knew the familiar confusion in his mind — what gave him inner exultation was the sense of strength and peace that seemed to fill the inside of the cab.

"Mij, I've never seen you cry before!" Debbie spoke shyly, watching her husband. He realized she was right.

They buried Eric beside the cab, digging a shallow grave with their hands and a few stones. Then they walked back to the road, crouching in the cover of the scrub bush, gazing silently toward the lighted Tower of the Ascension three miles away.

With the cab they could drive to the airport, and possibly board a plane and escape. They could get food and something to drink. Michael knew the World Alliance primary concern was that Omega appear as the returned Christ. He was sure police would be protecting the tower area, not the airport.

But the temptation to leave vanished as they gazed upon the Tower in Old Jerusalem, realizing even more deeply the abomination the World Alliance and WOEC were about to unleash. It was a hideous mockery of God's glory, a consummate lie. Nothing seemed more ugly than that which loomed only hours away. And they were the only people alive who could see it as it really was. Slowly, they knew without a doubt that it had been given into their hands to prevent it.

"Why us?" Debbie said, her voice wavering as she spoke the unsaid question.

"How can we possibly stop it?" Gabe sat on the ground and rubbed his beard stubble. "The Lord will have to show us. I haven't any ideas. I think we need to pray." He smiled wearily. "This is so big, and we're hungry, tired, and unarmed. There's no way we'll figure out what to do, or how. We can't act without Him."

They sat on the ground in a small circle. Gabe, accustomed to leading, opened his mouth to begun. But another voice spoke. "Jesus," Michael said softly, almost tentatively. The others tuned to him, conscious of the Spirit's presence. "You promised you are where two or three of us are gathered in Your name. There are five of us. And we're here in Your Name."

There was a long pause. Michael sensed a peculiar wonderful energy, and his words flowed and glowed in the center of that energy. He spoke again. One more word came out, a simple, heartfelt believing plea.

"Help."

They looked up at the dawn just breaking in the eastern sky. The day of abomination glowed with new life and hope. Then the World Alliance caravan slowly passed, small banners fluttering on their rooftops. As the line of pale blue and black limousines disappeared down the road, Gabe stood up.

"I felt a chill just then, as if the Antichrist himself had just gone by. It's clear that we've been led here to act against this terrible thing. You must each decide for yourselves. For me, I know what I must do." He looked at them with compassion. His own realization, acknowledgement and obedience was no less difficult for him than for the others in whom real struggle now rose. Knowledge is one thing — obedience is quite another. Serving God takes on a different perspective when the time to act is at hand and life itself is in the balance. Real priorities quickly sort themselves out.

Em sighed. "Long ago God said, 'Who shall I send?' " He looked at Gabe, then toward the rising sun. " 'Here am I, Lord. Send me.' "

Michael and Debbie, hands clasped tightly together, watched Ben, sitting cross-legged, head bowed and the palms of his hands up, remembering the time with him in their home. Fresh regret filled Michael at the memory of his motives then, and of his derision for this big man for whom he had now developed such respect and affection.

Ben opened his eyes. "I've known what I must do, friends." He spoke quietly, sensing the pure, sweet aroma nearby. "I've just been asking God to strengthen both of you and show you the way. You're in the power and grace of the Lord Jesus Christ. In His will nothing can defeat you. But in human terms the risks are real."

Ben's simple eloquence touched them. He had plucked at their exact thoughts. The sun rose fully above the horizon at that moment and poked rays of daylight across the landscape. Ben's grizzled, peaceful face was bathed in the warm glow of morning. He stood and joined Gabe and Em.

Michael thought of Milton Franklin and Pankie Retson and their ruthless dedication to do whatever it took to achieve their own ends. Truth, honor and compassion had nothing to do with it. He remembered O'Keefe's leer as that poor, shackled man — criminal or not, it didn't matter — was killed during the Omega rehearsal. He could not just walk away and leave the devils to their playland. God's word had seeped from his mind into his heart like precious nourishment and given truth and the ability to recognize and acknowledge it. He was no better, indeed, than Milton Franklin or Pankie Retson. And for however offended his sensitivities might have been at the moment of the murder of an innocent, he was able, he knew in his heart, to do the same to another as long as he served himself. He, as all men, could not only rise to the occasions presented to them, but could sink to them too.

But Michael knew what he had to do with all the power the freshly washed spirit of a baby Christian can convey. Jesus, too, was murdered as an innocent — and until a few hours ago he willingly participated in it. "Deb," he said, gripping her hand. "Let's do it." Debbie had already made her choice. She had been waiting patiently for his leadership. They went over to the others.

"Hallelujiah," Gabe said. "Lord God, We are Yours. Guide us as You will." They looked toward the Tower of the Ascension. Seven hours remained before the ceremony would begin.

Pankie Retson regained consciousness and became aware of excruciating pain. Her vision cleared, helped by the chilly morning air. Dim light struggled through a dirt-encrusted window and revealed the inside of a garage. She had trouble breathing, and felt sharp aching in her arms. Slowly she realized she was naked and hanging by her wrists locked in manacles chained to the top of a cage. She tried to scream but pain pushed her mercifully back into unconsciousness.

Chapter 42

The pomp and circumstance surrounding Milton Franklin and Anton Jedesky surpassed all prior occasions of state. News coverage extended across the globe. The larger WOEC churches focused their service around large videoscreen coverage of the Visgate's morning speech, a stirring call to "rise to the potential in every one of us." Jedesky had closed his message with a prophesy carefully planned to happen within hours of its utterance:

> ". . . I remind you once again how close we are to a world united in peace. We owe much to the concept of Jesus Christ as we near the achievement of this goal. But there are those who lurk in dark and narrow passageways insisting that allegory is truth, insisting that the Christ concept which embodies all the great teachings of the ages is a lie. There are those who, even as we gather to celebrate the new World Temple, nip at our heels and nay-say the happiness that is so near our grasp. They are terribly misguided and horribly lost. Unite your wills, in which resides the supreme power, that they might not spoil your hope with empty words and meaningless euphemisms. They are desperate and will not stop

short of any possible trickery and deceit against the peoples of the world. Beware. Beware."

Milton Franklin had used the occasion to improve his hold on the disintegrating helm of power. Stating that "the consummation of world peace will enable us all to lay down our weapons and turn to the advancement of prosperity," he announced a series of economic reforms and income guarantees and committed to a drive toward eliminating world hunger. It was an "everyone wins" speech. Coming on the heels of Anton Jedesky's emotional rallying cry, it seemed almost possible to hear the world roar in approval.

And well it might, for all it had suffered. In the disasters, turmoil and miraculous events of the past week which had begun with the Global Voice, more had occurred than anyone could assimilate. Across the globe rational calls for investigations and clear thinking had first yielded to urgent cries for answers. With the unplanned destruction of the Soviet flagship and her premier off the coast of Sicily, a panic-laced need for relief and stability dominated. The crisis had nearly peaked, and the Omega Plan timing seemed perfect. Despite their exhaustion Franklin and Jedesky were in high spirits, caught up in the headiness of accelerating adulation and the soon to be realized success of an incredibly intricate process.

They moved through cheering confetti-tossing crowds along the streets of Jerusalem toward the Tower of the Ascension. The sky was blue and cloudless, the sun warm and bright. As the caravan drove through the south Gate, still about a mile away, Major O'Keefe glimpsed them from his third floor room in the Mischa. He and Becker Simpson, he wearing the ceremonial uniform of the World Alliance Elite Corps and she hunched over in peasant garb, walked across the corridor and into the briefing room. The entire team except Professor Schmidt and Omega was assembled. They rose when he entered, applauding. He waved, all threats of the prior night forgotten in the halo of the congratulatory call he'd received earlier from Milton Franklin himself. The swelling in his jaw was down and the pain had lessened. Rest and recuperation could come later. For now the moment of triumph was at hand, and he intended to gather up as much of it as he could.

They sat down at the major's signal. "I salute your courage, your skill, and your accomplishment!" he shouted. "Hail to the World Alliance!"

"Hail!" they shouted in reply.

"Prepare now to welcome the star of the show." Becker shuffled out, returning moments later with Professor Schmidt. Then Omega entered. The team cheered. Omega walked slowly across the front of the room toward O'Keefe. His white tunic was so bright it hurt the eye to stare at it, and a soft glow surrounded him. Slowly he raised his hands, as if to pronounce a benediction. "I am ready, sir."

Even the major gasped with astonishment. Omega's voice echoed with richness as he spoke through a tiny microphone pinned next to his throat. O'Keefe grinned proudly, and put his hand on Omega's shoulder. The crackling of static electricity made his hand tingle. The team cheered and stomped their feet. Omega laughed, enjoying his adulation.

"Now it's for real," O'Keefe said. The group quieted. "I want clean, crisp answers. Magnets!"

"Ready," a voice from the back replied.

"North generator!"

Ready, major!"

The list continued . . . imploder, lights, fountain girdle, macro-electron guns, computer prompts, voice actuators, cage and tractor, communications networks . . . . it was all ready.

O'Keefe checked his watch and held his hands up for silence. "We go to stations in exactly five minutes. You know your own duties. Good luck." He turned sharply on his heel and walked out of the room. Two floors below, he would form part of the personal welcoming unit for the World Alliance chairman and the WOEC Visgate. 'It all feels worth it,' he thought, going down the steps. 'And it's too late for the traitor to do anything. Let him rot wherever he is, he and the rest of them.'

He walked outside just as the caravan pulled onto the cobblestones. The square was packed — correspondents and cameramen filtered among the colorful uniforms of officials from every World Alliance nation and the ceremonial robes of WOEC's College of Prophets. Squadrons of World Alliance attack jets streamed across the sky in criss-crossing flight patterns. Banners fluttered from the Tower. The WOEC orchestral band and choir filled three tiers of the gigantic platform, performing now with vigor. Franklin and Jedesky stepped out of their limousines and waved to the crowd and the cameras.

They stood a block away from the south Gate dressed in sunrobes purchased in a small shop earlier in the morning.

"You know what to do?" Michael whispered. They nodded. Many of their earlier worries had proven foundless. They'd driven the taxi into the city, stopping at the first clothier they found. To the merchant they were just five more customers, and a flash of paper money from Em's envelope had earned immediate attention. In new sunrobes, and Michael carrying a white tunic wrapped in paper, they strolled out of the shop and into the morning sunlight, anonymous. An hour later they had showered and shaved at a public bath and eaten their fill. They left the taxi in a side street near the south Gate. The Lord's power was with them, and their courage and boldness multiplied. Michael and Debbie couldn't understand the sense of joyful confidence that bubbled up like a spring. Their infectious enthusiasm spread to the others until all were without concern for the momentous issues they were shortly to confront.

"All right," Michael said. He looked at Debbie, then leaned over and kissed her. "Be careful, Deb. Stay close to Ben."

"And you, Mij . . . Lord be with you!" Debbie smiled sweetly and shyly as she spoke the new and beautiful words.

A distant bell chimed. It was one o'clock. The World Alliance band began the fanfare. Above the low buildings separating them from the square a crane boom swung into sight, a cameraman perched in its bucket to record the start of the ceremony. They huddled briefly and said a quick prayer. Then Ben and Debbie went back to the taxi, and Gabe and Em disappeared around the corner.

Michael waited in the shadows close to the Gate, watching the four guards. His memory was proving to be priceless once again, for the day's schedule was crystal clear in his mind. Back down the hill the taxi eased out of the alley and into the street. He could see Debbie in the back and Ben at the wheel, and signalled that all was ready.

Ben eased up the crowded street until the cab came to the wide flagstones just in front of the Gate. Michael noticed the guards eyeing the cab and readying their weapons.

Like an angry tourist Debbie got out of the cab complaining loudly about the fare. Soon she and Ben were shouting at each other and a small crowd had formed. Debbie swung her hand through the driver's open window. Ben ducked down as if to avoid the blow, and wedged the rifle between the seat and the accelerator. The engine roared, and people in front of the cab jumped away. As he opened the door and jumped out, holding one hand up to protect himself from Debbie's angry attack, he pushed the shift lever into gear. Tires squealed and the cab lunged forward. The guards, caught by surprise, scrambled out of the way as the taxi jumped the flagstone curb. Debbie ran through the crowds, shouting angrily over her shoulder. Ben chased her, calling after her like a man intent on recovering his money.

The taxi crunched violently into the stone wall near the Gate. Michael ran out of the shadows and pushed through the crowds toward the Gate. Two of the guards ran after Ben and Debbie. Michael slipped through the Gate during the few moments when the attention of the other two were on the smashed, steaming taxicab. Inside, he ran toward the cobblestone street along the buildings where he and Gabe had rescued Eric and the others the night before. He leaped over the low wall they'd hidden behind and crouched down out of sight, listening for any sound of pursuit. The wail of sirens told him that the police were already at the Gate. His timing had been very close.

The guards chased Debbie and Ben for about a block before giving up. The other two had resumed their positions, preventing access to the square.

Michael unwrapped the white tunic he'd purchased and pulled it over him, then hung a small battery-powered microphone speaker set arount his neck. Peeking over the wall, he could see through the garage windows and into the square. He had a clear view of the reviewing platform, filled now with dignitaries, and of part of the fountain. He began to feel nervous. For him the most dangerous part of their hastily conceived but divinely inspired mission was just ahead.

Gabe and Em were three blocks away from the square when the taxicab hit the wall, standing by a stone building which, centuries before, had been a prison. The building served now as a seasonal pumping station. Drawing from underground springs into several ten thousand gallon holding tanks, it was used as an auxiliary water supply. During this time of the winter the main station in New Jerusalem was able to meet the city's demand, and the auxiliary station was not used. Its doors were padlocked, but Gabe and Em broke a window in the back and worked it up high enough to crawl in.

"There — that must be the valve header." Em pointed toward a large stand of pipes poking through perforated steel flooring. "The tanks must be below, and pumps mounted above them. They would pull from the tanks through these pipes and out into the distribution system."

Gabe nodded, playing the flashlight beam over a tangle of pipes and valves. "The question is: which one controls the piping into the square?"

"And, is there water in the tanks?" Em added.

They found a steel ladder leading down to the storage tanks. Only one contained water, and only a little bit.

"I was afraid of this, Gabe. This is only enough to prime the main pumps. If we're going to get water to the fountain we'll have to pump it from the springs into the tanks first. We don't have time for that."

"We don't need much. Isn't there enough to do it?"

He estimated the amount required. "We probably need six thousand gallons just to fill the pipeline." Em checked the glass level indicator and shook his head. "Not enough. Not nearly enough."

"Michael will look for the flow through the fountain as his signal, assuming he got in all right."

"We have to trust the Lord for that."

"No reason to stop trusting him for this, then." Gabe patted the side of the holding tank.

"Let's get to it," Em said. "Lord, You made wine out of water — please make water out of . . ." Suddenly he stopped. "Did you hear something?"

It came again — the sound of air brakes. Gabe scrambled back up the ladder. As he came through the grating he saw something large through the dirty windows, glinting in the sunlight, moving up against the back of the building. His heart raced. Moving in a crouch across the grating to the window, he peeked above the sill. His jaw dropped with astonishment. A tanker truck was backed up against the window. The driver's door was open, and Ben stood in the dust, peering at the truck and scratching his head.

"It's Ben!" Gabe called. He heard Em's sigh of relief.

Though muffled by the window Ben heard Gabe. He spotted him, and his face lit up with smiles. Debbie came around from the other side of the truck. Gabe flicked the locking latch and pushed the window open.

"Michael got in. Where's Em . . .oh!" Ben saw Em coming up the ladder through the steel grating.

"What is this?" Gabe asked, looking at the gleaming truck.

"It's a little complicated," Ben said with a twinkle. "After we escaped we walked a block or two. It really went well, Gabe — you should have seen it!"

Debbie was bouncing with excitement. "We turned a corner and there was this truck parked right across the street!" she interjected, her eyes sparkling. "Ben said 'Let's take that thing over to Gabe and Em . . . I have a feeling they may need it!' Can you believe that?"

Gabe thought of Jesus' disciples taking the young donkey for His entry into Jerusalem. He nodded, chuckling.

"So Debbie and I and friend truck, here, just drove on over!" Ben's eyes twinkled. Gabe told them of the need for water. As their situation became clear they were amazed.

Gabe checked his watch. "We should have had water running through the fountain by now. We've got to move! Ben, what's in the tanker?"

"Don't know," he said, pulling the feeder hose from the undercarriage rack. He connected it to the outlet, then scrambled up the tanker ladder and opened the vent. "Did you learn all that when you drove for me years ago?" Em said, impressed.

Ben smiled and shrugged, aware of that sweet, pure hovering aroma. "Here," he said, pushing the other end of the hose through the window. "Knowing Who's running this show, I think friend hose will reach right where it needs to."

Gabe pulled the hose through the window and shined the beam of the flashlight down through the grating. It illuminated the open-topped partly full water tank. "Turn it on, Ben!"

The valve wheel cranked open and the tanker's contents gushed through the hose. Gabe struggled to hold steady against the force of the flow. A dark liquid exploded out of the nozzle and tumbled down through the grating into the tank. Em smelled something familiar. Puzzled, he bent down and touched his fingers to the rushing liquid.

"What have we got, Em?" Gabe shouted to make himself heard above the noise of the flow.

Em stood up with an amused look. "Root beer."

Gabe almost dropped the hose. "Root beer?"

"Root beer!"

Ben and Debbie, watching through the open window, heard the pronouncement. They could hardly contain themselves.

Em went across the grating to the header stand. Four distribution lines, each with a main valve, exited through the wall. He studied the first valve. NEx1250 was stamped into the metal valve body. The second valve revealed Sx2247. Direction and run length? He had no time to think further. The pumping station was almost due north of the square. The second valve had to be as good a guess as any. He turned the valve wheel, expecting stiffness and resistance, but it turned easily in spite of the metal stem creaking against its dried-out packing.

"Quick!" Gabe called. "The tank's almost full!"

Em ran to a large power panel mounted near the ladder. The flashlight revealed eight identical switches, one, he presumed, for each pump. He held the light down through the grating and counted. The tank they were filling was the third from the end. Em reached for the third switch and grasped its handle.

"Hurry up!" Gabe called.

"Please Lord," Em murmured, throwing the switch. "Let it work."

"Hurry up," Michael muttered, crouching behind the clay wall. He had less than two minutes before he would have to move on his own. His nervousness increased as the seconds ticked by. He'd seen his three friends go through tense circumstances in peace and power during the past two days. They had prayed often. He remembered his own prayer early that morning in the field, and the confidence it had given him.

It was almost time. "Lord Jesus . . ." He was amazed at the inrushing sense of strength which just the believing mention of His name brought to him. He had said that name many times while memorizing the scriptures in the early days of his assignment and had felt nothing. But he had acknowledged Him now as his Lord. Where he'd found only unanswered questions, now he found power and peace. Calmed and made confident, he continued.

"Lord, please help. I ask in Jesus' name." He looked up, then closed his eyes a moment longer. "Thank you."

The time they'd agreed on had passed. He focused on the task at hand. Vaulting over the wall, he walked briskly as though he had every right to be in the narrow alleyway between the end garage and the fortress-like stonework of the

Mischa. The alley led directly into the square. He stopped and took a deep breath, listening to Jedesky ending a speech which boldly proclaimed the square as holy ground and which prophesied that the Global Voice was certain to be manifested soon. Michael looked up to the sky, and shrugged. "I'm Yours, Jesus. If You want this abomination stopped, now might be a good time to do it."

With white tunic flowing he strode purposefully through the alley into the square. He was in full view of three hundred political and religious leaders, and cameras from every major broadcasting network.

Chapter 43

Sunlight streamed through the window opening and into a small chamber midway up the Tower. Omega and Professor Schmidt stood in the shadows of the room, waiting for the counterfeit Christ to be transported through the air to the fountain at the center of the square.

Omega checked the magnetic girdle once again to insure that the straps were secure and comfortable. He was tense, and wished now that he'd paid closer attention to the professor during the intensive instruction sessions.

"You haff two minutes Omenka, until der luftpassen. Are you ready . . . Herr Omenka, please. Taken der gumchew out of your mouthen!" The professor rolled his eyes and shrugged in exasperation. Omega spit his gum out onto the stone floor, trying to remain non-chalant.

"I'm ready, prof. Make sure the money's ready when this show is over."

"Ya ya. Sure, Omenka. Not to vorry."

"I'll bet," he said disdainfully, looking through the window. Suddenly his eyes widened. "What the . . . what is this!"

"Huh, Omenk . . . Aieee!" Professor Schmidt spotted Michael striding casually toward the fountain in front of the

platform of officials. "Omenka!" He said softly. He looked at the man in the linen tunic standing next to him, then back through the window. "You are der same . . . der iss no difference! Oi oi . . . . vat now, vat now?" He paced the stone floor, wringing his hands.
"Is this in the plan, prof?" Omega said sarcastically.
"Nien, nien! Dis iss dischunderpfiggen!"
"Say wha?"
"Iss terrible, jerken, dat's vat! Und less den ein minuten until . . . . oi, oi . . ."
"I'm not going down there now, prof. You can count on that. Whoever that looney tune is, the brass aren't gonna be pleased." He began to unstrap his left shoulder harness.
"Nien, Omenka, you not understanden — iss too late! Ve must go through mitt der plan now!"
Omega smirked. "Too late for you, maybe. Not for me."
The professor grabbed his arms, struggling to prevent his removing the shoulder strap. They fell to the dusty stone floor wrestling. Omega cursed so loudly that he could be heard faintly on the square below. The professor wished with new fervency that he was back in Bavaria.

Michael walked into view just as the World Alliance chairman began his address. According to the plan Omega was to appear during that speech and name him the true and proper world leader. Astonished, Franklin stopped in mid-sentence, staring as the young man in the white linen tunic strode toward him, waving to the crowds and cameras on the reviewing platform. 'Did I miss something?' Franklin thought. 'Is this how Omega is to appear, walking in through an alley?'

Michael reached up to Franklin as he passed in front of the speaker's platform. Unthinking, the chairman grasped it in a handshake, and yelped with surprise as the tiny windup buzzer button Michael had concealed in his palm zapped him. Michael smiled innocently. Then he came to the fountain and climbed part way up, moving his arms with exaggerated gestures as if taking measurements.

Recovering from his initial shock, Anton Jedesky became apoplectic. In one stroke the credibility of the Omega Plan had been destroyed. They had provided for every contingency, thought through all possible obstacles, developed alternative plans for anything that could go wrong. But they had never considered the impact which one man who looked like Omega, simply walking in front of the officials, could have. In the twinkling of an eye billions of dollars had been wasted and the dreams of those who sought the highest levels of power and stature had been dashed.

In the minute which followed, many of those present could have done things very differently than they actually did. Major O'Keefe could have signalled the generator station fifty paces away not to power up for Omega's flight through the air. Franklin could have continued speaking, ignoring the intrusion. The security forces could have dragged Michael back into the alley and out of sight before anyone noticed him. Becker might have created a diversion to distract the crowd's attention. Cameras could have been stopped — live broadcast was on a five minute delay precisely so that mistakes, if any developed, would not be seen by several billion people. Matters could be dealt with, given even a little time to think through the situation.

But logic was not to prevail in the suddenness of Michael's shocking appearance. No mind could grasp what had happened before it had happened already. All Michael had to do was appear and then disappear. That alone, they'd realized earlier that morning, was all that was necessary to discredit the whole of the Omega Plan.

Michael started back toward the alley, cool as ice and waving toward the cameras. Jedesky, trembling with rage, stood and pointed toward him. "Behold the evildoer!" he bellowed. "Behold him who dares to mock the concept most sacred to all of us! Seize him! SEIZE HIM!"

Michael stopped and pointed at Jedesky, and his amplified voice echoed with richness. "SIMBAR SANECH ES-SAMECH!" He had no idea what he'd spoken but the effect was momentarily electrifying. Then he broke into a dead run toward the alleyway.

In the generator room Jed Frost counted the seconds as he watched the clock on the wall. He remembered the tongue-lashing O'Keefe had given him at the last rehearsal for switching on the power an instant later than scheduled. "Not today, nosiree," he breathed. ". . . three . . . two . . . one . . ."

"Wait! Jed — wait!"

He thought he heard a voice floating down the staircase as he plunged the switch into the "On" position, but the whirring scream of energized generators drowned everything with ear-splitting noise, and power pulsed up to the macro-electron guns seventy feet about him. Jed adjusted his earplugs and sat down in a torn plastic-covered chair, his job completed.

On the top floor of the Mischa, seated behind the two giant macro-electron guns, the operator aimed the nozzles at the Tower waiting room. He finally detected the girdle and locked the guns onto it. His instruments showed the lock-on location three feet lower than it was supposed to be.

"Must have been lying down, snoozin' or something," the operator muttered admiringly. "Cool dude, that one. All right, baby, here we go!" He increased the energy gain flowing through the twin guns.

Wrestling on the dusty flatstones with Professor Schmidt, Omega had managed to loosen both shoulder harness straps and was trying to work the crotch band off. Suddenly he felt the girdle energizing, and his body was lifted off the stone floor. He screamed.

"Ho boy, ho boy," the professor gasped. In a last effort, he grabbed Omega around the neck, hoping his added weight would overpower the magnetic forces pulling him through the open window.

Below, it was chaos. The interruption of the World Alliance chairman, Jedesky's frantic shouting, and the confusion of Omega team people running about changed the formal atmosphere of the ceremony into a circus carnival. Franklin signalled wildly toward the band to play something loud. O'Keefe was directing police toward the alley where Michael had disappeared, waving his revolver in the air. Cameras whirred and panned from every corner to capture the turmoil of the world's gathered officials pouring off the reviewing platform, pushing and bumping into one another.

But the hoarse, frightened twin screams which came from above their heads overcame the bedlam. A figure bobbled through the window in the tower as if pulled by shaking unseen fingers, dangling upside down from an invisible skyhook. His white robe hung down from his upended body, covering the face and shoulders of a second man frantically clasping his arms around the chest of the first, his short stubby legs striding feverishly in mid-air. Cameras swung upward in wild arcs to record Omega and the professor geeing and hawing through the air like two inept acrobats shouting in panic, cursing in fear.

Perspiration broke over the gun operator's forehead when he saw what had happened. But it was too late — they were free of the window. He gripped the guide handles of the twin guns tightly and turned the power up to maximum. In his nervousness the guns were not moved as smoothly as they might have been. Omega and the professor darted back and forth in the air like mating dragonflies as they were manipulated toward the fountain.

Most of the assembled leaders were off the platform now, shouting, angry, and demanding answers. Some surrounded Franklin, shaking their fists and hollering over the noisy uproar at the World Alliance chairman. Franklin, gesturing and shouting back, disclaimed all knowledge of the incident. Omega and Professor Schmidt suddenly appeared above their heads. They stopped arguing and looked up with disbelief. Few heard the rushing crescendo of air which began hissing through the fountain, so loud was all the noise. The hissing became a gurgling like a huge percolating coffee pot. Suddenly brown liquid gushed through the ugly gargoyles and sprayed into the air from the ring of openings at the top. The sticky fluid soaked everything within fifteen feet of the fountain, including Omega and the professor who hung directly overhead. Flash bulbs exploded like popcorn. Jedesky, stomping around in small circles near Milton Franklin, was swearing and waving his arms at Major O'Keefe when the fountain erupted. The Visgate was soaked in seconds, his purple silk robe covered with the brown stain, his crown-shaped cap knocked off his head and laying in the mud. "Root beer!" he said with amazed disgust, spitting the taste out of his mouth. "Root beer!"

Omega and Professor Schmidt dropped heavily onto the muddy dust just behind Jedesky. The professor rolled over against the Visgate's legs and Jedesky's knees buckled. Livid, certain someone had knocked him down deliberately, he rose to his knees, glaring at the shaken professor, and swung his fist. He connected squarely against the professor's nose. Schmidt howled in pain. Someone standing nearby reached over to grab the Visgate's arm before he swung again. Wet with root beer, his grip slipped and his arm backlashed behind him and smacked against the back of a dignitary. The brawl was on, and heads of state rolled in root beer dust, pummeling away at one another.

Michael found the last few steps of his escape quite easy. He bolted through the alleyway and up to the low wall, leaping over and crouching down. He might have been seen by a dozen people and would not have known, for in his rush away he'd thrown caution to the winds. He waited, motionless and breathless, set to defend himself. No one came. He was hardly able to believe what he'd just done or the effect it had created. He peered cautiously over the wall. The area was empty. Through the windows in each wall of the garage it looked like a costumed crowd in a street fight, the din punctuated by panicky crow-calls of distress from Professor Schmidt.

Then Michael noticed something else through the window. There in the dimness of the garage was the cage, and inside it the body of a woman hung from wrist shackles. Inexplicably he thought it was Debbie, and leaped over the wall and up to the door. It had been newly padlocked, bolted on steel plates. He rushed to the window, pressing his face up against the glass to see inside. Relief flooded through him — the woman inside the cage was not his wife. He reeled against the garage wall. "Pankie Retson," he gasped. His mind locked in combat between leaving her and rescuing her. He shrugged. "Who am I to judge?" He hefted a nearby trash can and smashed the window, then jumped onto the ledge and into the garage. The keys were not in the tractor. He pawed hurriedly under the seat and over the sun visor, and then opened the glove compartment. The keys were inside. Michael felt a giddy excitement, and all sense of danger evaporated. He hastily unlocked the cage door, then opened the steel bands around Pankie's wrists and eased her limp body to the floor.

"There she is, the ultimate SelfGuide in a perfect world," he said, feeling unusual compassion. Pankie's eyes fluttered open. He lifted her off the planked cage floor and onto the tractor, gently easing her into the front seat. Then he got in, pushed the key into the ignition, and turned it. The tractor engine coughed into life. Pankie stirred and sat halfway up, still dazed.

"Relax Miss Retson. I've done this before." Michael's teeth were clenched with determination. The tractor lunged forward and splintered through the wooden garage door.

It wasn't like a limo but it was fast enough. This time he knew which way to go. They careened into the narrow alleyway just as police appeared. Spinning to the right, they jounced along the rough-cobblestoned downhill run and into the main bazaar area. They hit the concourse at fifty miles an hour and veered among merchants' booths and canopies toward the east Gate. Once again chickens, tapestries, beads, fruit and pottery sprayed in all directions.

The Gate came into sight several hundred yards ahead. Michel saw the sentries raise their rifles to their shoulders. He ducked down as far as he could, holding the accelerator tight to the floor. The wink of an orange flame kissed the tip of one of the rifles, and a bullet pipped through the windshield and thudded into the seat directly behind his head. If he hadn't ducked it would have gone through his neck. Two more slugs crashed through the glass, crackling the windshield. He had to steer now by watching the pavement spin by outside the side window, still hunched down low. The inside wall of the gate flashed by, lurching toward him and then away as the right wheel bounced against the other side of the archway. The wheel caught one of the guards against the Gate wall as it grazed by, tumbling him head over heels into the scrub bush just outside.

They bounced down the road, careening from one side to the other as Michael tried to steer the right path. They came to the road intersection without slowing and he pulled the tractor into a sharp left turn which almost tipped them over. He checked the side mirror for pursuers. So far none appeared. He felt hopeful.

"And there, Miss Retson, is your exciting tour of Jerusalem. That'll be six dollars, please." There was no response. He looked over, and almost swerved off the road with shock. Pankie sagged against the door, a tiny round wound red in the center of her forehead. A small rivulet of blood ran down the side of her nose. Michael shuddered, and checked the mirror again. Far behind a car was speeding toward them. With a flash of inspiration he bounced over the crest of a hill, momentarily out of view, and braked to a stop in the middle of the road. Then he jumped out and sprinted up into the scrub bush toward a grove of trees two hundred yards away.

Chapter 44

The storage tank emptied with a loud gurgling. Em shut the pump off while the others detached the truck cab from the eight thousand gallon tanker. Wedged together in the wide seat, they drove back toward the Tower square to meet Michael. They pulled up to the street in front of the south Gate and stopped against the curb. Ben pointed to the damaged wall where the taxi had crushed into it earlier, to Gabe and Em's delight. Suddenly, two police appeared, pointing and running toward them.

"Uh oh, . . ." Debbie said. Ben had already restarted the big diesel. "We shouldn't have driven this back — by now it would have been reported," he said, accelerating into a U-turn. Shrill police whistles cut through the throaty roar of the engine. People and animals scattered as they raced back down the cobblestoned street.

"They'll be after us soon," Gabe said, looking back through the rear window.

"Turn right! I think that's the way to the East Gate."

"Got it!" Ben pressed the accelerator. The truck jounced and careened past a row of shops and skidded to the right down a side street.

"Left now!"

Several frenzied turns later the bazaar mall was in sight. Sirens wailed faintly behind them.

"Go, Ben! Over the curb — then right."

Ben leaned into the wheel as if to urge more speed. They hit the high flagstone curb of the mall and bounced hard, all wheels momentarily in the air. The truck spun and skidded as it landed. Ben braked hard, stopping just a few feet from a gaping jewelry merchant immobilized with fright. Realizing he was safe, he began to shout and curse. Ben waved apologetically as he backed up. Suddenly a tractor swerved out of a side street and skidded into the mall, nearly clipping the truck as it passed. The merchant stopped railing in mid-sentence, staring in disbelief at the tractor now racing toward the East Gate. He threw his hands up and walked away, shaking his head.

"I think that was Michael!" Debbie said excitedly, bouncing up and down on the front seat, laughing and crying at the same time. "I think it was him!"

They raced down the mall trying to catch up with the tractor. "It must be!" Gabe shouted, equally excited now. "That's where we came out last night. Besides, who else would drive like that!"

Debbie squealed with joy and hugged Em tightly around his neck. Em sat motionless and pale, knuckles white and feet pushed against the floorboard as the truck careened around corners and narrowly missed pedestrians, parking meters and merchant stalls. He smiled bravely but was much more intent at the moment on avoiding fainting with fright from Ben's driving.

Lights flashing and sirens wailing, two pursuit cars ded into the mall behind them. Ahead, the tractor swerv it neared the Gate, clipping a sentry and hurling him ground. The other sentry spun away from the tractor as it eted through the entrance and aimed his rifle directly truck.

"Down!" Ben shouted. The others had seen the danger and ducked below the dashboard. They heard two staccato shots. One bullet crashed through the truck's radiator. The other pierced the hood and firewall, shattering the steering wheel as it ripped into the cab and crunched into Ben's left arm. He yelped involuntarily from sudden pain and surprise. Without steering the truck swerved out of control just as they reached the Gate, brushing against the other sentry and knocking him down. The bumper caught the Gate wall and the truck spun sideways and crunched to a stop, wedged tightly into the entrance arch.

"Ben!" Debbie screamed, seeing the blood.

"I'm okay — Get out! Out that side!" Gabe already had the right door open. They tumbled out and ran, Ben holding his numb and bleeding arm.

Sirens wailed down, and they could hear the squeal of tires as pursuit cars screeched to a stop, blocked by the truck cab.

"Over there!" Gabe pointed to the cordoned guard parking area. They dashed toward the nearest car. "Please Lord, let there be keys," he breathed, peering through the window. No keys. But in the next car, a dilapidated sedan, keys dangled from the steering column. They piled in and sped away.

Far ahead down the hill they saw the tractor skid to the left and accelerate onto the country road.

In the back seat, Debbie tore the hem of her sunrobe and bandaged Ben's wound. Pain was coming now. The bullet was imbedded in his bicep and his arm was broken. Gabe pushed the protesting sedan around the turn and into the main road without slowing. Ben grimaced in silence.

"Here they come!" Em gasped, looking back through the rear window. "Oh me, oh me . . ." Visions of another frantic ride worried the gentle scientist far more than their pursuers.

The shimmying car was going about as fast as it would, and they were gaining on the tractor when it disappeared over the crest of the hill a quarter mile ahead. Gabe pushed his foot tight to the floor to gain speed for the long upward slope. Shaking and rattling, the car tried, but before they made the crest they were slowing fast. Disgustedly, Gabe down-shifted, needing power now more than speed. The engine whined, turning far beyond its tolerance. Something under the hood snapped like a rifle shot, and the engine sounded like it was being ground into pieces. They eased over the crest at the pace of a fast walk.

Their slow speed saved them. Gabe skidded to a halt with only a slight bump against the tractor abandoned in the middle of the road. The sedan coughed to a grateful stop, and silence of the countryside settled around them like a blissful fog.

"That was close," Gabe said, swallowing hard.

"They'll be right behind us," said Em, worried.

"If that really was Michael he must be nearby."

"Let's go!"

Helping Ben, they jumped out and ran for cover. When they passed the tractor Debbie glanced inside, and stopped, stunned. The body of a woman, naked gray and lifeless, was slumped down in the seat.

"Debbie, come on!" Gabe took her arm and pulled her away. Frightened and uncomprehending, she turned and ran with him up the slope and onto the scrub bush plain.

"There he is!" Gabe shouted, glimpsing Michael's white robe just before he disappeared into the cover of an olive grove. They shouted but he was too far ahead to hear. Debbie raced ahead, running her soul out across the bumpy scrub plain. Gabe and Em, helping Ben, hurried after her as best they could.

Then they heard the screeching of braked tires back on the road, and a loud metallic crash as the pursuit car rammed headlong into their abandoned sedan.

Safe in the grove, Michael stopped and leaned against a tree, gasping for breath. He heard his name floating through the air. It sounded like Debbie's voice. An instant later he heard the crash. He spun around. There, through the trees, he saw her running toward him as if it was her last race, and the others coming along more slowly behind her. A cloud of dark smoke billowed up from the distant road. He bolted out of the grove and leaped across the field like a gazelle, legs pumping across the rough ground, mindful only that Debbie was safe. Their arms opened and they came together and fell down laughing, crying, reunited.

The brawl in the Tower square ended as fast as it began. Most dignitaries were exhuasted, much more fit in mind than in body. Police had arrived and moved quickly to restore order. They expected anything other than what they found. Wading into the thick of the fighting they pulled presidents apart from prime ministers, visgates apart from rabbis, bodyguards apart from Omega team members. And everything smelled like root beer. Only the media remained aloof from the melee, capturing the historic debacle on videotape. Violence of the most primitive kind broke through the sheen of civilized behavior, revealing the hair-trigger tension among the world's power elite.

"They're not gonna believe this in Kansas," a photographer remarked, flash bulbs popping and shutters clicking like automatic weapons.

"Get that guy, Chuck — over there!"

The camera panned over to the WOEC Visgate. Anton Jedesky was on his hands and knees, dazed, looking around.

Much of his anger had been pushed aside by embarrassment and astonishment. As usual, emotion which may have focused briefly on others yielded now to concern only for himself. He stood, separated by a hair from complete mental breakdown, trying to restore what dignity he could. The hem of his purple silk robe caught under his foot and ripped. It was his last straw. Frustration exploded and insisted on vengeance. He spotted Omega getting to his feet, the once-white robe matted with root beer mud. His ambitions and dreams had centered completely in this creature of his own creation. He was the one who was to have returned in power and glory. Now, in him he saw his loss, his defeat, his humiliation. His vision blurred from inner rage. He reached the border of his rational mind with no one guarding the gate, and stepped across. "Seize him!" he shouted in a trembling high-pitched voice. "Seize him!" No one moved. No one noticed him.

Anton Jedesky could take stress. But he could not stand to be ignored. "Kill him, kill the evildoer — Take him and burn him up!" He twitched up and down in quick hopping steps, dancing around the bewildered Omega. O'Keefe came to his assistance but stopped quickly when he saw the wild irrational panic in the WOEC leader's eyes. Then he reached out to try to calm him.

Jedesky pulled away. "Do not touch me, animal. For I am holy!" He was shrieking now. Many dignitaries were back on their feet trying to clean themselves off, and heard. Some ignored him, escaping to the sanctuary of their limousines, desiring only to leave this place of sudden madness and political disaster. Others watched, fascinated. And the cameras continued rolling.

"Capture the beast! Capture him!" The Visgate pointed a trembling finger at Omega. O'Keefe looked at Milton Franklin, who had pushed through the people now surrounding them. The Visgate lunged for Omega and grabbed the folds of his tunic.

"Hey man," Omega said, alarmed at his quivering face. "Get off my case."

Jedesky looked down and kicked as hard as he could. Omega howled in pain and broke away from the Visgate's grip, hopping up and down on one foot, clasping his shin in his hands.

Professor Schmidt, still on the ground and covered with root beer mud, shook his head sadly. "Oi, mama, vhy not I lissen up to you — ya, I had to be a biggenschdealer und do dis ting here. Next time I lissen better, ya." He got up slowly and limped toward the Mischa. "I goink to Bavaria now, mama. Pour der schnopps, my leibchen. Enough nonschundsensenstuff."

O'Keefe stiffened to attention as he approached the World Alliance Chairman. "Sir, what are your instructions? We're prepared to pursue the other Omega immediately and bring him to justice!"

Franklin peered through swollen, burning eyes, exhausted beyond endurance. Revulsion for O'Keefe filled him, particularly as Michael's daring and courageous interruption replayed through his tired and defeated mind. He fixed his stare on the major's bruised jaw. "Who hit you, major?"

O'Keefe reddened in embarrassment. "It's a long story, sir."

"I'll bet it is," Franklin said dully. "Look around, major. What we have here is not just a mess that never would have happened if you'd handled things properly. What we have here is the end of the World Alliance. It's the end of unity, the end of our dreams and hopes."

O'Keefe shifted uncomfortably, worried about the anger building in Franklin's heavy face.

"Look over there, major." Franklin pointed toward one of the whirring videocameras, focused now on the two of them. O'Keefe fumbled for his holstered pistol and pulled it out. "I'll take care of that!" he said excitedly.

Franklin pushed the barrel away with a swoop of his hand. "Give me that thing, you idiot," he said disgustedly. O'Keefe looked at Franklin, now hefting the pistol in his hand, with cringing surprise.

"So you're going to shoot the cameraman, is that right major? You should have used this thing an hour ago when Michael Ames waltzed in here like he owned the place and ruined the work of three decades. We put all the nickels in one roll, O'Keefe, and entrusted it to you. This was it. And the world was watching."

O'Keefe was pale and trembling.

"What shall I do now, major? Call a news conference? We have enough of the press here for that. I could tell the world we were only kidding, and that their eminent religious leader, the Supreme High Exalted Visgate of WOEC will be out for a bow as soon as he cleans the root beer off his robe and gets his sanity back. How about that?" Franklin clapped the major on the back, much harder than he needed to. "Or I could say 'Welcome to the World Alliance Wrestling Tournament! Hope you enjoyed the opening number!'" O'Keefe shrank away, terrorized by the chairman's sarcasm.

Most of the people had left by now, retreating into whatever sanctuary they could find. They knew when defeat was absolute. But they could not comprehend its ease and suddenness. Several police hovered nearby, and one camera crew continued to record the priceless expressions of the World Alliance chairman and his Omega team leader now sitting on the rim of the fountain.

For Franklin, as his exhausted mind processed what had happened, there was no way out. He knew the World Alliance well enough to know it was far less potent a governmental force than the illusion it had created. Like papier mache and mirrors, he remembered thinking once. His company was buried now under solid volcanic rock. He had been irretrievably humiliated, for this day was the child of the World Alliance and he was its head. Never again would he be taken seriously. Leaders of the nations would be back in their capitols tomorrow with the unforgettable experience of this day seared into their memory. They would disassociate themselves from the World Alliance with scorn. The scenes and sounds of this day would be viewed around the world. He would be the laughingstock of all people. He would go down in history as the bungler, the dealer in sham, the one in whom lofty hopes and trusts of people everywhere had been vested, and now lost. Ironically, the former chairman would probably be venerated.

"Gotta give 'em credit, O'Keefe." Franklin said. He spoke so softly that the major could hardly hear him.

"Sir?"

"The Christians, major. They defeated us today you know. I don't know how, but they did."

O'Keefe's voice strengthened. "Sir, in just a few hours we can mount an attack on . . . ."

"Shut up major." Franklin looked dully at the ground. Slowly, then, purpose straightened his sagging shoulders. He looked up at the remaining camera crews. "Turn those things off. Just for a minute."

The police jumped at his command and moved toward the cameras. The crews shut the equipment down. Franklin lifted the pistol to the underside of O'Keefe's chin. The major looked at the chairman with the kind of fright that prophesied.

"Goodbye, major. You did a lousy job." He pulled the trigger. Then he turned the pistol on himself. Two shots echoed from the stone walls surrounding the square. The crews hastily restarted their cameras.

Epilogue

Brilliant white clouds gleamed in the sun, billowing into majestic patterns and figures. The faint vibration was like a soothing reminder that all was safe and under control. Gabe and Em stretched back in their seats, the relaxing comfort sweet indeed. A flight attendant stopped by Debbie and Michael, nestled together across the aisle. "Newlyweds?" She asked, her eyes twinkling.

Michael blushed, surprised. Then it occurred to him — in a sense they were new, and therefore newly wedded. "Sort of, yes!" he said.

"How nice!" The attendant beamed. "May we bring you champagne?"

"Yes. And could you bring some for my friends across the aisle and for the man just in front of them?"

The attendant nodded and disappeared into the forward galley.

"Do you mind some bubbly wine, pastor?" Michael chuckled, nudging Gabe.

Gabe stirred and opened his eyes. "And what's the occasion?"

Michael and Debbie laughed. "We're newlyweds."

Gabe understood. "Ah, yes! And there's even more cause to celebrate — 'I tell you, Michael, there is more joy in Heaven over one sinner who repents than over ninety-nine righteous persons who need no repentance.' "

Michael pictured the scripture in his mind. "Luke, Chapter Fifteen!"

"And for both of you I will indeed drink with celebration!"

"Count me in too," Ben said, looking back over his seat. "A little wine for friend stomach's sake, you know. But someone will have to pour it for me." He pointed to his splinted and bandaged arm hanging in a sling strapped to his body.

Their journey from the olive grove to the airport had been difficult, more on account of fatigue and Ben's wound than for any other reason. Although Michael was the most able-bodied the risk that someone would recognize him in Jerusalem was too great. Gabe had insisted on venturing back out, arguing that he could be anonymous and that he alone knew enough of the language to get by. He had worked his way back to the road, keeping behind as much cover as possible, alert for any sign of pursuit. Flashing lights warned him that ambulances and tow trucks, and probably police, were at the crash site. He had moved along the scrub bush edging the road until he was safely out of view, then jogged through the countryside toward Jerusalem. An hour later he had reached the fork in the road. It was night by then, and vivid recollections of their pause there, wondering whether to go to the El Shar or to Jerusalem, flooded him.

Jerusalem was in turmoil from the aftermath of the incredible events in the Tower square that afternoon. He had easily been able to rent a car, check flight schedules, and get needed supplies. By nine o'clock, fresh groceries and jugs of water on the front seat, he was on his way back. He shivered as he passed the East Gate access road and the spotlighted wall farther up. The wreckage had been cleared away as he came over the hill. Its only remaining evidence were tiny shards of glass scattered over the pavement, glinting in the headlights. By the time he had returned to the grove the others had removed the bullet from Ben's arm, suffering with him through the pain of the experience.

Hunger eased and thirst slaked, they had carried Ben to the car and driven back to Jerusalem, stopping first at a hospital. The on-duty intern had looked suspicious as he cleaned and dressed the wound, but said nothing.

It was one in the morning when they'd checked into a small hotel on the outskirts of the city, the Star Hostel. They fell exhausted into their beds, sleeping until late the next afternoon. Then, showered and refreshed, they had gone to the airport, by then settled back into nearly normal operations, arriving three hours before their flight. Em had insisted that they fly first class, especially for Ben's sake. They bought the tickets for the nearly empty flight, got a newspaper, and caught up on world events with amazement. Clearing customs and immigration without incident, they boarded. The flight had taken off on schedule. They were on their way home, safe. Though home would not be what it had been, it was home indeed.

Michael Ames returned to a very different city than the one he had left nearly a month before. After restorative surgery on his face he continued to work for Robinson A. Peary Associates, and travelled extensively across the country, talking about the Omega experience. He accompanied Gabe Diehl often on his crusades, and his testimony touched many who heard him.

Debbie Ames rebuilt her photographic studio, and it prospered. One year to the day after their flight from Jerusalem touched down on American soil, she gave birth to twin girls, Jennie and Lucy. She grew and matured in the Lord and was a co-founder of WICK (Women in Christ's Kingdom).

After a lengthy recuperation with *Em* and *Lucy Prantzer, Ben Crockett* returned to the Binzoe District where he felt he could best be of service. He passed on to the Lord Jesus and to his many-jewelled crown of glory seven months later. More than a thousand people attended his memorial service. Every one of them had noticed a sweet and pure aroma that filled the sanctuary that day.

Emerson Prantzer served as Secretary of Peace in the rebuilding of the nation's government. He and Lucy moved to Washington just before Ben's passing. He became known as a trustworthy and far-sighted leader who loved his country and its people, and was instrumental in getting laws rescinded which banned the Bible and non-WOEC public worship.

Gabe Diehl pastored a church which flourished with love and rapid growth. His crusades took him all over the continent, and through his anointing many were given the truth, responded at the time of their call, and came home.

Tedrick Shriver took over SelfGuide, working to reestablish its credibility after the never-to-be-forgotten Omega disaster. But membership declined steadily. Three years later SelfGuide went bankrupt. Ted Shriver escaped with its last several million dollars.

The World Alliance crumbled publicly within a week of the Omega disaster. The consensus of poltical historians, found in many books published in the first few years afterwards, was that it was doomed by its founder's death regardless of what the success or failure of the Ultimate Sham might have been. Milton Franklin was no more than a footnote in their accounts.

Anton Jedesky was admitted to an asylum in Warsaw, where he remained catatonic. Five years later doctors turned off his life support equipment.

The World Organized Ecumenical Council purged its leadership and continued to operate, pausing only briefly following the Omega experience. Without missing a beat it continued promoting lines of belief similar to those followed under Jedesky's policies.

The number and severity of natural catastrophes abated. Two years after the horrible year in which new volcanoes, massive earthquakes, floods, famines and disease ran rampant across the earth, occurrence frequencies had dropped to near-normal levels. In their aftermath the world suffered intense economic depression. Recovery began only after several years.

The Day came, then. Michael and Debbie were taking the twins to a movie. Suddenly their car stopped, and no one was inside. Em Prantzer was in a cabinet meeting at the White House. Suddenly his chair and several others were empty. Gabe Diehl was holding a counselling session in his study. Suddenly he disappeared. The sky seemed to flash from east to west like lightning and a voice was heard like a heralding trumpet. The Lord of Lords and King of Kings had returned to His beloved creation and gathered His own, both those alive and those who had passed before, just as He had promised. They had endured to the end, their work and trial completed. And the King said to those He had gathered, "Well done, My good and faithful servants. You have been faithful over a little — I will set you over much. Enter into the joy of your Master."

About The Author

Kurt S. Johnson is a management consultant with a leading international business consulting firm. He travels extensively throughout North and South America and Europe, working with large corporations. His experiences in different cultures and in arenas of dramatic change have produced insights which have been helpful in developing *The Omega Plan*.

Years ago, with life and career in a shambles, he let go of it all and called out for Jesus Christ. Since then his Christian faith has grown and deepened, and spawned a desire to share God's certain joy and peace — and humor — in unconventional ways with busy people. *The Omega Plan* is one outcome of this desire.

He has completed a second book, *The Visions of Kinchipan*, and is writing a third novel, this one about consulting.

He lives in Oak Park, Illinois, with his wife, Liz, and cat Quat (to call the cat say "kumquat!") His son and daughter, and his wife's three daughters, are grown. Woodworking, writing, painting and tennis are among his weekend hobbies.